GIPSY MOTH

Jean Bull

PUBLISHED BY JEAN BULL

GIPSY MOTH

ISBN 978-0-9569969-2-3

First Published 2011 by
Jean Bull
jeanbullwriter@yahoo.co.uk

Printed in Great Britain by
www.direct-pod.com

GIPSY MOTH

To Adam

Best wishes,

Jean Bull

This book is dedicated to my wonderful family and friends.

Prologue

September 8th 1929

The old tartan rug didn't stop the dry straw sticking in my back, as the sun shone red through my eyelids. I touched Ben lying beside me, and electricity fizzled up my arms. He kissed me. His lips tasted of the wild plums we'd picked by the River Thames. He pulled me closer, and the pleasure still throbbed through my very being.

'Ben, what we did, I mean, it was all right, wasn't it?' I murmured. 'I'm not going to get myself into trouble, am I?'

'Of course not, Kathy, I was careful. Don't worry, you'll be quite safe.' He ruffled my hair.

'It was so wonderful, I do love you.' I couldn't help smiling into his eyes, shiny brown like the chestnuts scattered all around us. 'I didn't expect it would be like that; in fact I don't know what I thought it *would* be like.' I bit my lip. 'Oh dear, perhaps we shouldn't have . . . you know . . . but . . . it's too late now.'

'Don't be silly; it'll be fine, I promise.' He hugged me tight. 'I love you too. You mean everything to me.'

'I wish that you didn't have to go off to Cranwell in the morning; Lincolnshire is so far away. What time are you leaving?'

'Five thirty; to catch the six o'clock train.' He ran his hands through his tousled, brown hair.

'Do one of your whistles for me, and I'll wave from my window.' I made a piercing sound as a demonstration.

'Ow! Kathy!' Ben covered his ears. 'No, we'll wake up the whole road! You know that I'll be back for the Christmas holidays.'

Just then, a cherry red bi-plane buzzed across the sky, the sun glinting off its silver wings. He shaded his eyes. 'Look, Kathy! A Gipsy Moth! That's a good omen! You see, it will all work out, trust me.'

'I hope so; I'm really going to miss you.' I held on to him for dear life. 'I love you so much.'

We lay together in each other's arms until the sun began to set, and the Gipsy Moth returned, cutting through the silence.

'You know, I can't believe that you're going to become an RAF officer and fly one of those.'

'I'd much rather stay here with you. I could set up a business as a courier pilot.' He kissed my forehead. 'I don't know how I'll cope without you.'

I sat up and searched for my cigarettes and, lighting two, passed one to him. 'I wish that I could fly. It would be ripping to soar over the treetops and see the world spread out below! I saw an advertisement in the paper for lessons the other day, but they'd cost more than a week's wages.' I blew out the smoke which curled upwards in the still evening air. 'I'd fly to France perhaps. Oh, I don't know. I'd love to get up there in the sky and fly anywhere I wanted.' I knelt beside him. 'Do you remember Dad taking me to Croydon Aerodrome when I was little? There were these huge Handley Page bi-planes; so big that a man could stand under a wing. They filled the air like enormous dragonflies, flying off across the sea to Paris or Amsterdam. I asked him if we could go up in one, but he said we'd only come to watch. But when we got home, he built me a plane of my own with orange boxes and an old ladder.'

'Yes, I do. We could fly anywhere our imaginations took us, until that storm came and it really did blow away down the garden and get wrecked.' Laughing, Ben pulled me down and kissed me again.

'Mind my cigarette, you'll burn a hole in something!' I grabbed his hand to stop him, and then caught sight of his watch. 'Gosh! Is that the time? We must go; Mother will wonder where on earth I am.' I began to straighten my clothes.

'No, she won't, she's gone to the pictures, hasn't she?' He kissed me again, and the hairs on the back of my neck prickled to attention.

'No, we must get back; we've been here for ages.' I stubbed out my cigarette, and struggled up to find my shoes. 'Can I drive the Norton home?' I ran over to Ben's cherished motorbike, and grabbed the handlebars.

He laughed as he tucked in his shirt, 'Yes, if you want to!' Then, he shook his head in wonder, 'I don't know another girl quite like you. They're all dolled up like Abigail. Mother quite despairs about her sometimes: she's only interested in film stars, and bleaching her hair. But, look at you; you don't mind getting your hands oily, and I can really talk to you. You understand how things work, and . . . Hey, Kathy!'

As he talked, I'd rocked his bike off the stand and was kick-starting it. Now, it growled into action, and I rode it around the field in triumph, my hair streaming in the wind.

'Be careful, wait!' Ben shouted, running after me.

Chapter One

October 24th 1929

'So, how long's Ben been away then, Kathy?' Abigail had to raise her voice. It was half-day closing, and we'd managed to get the last table in the Vaudeville Cinema café on Broad Street.

'Six weeks, four days, ten hours and,' I checked my watch, 'twenty minutes.'

She smiled as she poured out my tea. 'Well, it's much quieter at home when he's not there, *and* tidier. Mother says she can dry her hands safely now, without getting them black from his oily handprints. He really is the limit.' And, raising her fine eyebrows, she asked, 'Have you heard from him yet?'

'He writes to me nearly every day.' I pulled out a bundle of letters from my handbag and hugged them.

'How many have you got? You surely don't carry them with you everywhere?'

'There are thirty-seven, no thirty-eight; one came this morning.' I waved the blue envelope at her.

Abigail grabbed it. 'He's drawn one of his little cartoons.'

'Yes, he always does that. It's me, isn't it? I'd know those long gangly legs and that frizzy hair anywhere.'

Smiling, she handed it back. 'It's so funny that you've fallen in love with each other after all this time. But, you know, you are lucky; he only writes to me once a week.'

'Well, you're his sister, aren't you, what do you expect?'

Abigail shrugged her shoulders. 'How are you getting on at the bookshop without your aunt?'

'It's not so good,' I moaned. 'The new manageress, Miss Snead, thinks she's God's gift to the broadening of women's minds, but all the girls are frightened of her. If you're a minute late, or even have a ladder in your stocking, she'll dock your pay. I missed the bus the other day and she said she'd take half a crown if I did it again. Aunt Sylvia would at least listen to us after she'd let off steam. I really wish she hadn't got married and moved to

Devon; it was just about bearable when she was there. I sipped my tea. 'Ugh, this tastes a bit funny; do you think the milk's gone off?'

'No, mine seems okay.' Abigail nibbled a chocolate éclair. 'Ooh, but these are delicious, Kathy, aren't you going to have one?'

'No, my tummy seems a bit upset. I don't really feel like one, thanks.' I pushed my cup and saucer away, and lit a cigarette. 'Tell me what you've been up to.'

'Oh, I had lunch in McIlroy's with Maureen and Hilda yesterday, and I bought this coat. Do you like it?' She stroked the collar.

'Yes, it's lovely. The blue suits you.'

'Kathy, why don't you come with us sometime? They're always asking after you. We all had such fun at school together.'

'I can't, Abigail, I have to go out to work; it's all very well for you.' I twirled my cigarette in the ashtray. 'I wish I didn't have to. I'd rather earn a living fiddling about with bikes, or cars, or even aeroplanes. I used to love helping Ben take his motorbike to bits, and put it back together again. But, how can I ever have a job like that? Mother and Dad won't hear of it.' I sat up straight and copied Mother's voice, '*You must do something suitable for a young lady*.' I stubbed out my cigarette with vigour.

'Sorry, Kathy, but I don't like to think of you missing out on all the fun.'

'It's fine,' I sighed. 'Anyway, I don't have an allowance like you, so how could I manage? If I'd had some money, I'd have gone to Brooklands a couple of weeks ago for the Five Hundred Miles Race. Well, it would have been even better to have gone with Ben. Did you see the newsreels?'

'Yes, but . . .' Abigail shrugged her shoulders again. Then she studied my face and frowned. 'Are you feeling a bit poorly? You don't look very well.'

'No, really, I'm fine.' I stood up, and gathered my hat and coat together. 'Come on, the film will start in a minute.'

‘Let me take your arm, you do look a bit peaky.’ Abigail squeezed me tight.

Secretly, I felt grateful for her support because I did feel a bit strange inside.

October 25th 1929

‘So, you’re here at last, Miss Mason. What’s your excuse this time?’ Miss Snead stood at the door of Auntie’s old bookshop in Friar Street with her hands on her generous hips, barring my way. ‘It’s nearly a quarter to ten.’

‘I’m sorry, Miss Snead.’ I hesitated, feeling really ill. ‘Can I come in? I think I’m going to be . . .’ I rushed past her, through the Women’s Poetry section, to the cloakroom. And five minutes later, I heard her black leather shoes squeak to a halt out outside the door.

‘Now, what’s all this about?’ I imagined her straightening her glasses which she wore on the end of her long nose.

‘I don’t know; I’ve got some sort of stomach upset,’ I mumbled as I washed my face. ‘I think I’ve had some milk that’s gone off, Miss Snead.’

There was silence for a moment. Miss Snead coughed, then her voice sank to a low, confidential whisper. ‘You don’t think that you could be; let me see, in the “family way”, Miss Mason? You’ve been late several mornings this week.’

The family way? That sounds awful. I can’t really be pregnant can I? I gripped the washbasin. A pulse throbbed through my head, and my heart drummed in my chest. *Ben said he’d been careful. I can’t be pregnant. It’s just a tummy upset.*

‘Miss Mason?’ Her voice came through strong and clear. ‘What are you doing?’

‘I’m coming, I’ve just eaten something that’s disagreed with me, that’s all.’

‘I’ll expect you to work your lunch hour today to make up your time. ‘ Her footsteps faded away.

'Don't worry, Miss Snead, I shall be glad to,' I called, as I dried my face with shaking hands.

On the bus that evening, I sat opposite a young mother struggling with two wriggling children. *In the family way?* Miss Snead's words echoed in my head. *No, I can't be. Can I?* I tried to think what I knew about being pregnant. *Well, you get a big stomach . . . and a baby. Jeepers.* I looked at the woman in horror. *What else?* I had no idea. Mother had never talked to me about having babies, and what I did know had only been gleaned from giggling whispers and rumours behind ink-stained hands in the changing rooms at school.

'Fare's please!' The conductor came along. 'Have you got a ticket, young lady?'

'No, sorry; a tuppenny one, please.' I managed to smile.

'You look a bit under the weather, if you ask me. I should go home and have a nice cup of tea; it'll do you a world of good.'

Home? What will Mother say when she finds out? Or Dad? My stomach churned like goldfish racing giddily round a bowl. *What shall I do? I can't face them yet.* So I decided to call in at Abigail's house on the way.

The Hunter's square Georgian house basked in the late autumn sunshine on the opposite side of the road to ours in Reading, where Dad had built a row of more modest semi-detached ones.

'Kathy? How jolly! Come in.' Abigail stood back looking perfect as usual, like a freshly unwrapped doll.

I'd always felt rather shabby compared to her, and now my heart was beating loudly, proclaiming that I was perhaps, truly shabby: a fallen woman.

'That's an adorable dress, shame about the colour. That mustard makes you look a bit jaundiced, and it really doesn't do anything for those hazel eyes.' Abigail went on, 'Wait a minute; you really don't look at all well, I told you so yesterday. Come along, I'm just having a cup of tea.'

'Thanks, but I don't seem to be able to keep anything down at the moment. I just want to ask you something.'

'Really? You haven't found a new beau, have you, now Ben's away? You minx.' Abigail screwed up her pert little nose and laughed.

I followed her into the sitting room. There, amongst all the family treasures, including Wing Commander Hunter's medals from the Great War, and his wife's embroidered antimacassars which she had been making whilst recuperating from tuberculosis, were Ben's drawings of motor cars and aeroplanes, proudly framed. I couldn't bear it. I wanted Ben to be there just like in the old times, when we would escape to the garage and mess about with his motorbike, without a care in the world.

'Oh, Abigail.'

'What ever is it, Kathy? It can't be that bad, Ben will be back at Christmas.' She patted the velvet cushions on the sofa. 'Kathy? Sit here and tell me all about it.'

I slumped down beside her. 'Abigail, we've been friends since before we can remember, haven't we?'

'Yes, of course. You and me and Ben. You're the sister that I never had. Believe me, when you have a brother like mine, you need some female company.'

I picked up one of Ben's Meccano aeroplanes from the table. I could feel his touch somehow vibrating in the metal. I spun its propeller, and put it down.

'Abigail, I don't know how to ask you this.'

'What? Come on, spill the beans.'

I took a deep breath, 'What do you know about getting in the family way?'

Abigail's clear blue eyes opened wide. 'The family way? Pregnant, you mean?'

My heart pounded. I could feel the colour rising in my cheeks. 'Er, yes, one of the girls at the shop . . . Annie . . . thinks she might be, you know . . .' I shook my head in amazement.

'Didn't Maureen's sister get pregnant? I thought she might have mentioned something to you about it.'

'Beatrice?' A smile flickered over her lips.

Dry mouthed, and unable to speak, I nodded.

'Yes, she did. What a jolly nasty fix. She had to be sent away to a Maternity Home, you know one of those Salvation Army ones. The shame! Her mother didn't know what to do. She worried herself sick in case the neighbours found out. Beatrice had to have it adopted in the end.'

The colour drained from my face faster than it had come, and I had to clutch my clammy hands together to stop them shaking.

'How . . . how did she know she was pregnant?'

'I'm not sure. Please, have cup of tea, Kathy, you look awful.'

'No, no, really, thanks.'

Abigail poured one out for herself. 'I think Maureen said that she stopped being "unwell".'

Alarm bells went off in my mind. *When was I "unwell" last? I can't remember*. I gently rubbed my stomach.

'Beatrice had terrible morning sickness though. Lost a lot of weight, but those Sally Allies fed her up. No good putting a baby up for adoption if it's scrawny, is it?'

I shook my throbbing head.

'She did say that some of the girls there had tried to get rid of their babies.'

'How? What did they do?' I fiddled with the Meccano plane again, hoping that Abigail wouldn't notice my trembling hands.

'I'm not sure. They took things like Beecham's powders, or Epsom salts. Gin, that was it. Gin and raspberry leaves; I think she said nutmeg was good too. Some of them tried very hot baths, and one girl even tried to throw herself down the stairs. None of it worked of course, or they wouldn't have been there.' Abigail stopped and stared at me for a moment. 'It's not poor Annie that's pregnant, is it? It's you, Kathy. You're pregnant, aren't you?'

The propeller came off the little plane at last, and clattered onto the floor. 'I don't know. I hope not.'

'Oh dear, what a fix you're in.'

November 4th 1929

I punched my pillow into submission, and peered at my bedside clock. Its hands had been crawling like sluggish glow-worms. *Only half past two? I've been tossing and turning for hours.* I stared at the shadowy ceiling and my thoughts twirled round and round, in and out of the corners of the room like grey mist. *Let's work it out again. When did I have my "friends" last? It was at the Church picnic, wasn't it? At the end of August. I couldn't go in the sea, and Abigail and I watched Ben and his chums swim out to that high rock and dive off all afternoon. Yes, that was it. End of September, end of October,* I counted on my tummy, *and it's Bonfire Night tomorrow, so that means I should have been "unwell", but I haven't. Was I at the end of September? I can't remember. I had that tummy upset . . . Please God; don't let me be in the family way. Ben said he was careful. What did he mean by that? I wish I knew. Oh, God, please make my "friends" come. Please God.* I tossed and turned again until my brain was so tired that at last I drifted to sleep.

The clock had managed to arrive at five to six when I woke up, but it was still dark. *It's morning at last, thank goodness. That was strange; I dreamt that I was pregnant.* I rubbed my tummy. *Well, I'm glad that's over. How awful. What would . . . Wait a minute. No, it's true, I might really be pregnant. It wasn't a dream at all.*

My temperature soared, so I threw off the bedclothes, and tiptoed over the chilly lino to the window. The frost made the casement stick, but I forced it open and took some deep, icy breaths. Across the road, amongst the frozen trees, Ben's house slumbered. *If only he was there, I could talk to him. What shall I do? Shall I tell him? What would he say?* I shivered, and hurried back into bed with my teeth chattering. I decided to have a very hot bath as Abigail had suggested.

Later when Dad had left for work and Mother had gone to town, I ran the bath and dipped my big toe in to test it.

'Jeepers! Ow!' I hopped around the bathroom, then turned on the cold tap, and winced as I managed to step in, and lower myself down. The hot water licked around my stomach, making the submerged skin red and mottled. I leant back, the heat prickling exquisitely like scratching an itchy rash. *I do hope this is going to work. If I am pregnant, Mother will have to make Ben come home and marry me. But what about his training?*

I got out when the water began to cool down, and caught sight of myself in the large bathroom mirror. Apart from glowing red, my tummy appeared as flat as ever. *Didn't it?*

The bath gave me a heat rash, nothing more. I went to Abigail's Guy Fawkes Night party, but it wasn't the same without Ben, and the fireworks didn't seem to have any sparkle at all.

Chapter Two

November 10th 1929

On Sunday, I didn't go to church. I told Mother I had a headache and stayed in bed. I waited until the front door banged and two pairs of footsteps crunched away down the path. For the millionth time, I pressed all round my tummy. It all felt the same as usual but, when I squeezed in a particular spot, it made me want to spend a penny. *Not again, I've only just been.* I trudged off to the bathroom. *I'm still not "unwell". What am I going to do? I think Abigail said the girls in the Home tried gin and Beecham's Powders. I'm going to have to try some, I wonder if we've got any?*

Padding downstairs, I rooted in the kitchen cupboards only to find some Lucozade, but there was a bottle of Stone's Ginger Wine left over from last Christmas in the sideboard. That would have to do. The cap was cemented on with sugar crystals, so I feverishly ran it under the hot tap, and unscrewed it with a rubber glove. My hands trembled as I poured out a large glassful, and unfolded six packets of Beecham's Powders and stirred them in. I skinned my knuckles grating some nutmeg on the top for good measure.

I climbed into bed, and stirred the potion. The morning sun shone through the swirling amber liquid and made patterns on the counterpane. *This magic draught could put everything right.* I took a sip, and screwed up my face; it was too sweet and gingery, yet bitter with the powders. I gulped the rest down fast, so I wouldn't taste it. Then, like Alice in Wonderland, I lay back and wondered what would happen next.

I was just thinking that I felt a little light-headed when the doorbell rang. I pulled the bedclothes up around my ears. I didn't want to go down; I'd pretend I was asleep. But then, I thought I could hear a voice calling my name.

Mystified, and my head beginning to spin, I crept down the stairs in my bare feet. Peering through the starry glass panel in the front door, I saw an azure RAF uniform and above it Ben's dark hair and eyes. My heart began to pound. I flung the door open wide and hugged him tight. 'What *are* you doing here? I can't believe it's really you!'

'Steady on, Kathy, I can't breathe. It's a bit of luck; I've got a twenty-four hour pass. I have to report back tonight though.' He held me at arm's length. 'How are you? Abigail said that you'd been ill. Why didn't you tell me?'

I couldn't understand why I could see two of him. 'It's nothing: just this tummy upset I can't seem to get rid of it.'

He appeared to be rocking slightly to and fro. Smiling, but frowning at the same time, he studied my face, 'I have missed you.' He kissed me, and my knees turned to jelly. 'Phew, have you been drinking, Kathy?'

'I thought a glass of ginger wine might help. Warming, you know. Come in and let's *slhut* the door, we don't want the neighbours *sheeing* me in my nightie.'

Although I'm not a dainty little thing like Abigail, he picked me up and carried me to the sofa in the front room. His familiar smell of engine oil, hardly masked by his cologne made me feel so safe. I clung onto him and couldn't get enough of his eager kisses. For the first time in several weeks, I didn't feel sick. I wanted to gobble him up like a box of chocolates. Then . . . everything went black.

When I opened my eyes again, it was dark, but the light from a small lamp made the silver threads in Mother's hair look like a halo.

'Mother? Is that you?' I croaked.

'Yes? Oh, thank goodness!' She dabbed my forehead with a cool cloth, and then cradled my hot sticky hands in hers. 'Kathy, what have you done to yourself?'

'I can't remember.' I rubbed my throat and swallowed. 'Ooh, it's so sore.' I tried to sit up, but the strange room spun like a merry-go-round, and I sank back into the pillows. 'Where am I?'

'In hospital, dear.'

'Hospital?'

'Yes, you've made yourself very ill. You've been unconscious since this morning.'

'Where's Ben?' I raised my pounding head again.

'He's had to go, dear. He tried to wake you when you passed out, but he couldn't, so he called the doctor. He did stay as long as he could, but it's gone ten o'clock now.'

'Ten o'clock? At night? But, why am I here?'

Her face looked pale and drawn in the shadows. 'Kathy, I think that's what *you* should tell me.'

I pressed my forehead to try to conjure up any memory, but my mind was as empty as a paper bag.

'Doctor Ford said that you've tried to poison yourself.'

'What? My eyes shot open. 'I've tried to poison myself?'

Mother dabbed at her tears. 'Yes, six packets of Beecham's Powders and a large glass of ginger wine, I should think that was enough. They've had to pump your stomach out.'

'Have they?' I massaged my raw throat. 'I wasn't trying to poison myself, Mother.'

'What on earth's wrong, Kathy? Why did you do it?' Her hands trembled as she twisted her damp hankie.

'I . . . Er . . . I don't know.'

Her face flushed bright red as she leant forwards and whispered, 'Doctor Ford thinks that you might be in the F.A.M.I.L.Y. W.A.Y.'

'In the what?' Then, to my horror, I remembered what Miss Snead had said. 'The family way?' I whispered.

'How can that be, Kathy? Please tell me it's not true.'

'But I'm not in the family way.' I crossed my fingers under the sheet so hard that they hurt. 'How does he know anyway?'

'He saw what you'd taken. He said that some women take those powders instead of Beecham's *Pills* thinking they'll bring on an ab . . . an abor . . . a miscarriage. It's very dangerous, Kathy, you could have killed yourself.' Mother hugged me tight. 'Oh dear, please tell me you weren't trying to do that?'

'I don't know.'

'How can you not know?' She got up and paced round the bed. 'You must know what you've been doing. You've been brought up to be a good girl, to be above all those things. What will they say at Church? Who have you been with, Kathy?' Raising her eyebrows, she studied my face. 'It's not Ben, is it?'

My cheeks blazed.

'Who'd have thought it after all these years?' Her green eyes narrowed and she clenched her fists. 'How could you? Just wait until I get hold of him.'

'No. It wasn't like that.' I clutched her arm. 'We love each other.'

She shrugged off my grip. 'What on earth possessed you? I wish I'd never let you go out with him alone on his fancy motorbike. I knew no good would come of it.'

'But, it was *Ben*, nothing's ever happened before.'

'Well, it has now and what *are* we going to do?' She gathered her coat and bag together. 'We shall have to tell him.'

I don't know how I'm going to . . .

November 11th 1929

The next afternoon, tired of the nurses' disapproving stares, I flicked through an old copy of *Good Housekeeping* until, at last, Mother bustled back.

'How do you feel, Kathy?' She looked around for a nurse to take her dahlias and put them in water.

'My head hurts, and I'm bored. When can I go home?' I tossed the magazine on the bed, and sighed.

'Doctor Ford says you must rest here for a few days.' Mother perched forward on the small, hard chair, and took my hand. She leant closer. 'He asked when you were last "unwell", Kathy.'

'Well, that's the problem,' I frowned, 'I don't think I have been since August.'

'There you are then, that answers it, doesn't it?' Mother sat back and folded her arms.

'You mean that I really am pregnant?' The whole ward seemed to tip sideways. 'Jeepers! Oh my God!'

'Kathy! For goodness sake!' She put her finger to her lips. 'I do wish you wouldn't use that language. You're not in a Hollywood film.' She looked around to make sure no one had noticed. Then she added quietly, 'Yes, I should think you are pregnant. Why didn't you tell me?'

'I couldn't. I didn't want to upset you.'

'But, you are doing a good job of upsetting me now.'

'I'm sorry, I didn't mean to.'

Mother adjusted her fox fur round her shoulders. 'The other thing is: I don't know how we're going to tell your father. He'll be here in a minute.'

I slithered down the pillows and pulled up the blankets. *Oh no, I've got to tell him too.*

The doors of the ward opened, and I held my breath as Dad came in clutching a brown paper bag of fruit which he plopped on the bed.

'Kathy!' He hugged me so close that I'm sure he could feel my heart pounding. His putty-and-wood smell reminded me of being rescued from a nasty fall in his building yard when I was little. 'Oh, Kathy, I thought we'd lost you.' He held me at arms length and stared at me, as if to be sure that I was truly alive, and shook his head in wonder.

I couldn't meet his gaze, so I fussed over the bag of fruit and pulled out some grapes.

'Kathy? What's wrong?'

My throat, still sore from the gastric pump, tightened up, and I couldn't speak.

He looked at Mother who patted my arm. 'You'd better tell him, dear.'

'No, you.' I whispered.

Mother sighed, 'No, I think it would be best coming from you.'

'What's going on?' Dad, bemused, looked from one of us to the other; he was used to our scheming ways.

'Daddy? Dad, I've got something to tell you.' I took his big, strong hand. 'Oh dear, how do I say this? Daddy, I . . .I'm in the family way; I'm pregnant.'

'What? In the family way?' He whipped his hand away as if it'd been stung. 'Not my little girl? You're not, are you?' His face flushed purple and his eyes bulged red, I thought he was going to explode. 'Who's been messing around with you? Who's the father?'

Mother put a restraining hand on his shoulder. 'It's Ben, dear.'

'Ben? He should be ashamed of himself.' Dad bounced up as if he was going to catch the next train north to Lincolnshire, and pin Ben against the nearest wall. 'Kathy, how could you let this happen?'

'I don't know. I love him.'

'You don't know what love's about.'

'Yes, I do, I'm eighteen. You think that I'm just a little girl.'

'Kathy!' Mother warned.

'So, is he going to do the decent thing and marry you?'

'He doesn't know, Joe.'

'Well, I know what I think: we should get that boy home straight away, and make him marry you.' Dad pounded the bed with his fist.

'Shh!' Mother glanced around at the other patients and their visitors.

'No, Dad, I don't want him to know yet.' The tears that I'd fought all day, threatened to overflow. 'I don't want to be pregnant.'

'Don't be silly, Kathy, you are pregnant and you've got to tell him as soon as possible.' Mother gave me her clean handkerchief, which smelt of Californian Poppy, and took Dad by the arm. 'Come on, Joe, we'd better go.'

Oh, why did I get myself in this mess? I thought, as I huddled down under the bedclothes again.

November 18th 1929

Mother brought in some writing paper the next day and a letter from Ben. When she'd gone, I propped myself up on the pillows, and chewed my fountain pen. Screwed up pages littered the blankets, and one or two inky fingerprints decorated the sheets. *How am I going to tell him? I can't just say 'Dear Ben, I'm pregnant'.* And heart thumping, I began a fresh page.

Dear Ben,

I'm always as pleased as Punch when your letters arrive, and the one that came today was really exciting. What sport to fly on your own, I'm so envious!

You know, I love you so much, and I miss you terribly. I am feeling a little better, but I'm really bored in hospital, and I do wish you were here in person to cheer me up.

I can't believe that I'm writing this, Ben, but I have to tell you that I've got myself in a bit of a fix - I'm in the family way. I'm having your baby, our baby. I didn't want to give you something to worry about when your training was going so well, but Mother said that I must tell you.

I love you, Ben, and I'm sorry to bring you all this bad news.

All my love,
Kathy

PS I want you to be sure that I don't regret what we did on that last afternoon one little bit.

I had to stay in hospital for a week. The days seemed so long; there was nothing to do. Mother managed to get me some back copies of *The Autocar*, which I enjoyed much more than the womanly advice in *Good Housekeeping*. Then a nurse heard that I was interested in flying, and brought in an Air Race board game which had belonged to her son, but it wasn't until Abigail came to see me that I had anyone to play it with.

'So there it is, Abigail, I really am pregnant.' I shook the dice and moved my little red plane five spaces round the board.

'I can't believe you're having a *baby*, Kathy,' she whispered. 'I never thought that you and Ben . . . Well . . . I *never*.'

'I'm worried though.'

'Why?' Abigail rattled the dice.

'I want Ben to pass his exams. I don't want the baby to get in the way of his career.'

'But the baby's his too, Kathy.' She moved forward one space.

'Yes, I know, but this isn't the right time.'

'Don't be silly. You're going to have to marry him, aren't you? The sooner the better, I should say.'

'Do you think he'll ask me?'

'I certainly hope so.' She handed me the dice and smiled. 'I could be a bridesmaid.'

I sighed, and moved forward to '*You've come down in the sea - miss a go*'. I twisted my little plane about in its square. 'It happened that last afternoon before he went. He was going to be away for *months*. I didn't think I'd get pregnant doing it only once. It was the very first time; I'd never dreamt of doing anything like that in my life before. What am I going to do?'

Abigail picked up the dice. 'Marry him, Kathy. You must.'

Chapter Three

November 19th 1929

With the doctor's approval, I escaped hospital the next day on the understanding that I stayed in bed. And there at home, waiting on the doormat, was another letter from Ben. I hurried upstairs, as fast as I could under the circumstances, to read it alone.

Dearest Kathy,

What a surprise! You're having a baby! What a clever girl you are. I'm going to come home as soon as possible and marry you - if you'll have me.

Jeepers! He does want to marry me! I fanned my face with the letter.

I'm just crazy about you. Please say yes. Believe me, I didn't mean it to happen, and I really thought I was careful, but now this means that we can be together for ever and ever!

All my love,

Ben

He finished it off with a cartoon of a Gipsy Moth flying a banner saying, 'Kathy is the girl for me!'

'Oh, my God! He wants to marry me! He wants to marry me!' I shouted, my heart looping the loop like an aeroplane in a flying circus. I wanted to get out of bed and dance around, but my head spun like a propeller.

'Mother, Mother!' I called down the stairs. 'Mother!' Until, drying her hands on a towel, she hurried up to see if I was being murdered.

'What ever is it?' she said, rushing into my room.

'Mother, Ben wants to marry me!' I waved the letter like a flag.

'Thanks be to God,' she said, hugging me tight, and then sitting on my bed to read it. Sniffing, she wiped a tear away with her towel. 'Oh, Kathy, I'm so glad. Thank goodness, this will solve everything. Write back, Kathy, and say yes. I can catch the next post, if you hurry.'

'I will, Mother.'

I can't believe that Ben wants to marry me!

November 23rd 1929

On Saturday afternoon, whilst Abigail and I toasted crumpets by the fire, Mother came in with a pot of tea on a tray.

'Ben's coming back tomorrow, isn't he, Abigail?' she said. 'Kathy, you must get him to arrange the wedding as soon as possible. Then when the baby's born, you can just say that it was early.' She poured out the tea. 'Now, what can you wear? You can hardly choose white.'

I rolled my eyes at Abigail.

'You've got that cream shantung dress. You know, the one you wore for the Harvest Supper?' she said. 'It's low waisted with plenty of room. That should hide your embarrassment nicely. It's a pity we can't afford a new one, but business hasn't been so good for your father recently, but we could dress it up with a new sash, and find you a nice hat.'

'You're so impatient, Mother.' I speared a crumpet with the toasting fork. 'I do wish Ben was here to make these plans with me. He hasn't even asked Dad properly yet.'

'Hasn't he?' Abigail shifted her legs from one side to the other to get comfortable.

'No, of course not, he's got to do it in person. Dad better say yes.'

'But, your dad knows that Ben's going to ask him, doesn't he?'

'Of course, but I hope he doesn't mess things all up. He nearly exploded in the hospital when he found out I was in the family way.' I licked my buttery fingers. 'Oh, I can't wait to be married to Ben. I can't believe it. He'll be back by this time tomorrow, and he's coming over to ask Dad before lunch.'

November 24th 1929

Ben arrived on the dot of eleven. I'd washed my hair, and put on my best red woollen dress decorated with black beads which I'd been fiddling with since ten o'clock. One came off in my hand as I hurried to answer the door.

'Ben, what ever is it?' I looked in dismay at his ashen face. 'It's not your mother, is it? She hasn't had a relapse?'

'No, Kathy.' Tears shone in his brown eyes. 'I don't know how to put it without hurting you.' Then he hugged me tight, and whispered, 'My parents won't let me marry you.'

'What? Why?' My world spun out of control like a bi-plane twirling to the ground. 'But you want to, don't you?' I imagined his parents' disapproving faces. 'They don't think I'm good enough for you, do they?' I grasped the door handle. 'I'm going to . . .'

'Kathy.' He caught my hand. 'It's no good. They want me to finish my training and become an officer like Father, and then perhaps . . .'

'Perhaps you'll marry some other officer's daughter with plenty of money.'

'They didn't say that, Kathy.'

'Yes, but that's what they mean. They've always made me feel that I was different from you and Abigail. Not quite good enough. A builder's daughter, that's me.'

'What's all this?' Dad stormed out into the hall, his face angry red and his eyes blazing.

'Not now, Joe.' Mother tried to hold him back.

'My daughter's not good enough for you, is she? After *you* got her into this trouble?' Shaking off Mother's grip, he flexed his biceps, stretching the fabric of his best jacket to almost bursting point.

I jumped in front of Ben.

'Stop, Dad! It's not his fault.'

'Oh, no? I'm going over to have a word with his parents.'

'Dad!'

He pushed past us, opened the door, and stormed out, giving it a satisfactory bang.

Ben began to follow him. 'I'd better go.'

'Wait!' I threw my arms around him. Holding him close, I wished he could stay for ever. 'Perhaps your parents will change their minds. I want to marry you so much, Ben. I'm sorry about what Dad said. He's cross, that's all. It took him long enough to get used to the idea of me being pregnant in the first place.'

'I'm sorry too, but I'm going to have to do as my parents say if I ever want to be a pilot. I'll be twenty-one next August, and then they can't stop me. If we marry before that they say they'll cut off my income.'

'Oh, Ben!'

'I want to marry you, and see our baby grow up. Please be patient. Trust me, everything will turn out fine.'

I smiled. 'That's what you said last time, and now look at me.'

He took my hands. 'What have you got there?' he said, unfolding them.

'It's just a bead off my dress.' I rolled it in my fingers. 'Take it, and keep it with you all the time until you can come back and marry me.' I kissed him, and the longing was so strong that my knees turned to jelly again. 'I love you, Ben.'

'I love you too, and I promise that I'll marry you.'

'I promise that I'll marry you too.' I hugged him tight.

'I'll see you at Christmas anyway, won't I?'

'Yes.' He ran his fingers through my hair, and caressed my face, then he gave me one last hug, and rushed off down the path.

I sat in the kitchen, listening to the clock ticking and watching Mother peel the potatoes and trim the Brussels sprouts. I felt as if I was becalmed in a hot air balloon, waiting for the wind to blow, and not knowing whether it would sweep me into the high mountains or to the safety of the riverside meadows. Then, we heard the front door slam, and rushed out into the hall.

'What did they say?' Mother asked the words, that I didn't dare to speak.

Dad stood there, his eyes bulging and a vein in his forehead pumping in anger. 'They won't listen to reason. They won't let Ben marry her.' He clenched his fists in desperation. 'I don't know what's the matter with them. I'm sorry, Kathy.'

The fire went out from under my balloon and it sank to the ground.

'But why? What did they say?' Mother brandished her vegetable knife.

He took a deep breath. 'Wing Commander Hunter said that Ben must finish his training. He doesn't want him to jeopardise his future. And he said that under the circumstances, a wedding would be too much for his sick wife.'

Mother prodded the air. 'But what about Kathy's future? And the baby's? Doesn't he care about jeopardising that?'

'He said that Ben's career was paramount. He wants him to become a high flying officer like him.'

At last, I found my voice. 'But, Dad, that's not fair. Ben and I love each other. We want to get married. The baby needs us to be married. Can't we do anything?'

'No, it doesn't look like it. They won't give their consent. You'll have to wait until he's twenty-one or they'll cut off his income which should double on any marriage in the future.'

'But, he will be twenty-one next August, Dad. Can't we ask Reverend MacAulay if something can be done?'

Mother shook her head. 'I don't think so. His wife said the other day that she heard of a young man applying to the Bishop for a special licence because his fiancée was pregnant, he was nearly twenty-one too, but the Bishop said they must wait.'

'Couldn't we go to another parish and not tell them he's under age, Dad?'

'You could, but it's risky. Remember my cousin Betty's boy? He did just that and ended up having his marriage annulled.'

'We'll run away to Gretna Green then. I can't believe that we're not allowed to do the one thing that would put everything right.' I scanned their faces for some hope, but Mother shook her head again.

'There was a bit in the paper yesterday. You have to live there for three weeks now, you can't just turn up at the blacksmith's and get married over the anvil, Kathy. The RAF would never release Ben to do that. I don't think you've got any option but to wait, especially with Mrs Hunter in such frail health.' Mother glanced at Dad for his agreement. 'She won't be able to cope with any scandal in her condition. But, you know, Joe, I'm worried that there'll be an even bigger furore if Ben marries her after the baby's been born. They can hardly hide the fact they have a young child then.'

'I can't think straight any more,' he said, heading for the back door. 'I'm going to go and get some more coal in for the fire.'

'The Hunters don't want Ben to marry me at all, do they?' I followed Mother into the kitchen, whilst outside, Dad bludgeoned some large blocks of coal into smaller chunks with his mallet. 'What are we going to do?'

'Kathy, I've been wondering.' She shut the door. 'We really can't have any scandal here either.'

'What do you mean?'

'If Ben can't marry you, we mustn't let the neighbours know that you're pregnant. We've got to keep it quiet.' She patted my stomach. 'It doesn't show at the moment, that's good. But I thought we might have a bit of trouble with Ben's family, so I've written to Sylvia and arranged for you to go and stay with her at the end of the month until the baby comes.'

'What?' A picture of my aunt appeared in my mind: tall, elegant, rather like Coco Chanel, finished off with a double string of pearls. 'Aunt Sylvia? But she lives in *Devon* now. It's one thing working in her shop, but I wouldn't want to go and live with her. It's so far away.'

'Well, you should've thought about that before you got yourself in this predicament, shouldn't you?' Mother stuck her hands on her hips.

'But, Ben's coming home at Christmas. You've just said the baby doesn't show; please let me stay until then?'

'I don't want you to go at all, Kathy, but we can't possibly have the neighbours talking.' She raised her eyebrows. 'You'll just have to go away, and pretend that nothing's happened.'

Dad came in to wash his hands and made us jump.

'I'm going to send her to Sylvia's in Devon, Joe, until the baby's born and we can sort something out.'

'Sylvia's? Where do I come into this? What about what I think?'

'We've got to do something, Joe.' She touched his arm. 'She can't stay at home like this in the family way, what will everyone say?'

Nobody felt like having any Sunday lunch. Dad went at the beef with the carving knife as if it was Ben's father, and Mother pushed her peas around her plate without actually eating any. I stared at the bare winter trees in the garden, my Yorkshire pudding tasting like cardboard.

'Don't worry, Kathy, I'm sure Aunt Sylvia will be fine.' Mother finally popped a forkful in her mouth.

'I don't want to go, Mother. I want to marry Ben. Can't *you* go and see Ben's parents and ask them to change their minds?'

'No, I don't think I could make a scrap of difference, what with Mrs Hunter convalescing too. No, the best thing is for you to go away. Perhaps they'll let you get married after the baby's born. It's not what I would prefer, but we'll have to see.'

'It's the best thing for you, isn't it? To send me out of the way?' I put down my knife and fork.

'Kathy, do *not* speak to your Mother like that.' Dad pointed a warning finger.

'Sorry, Mother, but you're the one who's worried about what the neighbours will say.' I stood up and smoothed my dress over my tummy. 'It doesn't really show yet. Please could I stay here until after Christmas? I must see Ben again. I won't see him until the summer if I go. And I'm really worried that his parents won't ever let me marry him, because I'm not up to scratch.'

'Why do you say that? I paid good money for you to go to that private school with Abigail.' Dad prodded the air with his fork. 'You're as first rate as anyone, Kathy, and don't you forget it! Oh, I've had enough; it's up to your mother.'

'But Joe, she can't stay here like this, in the family way.'

'Won't she still be "in the family way" in Devon? She can't run away from it, you know, Emily.'

'Please, Mother?'

She glanced at Dad. 'I don't have much choice do I? But you must be off by the New Year. You'll be about four months gone by then, and it'll be obvious.'

Dad sighed. 'She'd be far better off marrying the boy, if only they'd let her.'

The doorbell rang, and we glanced at each other.

'If that's Ben again, I'll give him another piece of my mind to take home to his parents.' He flung his chair back.

'No, I'll go, Joe.' Mother was on her feet, but I was already halfway into the hall. 'You stay here, Kathy. I'll handle this.'

She went out and shut the door.

'I can't hear anything.' I pulled it open a crack, 'I can't see anything either.' Then Mother pushed it from the other side, making me topple backwards.

'Kathy, what ever are you doing?' Then, over her shoulder, she said, 'You'd better come in.'

'*Abigail?* I thought it was Ben.' I grabbed a chair for balance.

‘Kathy, I had to come. I’m so sorry. We’ve had the most frightful row at lunchtime. Ben’s gone back already; Father won’t speak to him about it any more.’ She screwed her handkerchief into a wet ball. ‘I wanted to tell you yesterday; to warn you.’

‘You knew?’

‘Yes, Father is adamant that Ben finishes his officer’s course.’

‘What about afterwards, do you think he’ll let Ben marry me?’

‘I don’t know, Kathy, I just don’t know.’

Chapter Four

December 1st 1929
The days ground by, and the rest of November disappeared under a blanket of cloud and fog. I wondered why Ben's parents were being so mean? Why couldn't his mother cope with a wedding? I was good enough, wasn't I? I wished that he could make them change their minds. I really didn't want to be sent away.

I felt so empty each night; I wanted to see Ben and tell him how much I missed him, but all I had were his letters. I couldn't wait to sit on the stairs in the morning, eager to grab the post as it came through the letterbox. I would search through the brown bills, scented letters from aunts, or airmail letters from cousins in Canada, until I found the blue one with Ben's spiky handwriting. Then letting the rest fall, I would open it with a beating heart. His little cartoons made me smile. This time last year, marriage was the last thing on my mind, and Ben, along with Abigail, were just my best friends. Now I was expecting his baby, and I needed to be with him more than ever. The fact that we weren't allowed to marry made it all the worse.

Today, a large mysterious envelope, with his familiar writing, burst through the letterbox with the usual post. I only just caught it as it sailed to the floor. Inside was an Advent Calendar, but instead of a Nativity scene, there was a red Gipsy Moth flying a banner which said, 'Happy Christmas, Kathy!' and a letter.

Dearest Kathy,

I love you so much and I miss you every minute of every day. Even though the chaps here are friendly, like Archie McCall who's really looked after me, I feel lost and alone without you. I've made this calendar so you can open a door each day and count the time to Christmas when we can be together again.

I gently opened number one, and there was a cartoon of Ben wearing a paper hat from a cracker and smiling, with my little black bead around his neck. I stroked it with my finger and kissed it.

It's only a few weeks till I come home, and I can't wait. I'm so cold and lonely without you. Remember, every day that passes is a day less to wait. It won't be long, until I am there and you are my arms. I love you, Kathy, with all my heart, and I'm going to talk to my parents when I get home and see if they will change their minds.

All my love,

Ben

I hugged the letter and calendar to my heart as if I could somehow draw him into my body. Then I felt my hard little tummy; he was there already.

As always, I sent him a reply by the next post. I had a large stack of his letters, and I imagined that he did too, tucked in a drawer. I often wondered if there was enough room for his RAF socks.

Dear Ben,

Only you would think of making such a wonderful Advent calendar. Thank you so much. I'm just itching to peep inside all the doors, but that would spoil all the surprises.

I miss you too; time drags by so slowly without you here. I even miss the shop, and find myself longing to go back to work, at least that would make the days and weeks crawl past more quickly.

There's nothing to do. No motorbike to tinker with and no trips into the countryside, hugging you for dear life as we breeze along the lanes. I'd really enjoy that, even though the weather's turning cold and damp now. No poring over the latest magazines together, and dreaming about shiny new motor cars. No holding hands in the pictures and watching newsreels of aeroplanes and adventurers. Ben, my life is so empty without you. I can't wait for Christmas to see you again. But afterwards, I'll have to go away to Devon, and I'm dreading that. I really hope that you can talk to your parents soon and they will let us marry.

Hurry up and come home,
Your loving Kathy

Every day when I woke up, my mouth actually watered at the prospect of opening another door; it was like choosing a chocolate from a box. I found a Gipsy Moth, Ben's motorbike, an orange-box go-kart, even some wellingtons, amongst Christmas candles, holly, mistletoe, parcels, snowmen and robins; all drawn lovingly in pen and ink and painted with watercolour. He was so clever; I couldn't draw for toffee. Every tiny picture brought me closer to him for a few minutes, but when I saw the day stretching away in front of me again, despite the possibility of another letter tomorrow, the pain was almost too much. But when the letters came, although they were full of love, he didn't mention any more about tackling his mother and father about the wedding. How I wished he'd do something.

December 21st 1929

Two o'clock in the afternoon of the shortest day of the year, and with heavy snow clouds in the sky, it seemed to be getting dark already. Dad had gone to the football, Mother was knitting, and I was roasting nicely by the fire, lost in thoughts of Ben coming home in only three day's time, when the doorbell rang. Sorry to be roused from such a delicious daydream, I shuffled off in my old slippers to see who had disturbed us.

Abigail stood at the door, wearing a camel coat and hat trimmed with honey coloured fur that framed her pixie face, and matching tiny ankle boots with buttons up the sides. Snowflakes clung to her like sugar sprinkled on a cake.

'Oh, Kathy, may I come in?' She took a step forwards, her eyes glistening, as if she'd been crying.

'Yes, of course, what on earth's wrong?'

'Mother is driving me mad. I've been trying to make her see reason about you and Ben, but she won't listen. It would be so nice if you could come over to our house on Christmas Eve, like you used to, and sing carols, but she won't hear of it. Oh, Kathy, she seems to think that it's all your fault, and that you led Ben on. She even thinks that you are jeopardizing his time at Cranwell.' Puddles of melted snow gathered round her feet on the doormat.

I nodded, and sat down on the stairs. I'd heard it all before. Abigail had been trying her best to make amends, build bridges and generally smooth things over between me and her parents, but they wouldn't budge.

'Oh, do come shopping with me, Kathy? I can't bear it at home any longer.'

'But it's snowing!' My thoughts went back to the warm fireside and my dreams of Ben. 'No, I don't really feel like it. I went with Mother last week and the shops were so crowded that we were squashed to bits. We could hardly carry our bags; they were nearly ripped out of our hands in the crush.'

'Oh, come on, it'll do you good to get out. You can't spend all your time hiding indoors.'

'I . . . but . . .'

'I've got the car; Benson's outside waiting.'

'The Alvis Silver Eagle? I've been itching to go for a ride in that. But, I can't, Abigail, what would your mother say?'

'Oh, she's busy this afternoon; she's got her ladies round for bridge, and Father's gone up to London for some Reunion Luncheon. Please Kathy, I'm all on my own. I miss Ben, and I never see you very much these days, please come?' She begged with her large blue eyes.

'I've got all the presents I need; I really can't face all those bad tempered shoppers and gaudy gifts. Everything seems so glittery and false this year.'

'Please, Kathy?'

Abigail's earnest expression made me relent. 'Oh, all right, but I'm only coming so I can have a ride in that car.'

Mother fussed that I was going out in the snow and made sure I wrapped up warm, but she was as keen as Abigail to keep the channels of communication open between our families.

Benson had the engine running at the kerb and the headlamps lit up the falling snow like a sky full of shooting stars. We sat back in the leather seats as if we were on a sleigh ride to fairyland.

Every shop window bulged with Christmas food and gifts, from pheasants to mistletoe, and from toys to crackers. There wasn't room to walk on the pavement and we were pushed into the gutter. Abigail's boots kept her feet dry, but mine were treated to a dose of icy slush which oozed through a hole in my shoe that I hadn't bothered to get mended. My fingers were frozen too because my gloves needed a stitch. I felt like an absolute tramp against my fairytale friend.

Abigail sensed my distress, 'Let's go into McIlroy's for a cup of coffee.' She guided me through the revolving doors into a warm world that smelt of expensive perfume. 'Come on, the lifts are over here.' Then, she grabbed my arm. 'Look! See that sign? There's Father Christmas on the third floor! Would you like to go and see him?' Her face lit up with excitement.

I would've rather sat down with a nice hot drink, but I couldn't disappoint her.

We took the lift to the third floor, but the attendant was telling people to get out at the second to join the queue on the stairs. So along with mothers and fathers loaded with bags and brown paper packages, and boys and girls waiting patiently or trying their parents' patience, we shuffled up the stairs, one at a time, to the Grotto on the next floor.

A magician with a top hat and cloak covered in moons and stars was entertaining the crowd. He shook hands with a man, and then with a flourish of his wand, produced the man's wristwatch from behind his ear to rapturous applause. He spotted Abigail and asked her for her signet ring, she refused; she'd seen what had happened to the watch, so he asked the next young woman.

Her scruffy little boy, beaming at the crowd with excitement and importance, whispered, 'Go on, Mum.' But she shook her head, unconsciously touching her stomach.

'Well, I never did,' a woman whispered behind us. 'Look at her, no wedding ring, and in the family way.'

'*And* with a young'un too,' added a second lady.

The young mother froze like a cornered rabbit, as the women went on.

'Oughtn't be allowed.'

'Fancy throwing herself around to get like that.'

The magician coughed and asked another lady who proudly lent him her diamond ring, as the young mother grabbed her son by the arm and fled down the stairs. We heard him crying out. 'Why aren't we seeing Father Christmas, Mum? Why? You promised!'

'That poor woman and that poor little boy.' I whispered. 'Why are people so cruel, Abigail? Look, I can't stay here, please can we go and have that cup of coffee now?'

'Yes, of course.' She took my arm and steered me towards the restaurant. 'Golly, you're shaking. I'm sorry, Kathy, I shouldn't have made you come.'

'It was as if those women were talking about me. *"No wedding ring and in the family way." "Throwing herself around."* I haven't done that, Abigail, I haven't. It was just love; love between Ben and me. Oh, why did I have to get myself in this mess?'

One or two ladies in smart hats and coats raised their eyebrows at me, but I walked past and ignored them.

Abigail ordered two coffees and some mince pies. 'They'll do you good; keep your strength up.'

I took one, but my throat tightened at the thought of eating the warm, spicy fruit and pastry. 'I can't get that young mother out of my mind. She didn't look any older than us, but she had one child and another on the way. I wish I could give this to her.'

'Don't be silly, Kathy, you'll never find her in this crush. She'll be all right, don't worry. Drink your coffee, there's a good girl.'

I glanced round at the other women posing in their expensive clothes and furs, like extras on a film set. *Against Abigail, my clothes are old and drab, but I'm more fortunate than that young mother, I have Ben, and with any luck we'll get married one day. I really hope so.* I crossed my fingers. *It's torture that he's not here. It's torture being kept apart.*

'A penny for them?' Abigail smiled at me.

I wiped my mouth on a serviette. 'Sorry, I was far away.'

'Kathy, would you mind very much if we looked in Ladies' Fashions afterwards? I need a dress for New Year's Eve.'

My face fell.

'Sorry, I know you won't be able to go,' she patted my arm, 'but I've been invited to Maureen and Hilda's party. I do so wish things were different.'

'It's all right, let's see what we can find for you.'

There were so many things I'd have liked to put right in my life: not being pregnant was at the top of the list, being petite like Abigail and able to look gorgeous in the latest fashions was quite close. But yet again, they'd be wasted on a tomboy like me.

Ladies' Fashions were on the same floor, and we threaded our way through the rails of dresses on the thick luxurious carpet. Abigail picked a handful of gowns and went to try them on whilst I sat outside.

'What do you think of this one, Kathy?' She emerged in a sea green silk dress with a matching coatee. 'It's got the new higher waist,' she said, placing her hands on her hips and admiring the embroidered panel which accentuated her flat tummy.

'It's lovely, Abigail,' I said, as she disappeared to try on another one.

To pass the time, I looked round the department at delicious frocks that I could never afford on my meagre wages at the bookshop. Then I came to the rail of white satin wedding dresses cut on the bias, with floaty feathers sewn around the hem. I fingered the heavenly material and closed my eyes, dreaming of walking down the aisle to meet Ben at the altar. I held the dress in front of me, and twirled round as if I was dancing.

'Excuse me, miss, would you like to try it on?' The sales assistant regarded me over her half-moon spectacles, and tapped her lip with her pencil. 'I think it would suit you. You need your height to carry off those feathers, now they're making skirts longer.'

'Oh, no,' I protested, 'I'm just waiting for my friend in the changing room.' But then I thought, why shouldn't I? I would be getting married if I had the chance.

A few minutes later, Abigail emerged. 'How about this one? I quite like the black and white crêpe de Chine with the white georgette bodice' Then she saw me . . . 'What *are* you doing, Kathy?'

Somehow, the assistant had managed to hook and eye me into the gorgeous dress, the waist wasn't quite as high as Abigail's, and top it off with a cloche style veil made of scalloped lace.

'Oh, Kathy! If only Ben could see you know. If only Mother and Father could see you now! You look like a film star. Oh, you look beautiful!'

I smiled at myself in the mirror. 'If only, Abigail, if only.' Taking a final glance, and feeling a bit like Cinderella, I swished into the changing room to change back into my old clothes.

Too overcome to buy anything herself, Abigail squeezed my arm as we wound our way back to the lifts. 'It really suited you. I hope it won't be too long before you marry Ben.'

'It's a wonder it fastened up. Do you think she knew I was pregnant?'

‘No, I shouldn’t think so; she wouldn’t expect you to be, would she?’

I blew air onto my forehead. *Was it hot in there or was it me?* ‘No, I don ‘t suppose she would.’

But none of this altered the fact that I was pregnant, and although I couldn’t wait to see Ben at Christmas, very soon afterwards I would be packed off to Aunt Sylvia’s in Devon.

Chapter Five

December 26th 1929

Ben was due back on Christmas Eve, but it was Boxing Day afternoon before he could manage to escape from his family. Every time someone came to our door or the telephone rang I thought it was him. But, I didn't dare telephone his house, or turn up at his front door for fear of what his parents would say. At last, however, there he was at ours, muffled with a long red scarf, and stamping the snow off his feet. We clung to each other like two children lost in a blizzard.

'Happy Christmas, Kathy. I've been waiting for this moment for so long.' His kiss was soft, warm, desperate. And that faint smell of engine oil on his clothes made me feel safe and reminded me of all the good times we'd had before I got pregnant and he'd gone away.

'I've missed you too.' I could hardly speak.

He touched my tummy. 'There's definitely a small bump.'

'Yes, but it doesn't show too much yet, does it?' I held in my muscles and smiled.

'No, but it will soon.'

'I know, but it would be a lot easier if we could get married. Have you talked to your parents yet?'

'I haven't had a chance. You know what it's like at Christmas. They're so busy with the visitors, I've hardly spoken to them at all.'

'Oh, Ben, you said you were going to, and I've been hoping and hoping that you would. Don't you want to marry me?' I made a puppy face with doleful eyes.

'Of course!' He kissed me again.

'Oh, Ben, can't you get them to change their minds? Then I could come up to Lincolnshire and be near you all the time.'

'Look, I've got your little black bead here on my ID chain.' He dug it out to show me. 'It brings you to me, any time I'm lonely.'

'I know, but I want you, Ben,' I said, kissing him back.

Voices rose in the front room, and the door opened.

I let go of him. 'Mother's sisters are here with their families,' I whispered.

'Let's go for a walk then,' he whispered back, smiling.

Making excuses and getting disapproving looks from my aunts, we escaped into the sparkling wintry wonderland. I'd had a black fur muff as a present, and we held hands inside it, keeping our other ones warm in our pockets.

Putting my worries behind me, I squeezed his hand, deciding to make the most of having him here. 'Did you have a nice Christmas?'

'No, of course not without you. Everyone was so boring; Great Uncle Peter, Great Aunt Jane, cousins I never see from one Christmas to the next. I'm not sure who half of them are. Even the table was groaning under the weight of all the food.' He made a snowball and hurled it at a tree. 'What about you?'

'How could I have a nice Christmas, knowing that you were just a hundred yards away over the road, and I couldn't see you? If I'd had my own aeroplane, I would've flown by and carried you off to, I don't know, the Northern Lights, so we could fly round amongst all the shimmering colours. That is, if your parents would have let you come.' I aimed a snowball fair and square in the centre of his. 'Bullseye!'

'Should you be doing that, er, in your condition?'

'I'm blooming like a Christmas rose now you're here. Never felt better.' I gathered up some more snow and threw it at him.

'Hey, Kathy!' He seized my hand, then kissed my icy blue fingers. 'I'm so sorry about this awkward business.'

We walked on in silence, through deep drifts of snow which stretched across the river meadows like frozen waves on the Arctic Ocean, and the winter sun shone through our cloudy breath and turned it into rainbow colours.

'What do your parents say?' he asked.

'You know, don't you? They want us to be married, but if we can't, Mother wants me out of the way. She doesn't want the neighbours to gossip.'

'I've been thinking, she might be right to send you to Devon. I don't want people saying awful things about you. You've got to be strong, Kathy.' He ducked under a branch which hung heavy with snow, and created a little snowstorm of loose flakes. 'When are you going?'

'The day before New Year's Eve.' I brushed the snowflakes off his shoulder. 'I used to love those New Year's Eve parties at your house. We were so happy then, when your parents weren't afraid that I might marry you.'

He kissed me on the forehead. 'I won't be there either this time, and Abigail's going to Maureen and Hilda's party, isn't she?'

'Yes, so everything's changed.'

Ben stopped, and faced me. 'Listen Kathy, I've got to go back tomorrow.'

'Tomorrow? But I thought you were going to stay a few days.' I held him tight. 'I've only just got used to having you here.'

'I'll get some time off at Easter, but I don't know whether I'll be able to get down to Devon. When is the baby due?'

'I'm not sure, around the end of May, I think.'

Ben stopped in his tracks. 'You mean that the next time I see you, our baby might be born? I'll be a father.'

'Yes, and I'll be a mother. I don't know how I'll ever cope.'

'Wait for me, Kathy. I will come back and marry you, I promise. August is not that far away. I wish Mother hadn't been so ill. Things might have been different.'

'Oh, Ben, and I really wish that you would talk to them and make them understand. It's terrible we have to be apart.'

'They wouldn't listen anyway, Kathy. They want me to finish my training and become an officer like Father.'

'That's not fair. They won't really know how we feel, or care about what we want or what would be best for the baby, unless you tell them, Ben,'

'I tried before I went away, but they won't listen. There's nothing I can do, Kathy, I'm sorry, but there it is.' He put his arm round me. 'I suppose I'd better take you home before it gets really cold.'

'Do we have to go back? I can't bear you going away again. I miss you so much. It would be bad enough even if I wasn't pregnant.' I hugged him again. 'Oh, Ben, I'm not looking forward to spending all those months in Devon with Aunt Sylvia.'

'It'll be fine, Kathy. They'll fly past, believe me.' And despite my misgivings, his kiss warmed me all the way to my frozen fingers and toes, as the sun dipped behind the snowy trees.

'They might fly past for you in your Gipsy Moth, but I don't think they will for me.' I sighed, as we trudged back.

At home, everyone was wearing paper hats and noisily guessing at charades in the front room.

'Come and join us, Kathy.' Mother beckoned.

'No.' I looked round the room and even the tinsel had lost its sparkle. 'I think I'll just go and lie down.'

Upstairs, I hugged my pillow and replayed every moment of our walk in my mind. *I love you, Ben, but I wish you would make your parents listen. I don't want to go away on my own.*

Abigail popped in the day after with a box of lavender soap tied up with a pink ribbon.

'Just a little gift for you to take away.'

I smiled, 'Thank you very much. It's just like you to give me something so pretty.'

'Lavender's very calming, Kathy; it'll do you good.' She picked up some dresses and skirts which were draped over the sofa. 'What are all these? Is your Mother throwing them out?'

'No,' I groaned, 'she's borrowed them from her sisters for me to wear as I get bigger.'

'But you can't wear *these*; they must be at least ten years old.'

'I know, but Mother refuses point blank for either of us to set foot in a shop to buy some proper maternity clothes.'

'Poor Kathy, you could get both of us in one of these.' She struggled into a dress; it was like a tent. 'Come on, let's try it. Mind my hair, though.'

'No, it's no good, there's not enough room for us both.' I laughed, trying to get my elbow through the sleeve.

Abigail grabbed a cushion from the sofa. 'I'm going to stuff this up the front instead. You try one on, and do it too.'

I scrambled into another dress and we fastened up the belts, and pummelled the cushions until we looked like two kangaroos. Then, giggling, we pushed each other out of the way so we could look in the mirror.

Nearly toppling over, we bowed at each other, and paraded about in fits of laughter.

'How do you do?'

'How do you do?'

Suddenly, Mother was at the door. Her smile soon disappeared when she saw what we were up to.

'What are you doing, Kathy?' She put her hands on her hips. 'Abigail, I thought you'd have more sense.'

We let the dresses and cushions fall to the floor.

'Your aunts have lent you those clothes out of the kindness of their hearts, and I'd thank you to look after them.'

'But, they're so out of date.' I hung my dress back on its hanger.

'Since when have you cared about being *up to* date, Kathy? They are good clothes; they came from Heelas's. I wish I could afford clothes from there.' She stoked them lovingly.

'But . . .'

'That's enough, I don't want to hear any more.' Mother marched out, and like party balloons that had been popped, Abigail and I drifted onto the sofa.

'You know,' I said, 'that was the best fun I've had for months. I wish I didn't have to go, I shall miss you, Abigail.' And we hugged each other, as if I was flying to the ends of the earth.

December 30th 1929

I kept waking up all night. *I'm going away in the morning; I'm going away to have a baby,* I repeated endlessly, but I still couldn't believe it. For once, the morning came far too soon.

Mother and I were standing at the bus stop, when Reverend MacAulay and his wife purred along in their blue Morris Oxford, the slush spraying up behind like a winged chariot.

Mrs MacAulay rolled down her window.

'Could we offer you a lift somewhere?'

'No, thank you, it's very kind,' Mother said, 'but the bus will be here in a minute.'

'Where are you going?'

'Oh, to the station.' Mother tried to make light of it.

Mrs MacAulay caught sight of the large label on my suitcase: *Mason – Passenger to Teignmouth.*

'Who's off to Devon then, is it you, Kathy?'

She must have eagle eyes and the brains of Sherlock Holmes, I thought as I studied the buckles on my new shoes like a naughty schoolgirl.

'That's nice. Is it for a little holiday?'

'No, she's going to be a companion for her aunt.' Mother clamped her mouth shut, already sensing she'd said too much, as Mrs MacAulay's eyes slid to my stomach.

'I see.' She gave a knowing nod.

Mother's face turned the colour of her maroon winter coat, and her eyes glittered like the brooch on her lapel. 'Oh, look, there's the bus,' she said through clenched teeth. 'Goodbye, Mrs.

MacAulay. Thank you for offering us a lift. A Very Happy New Year to you.'

'Yes, and a Happy New Year to you all,' said Mrs MacAulay, raising her eyebrows and pursing her lips, as they drove off in a cloud of exhaust.

'How dare she?' Mother fumed as the bus drew up. 'That's only the beginning of it, Kathy, you'll be far better off in Devon, before the neighbours start to gossip.'

I hope you're right, I thought, as she heaved my case onto the bus.

The bitter taste of Mother's face powder clung to my lips, as I leant out of the railway carriage window. *I wish I didn't have to go.* My throat tightened, and I struggled to whisper goodbye.

'Take care, dear,' Mother called, 'Uncle Jeremy will be there to meet . . .' But, her voice was drowned out by the shrill whistle as my train pulled out of the station.

Shivering from the draught, I hauled up the window with the leather strap and flopped onto the seat. The late December sun caressed my face. I closed my eyes, remembering that last, hot afternoon of the summer with Ben: the exquisite pleasure of lying together in the heat; the soft breeze that cooled our damp skin, the solid certainty that we were in love. *If only you'd got your parents to change their minds.*

The train steamed relentlessly southwest: past the graveyard where Grandfather was buried, and on past our house away over the fields. As a child, I lay in bed and pretended I was an engine driver roaring down the line to exciting faraway places, but this was one trip that I hadn't planned. We entered a tunnel and the reflection of my worried face rushed alongside in the dark.

What's Aunt Sylvia going to say? What will it be like living with her for months? I sighed, and my breath made a damp patch on the glass. I sketched a little picture of Ben in the moisture with my nail. *Perhaps I could get off in Bristol, and catch the next train north to Lincolnshire. But then, I'd only be sent back. How have we come from children, playing with orange-box cars on pram wheels, to having a baby of our own?*

As the train came out of the tunnel, my thoughts swirled around like the snow which had begun to fall. I looked at my watch; it was already four o'clock, time for tea. I swayed along the dim corridor to the busy buffet car, but I only drank half a cup, and picked at a few crumbs of fruitcake.

The train stopped at Bristol and when I returned to my seat, an elderly lady sat opposite.

'I hope that you don't mind me sharing your carriage?' She gathered her black fur coat around her as if to take up less space.

'No, there's plenty of room.' I said, but secretly wished I could have it all to myself.

The door glided open again, and the draught from the corridor blew around my legs. A man with a large suitcase thrust his way into the carriage. He was taller than Ben, but I gasped when I saw his face, because with his fair hair and blue eyes, he looked just like the Prince of Wales, only younger. I bet he has girls falling at his feet all the time, I thought.

'Excuse me,' he said, as he struggled to hoist his case up onto the rack, bumping into my knees in the process. 'All the other carriages are full.'

I just smiled, not knowing what to say. It was like sharing a carriage with a film star.

'Tickets please!' The ticket inspector put his head round the door that the man had forgotten to push shut. 'Tickets please, from Bristol.'

I dug mine out of my handbag, as no one had checked it yet, and the man produced his out of his wallet. The ticket inspector punched them, and looked expectantly at the lady who rifled through her handbag, and then her pockets.

'Do you think you could get my holdall down for me, please?' she asked the ticket inspector.

'Here, let me help you.' The good-looking man hauled down her bag and rested it on the seat.

'Thank you very much.' The lady opened it up, and rummaged through her belongings. The ticket flew out and fluttered to the floor, and the man and I bent down to pick it up and knocked our heads together.

'Ooh, sorry!' we said. Then, he smiled, his blue eyes twinkling like the sea on a sunny day. To my horror, I blushed. *What on earth is wrong with you, Kathy?* I quickly handed the lady her ticket, and settled back into my seat.

He sat down, stood up, took *The Times* out of his bag, flapped it open, and folded it again so he could read an article. Whilst he engrossed himself in the paper, he seemed to produce a two-shilling piece out of thin air, and flip it around his fingers, up and down, never dropping it, like a Hollywood gangster. It mesmerized me so much that my fingers itched to copy the wave-like movement.

Suddenly, he looked up. I was caught red-handed and red-faced. I hunted in my bag for the book Auntie had sent for Christmas and tried to immerse myself in a story about a female detective and a murder in an amusement park, but I couldn't stop being aware of the handsome man, sitting with his knees only two feet away from mine across the carriage.

Chapter Six

Eventually, the train rumbled on over some iron bridges, and the rhythmic girders lulled me to sleep. I dreamt that I rode a roller coaster, creaking and groaning up a steep slope, and then plunging down into an endless tunnel, out of control, riding up and spiralling over the curved walls. I opened my eyes in panic, and glanced around, gripping the arm rests. I was relieved to find myself safe in the carriage with the two others chatting away like old friends.

It was almost six o'clock when the signs: TEIGNMOUTH, TEIGNMOUTH sped past the window, and the train came to a halt amid clouds of steam. There was a jolt as I stood up to pull down my case, and I stumbled against the man.

'Jeepers, I'm so sorry.' My body glowed with heat as if I was inside an electric oven. *What is the matter with me?*

'Don't worry; I'm still in one piece.' He smiled, and my temperature rose a few more degrees. 'Can I get it down for you?'

'No, thank you, I can manage.' I didn't dare make eye contact with him again, but swung my bag down, and got out as quickly as possible.

I searched up and down the platform for Uncle Jeremy. I nearly spoke to one man who looked the right sort of age, but a young girl ran up to him instead, calling 'Grandad!'

Where is he? Eventually, the station emptied, and the bright train pulled away into the darkness.

A porter hobbled up. 'Can I get you a taxi, miss?'

I looked around: no sign of Uncle Jeremy.

'I'll just wait a while; my uncle's coming to meet me.'

Ten minutes passed, but still no sign of him. The old porter came back.

'Let me help you to the taxi rank.' He loaded my case onto his trolley and led the way outside. I could smell the sea, and the lights from the promenade shone at the end of street, but these remnants of summer made me feel even more lost and alone in the middle of winter. Sinking down in the taxi seat, I lit a cigarette; I hadn't smoked one for months.

The driver stopped at some wrought iron gates. 'Here we are at Hillfields, miss,' he said. The black-and-white Edwardian house sat elegantly at the top of the drive, stretching its long front garden down towards the river. Peering into the shadows for ghosts or murderers, I trudged up the gravel with my case, passing several parked cars. The enormity of the situation hit me. I'd been sent away from home so I wouldn't disgrace my parents. I'd never been anywhere on my own before like this. I felt as if the jolly rubber ring that had been keeping me afloat had burst, and I was floundering about in choppy water. I wished Mother was there to tell me what to do. A shoal of fish darted about inside my tummy. They swam faster, round and round, as I spied Aunt Sylvia's silhouette on the bright dining room curtains, the feather in her headband bobbing as she talked to some visitors. I tried to keep the surging in my stomach under control as I crunched over the stones to the door and rang the bell. My heart thumped away so much, I didn't hear anyone coming until the door opened.

'Kathy! Oh, my goodness!' Aunt Sylvia, wearing a chic little black dress, took a step backwards. She clamped her hand over her mouth, and her silver bangles jangled down her arm. 'We forgot you were coming: we've got a little cocktail party on this evening. How on earth did you get here?' She looked out, as if to see Cinderella's coach, or a magic carpet waiting for a tip.

'I got a taxi from the station, Auntie.'

'Oh well, come on in. My goodness, look at you, you must still be growing; you're nearly as tall as me.'

'Thank you very much.' *At least she didn't mention I was pregnant.*

'Are you hungry after such a long journey? Come and have some supper.'

I can't meet all these people. How am I going to keep my condition a secret?

The fish raced round in a frenzy as she helped me out of my coat, hung it on the hat stand, and then, to my relief, led the way to the kitchen, her heels clicking on the black and white tiles. Music danced out of the dining room as we passed, and I kept my head down, not wanting to meet anyone's eyes.

She opened the kitchen door. 'You'll have to excuse me, Kathy; I must get back to my guests. Mabel?' she called, 'Kathy's here, can you find her something to eat?'

'Certainly, Mrs Trevelyan.' A rosy-cheeked woman in a starched white apron clattered oven trays onto to the table. 'I'm sorry, ma'am, I didn't hear the door. It's all this party food.' She blew on her fingers to cool them, and brushed some stray, grey hairs off her damp forehead.

'Thank you, Mabel.' Aunt Sylvia swept back to her guests.

A golden retriever yawned and stretched in its basket near the Aga.

'That's Rosie, don't mind her,' Mabel explained, as the dog raised her head sleepily. 'Would you like one of these vol-au-vents? Or I could do you some cold meat and salad, if you give me a minute.' She pulled out a chair for me. 'There's some trifle left over from lunch, if you like.'

My stomach lurched. 'Do you mind if I just have a cup of tea, Mabel? I really don't feel hungry.'

'No, of course not, let's make you a nice cup.' She drew the kettle onto the hotplate. 'How was your journey, miss?'

'Not too bad.' I caught my breath as I remembered the man on the train, and shook my head.

Mabel frowned. 'You must be tired, miss.'

The tea was hot and soothing, and I could feel my eyes beginning to close, as Mabel arranged the party food on silver platters. She wiped her hands on her apron.

'I've got a moment now: let me show you up to your room, and you can get an early night.'

I agreed, and followed her upstairs. A fire burnt in the grate, so at least *she* must have been expecting me. The room appeared tidy and bare, compared with my own which was always littered with Meccano models and motoring magazines. I pulled open the wardrobe door, and it smelt of mothballs. Auntie had stored some spare clothes in there and there was hardly room for the few dresses I'd brought. I chose the bed beside the window. The springs complained, and the sheets crinkled with starch as I climbed in and settled down with my writing paper.

Darling Ben,

Well, I've arrived here in Devon. Would you believe it? Aunt Sylvia had forgotten that I was coming, and Uncle Jeremy didn't even meet me off the train! She's having a party downstairs, but I don't think it'll stop me going to sleep; I'm so tired. I'm so lonely too; I wish you were here with me. It was such a long journey, and we're further apart now, than we've ever been.

I hope that you will have a Happy New Year, and it'll be a better one for both of us. It won't be half so nice without you though.

Your loving,
Kathy

I dashed off a quick note to Mother and Dad to tell them I'd arrived safely, and decided to post them both in the morning.

I tried to go to sleep in the dying firelight, but I couldn't help thinking about the happenings of the day. It seemed ages since I'd left Mother on the platform, and Ben was now a world away. As I finally dropped off, a picture of the man on the train with the deep blue eyes floated across my dreams, like the summer sun sparkling on the sea.

December 31st 1929

As I lay in the dark of the mid-winter morning, I thought about Ben and Abigail's party last year. They'd ordered over a hundred balloons, and we'd laughed so much that we could hardly blow them up. It must have been lack of oxygen or something. *I wish that we were doing that today. Though I'm sure I've heard Mother say that you shouldn't blow up balloons if you're pregnant.* I sighed. *Pregnant: what a heavy sounding word.*

I heard voices, and a clattering in the kitchen, and wondered whether to get up. The next minute, there was a knock on the door and it opened, letting in the light from the landing. I blinked as Mabel came in with a cup of tea.

'Good morning, miss. I thought you'd like this before you got up.' She placed it beside the bed. 'It's another cold morning out there.'

'Thank you Mabel, I'll get dressed soon. Is Auntie up yet?'

'Yes, she says there's quite a lot to do for the dinner tonight.'

'Dinner?'

'Yes, it's New Year's Eve,' said Mabel, as she went out.

I groaned and sank back into the pillows. *Am I invited?* I prodded my tummy. *I hope Auntie's guests don't ask too many searching questions.*

I put on yesterday's brown dress which was already beginning to feel a bit tight. *I'll soon have to wear those other awful dresses. I wish I'd got some more fashionable ones.*

Uncle Jeremy was pouring out some coffee in the dining room when I got down. He turned, and smiled. 'Good morning, you must be Kathy.'

I gasped.

'What is it, my dear girl?'

'Nothing, you just remind me of someone, that's all.'

'Really? Handsome, I hope.' He handed me a cup. 'I'm sorry I wasn't there to meet you last night. Your aunt roped me in to help with her little cocktail party, and the time just flew by, let me give you some money for your taxi fare.'

'No, really, it's all right.' I sipped my coffee.

He spooned some bacon and eggs onto his plate. 'It's a pity, because you could've had a run in my new motor car.'

'Oh, what sort have you got?'

'An Alvis Silver Eagle.'

'Six cylinders and eighty-five miles an hour!' I chimed in.

'I am impressed, Kathy. How did you know that?'

'Our neighbours across the road have one. Ben, that's their son, told me all about it.' I buttered some toast. 'I've only been out in it once though.'

'We'll have to put that right then, won't we? But, Ben, eh? Is he your young man?'

My face blazed red, and I nodded.

'Poor girl,' he added. 'Damned awkward situation for you.'

Aunt Sylvia bustled in. 'Ah, there you are, Kathy, apologies for yesterday evening, dear. Just one of those things.' She drew on her cigarette through an elegant black holder. 'We have some friends coming for dinner tonight.'

I forced a smile. 'Oh, that'll be nice.'

'By the way, they're under the impression that you've come to be my companion. I think it's best to keep it that way, don't you?'

I nodded, relieved for a moment.

'What are you going to wear?'

The shoal of fish darted about inside my tummy again. *So I was invited to the dinner. I'd been sent away from home so I wouldn't disgrace my parents. And now, I'm going to be introduced to Aunt Sylvia's friends and pretend that everything is normal.*

'I've got a cream shantung dress, would that do?'

'I shall have to see it. Run and put it on after breakfast, will you?'

Aunt Sylvia fingered the material. 'Heelas's, isn't it? I think I saw them in there the last time I was in Reading.'

'Yes, Mother got in it in the Sales.' I smoothed the silky material over my tummy. *This would have been my wedding dress, if only Ben had convinced his parents.*

'Stand up straight, that's right. You know,' she added, 'it is a bit passé, but it will do. The hem's coming down just here though, isn't it?'

I swished the handkerchief skirt to and fro. It wasn't the most fashionable dress, but how I wished I could have walked down the aisle in it to join Ben at the altar. Heaven knows when that will be now, I thought, my head starting to swim.

'Kathy, sit down, dear; you look a bit pale.' Aunt Sylvia appeared concerned for once. 'How about mending that hem? I've got a needle and cotton somewhere.'

'I'm no good at sewing, Auntie.'

'Nonsense girl, here you are.'

The needle floated about in front of my eyes as I tried to thread it, and struggled to make neat stitches. 'It's not very good, I'm sorry.'

'Here, let me have a look,' she said, pulling it to her. 'It's not the best needlework, I've ever seen. Do it like this.' She took the needle and began to sew.

'Golly, you're doing it left-handed like me. How did you learn how to do that?'

'I am left-handed, Kathy. Didn't you know?' She looked at me over her glasses.

'No, I've never seen you sew before.'

'Well, it's surprising what you learn when you keep your eyes open.' She bit the thread off. 'There!'

Uncle Jeremy fussed Rosie's ears, making her frown at him sleepily. 'What ever is the matter with her? She's not normally this lazy. Do you want to go for a walk, girl?' But, she rested her heavy head on her paws, so he turned to us. 'How about you two coming to town with me instead?'

'No, Jeremy, I'm far too busy getting ready for tonight.' Auntie began to search through a recipe book. 'This is the one I was telling you about, Mabel. You go Kathy; a breath of sea air will do you good,' she added without glancing up.

'I'd love to. I do have some letters to post.' I said, relieved to escape.

I got changed again, and met Uncle by his gleaming car. He opened the rear door for me with a flourish and the smell of new leather wafted out.

'Could I sit in front instead, it's much more interesting?' I asked.

'Certainly! I think that you're even more excited about my lovely motor car than your aunt was, Kathy.'

He helped me in, and we scrunched down the drive as the winter sun glinted off the bonnet.

'Well, what do you think of her?' Uncle Jeremy asked.

'Of my aunt?'

'The car, Kathy. It was a little Christmas present to myself: might as well make the most of my money before we feel the effects of the Wall Street Crash.'

'It's wonderful. I'm really interested in anything with an engine, and these are the best cars I've ever been in.' I inspected the dials on the dashboard whilst Uncle grinned.

'I'm going to buy a wireless as a surprise for your aunt,' he said, as we drew up outside Scott's Wireless shop.

He pushed open the glass door, and the sounds of music, male voice choirs, and even a weather forecast greeted us. I had seen wireless sets in the shops at home, but Dad couldn't afford one. I stroked the polished mahogany cabinets. It was like fairyland. One had the design of a setting sun radiating from the corner, and I traced the cut-out rays with my finger. I whispered the names of the broadcasting stations on the dials: London, Prague, Vienna, Stavanger, Brussels, Lyons, Marseilles, and my jaw dropped open when I realized that the sounds I heard came from those far away places.

Mr Scott shook hands, and when Uncle introduced me, my heart beat faster and my hand went to my stomach; I couldn't help it. *What if he's noticed? I don't think I'm ever going to get used to this.*

He waxed lyrical to Uncle Jeremy about how the voices and music floating in the air, passed down through the aerial to the wireless, whilst I wandered about the shop, listening in to the various programmes. The lady behind the counter stared at me, and whispered to her assistant.

Perhaps things are going to be just the same as at home. Coming here isn't going to make it any better; Dad was right.

Suddenly, one programme caught my attention:

'The Antarctic expedition, aboard the ship 'Discovery', is hoping to make an aeroplane ascent to explore the icefields.'

'What's that you're listening to, Kathy?' Uncle Jeremy came up beside me.

'It's about the South Pole expedition. Fancy spending the New Year in the icefields. I would love to go up in an aeroplane, and fly above the snow and ice. I wish I was there right now.'

Uncle raised his eyebrows, and smiled.

'Sorry, Uncle,' I blushed. 'It's very kind of you to have me to stay. But I've visited Croydon Aerodrome once or twice, and I've always thought it would be ripping to go up in a plane. That's all.'

'Well I never did, Kathy, I didn't know that you were such a modern young woman. Did you know we have an aerodrome near here?'

'Really?'

'Yes at Haldon, we shall have to go up there one day and do some aeroplane spotting.'

He finished paying for the Phillips set he'd chosen.

'Let's go to the Post Office; I need to get a wireless licence, and you can post your letters.'

I followed behind, fantasizing about flying high above the Antarctic with Ben.

Chapter Seven

'Let me tell you who's coming to our party.' Uncle Jeremy suggested as we drove out of Teignmouth along the river.

'Yes, thank you, that would help,' I agreed.

'Well, you'll meet my business partner, Bill Canlan, and his wife Mary.'

'You're running a business? But, I thought you'd left all that behind in London.' I hadn't taken much interest in the letters that Mother used to read out, only that he'd proposed to Auntie on his retirement, after a whirlwind romance.

'Yes, as a young man, I couldn't wait to get away to the bright lights.'

'What made you come back to Devon, then?'

'It wasn't the countryside so much as the sea.'

'The sea?' I looked towards the estuary. 'It's beautiful isn't it? Though I haven't seen that much of it yet.'

'I've missed it so much being up in town. Yes, you've got the River Thames there, but it's nothing compared to the Devon coast. So I wanted to start up a little business for my retirement down here.'

'What are you going to do? Fish?'

'No, Bill and I are going into the pleasure craft business. We've come across a second-hand passenger launch, called *Lady Valentine*, and Bill has been renovating her all winter. I've been helping him of course, but Sylvia gets in a flap about all the time I spend down at the boatyard, so I'm very glad that you're here to keep her company.' He gave me a reassuring smile.

'Who else is coming?' I asked, hoping she felt the same.

'Well, there's our neighbours, and my son, Paul . . . What the blazes?'

A sheep jumped straight out in front of the car. Uncle jammed on the brakes, but couldn't help knocking it over sideways. He got out. 'You stay there, Kathy, I'll just see if it's injured.'

I felt sick at the thought of the poor animal, but it stood up and staggered about, just a little dazed. Uncle pushed it back through the hedge, and blocked up the hole with a branch.

'All the joys of living in the country,' he said, as we set off again.

That night, the moon hung in a clear sky, the stars shimmered like diamonds, and the Christmas tree lights made the frosty lawn sparkle like coloured sugar: a perfect evening, unless you're about to have dinner with complete strangers. I walked round the table, my fingers trailing up and down over the chairs. Before I fell pregnant, I'd always looked forward to parties and meeting new people, but now that I could see some cars coming up the drive, those fish that had been floating about quietly inside me, lurched into ferocious action again. Uneasy, I waited in the hall.

The bell rang. Tingles shot to my fingers and toes. Uncle Jeremy hurried to the door followed by Sylvia, and Rosie, revived after her sleep, barking and wagging her tail. I shrank back into the shadows.

'Bill and Mary! Come on in.' He opened the door wide.

'Hello, hello!' said Bill, whose weather beaten face creased into a wreath of smiles around his sea green eyes. He shook Uncle's hand and gave Auntie a kiss on the cheek. 'I thought we'd make a little contribution to the proceedings.' And he handed her a bottle of wine decorated with a bow of red ribbon.

'Thank you, Bill,' she said. 'This is my niece, Kathy. She's come to stay for a few months as my companion.' I wished I could disappear altogether, but she put her arm round me and pulled me forward. 'Would you mind taking their things, Kathy?' she asked.

Whilst I bundled their hats and coats upstairs, Bill and Mary were ushered into the sitting room, and Uncle welcomed another guest.

'Ah, Kathy, this is my son, Paul. He's a doctor at the new hospital in Teignmouth.'

'How d'you do?' he said, his blue eyes twinkling just like his father's.

'Oh my goodness, it's you! The man on the train with the two-shilling piece!' My heart skipped several beats, and the colour rushed to my cheeks. I had to grip his firm handshake to steady myself.

'Pleased to meet you again, Kathy.' He rubbed his temple where our heads had bumped. 'We'll have to be careful not to do that again!'

I smiled. Then to my relief, the bell rang again, releasing me to take the coats of the neighbours who stood on the doorstep.

Eventually, we all gathered in the sitting room. I hid myself in a deep armchair in the corner. Uncle stood with his back to the fire and raised his glass of sherry, beaming around at the gathering with pride.

'To my family and friends!'

Although, Uncle Jeremy and Aunt Sylvia had been quite kind including me in their party, I wished that I was with Ben instead on this New Year's Eve.

Just then, Mabel sounded the brass gong, and I held back, letting the others go in first. The table reminded me of the one I'd glimpsed in the Hunters' dining room: crisp white linen, sparking glasses and polished silver with bright candles trimmed with prickly holly.

I didn't feel hungry and I toyed with my lobster soup, until at last Mabel took it away.

'Don't you feel well, Miss Kathy?' she whispered.

'I'm just a bit tired, that's all.'

I had no appetite, even though I hadn't had a proper meal since I left home. The roast beef and Yorkshire puddings smelt delicious, but somehow, I couldn't bring myself to swallow them. I tried to concentrate on the conversation around the table, but my mind kept returning to Ben.

'Don't you miss Reading, Sylvia, with all these gales we're having? I didn't think you were cut out for the country life,' Bill asked.

'I'm not, but I'm learning.' Auntie smiled.

'What about you, Kathy?' asked Paul. 'I understand that you're going to be staying here for a while.'

I'd been hoping that no one would speak to me, and they'd forget that I was there, but then everyone turned my way and paused, waiting for my answer. I'd just taken a sip of water, and it tickled the back of my throat, threatening to make me choke. It took all my self-control to swallow it without spraying it everywhere. I dabbed my mouth with my serviette.

'Yes,' I eventually addressed the table in general. 'I'm going to be acting as a companion for Aunt Sylvia whilst your father is busy with his affairs.' My hand was drawn to my stomach like a magnet, and my cheeks burnt again. *I can't go through with this. I wish I could go home.*

At that moment, Mabel made an entrance with a piping hot apple pie, drawing everyone's attention from me. Thankful, I busied myself with the sweet and comforting pudding.

I didn't want to risk going through to the sitting room for coffee and brandy, so I helped Mabel to clear the table until she shooed me away. Then looking for a means of escape, I grabbed my coat and went outside.

The full moon rose high on silver clouds, and the icy air hurt my lungs as I gulped deep breaths to calm myself. 'Ben, why didn't you talk to your parents? We might have been married by now, and be spending New Year's Eve snuggled up together, instead of so far apart.'

'Kathy?' I turned; Uncle Jeremy stood at the door. 'Who are you talking to? And what ever are you doing outside?'

I shook my head, unable to speak.

'Come in, dear, you'll catch your death of cold. Come and have some nice hot coffee.' He patted my arm.

'I want to go home.' I shivered. 'I don't belong here. Auntie even forgot I was coming.'

'She has a lot on her mind at the moment; she's busy trying to open a new bookshop.'

'A new one? But I thought she'd left all that behind.'

'Yes, I think she regrets making such a big move.' He smiled wistfully. 'Give her time, Kathy. It's early days yet.' And he guided me inside where we joined the others gathered around the roaring fire.

He looked at his watch. 'It's nearly midnight. Who's got the right time?'

'Let's put on your wireless,' Aunt Sylvia suggested, 'and find out.'

'Yes, let's. How Scott's managed to deliver it today, and get it to work, I'll never know.' He turned the knob. It took a few minutes for it to warm up, then we marvelled to hear church bells being broadcast.

'Are they ringing out the Old or ringing in the New?' she asked.

Then Big Ben began to chime.

'Happy New Year!' They raised their glasses, and I obediently joined in. 'Here's to 1930!'

Ben's welcoming in the New Year at this very moment in Lincolnshire with all his RAF chums. I was with him this time last year, and going home, in an hour or so, to my own familiar bed. Amid the laughter and high spirits, my heart ached.

More bells rang out, and then *Auld Lang Syne*. Uncle Jeremy took my hand and squeezed it tight, whilst Mary grabbed the other, compelling me to join in the song with all those jolly strangers, I felt sick and alone.

The announcer broke in, 'Now, we are going to join Phil Spitalny and his Orchestra for some dance music.'

As the first bars were played, Aunt Sylvia jumped up and said, 'Let's dance!'

'Oh no, Sylvia, I've only just sat down.' Uncle began to light his pipe.

'No, Jeremy, up you get.' And she heaved him out of his chair.

Mary gave Bill a tug. 'If Jeremy's going to dance, then so are you.'

'Come on, Bill.' Uncle Jeremy cavorted about in front of him. 'You're not going to sit this out, and watch me make a fool of myself.'

My heart beat like a bass drum, *I'm not going to make an exhibition of myself either,* and I tried to hide in my dark corner. I watched the neighbours whispering to each other, and I thought they were going to sit it out, but they got up and began to dance as well.

Suddenly, Paul bowed low before me, 'Will you do me the honour?'

I shook my head. 'Oh no, I couldn't.'

'Oh, come on, Kathy,' he urged, 'it's the Charleston. Everyone can dance to this.'

Nevertheless, those blue eyes bewitched me, the bass drum in my chest beat a tattoo, and as if by magic, my feet began to jig about to the rhythm.

'There you are.' Paul drew me out of my chair, and for a few minutes, I danced like a film star.

Beads twirled, and dresses shimmered in the firelight, until all too soon, the music stopped, and Uncle Jeremy got out his handkerchief to mop his brow.

'Well, I'm really ready for bed now,' he said.

Everybody agreed, and said that it had been a wonderful evening and, as everyone was saying 'Good night', I realized that Paul was still holding my hand. I snatched it away as if it was on fire.

Chapter Eight

January 1st 1930

I lay in the bath, gently splashing water over my legs, and trying to relax with the scent of Abigail's lavender soap, as I hadn't slept all night thinking about Ben, and those long months that stretched out ahead until I saw him again. The sun reflecting off the chrome taps, dazzled my eyes, so I shut them and leant back with my head on a folded-up flannel.

1930, I can't believe it. I hate the moment when the old familiar year dies to be replaced by the New Year which is totally unknown. All the warmth of December replaced by the icy white of January. What is this New Year going to bring?

How I wish I had a crystal ball.

Before the water got too cold, I climbed out and dried myself, making wet footprints on the cork mat. I examined my tummy: if I held it in tightly, it appeared almost as flat as ever, but when I pressed it, there was definitely a hard, solid ball shape inside which wouldn't go away, however much I pulled in my muscles. Turning away, I wrapped myself up my dressing gown, gathered my sponge bag and towel, and opened the bathroom door.

Paul was outside, waiting for his turn.

'Oh, you made me jump!' I grabbed the door handle tightly. He did look rather dashing in his tartan dressing gown with a white towel slung around his neck. I didn't think I'd ever seen another man in his dressing gown, apart from Dad. Not even Ben.

'I'm sorry.' He moved aside to let me pass. 'Kathy?'

'Yes?' I said, feeling my cheeks glow red.

'We're thinking of going for a walk along the seafront after breakfast, would you like to come?'

Nodding like a wooden puppet, I gave him a quick smile, and fled to the safety of my room.

The wind blew, and the trees made broad bands of shadow across the frosty lawn, as I waited to be told which car to get into, like a boy hoping to be chosen for a football team. I half wanted to go with Paul, and my heart was beating like a drum on match day, but I was relieved in the end to be chosen for Uncle's car with Auntie, whilst Bill and Mary squeezed into Paul's Austin Seven . . . then got out again.

'It's my back.' Mary groaned, as she straightened up.

Uncle Jeremy sighed. 'Would you be a sport, Kathy, and go with Paul so they can come in my car? It looks as if it'll be a decided squash today with Rosie too.'

'Yes, of course,' I said, whilst wishing I could stay in the safety of Uncle's Alvis.

'Thank you, you saintly girl.' He grinned.

Paul scared me; he was so good-looking. I didn't know what to say to him. But, he leant over and held open the passenger door. 'Guess you're with me, Kathy.'

I tried to catch Aunt Sylvia's eye, but she appeared too busy settling Mary and Bill in Uncle's car to notice my discomfort, so reluctantly, I got in and clasped my clammy hands together on my lap.

I peeped at him. His clear skin glowed with a faint tan, and his hair, more golden brown than Ben's, curled gently behind his ears. When he turned my way, his blue eyes mesmerized me.

We began to speak at the same moment:

'I . . .'

'I . . .'

'No, you go first.'

'No, you.'

I took a deep breath. 'So, this is an Austin Seven, I've never been in one before, is it easy to drive?'

'Yes, fairly, if you don't mind double-declutching.' He raised his eyebrows and smiled.

'Oh, I know what that is.' I pushed my hands up and down like pedals. 'That's when you have to put the clutch in twice going through neutral to select the next gear.'

'My goodness, you know a lot about motor cars.'

'Yes, I always get *The Autocar* magazine. You should see the pile I have at home. I can't drive a car, but I can ride a motorbike though.'

'Really?'

'Yes, it's easy.'

'Whose do you ride; your father's?'

'No, Ben's . . .' I'm sure my cheeks glowed bright red, and I took a deep breath. 'My friend's brother's got a Norton, and I've had a go.'

'A Norton?'

'Er . . .Yes,' I nodded. 'A CS1: overhead camshaft. You know, won the Isle of Man TT race.'

'Well, I am impressed. Would you like to have a go in this? It'll be a bit different to a motorbike; no balancing for a start.' He smiled.

'May I? Are you sure?'

'Yes, of course, you can have a go on the way home.'

'Jeepers, thanks a lot. I hope I'm not going to make a fool of myself.'

'You'll be fine.' Paul grinned.

All too soon, we arrived at the seafront in Teignmouth. The stiff leaves on the palm trees shivered in the brisk sea breeze, as we got out and set off with the others along the promenade. But, before long, Bill and Mary lingered behind watching the waves splashing up over the sea wall, and Uncle and Auntie strode out in front with Rosie, leaving Paul and me alone.

We walked along in companionable silence, broken only by the shrill whistle of an engine muscling around the base of the cliffs, and disappearing under the bridge into the station like a model train in a toy shop window.

'Let's get out of this gale.' Paul pointed to a seat. 'It's quite sheltered here.'

We sat looking out at the gulls swooping down for fish in the wind whipped breakers.

'You're a doctor then?' I asked, turning up my collar, and pulling down my hat over my ears.

'Yes,' he laughed, 'All late nights and bandages! Well, I've just qualified; I'm getting some experience on the wards. What do you do?'

I took a deep breath. 'I've been working in Auntie's old bookshop until now.'

'What was she like to work for?'

'Wonderful, much better than Miss Snead, she's awful. I don't know what's the matter with Auntie now though; she seems to have changed. She didn't even remember that I was coming.'

'I expect she has other things on her mind.'

I raised my eyebrows.

'Sorry, I didn't mean that you're not important, Kathy. Would you like a cigarette?' He offered me a Player's Navy Cut.

'Yes, please.' I needed something to steady my nerves. I lit it with my lighter, took a long drag, and blew out a cloud of smoke which disappeared down the promenade in a rush with the wind.

'You're left-handed,' he said.

'Yes, they made me learn to write with my right hand at school, but it was so hard: the letters came out crooked and my left one twitched all the time to take over. I'm hopeless at sewing; I can't even turn up a hem. But, somehow I manage with mechanical things: screwdrivers and spanners. I've been helping Dad since I was small.'

Paul beamed at me in amusement.

'Sorry, I didn't mean to tell you all that, I got carried away.'

Bill and Mary arrived the next minute, then Uncle Jeremy and Aunt Sylvia returned, fresh faced from their walk beside the railway line.

'May we join you?' Uncle asked, as Rosie snuggled her head in my lap.

'Of course,' Paul and I said at the same time, and moved up closer together. I tried to make myself as small as possible, but that's not easy when you're five foot eight, and four months gone.

Exhausted from their walk, everyone flopped down beside us.

'Would you like a bullseye?' Uncle rustled up a paper bag from his pocket, and passed it round.

For a while, no one could speak until we sucked them down into a manageable size, so we studied a large gull strutting about in front of us, searching for scraps. Rosie growled.

'Don't be silly, Rosie, it's only a bird.' Paul ruffled her ears, as another train whistle made it fly off and wheel high above the cliffs.

'Look!' He pointed, shading his eyes. 'There's Andrew Black's Gipsy Moth from up at Haldon.'

'Oh no, not again.' Aunt Sylvia frowned. 'As soon as the sun shines, he's out. Noisy plane, I can't hear myself think. Spoils all the peace.'

Uncle winked at me. 'Do you remember me telling you about the aerodrome, Kathy?'

'Yes, I do. Is it far from here? I would've thought that it was a bit windy today for flying.'

'I didn't know that you knew all about flying as well, Kathy.' Paul turned to me, 'I'm learning to fly at the moment.'

'Really? I'd love to do that. Ben . . .' Then, I changed my mind. 'Are you learning on a Gipsy Moth?'

'Yes, I am.'

'Oh, Paul spends all his spare time up at the aerodrome, learning to fly, and patching up pilots who get injured,' Uncle Jeremy chuckled.

'Would you like to come with me and see the planes, some time, Kathy?' Paul asked.

'I was going to take her to do some aeroplane spotting myself, Paul.' Uncle Jeremy pretended to be hurt. 'Who do you want to go with, Kathy?'

'I . . . er . . .'

Aunt Sylvia made up my mind for me:

'I should let her go with Paul, Jeremy. I hardly see you as it is, with all the time you spend at the boatyard. I don't know about the rest of you, but I'm getting cold and hungry.' Auntie snuggled her fur collar around her neck. 'Let's get back, there's roast lamb for lunch.'

We walked back to the cars: Uncle and Auntie arm in arm, Bill and Mary following, then Paul and I.

'I'd really like to show you the aerodrome, but I'm working over this weekend. Perhaps we could go next week?' Paul said.

'All right, thank you.'

'What are you going to do whilst you're here?'

'I don't know really: be a companion for Aunt Sylvia, I suppose. I think that she misses her shop, you know: the girls and the gossip.'

'She's going to open a new one here, isn't she? All the nurses at the hospital keep moaning they can't get anything decent to read. They have to go to Exeter or Torquay.'

'All the nurses?'

'Yes, well, some. We often chat when we are on night duty.'

'Is there a particular one?'

'No!' he laughed as we reached the cars. 'Now what about this driving lesson?'

'Are you really sure?' My heart began to thump.

'Of course! It's easy!' His eyes sparkled like the sun glinting off the wave tops out at sea, as he opened the driver's door for me with a flourish, and I slid in, knocking my ankles on the pedals.

'Ouch!'

'Relax, Kathy, you'll be an excellent driver.' He sat in the passenger seat, talking about the controls and I prickled with excitement; I could hardly wait to drive at last.

'What are you doing?' Aunt Sylvia tapped on the window. 'You're never going to let her drive your motor car, are you, Paul?'

'Yes, she'll be safe with me. Don't worry.'

'I was more worried about your car.' Auntie shook her head, and stood next to Uncle Jeremy. I couldn't hear what she said to him, but he grinned.

They shivered in the icy wind with Bill and Mary, as I struggled with the throttle and the electric starter. The engine coughed, but nothing happened.

'I'll have to turn it over with the crank handle, it's too cold today.' Paul disappeared in front of the car, then gave me the thumbs up as the engine leapt into action. 'Right-o! Off we go!' He hurried back into the car, and everyone cheered as we crept forward.

'Shall I change gear now?' I could see that the speed was about ten miles an hour.

'Yes, have a go.'

Carefully, I double-declutched and selected second.

'Excellent, Kathy! That's right, keep up the acceleration. By Jove, you are doing well. Let's make a circuit of The Den before we head back.'

'This is fantastic! I've always wanted to do this!' I turned to him.

'Keep your eyes on the road! Good girl!'

Eventually, only jumping a little bit like a kangaroo, and swerving to miss an oncoming car, I headed out of the town.

'It's lucky there's not so much traffic today, but I think you are a natural driver, Kathy.'

‘Thanks, I don’t know why I’m doing so well; I’ve only ridden Ben’s bike a few times. The first time I managed to accelerate it too hard and ended up in the laurel bushes down their drive!’

Paul laughed, but by following his attentive instructions, I managed to finally turn into Hillfields, and make it to the front door without damaging any trees. I’d had a wonderful time, but was I damaging my precious love for Ben?

Chapter Nine

There were three letters on the hall table addressed to me. I picked them up, and my heart raced when I saw they were from Mother, Abigail, and Ben. *What on earth would they think of me learning to drive with Paul?* I saw Mabel carrying the roast lamb into the dining room, but forgetting I was pregnant, I rushed upstairs two at a time to read them. The gong sounded for lunch as I tore open Ben's letter, and my heart thumped away like Mabel's little wooden drumstick, as I read it.

Dearest Kathy,

Happy New Year! I miss you so much. My squadron had a Christmas party with some local girls, but I slipped away to look at the moon and stars, and think of you. I want to hold you Kathy and kiss you. I have your little black bead here round my neck and when I'm lonely, I touch it and think of you and dream about us being together soon.

Well, the New Year is nearly here, and the months will soon slip away, and we will be married. I can't wait until you're my wife. I can't wait to hold our little baby, our little bundle of love.

I love you, Kathy,
All my love, for ever and ever,
Ben

He had finished up with a drawing of a bouncing baby.

Curled up on the bed with my pillow, I thought, I can't wait either, Ben. Sighing, I opened Mother's letter and ran my finger over her familiar copperplate handwriting.

Dear Kathy,

Happy New Year! Dad and I are missing you already. The house is so quiet without you. I didn't know that you made such a noise. We seem to be rattling around on our own.

Got your letter this morning saying that you'd arrived safely. How are Sylvia and Jeremy? Have you met his son, Paul, yet? We were introduced to him at the wedding. I thought he looked rather like the Prince of Wales, but Dad said not.

He sends his love and wants to know where you put his wrench; he can't find it.

Lots of Love from,
Your Loving Mother

Smiling I tore open Abigail's letter.

Dear Kathy,

Happy New Year! I hope that you are well and had a good journey down to Devon. I'm going to Maureen's party tonight, but it won't be half so nice without you. I had nothing to wear, so I simply had to scoot out and buy a new dress. I got a lovely grey silk dress with beads and fringing in McIlroy's. It was to be reduced in the January Sales, but they let me have it in advance because I'm such a good customer!

When the weather gets better, I might come down for a few days, if that is all right with your aunt.

All the very best,
Your friend,
Abigail

I did miss them so. I'd brought some snaps of them which I'd propped up on the mantelpiece.

'Dear Ben,' I whispered, outlining his face, 'When are you going to get your parents to agree to us marrying? I wish I was with you, I'd tell you all about learning to drive today, but I don't think you'd want to hear about Paul.'

'Kathy! Lunch is on the table. Have you gone to sleep?' Aunt Sylvia called.

With my tummy rumbling after not eating properly for two days, I enjoyed the roast lamb; it must have been all the sea air that morning. I tried to join in the general conversation about the Wall Street Crash, and Uncle's new boat, but it was such hard work and I longed to be safely at home.

Afterwards, when Bill and Mary had left, and Paul had gone back on duty at the hospital, Aunt Sylvia sank into an armchair, placed a cigarette in her long black holder and lit it. 'Thank goodness that's all over, and we can get back to normal. Apart from you, my dear.' She patted me on the arm. 'I haven't had a moment to talk to you. Tell me how you are.'

'I'm fine, Auntie.'

I didn't want to linger in the sitting room; I wanted to go back upstairs and read Ben's letter again, so I made my way to the door.

'Kathy, come and sit down here.' She plumped up the cushion on the chair next to her. 'Mabel can bring us a nice cup of coffee.'

What could I do? I sat on the edge of the chair and warmed my hands by the fire.

'I'm going to open a bookshop in Teignmouth, Kathy.'

'Yes, I know, Uncle Jeremy told me.'

'Did he?'

'Yes, he said that you missed all the gossip in the shop, and you were bored.'

'It does sound strange when you're newly married, doesn't it?' she laughed. 'Well, I had to give it up, as you know, when I came down to Devon, and Jeremy is so keen on his pleasure craft business that he's never around.' She waved her cigarette holder. 'So I suppose it works out quite well that you're here instead.'

'Do you want me to help you open the shop, Auntie?'

'Good Heavens, no! You can help behind the scenes, but we can't have you on the shop floor, can we, what will people say? It won't do my business much good, will it?' She gave a bright smile.

'Oh . . . I don't suppose it would.' I didn't really want to work in there; it had been nice to get away from the old one. But, to be reminded I couldn't because I was pregnant, made things seem just as bad as at home.

'Chin up, Kathy! I hope to be open by Easter.'

Mabel brought in the coffee, and Aunt Sylvia busied herself pouring out a cup for each of us.

'Now, Kathy, I want to talk to you about Paul.'

'Paul?' I felt my cheeks go pink. 'Why?'

'Well, young lady, you danced with him last night, and walked with him along the seafront this morning, not to mention driving his car, for Heaven's sake.'

I shook my head. 'It was nothing; there was no one else to dance or walk with. We were just an odd couple. And, Auntie, you said yourself that I should go to Haldon with him.'

'I saw the looks he gave you.'

'Really?' My heart began to beat.

'Be careful, my girl, he's quite a charmer. A bit like the Prince of Wales.'

'Yes, he does look a bit like him.' I said, remembering how star-struck I was on the train. 'But, he's all right, Auntie, isn't he?'

She drew on her cigarette and blew out a perfect circle of smoke. 'The nurses he has at his beck and call at the hospital are nobody's business. No, you be careful, especially in your condition. Ha! He'd be the first one to notice you were in the family way, I should think.' Stirring some sugar into her coffee, she added, 'You're going to marry your young man at home, aren't you? Or so your mother says.'

I automatically stroked my tummy. 'Yes, when he's twenty-one.'

'I can't understand why he didn't marry you straight away, and save us all this bother.'

'His parents wouldn't let him. It was all too much for his mother. She's recovering from TB and they want him to finish his officer training first. To be honest, I'm not good enough for him in their eyes.'

'How ridiculous. You're as good as any girl, and better than most.'

That was fair praise indeed from Auntie.

'You have to believe in yourself, Kathy. I had to work hard building up my business; getting men to respect me. It wasn't easy, and it still isn't easy, but you just have to work at it. You'll come through this with flying colours, I'm sure.' She held my hand between her impeccably manicured ones. 'Now my dear, I've arranged for you to go to see Dr White tomorrow. It's best just to make sure everything's all right, isn't it?'

'Do I have to go?' I said, wishing I'd stayed at home and hidden away altogether.

'Yes, my dear, we'll take you down in the car.'

I didn't have much faith in what Auntie had said about flying colours, and eventually, I escaped upstairs to read my letters again. As I lay on my bed, I watched the winter sun sink low in the sky. Its red glow gave way to flickering shadows from the fire in the grate. I pulled the eiderdown over me for warmth, and held it close.

Oh Ben, if only you were here. If only I was with you. As the flames devoured the logs, the shadows rose and fell, in competition with each other on the wall, and I recited Ben's letter again and again in my mind. I knew every word. *'I miss you so much.' 'I can't wait until you can be my wife.'* If only you'd do something about it, Ben.

The room grew dark, and the moon shone through the window. Taking out my pen and paper, I began to write in the firelight.

Darling Ben,

Thank you for your lovely letter, it does mean so much to hear from you when we are so far apart. I love the little picture of the baby. Aunt Sylvia has made an appointment for me to see the doctor tomorrow, to make sure everything's all right.

After chewing my lip for a few minutes, I continued:

I had a driving lesson today! Aunt Sylvia's stepson, Paul, let me have a go in his Austin Seven. You'd have been so proud of me. I drove all the way from the seafront to Auntie's house. Double-declutching, and everything! Uncle Jeremy's got an Alvis Silver Eagle like your father's and he took me for a spin in that too. Aren't I a lucky girl?

Abigail says that she might come down to Devon for a few days. I bet you miss her as much as I do.

Oh, Ben, I want to cuddle up with you and feel safe and sound. You know I can't wait for us to be married.

Your loving,
Kathy

Chapter Ten

January 2nd 1930

Uncle Jeremy and Aunt Sylvia had parked in The Triangle to go to the bank, leaving me to walk round the corner to the doctor's. Hungry gulls swooped in the clear, blue sky and squabbled over scraps, and I felt like running off and walking for miles along the beach, because somehow visiting the doctor would make my pregnancy all the more official. But, checking the doctor's address on a piece of paper in my pocket, I found the surgery, and with my heart beating loudly, pushed open the heavy black door.

About half a dozen women waited on high backed chairs around the room which looked like a Victorian front parlour with potted plants and velvet curtains. As I entered, the buzz of conversation stopped. The clock ticked loudly, and the fire crackled and spat. The patients looked me up and down as I slid into a seat, then they carried on:

'Yes, Mabel's sister told me yesterday.' A heavily pregnant lady nodded with conviction.

'No, I don't believe it.' Her friend, holding a small baby, shook her head.

'Fancy, I wouldn't have thought Mrs Trevelyan would have a niece like that,' said a third woman who looked as if she might have been the baby's grandma.

'Yes, it's true. She arrived the day before New Year's Eve, bold as brass, from up country.'

Jeepers! The colour rose in my cheeks. I picked up *The Autocar* magazine from the chair beside me, and studied it carefully.

'She's come down here to have a baby?' The woman cuddled her own little bundle and patted its back.

'Yes,' confided the first. 'And, she doesn't wear a ring.'

A ring, I wish I had one, then I wouldn't be sitting here listening to these awful women. I wrapped my coat around me, and tucked my left hand inside. *Perhaps I should get one from Woolworth's, if I have a chance?*

The grandma had to join in. 'You mean to say that Mrs Trevelyan's niece has come down here to have a baby because she isn't married? Poor girl. Do you know who she is?'

'No, but I'll bet she's a little minx and no mistake.'

At that moment, the first lady was called in to the surgery and, rather like the Mad Hatter's tea party, we all moved down a chair. The other patients settled back into their magazines, whilst the mother and daughter with the baby fussed over their little treasure. Although still very tiny, it gurgled with a wet, toothless grin and wriggled its whole body in happiness.

I stroked the small bump under my coat. *I'm going to have a real little baby, just like that one, a real little person.*

They were talking again: 'Do you think she'll keep it?' whispered the daughter.

'What?'

'The baby: you know, Mrs Trevelyan's niece?'

'Well, what would she do with it in this day and age? Who'd look after it?'

'I don't know.'

'I expect she'll have it adopted.'

I cradled my tummy and frowned.

Nobody's going to have my baby.

Eventually, Dr White called me in to his office. He sat at his desk, a man about the same age as Uncle Jeremy, but with a shock of grey hair and a little goatee beard.

'Let me jot down some details first, Mrs Mason.'

'It's *Miss* Mason.' I perched myself on the hard wooden chair to his left.

'Yes I know, my dear, but we call everybody 'Mrs' here.'

I winced. *I would be Mrs Hunter by now, if only Ben's parents had let me.*

After making a few notes, he looked up. 'How far along are you?'

'I'm not sure.' I remembered the denial, the sickness, missing being "unwell".

'Have you felt the baby kicking yet?'

'I don't think so.'

'They tell me it feels a bit like a butterfly fluttering its wings. Anyway, hop up onto the couch, and I'll see if I can work it out.' His hands were warm and reassuring as he examined my tummy. 'Um,' he said, 'let's listen to its heartbeat.'

'Can you hear it?'

'Yes, of course.' He took something that looked rather like an ear trumpet from his table of instruments, and feeling for the right place, listened carefully whilst I held my breath.

'Your baby has a good strong heart. Give me your hand. You can feel it kicking . . . Here.'

'Really? I thought it was wind.'

'Well, your baby is a good size even though he doesn't show a lot yet; I think you are around four months. Let's see,' he consulted his chart, 'that would make it due in the first week of June, Mrs, er, *Miss* Mason.'

'June? That's only five months.'

'Yes, my dear,' Doctor White jotted down the date. 'Have you thought about what you're going to do with it afterwards?'

'Oh, I'm getting married. My fiancé is away doing his RAF officer training at the moment at Cranwell.' I certainly couldn't tell the doctor about Ben's awkward parents.

'Well, it is best for baby to have a father and a settled home as soon as possible.' He looked at me pointedly over his glasses.

Slightly troubled, I emerged again into the cold bright morning. I'd arranged to meet Uncle and Auntie at their favourite café, Ashley's in Northumberland Place, but I'd said I'd pick up an extra pint of milk for Mabel first.

The fresh, salty air blew away the methylated spirits smell of the doctor's surgery as I walked up the road towards the dairy.

The warm sun shone on my brown coat, making me hot. Of course, I knew it was only January, and that Mother would have tut-tutted at me and told me I would catch a chill, but I couldn't help undoing the buttons and letting it fly behind me like wings. I'm free, I thought, no one knows me here, and I enjoyed striding out down the street. But, I hadn't gone very far when I began to sense that people were watching me. Women were the worst, giving me disapproving stares, although men, whilst raising their hats, would also raise their eyebrows and give a curious smile. Had they all got eagle eyesight so they could see whether or not I wore a ring? Up to now, my coat had hidden all my sins. I caught my reflection in the shop windows. My dress clung to my body in the breeze, showing off my unmistakable pregnant bump, not very large yet, but definitely there, and put into sharp relief by my otherwise slim figure. I hurriedly did up my buttons. But, it was no good, I really was pregnant, and I felt completely naked.

I waited for my turn in the dairy, watching the assistant expertly shaping half a pound of butter with wooden paddles. Then I gasped, the two know-it-alls in the doctor's waiting room were right there in the queue; I tried to ignore them, but it was no use.

'She should be ashamed to be out in her condition,' one nudged the other and whispered, 'with no wedding ring on either.'

I grasped my left hand, cross that I'd stuffed my gloves in my coat pocket.

'Fancy being brazen enough to walk about in public.' The second woman pulled her pram in front of her, as if for protection.

My temperature rose, and I felt a trickle of sweat running down my back as I stepped up to the counter.

'Yes, madam?' The assistant held some greaseproof paper ready.

'It's *miss*,' I glanced back at the women. They tutted to themselves and shook their heads. 'A pint of milk, please.'

This is ridiculous! Perhaps I should buy myself a cheap ring, then no one would know, would they? But, why should I? Why should I have to apologize and lie?

Along the street, I passed a jeweller's shop, and stopped to look in the window at some trays of second hand rings. How sad, I thought, each one of these must have a story. An engagement broken off. A loved one died. A precious ring sold to pay the bills. But, they were cheap. I pushed open the door, and the bell jingled, summoning an old man with whispy white hair, and glasses perched on his nose.

I really didn't want to go into all the whys and wherefores so I pointed to a ring with a little five-petalled turquoise flower on a gold band.

'That's twelve and sixpence, my dear,' he smiled as I tried it on and twisted it round so it was plain. It fitted perfectly.

'Twelve and six?' I rummaged in my purse. 'I've only got ten shillings. I'm sorry, I'll have to leave it.'

'No, ten shillings is fine. You take it; it suits you. Would you like it wrapped?'

'Er, yes, please,' I said as I pulled it off. I wasn't quite ready to wear it yet.

'That's a good little ring that,' the jeweller said as he handed me the neat brown parcel, 'belonged to a young girl like you. Had to sell it for funds, you know.' He smiled and nodded knowingly.

I wondered if that girl had had to leave home like me.

As I approached Ashley's the warm aroma of roasted coffee beans wafted down the road, and when the door opened, undercurrents of chocolate and freshly baked cakes rushed out to greet me.

There was no sign of Uncle Jeremy or Aunt Sylvia, but I noticed a man, over by the window, playing with a coin which glinted in the sunlight as he rolled up it and down his fingers. My heart missed a beat. Then he stood up and waved to me. It was

Paul, of course. Wary of Auntie's warning, I threaded my way through the tables to him, patting my secret package in my pocket.

'There you are, Kathy, Dad said I should look out for you. I bumped into them in the bank,' Paul grinned.

Reluctantly, I sat down opposite to him. I had enjoyed the driving lesson, but I didn't want to get involved any further. The waitress came up, and I ordered a coffee.

'Shouldn't you be at the hospital, Paul?' I asked.

'I don't start until midday. I had to go to the bank,' he said, passing me the sugar.

I decided to tell him about Ben and the baby; that should be enough to put anyone off. 'Paul . . .' I began, 'Paul, I need to . . .'

At that moment, Aunt Sylvia and Uncle Jeremy arrived. They spotted us straight away and came over.

'Hello, Kathy,' said Uncle. 'Sorry we're so late, we got held up at the bank.' He winked. 'Well not really held up, but you know what I mean. Hello,' he added, turning to Paul, 'I see that you've found each other.'

'Yes, Father, I was just going to ask Kathy when I should pick her up to go to Haldon.' He turned to me. 'Perhaps you'd like to have a go at driving again?'

Auntie caught my eye, and raised her eyebrow.

The heat rose through my body, and I tried to unbutton my coat, but I was all fingers and thumbs.

'How about next Saturday morning?' His eyes glittered with excitement.

Searching for any excuse, I said, 'Auntie, I was going to ask you if we could go into Exeter to look at the January Sales; I've got nothing to wear.'

She shook her head. 'I'm sorry, Kathy, but I have to go up to London to see one of my old publishers.'

'Well, I guess you're mine then!' Paul laughed.

'Yes, I suppose I am.' I knew it was wrong to spend so much time with Paul, especially after the warnings I'd had from

Auntie and Uncle, but I loved having a go at driving his car and I hoped that Ben would understand.

The next morning, a van arrived with a huge bunch of daffodils and a letter addressed to me in unfamiliar handwriting. Mabel took the flowers to put them in a vase, whilst I opened the letter with shaking hands.

Dear Kathy,

I hope you like the daffodils.

I have to confess that the first time we met on the train, there <u>*were*</u> *empty seats in the other carriages, but when I saw you sitting in the corner, looking so bereft, I just had to come back to yours. After we bumped heads, I saw the mischief in your eyes, and the smile twitching at the corners of your mouth.*

I couldn't believe it was you at Hillfields. I learnt your face off by heart on the train as you slept: its oval shape like the Mona Lisa, serious but capable of transforming itself with an irresistible smile.

Not only that, you were born to drive!

Looking forward to our little trip to Haldon next Saturday,

Yours,

Paul

Jeepers! Ben never wrote to me in quite the same way. His letters were warm, safe and comfortable; his sketches made me smile. He loved me with all his heart, but somehow, even though I carried his child, it was an innocent love, which had been growing ever since I was four when we filled my brand new Wellingtons with wet mud to see if they were waterproof. Until now, that is.

Paul's letter excited me; it conjured up a Kathy that I didn't recognize. Was I really a Mona Lisa? I examined my face in the mirror. The same old Kathy looked back. Yet, maybe I could be? I brushed my hair, and borrowed some of Auntie's lipstick; I never bothered with the stuff myself. But no, I appeared just the same as ever, but perhaps a little guilty, a painted lady? Hurriedly, I wiped it off.

I just had to tell him that I couldn't go. I sat down to write at my dressing table by the flowers that Mabel had brought up, trying to ignore their fresh green perfume which filled my head and made me want to run with Paul through woodland glades.

Dear Paul,

Thank you so much for the gorgeous daffodils, and your letter.

I'm sorry, but I won't be able to go with you to Haldon. Although, I'm very flattered by your words, and, yes, I like you very much, I've been trying to tell you all along that I have a fiancé at home.

I think it would be best if we leave things as they are and not let them go any further.

Thank you again,
Kathy

Sighing with relief, I sealed it up, and put on my hat and coat. I found Ben's letter to post in my bag, and gripping them both tightly, went outside.

Uncle Jeremy's car glinted in the early January sunshine. The bonnet was up, and he was polishing the inside of the engine until it gleamed. After a few moments, he turned his head.

'Ah, there you are, Kathy, pass me that spanner would you?'

I rummaged in the toolbox on the ground.

'Will this one do?'

'Yes. I'll try it.' He looked up from under the bonnet.

'Is anything wrong, dear, you're frowning?'

'Am I?' I shaded my eyes. 'It must be the sun.' My fingers vibrated as I ran them over the tread of the spare wheel.

'Uncle, do you think that I could take you up on your offer, and come to Haldon with you after all?'

'Why, of course Kathy, but I thought you'd arranged to go with Paul.' He straightened his back, and rubbed his spine as it clicked into place.

'Yes, I did, but I think he likes me a bit too much, I don't want to create an awkward situation.'

'He's just being his charming self.' Uncle smiled, and his eyes twinkled just like Paul's, making my heart miss a beat. 'We could go for a run up there now if you want to. It's a nice clear day; I'll clean myself up.'

'Thank you, can I sit in the car while I wait?'

'Of course.'

The leather seats, heated up in the sun, warmed my body, as I sat back and pretended the Alvis belonged to me. *How lovely to be like Abigail and be driven about in luxury all the time, to have lots of money and beautiful clothes, and not have to work, but just have fun with my friends. I wouldn't mind being blonde and petite like her with a cute turned up nose. But, what is it about me that attracts Ben and Paul? Perhaps they don't feel threatened by a girl who's so much one of the boys?*

A picture came into my mind of Ben and I playing with his train set, and Abigail sitting beside us having a dolls' tea party. 'Come and have some tea, Kathy!' Her little face had looked so earnest, but Ben and I were in the middle of fixing some signals. Quickly, her blue eyes filled with tears, but trains were far more interesting to me than dolls. I knew I couldn't hurt her now by encouraging Paul. She'd be horrified if she found out, and would never be friends with me again. I checked the letters in my pocket; I was doing the right thing at last.

Chapter Eleven

Uncle Jeremy returned, pulling on his driving gloves, and off we went, bouncing along the flint roads, skipping over twigs which had fallen in the night and dipping through the shadows of the deep earth banks. He began to hum '*Button Up Your Overcoat*'. Well, I think that's what it was. My feet tapped along and I grinned, relieved to be escaping from Paul's spell at last.

We passed the golf course, and turned left where the flat hilltop had become a natural airfield. I heard an unmistakable drone, and rolled down the window to poke my head out.

'Oh look, there's a plane!' A Gipsy Moth skimmed the trees to our right and came in to land. It hovered over us like a huge bee, and slowly swung across the clubhouse, yawing from side to side in the breeze as it disappeared from view. Through the bare branches, I glimpsed more planes parked in shimmering lines. 'This is wonderful, Uncle Jeremy.'

'I'm glad you like it.' Then he looked over to the hangar as he pulled up. 'What the blazes? Look, someone's fallen off that ladder. They must have been trying to repair the roof. It blew away in the gales last week just like a paper hat from a Christmas cracker.'

We hurried over. 'Is he all right, Andrew?' Uncle asked one of the engineers gathered round a man who lay still and ashen on the ground.

'Bob came a cropper; I don't know how he managed it.' Andrew rung out a wet cloth and mopped the man's forehead. 'The doctor's on his way.' He looked around anxiously, and stood up, relieved at the sound of another car on the gravel.

We all turned, and I nearly collapsed with shock. The car was Paul's little red Austin, and he was at the wheel. He didn't see me, but hurried out with his bag to tend to the man.

'Oh, it's you, Dr Trevelyan.' Andrew let him through. 'Glad you could come.'

Uncle squeezed my arm, 'Would you like to go home?'

‘Yes,’ I said, ‘Would you mind?’

Then Paul, recognizing our voices, glanced up from his patient.

‘What are you doing here, Kathy? Father?’

‘It’s a long story.’ I shook my head as my heart thumped away. ‘I’ll explain when you’ve finished. But what are you doing here yourself?’

‘I volunteered; there was no one else to come and anyway, I like any excuse to drive up to Haldon.’

Uncle took my elbow, ‘Come on, Kathy, we’ll leave him to get on with it. I’ll show you around.’ He guided me past the clubhouse where the green expanse of the aerodrome spread before us, and Dartmoor rose up, grey, in the west.

‘Look at those.’ I pointed to a pair of blue and gold Gipsy Moths resting on their tails at the far side of the field.

‘They belong to Richard Westenra. He lives near here,’ Uncle said. ‘His sister, Lady Bailey was the first woman to fly to Cape Town and back.’

‘Really? I saw it on the newsreels; I would love to do something like that. Did you see Amy Johnson in the paper, working on a Gipsy Moth? She’s the first woman in the world to get her Ground Engineer’s Licence. I wish I could be like her, but what chance have I got in my condition?’

‘Well, not a lot at the moment.’ Uncle patted my back. ‘Let’s go and see Andrew, perhaps he can help.’

We walked over the short grass to a nearby Moth where Andrew was now working on a wing, and I wrinkled up my nose at the strong smell of aircraft fuel. I’d never been so close to an aeroplane before.

‘Is Bob all right?’ Uncle called up to him.

‘Yes, he’s got a bit of concussion, but he’ll soon be on the mend. The doctor’s sent for an ambulance.’

‘Can I introduce you to Sylvia’s niece, Kathy? She’s quite taken with aeroplanes.’

'Pleased to meet you.' He climbed down. 'I'm afraid I can't shake hands, they're a bit oily.'

'Andrew used to be in the Royal Flying Corps, but now he runs this place. You can't get away from planes, can you?'

Andrew grinned, and shook his head.

'What are you doing?' I asked.

'I'm cleaning the insects off the air speed indicator. Not much fun, but it has to be done, or you can't read it.'

I ran my hand over the glossy scarlet paint, and peered at the instruments in the cockpit.

'Would you like to see this one fly?' he asked.

'Oh, yes!'

Uncle smiled, 'I'm glad to see you so enthusiastic, Kathy. I don't think I've seen you so happy since you came here.'

'Can you help me to push it along to the airstrip, Jeremy?' asked Andrew.

I was amazed, considering Uncle's bad back, that they could bump the plane on its two little wheels over the tussocks to the smooth grass runway. Andrew fastened up his leather helmet, climbed into the rear cockpit, and adjusted his goggles.

'You can fly it from either seat,' he said, pointing to the one in front. 'But you actually get a better view from the back, because the wings aren't in the way.'

With all his strength, Uncle swung the yellow propeller and the engine sprung into action. 'Chocks away!' he called, pulling out the wedges. The little plane purred off over the grass which rippled in the wind, making stalks, leaves and dust blow into our faces. It circled at the end of the strip to take off, and bounded along, up into the air: its engine buzzing across the sky.

'It looks more like a ladybird than a moth.' I screwed up my eyes as the red fuselage reflected the sun, and its silver wings glimmered, just like the Gipsy Moth which had flickered above the trees on that last afternoon with Ben.

Andrew waved to us as he passed, and put the plane through its paces, giving an impromptu air show. I gasped as it looped the loop, and soared up straight, only to stall, spiralling down as fast as a sycamore seed, until Andrew recovered control again, and brought it carefully in to land.

He flicked off all the switches and jumped down. 'Well, I've been flying since the War, and I've never had a lady passenger, would you like to come up with me, Kathy, if you're so interested in aeroplanes?' His eyes crinkled up at the corners where the sun and wind had weathered his face.

I looked at Uncle Jeremy and hopped from one foot to another like a child on her birthday. 'Jeepers! I'd really love to have a go.'

He rubbed his chin. 'Andrew, will you take care of her, she hasn't been very well lately; she's come down here to recuperate. No, looping the loop or any barnstorming, please.'

I hugged him, and whispered, 'Thank you.'

'I'll just put her through her paces, nothing too dangerous, you'll be safe with me.' Smiling, Andrew went off to find me a spare leather coat and helmet; surprisingly, they were quite a good fit. Uncle helped him hoist me up into the front seat. There wasn't much room at all, and I could hardly see out over the high sides. It was like sitting in a barrel, or on a roller coaster slowly climbing up the steep ramp, waiting for the thrill of the release as the car reaches the top and races down through all the bends: impatient for the excitement, but scared at the same time.

When Andrew disappeared into the rear cockpit, I felt I was going to fly the plane all by myself and my heart raced as fast as the propeller. He made all the checks whilst the clattering engine built up into a whining scream which hurt my ears, and made the little plane vibrate in anticipation. At last he called 'Chocks away!' and I stuck my hand out and waved as the cold air rushed through my fingers. *If only Ben could see me now!*

The Gipsy Moth bumped across the field. Then, from my seat under the upper wing, I caught sight of its shadow scything through the grass as the plane picked up speed, faster and faster; relentlessly fast, roaring and rattling into the wind. I gasped as the ground fell away, and the plane circled up over the clubhouse which dwindled until it was the size of a wooden toy. *I'm flying!* All the worries of the past few months tumbled down and scattered on the ground like a sack of letters. *I'm free!*

'Eighty miles an hour.' I could just make out what Andrew was shouting over the engine noise. I'd never been so fast on land, never mind in the air.

'One thousand feet.'

As we turned, the sun glinted off the cross wires, and I got a view of the coast, and all the tiny boats forging through the waves leaving a white arrow of foam behind them. We flew back over the river, which lay in the valley like a silk ribbon, towards the misty Dartmoor peaks, and wheeled low over the grassy airfield. After one more circuit, soaring through the air like an eagle, we came in to land, juddering along the ground and making our fillings rattle. We taxied back to Uncle Jeremy who helped me down.

'Well, did you enjoy that, Kathy?'

'Yes, it was breathtaking; I've always wanted to fly, Uncle Jeremy.' I hugged him again, and I could feel the hugest grin on my face. 'It was all over so soon.'

Andrew got out, and I shook his hand, 'Thank you so much.'

'It was a pleasure. You can come any time.'

'Hey, Kathy!' We all turned to see Paul running across the field, his breath puffing out like smoke from a train. 'You never went up in that Moth did you?' he panted. 'Is there no end to your surprises?'

'Andrew asked me.' I couldn't resist returning Paul's hug, and he swept me up into the air.

Uncle cleared his throat, but Paul kept his arms round me, 'Kathy, you are *the* most surprising girl I've ever met. But, my goodness, you're shivering, would you like a cup of tea to warm you up? Doctor's orders.'

I *was* shaking; I didn't know whether it was the excitement of flying or the cold wind. I didn't think it was because of Paul's embrace . . . Nevertheless, he caught Uncle's eye.

'Don't worry about me, I'll stay here and catch up with all the news from Andrew.' Uncle gave me a wink.

I put my hand in my pocket and felt the letters: one for Ben and one for Paul, and the little brown package with the turquoise ring. *What am I doing? I've got to tell him.* So, with those uneasy fish swirling round inside me once again, I managed to say, 'Yes please, I'd love a cup.'

We walked back to the clubhouse, inside there was a huge stone fireplace where an enormous log fire roared up the chimney. I imagined pilots leaning on the mantelpiece telling tales of derring-do.

'Good Morning, Dr. Trevelyan, Good morning, miss.'

'This is Peggy, Kathy. She's Jim's wife, he's one of the engineers. She keeps the humans fed and watered whilst he looks after the aeroplanes.

She handed me the menu. 'What can I get you?'

'We'd like a pot of tea for two, please,' Paul smiled.

He steered me over to the fire and we sat down in deep leather armchairs beside a small table and looked out through the picture window at the airfield.

Peggy brought the tea. 'Would you like to be mother?' she asked.

I smiled ruefully as she returned behind her counter and busied herself, singing along to the wireless.

'Paul,' I whispered as I felt all the excitement and exhilaration of the day evaporate, 'I've got something to tell you: you're going to find out sooner or later anyway.'

'What on earth is wrong, Kathy?' His eyes turned a cloudy grey.

'I know how you feel about me, Paul, but . . .' A picture of Ben's warm smiling face, his eyes, brown and trusting like a puppy's, floated in front of me.

'Kathy?' Paul called me back. And like a reflection in a pool that's ruffled by the wind, Ben's face fragmented and disappeared. I frowned and took a deep breath.

'What is it?' He cradled my hand in his.

But, I grabbed it away. 'No, don't.' I glanced over to see if Peggy was listening. 'Paul,' I whispered, 'I'm going to have a baby.'

He looked straight at my tummy, making me cradle it protectively. 'No, you're not, are you? You can't be. You're joking; you've just been up in an aeroplane!'

'Shh! Yes, I know.' I forced a smile. 'Listen, Paul, you're not a very good doctor if you haven't noticed.'

'Good Heavens!' He sat back in his chair.

'The baby's due in June. I'd just been to the doctor's yesterday when I bumped into you in Ashley's.'

'Oh, my goodness.' Paul rubbed his forehead. 'Who's the . . .?'

'The father?'

'Yes.'

'It's Ben . . .'

'The one who's learning to fly?'

'Yes, in the RAF.' I felt for the letter again. 'He's asked me to marry him. And we will get married as soon as he's twenty-one.'

'But, why hasn't he married you already?'

'Because his mother isn't well and his parents want him to finish . . .' I rummaged for my handkerchief, and blew my nose; I wasn't going to let him see me cry.

'Kathy, it doesn't matter, I . . .'

'Of course it does. I've come down here to have the baby, and then go back to my real life. This isn't real.'

'It is, Kathy. It is for me.'

I shook my head.

Uncle Jeremy came in at that moment, rubbing his hands. 'Is there any tea left in the pot for me?'

'I'll get you some, Mr Trevelyan,' Peggy called.

I hurriedly stuffed my hankie back up my sleeve.

'Are you all right Kathy? The flight wasn't too much for you was it?' He sat down beside us. 'I don't know whether I should have let you go up in that contraption.'

'I'm fine. It was super, thank you; I wouldn't have missed it for the world.'

Paul stood up, 'I have to get back now, Father. Kathy please think about what I said.'

I smiled and shrugged my shoulders.

'You've told him, haven't you?' Uncle Jeremy whispered when he'd gone.

'Yes,' I sniffed.

'That's my girl.' He squeezed my hand.

I unpacked the little ring, and placed it on my palm. 'It's time to wear this now, Uncle,' I said.

And he nodded in agreement.

It wasn't until I got home that I discovered the letters to Ben and Paul still tucked in my pocket.

Chapter Twelve

January 10th 1930

Since that day at the aerodrome, I couldn't get Paul out of my mind. Whether I was reading one of Aunt Sylvia's many books, helping Mabel to peel the potatoes, or even writing to Ben, to my horror the picture of Paul running across the airfield and sweeping me up in his arms kept bursting into my consciousness like a scene in a Hollywood movie; only it had really happened. I hadn't posted the letter I'd written to him, I didn't think I needed to because I'd told him about the baby. But that didn't stop me thinking about him at all, even though I knew I had to fight my desires and be true to Ben. It was ridiculous that I should feel this way about a man that I'd only met about ten days ago.

Then, downstairs, I heard Aunt Sylvia reminding Mabel that Paul was coming round to see Uncle Jeremy at four o'clock, so I decided I must go out. As I didn't have any friends to visit, and I'd already been to the Post Office that morning, I thought I'd walk up to the paper shop to see if the latest issue of *The Autocar* had arrived.

Clouds rushed across the sky, and the wind whistled through the bare trees, as I battled my way up the garden path, through the gate, and into the lane which led to the village shops. Although it was only half past three, many cottages had their lights on, and I could peep in and see women darning socks, or playing with their children by the fire. It was hard to imagine myself caring for a family like that. But, if things worked out as they should, then by this time next year, a young girl, spying through a window, might see *me*. Those anxious fishes in my tummy churned around again: things were so much easier last January.

Large raindrops began to fall as I pushed open the door of the newsagent's and sheltered inside, brushing off my coat.

'Good afternoon.' The lady behind the counter folded her arms. 'You're new here, miss, aren't you?'

'Yes,' I smiled. 'I'm staying with my aunt at Hillfields.'

'Oh, Mrs Trevelyan's niece?' A frown dug between her eyebrows.

'Yes, I wondered if you had this week's *Autocar* magazine?'

'Did you order it?'

'No, I've only been here a few days.'

'Well, I'm sorry, but it must be ordered.'

'Oh, I'll take this *Daily Mail* then instead.' I picked one up from the rack and offered her the money.

At that moment, the door burst open, and a man backed in, shaking his umbrella outside. He left it by the door and made his way, dripping, to the counter.

'Ah, Mrs Brown, do you happen to have a copy of *The Autocar* magazine? There's an article I'm anxious to read. Do you keep it?'

'Oh, yes, Mr Kingston, certainly, sir.' She reached down behind the counter and brought out this week's issue.

Jeepers, she knows! She knows I'm pregnant, she must. Why else would she do that? I dropped my coppers on the counter, and walked out.

The rain poured down and I tucked the newspaper into my coat. *Now what? I can't go back to the house and risk bumping into Paul.* I looked up and down the street. The church loomed black in the early dusk, but a light seemed to be shining inside, so on the spur of the moment, I decided to see if it was open, and hurried along the road.

Gasping for breath, I pushed the heavy oak door. It swung back and, with relief, I crept in. Someone was practising *O God Our Help In Ages Past* on the organ. The deep music vibrated up from the floor and into my heart. Hoping no one could see me, I hid in one of the pews at the back. I felt so small and lost under the tall barrel shaped ceiling as the rain attacked the windows outside like gunshot pellets.

'Oh God, please help me,' I whispered. 'Help me to ignore Paul. And please help Ben to make his parents see sense so we can get married.'

All too soon, the organist finished, collected his music together, and walked down the aisle, his footsteps echoing in the empty church.

Putting on his coat, he said, 'I should be getting along home, miss, I'm going to lock up now. You look a bit wet, why don't you borrow one of those?' He indicated a brass container full of umbrellas, sticking out like flowers from a vase. 'Folks are always leaving them behind. I don't think it'll be missed.'

The rain still battered the roof like a thousand military drums. It was too early to go back, but I didn't have much choice.

'Thank you,' I said, choosing a black one with a bone handle, and venturing out into the deluge again. I fought to open it, and when I did, I found that one of the spokes stuck out, meaning there was only two thirds of the umbrella to shelter under. I decided to make a dash for it.

Splashing through the puddles, and drenching my shoes and stockings, I struggled up the hill to the back gate. The lights shone out over the garden. I couldn't see anyone in the kitchen, so I decided to creep upstairs until I was sure that Paul had gone.

Slipping off my shoes at the back door, I tiptoed across the kitchen and into the hall. To my relief, no one was about. Then the voices from the sitting room got louder as the door opened and Paul came out, followed by Uncle Jeremy. I shrank into the shadows by the hat stand, and tried to hide behind the coats.

'Lovely to see you, my boy!' Uncle patted him on the shoulder.

'Yes, I had hoped to see Kathy. I thought she might be back before now. Anyway must go. See you soon.' He turned get his hat and coat, and met my eyes, then leapt backwards like a surprised cat.

'Kathy, what are you doing there?'

'I . . . I'm just getting out of my wet things,' I said, peeling off my coat.

'I wanted to talk to you, but I've got to get back.' He took a step towards me, but I retreated into the corner like a convict on the run.

'I'm sorry, but I had to go out. To the shops.' I shook the raindrops from my newspaper.

'In this weather?' Paul smiled. 'Sorry I've missed you, but I'll come again soon, Kathy.'

Skilfully, Uncle Jeremy helped him into his coat, 'Still raining out there, Paul, now you be careful.' And he had him out of the door in a jiffy.

'Thank you, Uncle. He can't seem to keep away, can he?' I said, hanging up my coat.

Dry at last, and safe in my bedroom, I scanned the newspaper headlines: 'THE PRINCE OF WALES VOYAGES TO MADEIRA'; I'm not going to read about *you*, I thought, then I saw: 'MR FRANCIS CHICHESTER CONTINUES HIS ATTEMPT TO BEAT THE SOLO RECORD FOR FLYING TO AUSTRALIA IN A DE HAVILLAND MOTH'. *A Gipsy Moth? I should love to be able to do that, but what chance has a girl like me got?* I began to fold the paper up, then another article caught my eye: 'AMY JOHNSON IS ALSO PROPOSING TO BEAT THE RECORD FOR A SOLO FLIGHT TO AUSTRALIA IN A SECRET PLANE'. *Jeepers. That's why she's taken her Ground Engineer's Licence. Perhaps it is possible after all.*

For a few minutes, I forgot all about Paul. I lay back on the bed and shut my eyes. *I'm going to fly like Amy Johnson; I'm checking over my plane. It's a green Gipsy Moth, and it's filled with provisions for my ten thousand mile trip. Which exotic countries will I fly over? Which deserts, jungles, and seas? Flash bulbs are popping and blinding me with stars, as I taxi out onto the runway and fly up into the cool dawn light.*

Then the baby gently kicked me back to reality. *I'll never be able to do that; I'm going to be a mother, aren't I?* I rubbed my tummy, and sighed.

January 11th 1930

After yesterday's rain, the sun shone brightly and I was helping Uncle Jeremy polish his car. I couldn't resist getting my hands on the beautiful Alvis, and as I knew he wouldn't let me drive his pride and joy, polishing it was the next best thing. I had one of his old shirts on over my coat, and my hair tied up in a scarf like a factory girl. I hummed a tune as I buffed the paintwork to a gleaming shine. Then, I heard the familiar vroom of an engine as Paul's car crunched up the drive. I jumped and dropped the chamois leather, and busied myself by picking off the bits of grit that had clung to it. Don't take any notice of him. Don't get involved, I warned myself.

'Good morning, Kathy!'

It was useless, his voice sent delicious ripples right to the tips of my fingers.

'I've just come to see if Mabel has any breakfast left, I've been working all night.'

'Good morning,' I muttered, and a hot flush rose to the top of my head.

I watched him disappear into the house, and then noticed that Uncle Jeremy had straightened up and was looking at me.

'What is it?' I said.

'What is it with *you*?' He smiled.

'What do you mean?'

'I saw how you looked at him, Kathy.'

'I still don't know what you mean.'

'I think you're attracted to my son.'

'No, of course I'm not.' I shook my head, and turning away out of the breeze, found some Player's Navy Cut in my pocket, and shakily lit one. I'd been smoking them occasionally ever since Paul had given me one on the seafront.

'You're thinking about him now, I can tell, Kathy. You'd better be careful, my girl. What about your sweetheart at home?'

Before I could answer, Aunt Sylvia ran out waving her hands.

'Jeremy! Kathy! Come quickly! Rosie's having *puppies!*'

We looked at each other, and then back at her. 'Really? No? She can't be.'

'Oh, do come on!'

Uncle wiped his hands on his rag, I stamped out my cigarette, and we hurried indoors.

Rosie lay panting on her favourite blue blanket by the Aga. One tiny soft puppy already sucked greedily for some milk. Another one slipped out, and she licked and nuzzled it round to join the first.

Is having a baby as easy as that? I don't think it is.

Rosie's big brown eyes looked up at us. Uncle Jeremy gently stroked her head and fondled her ears, whilst Paul examined her stomach.

'Well, he said, 'I think that there are two or three more to come.'

'I never did,' said Mabel. 'What have you been up to, girl?'

I felt my tummy; they could quite well ask me that too.

'No wonder she's been so tired. It's not at all like her to be so sleepy,' Uncle said.

'Yes,' said Mabel, helping the latest arrival round to be attended to by the new mother. 'I thought it was strange that she was making a nest again. She always does it when she's on heat. Drags all the blue things she can find to her basket: scarves, socks, gloves, you name it. You do love blue, don't you Rosie?' The dog gave a small bark and licked Mabel's hand. 'You know everything we say, don't you?'

I hoped that such care would be taken of me; no one seemed to mind that Rosie had got herself pregnant with probably less love and devotion than I had. I watched the four pale bundles of life sucking away at their mother.

'Are they boys or girls?' I asked

'Three boys and a girl,' said Paul.

A strange mix of maternal feelings tugged at me, and my baby kicked inside. 'Aren't they gorgeous?'

'Just look at them squirming with pleasure,' said Mabel, giving Rosie a fresh bowl of water, which she lapped gratefully. Then she put the kettle on: 'Would anyone like a cup of tea?'

'No, thank you.' Aunt Sylvia pulled on her leather gloves. 'I've got to catch the bus today, as Jeremy's so busy fiddling with his car.'

'Well, I'll have one please, Mabel, but I'll take it outside because I want to get on,' he said.

'I'll bring it out for you. What about you, Miss Kathy?'

'Oh, I'd love one, please. It's so cold outside.'

'And you, Dr. Paul?'

'Yes, please, I don't suppose that you have any breakfast left over? That's what I came for after all, not to deliver puppies.' He gave me a wink, which made my cheeks burn.

'Well, there are some sausages and I could fry you an egg. Would you like that?' Mabel busied herself at the Aga, drawing on the kettle to boil, and heating up her black frying pan.

Paul sat down and rubbed his hands together. 'Yes, that'd be wonderful, thank you.'

How and why had I got myself into a situation with Paul again? I could have easily declined the tea, or even taken a cup outside and had it with Uncle. But here I was sitting at the kitchen table, just inches away. I pulled off my ridiculous scarf, and shook my hair free whilst Mabel placed a sizzling breakfast in front of him.

'Thank you very much, you didn't have to go to all that trouble.'

'Not at all.' And balancing the laundry basket on her hip, she went outside.

Paul took my hand. 'Kathy? Why are you avoiding me?'

But before I could answer, Mabel rattled the back door and we yanked them apart like a Christmas cracker.

'Just forgot my pegs,' she said.

Chapter Thirteen

I hurriedly drank up my scalding tea and excused myself to finish polishing Uncle Jeremy's Alvis. But, after a few minutes, Paul followed me out.

'Would you like to drive my car again today, Kathy?'

'Drive the Austin?' I squinted in the sunshine. 'No, I really can't come today. I've got all this polishing to do.'

But, Uncle Jeremy who was on the other side of his car, tinkering with the engine looked up. 'She's in a dream world this morning, Paul.'

'Uncle . . .' I began. *I thought he was meant to be keeping me away from his son.*

But he shrugged and smiled. 'I'm meeting Bill at eleven so I'll have to leave soon.'

I sighed. 'Paul, I've got some letters to write . . .'

'Don't worry, you can do them when you get back, you'll still be able to catch the afternoon post.'

I really wanted to have another go at driving. If only I didn't have to go with Paul, I thought. But he and his father were looking at me expectantly, so I pulled off Uncle's old shirt, and tied my scarf under my chin. And my heart thumped away like a bass drum as I sat in the driving seat once again.

'Do you remember what to do?' Paul raised his eyebrows.

'Yes, of course. Gear in neutral; handbrake on. Is the petrol on?'

'Yes, I've done it.' Paul nodded. 'Try the electric starter today, because it's been standing in the sunshine. Voilà!' The car moved off smoothly then stopped with a clunk, throwing us forwards. 'You've stalled it, Kathy,' Paul laughed, 'I think you let up the clutch too quickly. Try again.'

Frowning with concentration, I tried again and the Austin Seven inched down the drive. 'I'm jolly glad that I didn't have to turn it round as well,' I muttered. 'Where are we going?'

'Up to Haldon, let's go and look at the planes.'

Carefully changing down to lower gears to climb the hill, I made it to the top, and turned left into the aerodrome.

'I am proud of you, Kathy, though it could, of course, be my superior teaching,' he laughed, as I parked the car near the clubhouse.

We watched two pilots practising some stunts. Their heads looked like two small black dots. Suddenly, they took their planes up vertically into the azure sky. I held my breath as the engines stopped, and the little Moths silently twirled like autumn leaves back to earth, then the men took control again and sped off in opposite directions along the valley.

'Can you do that Paul?'

'Yes, I have with Andrew's help.'

'I'd love to have a go.' I slid my hand around the steering wheel, feeling the leather tickle my palm.

'You went up the other day.'

'Yes, but I'd really love to learn to fly like Amy Johnson.'

'Not all the way to Australia?'

'Why not? I'd love to be independent, and just fly off anywhere I wanted. It would be wonderful.'

'Let's ask Andrew to give you a lesson.'

'Really?'

'Yes, your wish is my command.' Paul hurried off in the direction of the hangar.

Jeepers, a flying lesson!

I pushed the seat back to make more room, and closed my eyes. The sun shone red on my eyelids. I remembered the tartan rug with Ben, and hoped that he didn't mind me having a go.

Paul ran back. 'Andrew says yes! Would tomorrow afternoon be all right? I don't have to work until the evening.'

January 12th 1930

For nearly twenty-four hours, I blew hot and cold, like a desert wind, worrying about the baby. It was one thing going up for a ride with Andrew as pilot, but quite another to learn to fly myself. Yes, he would be there, and there were dual controls because you could fly the plane from either the front or the back seat, but what if I did something really wrong and, Heaven forbid, the plane crashed?

But, I'd kept the article about Amy Johnson. I did so want to learn to fly like her. The freedom, the excitement. It had been a wish come true to go up with Andrew, and here was my chance to learn. I may not have another one until the baby was born. Surely it couldn't do it that much harm?

I thought about Ben learning to fly up in Lincolnshire and enjoying himself in the RAF. He didn't have to worry about us not being married, and he hadn't been sent away in disgrace like me. Why should he have all the fun?

And with that, I decided I should go ahead and have the lesson.

Paul arrived at two o'clock, and put his hand on my elbow to guide me to the car.

'What is it, Kathy, you're shaking?'

'Nothing, I'm just crazy to start.' I got in the passenger seat and tied a red scarf around my head. 'Let's go.'

'Wouldn't you like to drive again?'

'No, I'm far too excited.'

He grinned at me. 'So, you're all ready for your flying lesson, then?'

'Yes, I'm ready for whatever the day may bring. I want to take off into the wind, and soar over the sea. Is that how you felt when you learnt to fly?'

'Well, I was bit frightened at first,' he said, 'but, I love it now.'

'I can't wait!'

As we climbed to Haldon, snowdrops carpeted the woods. An image of Ben throwing snowballs on Boxing Day flashed in front of me, and I pushed it firmly to the back of my mind.

At the aerodrome, two ground engineers manoeuvred a fragile Gipsy Moth into the hangar. The bright sunshine glimmered off its yellow fuselage as it finally disappeared into the gloom of the shed, like a bee crawling into a hive.

'Could we go and look inside? I'd love to go and see what they do. Do think that they'd let me because I'm having a lesson?' I peered through the wide hangar door. 'What with Amy Johnson flying to Australia, they can hardly say no, can they?'

'No, Amy, I mean *Kathy*, let's ask Andrew. Here he is.'

Andrew walked up, wiping his hands on a greasy cloth. 'Hello, Dr Trevelyan. Hello, Kathy. It's a pleasure to see you again.'

'Hello,' Paul strained to be heard above the noise in the hangar. 'Can I bring Kathy inside to see what goes on for a few minutes before her lesson?'

'Why, yes, of course,' said Andrew, 'Don't slip on the oily floor.'

Paul held me tightly by the arm. The ground engineers looked up in amazement and stopped talking.

'Carry on, men,' said Andrew. 'This is Kathy; she'd like to see what you get up to in here.' He showed us around the collection of Gipsy Moths, in varying stages of maintenance.

My eyes darted around the shed. 'This is fascinating. I didn't know that it was so involved. I thought that you just put in the aircraft fuel, oiled a few points and swung the propeller.'

'Well, it is vital to be able to maintain your own plane, especially if you had to make an emergency landing all alone in the countryside.' Andrew patted the yellow Gipsy Moth.

'Just like Amy Johnson.'

'You and Amy,' Paul chuckled.

Andrew laughed and looked at his watch. 'Well, it's time for your lesson now. Shall I meet you in a few minutes?'

'Right-o. Thanks very much for the tour.' And Paul guided me out.

'Thank you, Andrew,' I added, and we hurried back to the clubhouse to find me a leather flying jacket and helmet.

'You look like a real pilot dressed like that. Let's finish it off with your red scarf.'

My knees felt so wobbly, I wondered if I'd be able to climb into the plane at all, as we walked towards the Gipsy Moth which Andrew was already checking for the flight.

'Are you ready?' he called.

I hesitated, thinking about the baby again, but the thrill of flying won me over. I crossed my fingers that everything would be all right. 'Yes, I can hardly believe that I'm really going to do it at last.'

'Right then,' said Andrew when I was strapped in. 'This is the drill.' And he went through all the various controls for gas, brakes, throttle and switches.

'Well, it looks easier than starting up Paul's car, Andrew.'

'I'm not so sure about that.' He fastened his chinstrap. 'I'll fly the plane from the rear, you just have to follow what I do.'

'If I can hear you.'

Andrew grinned. 'Ready?'

'Yes. I think so.'

He climbed in, but I felt again that I was on my own, going solo. I could hear my heart thumping in my ears, and a sick feeling sloshed about in my stomach.

'Good Luck!' Paul shouted.

'Right-o, CONTACT,' Andrew commanded.

I heard Paul grunt as he gave the propeller a hearty swing. I took a deep breath and cradled my tummy with one hand. But the Gipsy Moth did not come to life.

'Switches off,' Andrew called. 'Propeller back to swinging position.'

From my seat in the front, I could just see Paul wipe his face on his handkerchief, and roll up his sleeves.

'CONTACT.'

This time he swung it into action and the engine stirred itself and began to throb.

'Pull the chocks.'

With Andrew's help, I steered the little plane down to the end of the landing field, and then turned round to accelerate back towards Paul for take off. The Gipsy Moth bounded over the grass, and leapt up into the air.

'How does it feel?' Andrew called.

'Like riding the wind, I've always dreamt of doing this!' I shouted.

I'm flying like Ben! I'm flying like Amy Johnson! I'm free!

Then the engine started to shudder, and seemed to miss a stroke like a scratch on a gramophone record. I gripped the joystick for dear life.

Andrew appeared to be struggling with the controls. 'Sit tight, Kathy, we seem to be having some sort of mechanical problem. I think we'd better turn back.'

'Will we be all right?' I shouted as the plane began to nose dive like the Big Dipper on Blackpool Pleasure Beach. It felt as if we were going to flip over forwards and I could feel my body tipping, tipping. 'Andrew! Andrew!'

'Keep your head down and brace yourself!' he shouted, as the wind whistled past, faster and faster.

I wedged myself down into the cockpit with my arms over my head and my elbows banging on the control panel. And when I thought we couldn't possibly go any faster, BANG, we hit the ground.

Silence.

I felt as if we were still moving, still streaking downwards.

'Get out! Get out!' Andrew shouted. 'Kathy, can you get out?'

'Yes, I think so.' I fumbled with the catch and at last managed to unbuckle my belt. *Oh God! The baby!* I felt bruised and battered, but my arms and legs seemed to work so I hauled myself out and slithered to the ground. Andrew grabbed me, and dragged me away as the Moth burst into flames with a blast of hot air which propelled us out of danger. Glancing back through the suffocating smoke, I saw that we'd come down only about a hundred yards from the clubhouse.

Then Paul was there: holding me, supporting me. 'Are you all right, Kathy?'

'Yes, I think so,' I coughed.

'What about you, Andrew?' Paul asked.

'I'm fine, just bumped about a bit.' Andrew rubbed his knee.

'Let me have a look at it for you.'

'No, it's okay. Are you sure that you're not injured, Kathy?'

'No, really.' I smiled, but my head was swimming.

The engineers tried to put the fire out with a hose, but it just turned the water into sizzling steam, so we stood helplessly watching the Gipsy Moth burn down to a charred frame which crumbled onto the scorched grass.

Andrew shook his head, 'I'm sorry, Kathy, I don't know what happened, the engine just began to lose power.'

I rubbed my eyes to remove the itchy smuts. 'I'm sorry too.'

'It wasn't your fault, don't worry. It was just something mechanical, but we'll never know what now.' Andrew looked over to where the remains of the Gipsy Moth smouldered in the breeze.

'You were very lucky not to be badly hurt.' Paul hugged me tight. 'You were marvellous; you were really brave.'

I felt my tummy; I could still feel the baby kicking. *Thank goodness.*

The pale winter sun shone all the way home, picking out clumps of snowdrops which hid under the hedgerows. Paul drove, carefully avoiding the bumps and potholes in the country lanes.

Tired, I closed my eyes and re-lived my flying lesson. Despite being shaken up, I couldn't wait to have another go.

Chapter Fourteen

'What on earth have you been up to Kathy?' Aunt Sylvia opened the door and stood back in horror at my blackened clothes. 'You look like a chimney sweep! Take a look at yourself in the mirror.'

'She's fine, Sylvia, she just had a little accident at the aerodrome.' Paul had his arm round me and squeezed my shoulders.

'You didn't crash the plane, did you?'

'Yes, I did, but…'

Auntie sank down on a little red velvet buttoned chair.

' . . . there was some mechanical problem.'

'I thought that you were flying with Andrew. I should never have let you go.' She blew out a cloud of cigarette smoke which stung my sore eyes. 'I don't know what your mother will say.'

Jeepers, she better not find out about the plane bursting into flames! I rubbed my forehead to get my thoughts together. 'Auntie, I did go with Andrew, I'm not hurt, just a bit shaken, that's all.'

'You certainly look in a state. What about the baby, Kathy?' She shook her head, 'I don't understand you at all. How could you put your baby at such a risk?'

I glanced at Paul. 'I've felt it kick, it's fine.'

'Well, I hope that you've got that fancy idea of flying out of your head once and for all.'

I felt my cheeks flush.

'For goodness sake, go and have a nice hot bath and give your clothes to Mabel to wash.' She stubbed out her cigarette in the aspidistra on the hall table. 'I don't know, you young people these days: no sense of responsibility.'

The bath soothed my aches and pains and, feeling more relaxed, I decided I should write to Ben and tell him about my adventures.

Dear Ben,

I've got some exciting news for you! Yesterday, I went up in a Gipsy Moth! And today, I had a flying lesson! I drove up to the aerodrome in Paul's little Austin, and he arranged it all for me. (I told you, didn't I, that he's been teaching me to drive?)

It was wonderful to be up in the sky like you, and fly with the birds. I could see for miles. Oh, it was such sport; I can't wait to go again!

'I'm not going to tell you about the crash though,' I said to Ben's photograph on the mantelpiece, whilst rubbing my tummy to make sure that the baby was still alive and kicking.

I've been reading about Amy Johnson in the newspaper. It said that she might challenge the solo flight record to Australia too, like Francis Chichester. Fancy that! If things were different and I wasn't pregnant, I'd love to have a go. Wouldn't you? Maybe one day we could do it together as co-pilots. I'm so glad that I'm learning to fly.

All my love,
Kathy

The sun slipped down behind the hills, picking out the bare branches around my window in gold against the clear azure sky, and throwing long shadows across my room. Paul had lent me his Gipsy Moth manual and I sat on the bed against the pillows, like a pilot in a cockpit. And as the room grew dim, I pretended to take off into the wind at forty miles an hour. I banked left with my hairbrush joystick and the left rudder, using a couple of Auntie's dusty old books under my feet for the pedals, and then straightened up by turning right. All the time, imagining I was checking the altimeter to monitor my flying height. I hoped I would do much better the next time I had a lesson, because even though Andrew said the accident wasn't my fault, I couldn't help feeling that I did have something to do with it.

Thank goodness the baby didn't seem to be harmed at all. It kicked away like a little donkey as I tried to go to sleep, making me stroke my tummy to calm it down. The bump definitely seemed to be growing, and I knew that soon I wouldn't be able to fit in a plane, let alone fly one.

January 14th 1930

'What's that?' A bell was ringing in my dream. I turned over and peered at my little alarm clock. 'It's only half past seven.'

The bell continued for a while, then stopped. 'It must be the telephone,' I muttered. 'Thank goodness, someone's answered it.' And I settled down again, only to be disturbed by a knocking on my door.

'Miss Kathy?' Mabel's rosy face appeared. 'There's a telephone call for you.'

'For me?' I frowned. 'Is it Mother? I hope there's nothing wrong at home.'

'No, miss, it's your young man.'

'Paul? What does he want so early in the morning?'

'No, miss,' she shook her head, 'it's your young man, *Ben*. And you'd better hurry up; he's calling from Lincolnshire. It must be costing him a fortune.'

I struggled into my dressing gown, getting my arm tangled up in the sleeve in my haste. *Why is he calling?* Then, my heart leapt. *Perhaps he's got his parents' permission at last. Perhaps we can get married!*

I picked up the receiver, 'Ben?' I hadn't talked to him on the telephone before, and my heart beat with excitement. 'Ben? Hello?'

'There you are at last, Kathy, I've had to put some more money in.'

'What is it? Why are you phoning?' My feet were cold on the tiles and I hopped from one to another.

'I've just got your letter. Who is this Paul, Kathy?'

I swallowed. 'I told you, he's Auntie's stepson, why?'

'Why? *I* was going to teach you to drive, and to fly. I didn't expect you to do it with someone else!'

'I know, but I'm here, and he's here, and he's . . . he's just helping me.' I crossed my fingers, and shut my eyes.

'Are you crazy, Kathy? You can't learn to fly in your condition; you've got responsibilities. The baby to think of.'

'But, it's such a wonderful opportunity to have a go. There's not much else I can do down here. You know it's always been my dream to learn to fly, and I won't be able to fit in a plane much longer. So I thought I'd have a go whilst I could.' I bit my bottom lip. 'It's quite safe.'

He sighed, 'I wish you'd never gone away on your own, Kathy.'

'Don't you think I wish I wasn't here too?' I could feel tears welling up, but I bit my lip harder.

The operator came on the line to ask him to put in some more money, and I heard it go *ching, ching*.

'I haven't got much change left,' he said. 'Look, Kathy, I don't want you to see this Paul again.'

'Why?'

'It's too dangerous: learning to drive, learning to fly. You don't know anything about him.'

'Yes, I do. He's Auntie's stepson, Ben, and he's a *doctor*. He's learning to fly too.'

'Oh, I see. So that's all right is it?'

'Yes, and everything is fine; it wasn't a serious crash.' I clapped my hand to my mouth as if to trap in the words that I'd spoken, but too late.

'What did you say? A crash?'

I took a deep breath. 'Yes, there was a mechanical problem, just after we'd taken off. But, the plane came down smoothly, Ben, like a paper dart.'

'You're telling me that the plane crashed and you were in it? Was Paul in there with you?'

'No, it was Andrew, he runs the aerodrome.'

I'm certainly not going to tell him about the fire.

'I can't understand why you're being so irresponsible.'

'I'm not irresponsible!' Feeling guilty made me angry with him. 'Look, Ben, getting me pregnant was irresponsible.'

'But you were there too. It does take two, you know.'

'Yes, but look at me, banished down here in Devon, and you stuck up there in Lincolnshire. Look what's happened! I wish you'd talked to your parents and made them see how much we wanted to get married. You promised you'd speak to them again at Christmas, but you didn't.'

'They wouldn't have listened anyway. Apart from Mother being ill, I'm due to get an allowance on my twenty-first birthday, and Father said that he won't pay it if I marry you before then. Just be patient, Kathy. If we get married now, as you want, I'll have nothing.'

'Like me,' I said in a small voice. Then I added, 'I thought you wanted to get married too, Ben.'

'Of course I do.'

'Well, please do something about it. I can't bear it all alone down here.'

The operator came on the line again.

'I'd better go, Kathy, I haven't got any more money. Goodbye.'

'Goodb . . .'

But the line went dead.

I turned round to see Aunt Sylvia in the hall. 'Come on, Kathy, you'll catch your death of cold out here, let's go into the kitchen and have some tea.'

Gratefully, I padded over to the Aga and sat on Mabel's comfy chair tucking my feet underneath me to warm them up.

'I told you that he should have done the decent thing and married you,' she said, pouring me out a cup.

'But he makes me so mad!'

'Oh, Kathy, he's the baby's father.'

'I know, but I've never heard him so cross before.' I sipped the hot tea. 'And he hasn't even tried to speak to his parents again about the wedding.'

Chapter Fifteen

January 21st 1930

With my heart in my mouth, I stood at the dining room window watching a plane soaring out over the river, climbing up into the sky, invisible against the sun, and then spinning down and down until the pilot pulled it upwards again and sped off towards Dartmoor.

I wonder if that's Andrew? I want to go up again with him, but Aunt Sylvia says we won't be so lucky next time. I can't wait though. I adored it.

Then Paul's Austin rattled up the frosty drive between the lawns peppered with snowdrops and edged with daffodil shoots. Unfolding his tall frame from the car, he waved and hurried into the house.

'Kathy? Do you want to come driving?' His footsteps tapped along the hall. 'I thought we'd explore the other side of the bridge today and drive to Shaldon. What do you think? Better keep away from the aerodrome at the moment.'

My heart began to thump loudly because Ben had told me not to do any more driving with Paul, or flying for that matter, but I was cross with him: flying and driving were the only things I could do in Devon without people pointing out I was pregnant . . . for the moment. I was tired of being cooped up in the house too, whilst Aunt Sylvia investigated new premises for her shop, and Uncle Jeremy spent all his time at the boatyard. So, I grabbed my scarf and gloves, and followed Paul outside into his car.

He grinned at me and his blue eyes and fair hair reminded me of a poster of a matinee idol pasted up outside the Vaudeville Cinema, and I began to think that I'd like to be the brunette woman reclining in his arms. I shook my head to get rid of the unsettling image, and started the car, found reverse, did a three-point turn and headed off down the drive.

'Kathy, that was marvellous! How did you manage it?'

'Just watching and learning. At least your car isn't going to fall out of the sky!' I smiled.

Paul directed me along the river to the town, and I drove carefully through the narrow streets to the bridge. The sun shone off the water and made me squint, and to my annoyance, because I really wanted to prove that I could drive as well as any man, he had to grab the wheel to keep me on the left hand side of the road. Double-declutching, I moved down into second gear and climbed up the hill to Shaldon.

'Oh,' I said, glancing over my shoulder, 'you can see all of Teignmouth from up here!'

'It's like flying in an aeroplane!' we said together and laughed. As I drove up to the top, a worrying niggle told me it was wrong to be with Paul, but I was enjoying myself.

'I wish I'd got more time today; I'd love to take you all the way to Torquay along the cliffs,' Paul said, as we sped along with the sea sparking below on our left, 'but let's pull in here and turn around.'

I drove the car onto the grass, and gasped, 'This is wonderful! Look at the sea; it's so far below. Look at all the boats! Can we get out?'

'Of course,' he said, opening my door.

The wind almost whipped my scarf away, and I tied it round my neck tightly as we battled our way down over the field. Paul guided me to a log, sheltered by some bushes, and we sat down.

'Kathy?'

I turned to him, shocked that his voice saying my name, so gently with the slightest Devonshire burr, was like being dipped in melted chocolate: his warmth washed all over me. But alarm bells went off in my head, and I remembered Aunt Sylvia saying: 'Be careful, my girl, he's quite a charmer. A bit like the Prince of Wales . . .'

'Kathy, I see your name everywhere.' He made a sign up in the air with his fingers and thumbs. 'KATHY MASON on shops, newspaper headlines and even destination boards on buses.'

I nudged him with my elbow. 'Don't be silly, Paul.'

Then, lightly supporting my chin with his fingers, he turned my head from side to side. 'I see your face on coins, in the faces of my patients and even in Matron's face. She was surprised to see me looking at her so intently.' His eyes twinkled, but I tried to study the gulls which swooped and flapped, calling to each other on the wind.

'Listen to them! They're so noisy. They must be searching for their lunch.' I pointed, trying to keep my mind off that melting chocolate sensation inside. My lips tingled and burned, and for some crazy reason, I wanted to kiss him. My temperature soared, despite the cutting wind and Paul could have poured me into any chocolate mould that he liked. He put his arm round me, and electric shocks shot down to my toes. Then he gently pulled me towards him, so I could feel his breath on my face. *Kiss me, please!* I closed my eyes, but then snapped them open and managed to say, 'I think we should be getting on with the lesson, don't you, Paul?' I rubbed my clammy hands together. 'It's been such sport.' And desperate to get away from his embrace, I got up and walked back to the car.

He caught me up and took my hand. Turning it over, he began to kiss my palm. I closed my eyes; the pleasure was almost unbearable. 'Kathy, I love you,' he murmured into my ear despite the howling wind.

'No, Paul.' I tried to struggle away as he enveloped me in his arms, 'No, Paul. Really. I can't.'

But, it was no good. He gently brushed the hair out of my eyes and trailed his fingers over my cheek and across my lips. 'Kathy,' he murmured.

'Paul . . .' I tried to fight the spell he had over me, but it was like sliding into a warm bath of chocolate: wrong but irresistible.

'Shh, no matter what may happen, I love you, Kathy.'

'But I'm having Ben's baby. I've promised to marry him.' I tugged at his arms. 'I wish I'd never come to Devon.'

'Then I wouldn't have met you on the train.'

He kissed me and held me tight, until the baby kicked, and I pulled away, guilt scorching my cheeks and my lips burning as if smeared with fresh mustard. I rubbed them as if to wipe his kiss away, but it lingered there, and desire and disgust raced in equal measures around my body.

I pressed my hands on his chest. 'We shouldn't have done that, Paul. I'm having a wonderful time here learning to drive with you and learning to fly with Andrew. Don't lets spoil it.'

He lifted my hands and kissed them and it felt as if I'd been brushed with a live wire. 'You're so lovely, Kathy, when you're so earnest.'

That night I lay in bed, reading Ben's latest letter, trying to will all thoughts of Paul out of my mind. But then like the fickle flames in the fireplace, his image would rise up in the middle of the paper. Those eyes, that smile: I was smitten.

My eyelids drooped, and suddenly, I was grappling with the controls of a Gipsy Moth, flying low along a golden path to the sun, over an iron-grey sea. An enemy plane shot straight towards me out of the dazzling glare. I ducked. It fired at me, and as the bullets blazed past, I swerved left into the midst of planes diving and swooping through smoke and tracer fire.

Two aircraft flew beside me, and I knew that they were piloted by Ben and Paul. Together, playing cat and mouse, they drew the enemy further and further away, spiralling up, just out of reach of his incessant fire. Then CRACK, one of them was hit. The flimsy aircraft spun noiselessly down out of the sky, and exploded, before cascading into the sea like a firework.

Which one was it? Ben? Or Paul? Ignoring the battle surrounding me, I dived down to the small pieces of wreckage bobbing up amongst the waves. I circled, but I couldn't see a survivor. I cried out for Mother, Dad, Abigail: anybody who could help me. The remains of the plane sunk into the cold dark water.

I woke up in a sweat, panting. *Which one had it been?*

I stared at the shadowy ceiling.

Oh, Ben: that last day in the sun. I loved you so much; I love you now, but Paul makes me feel giddy. I'm under his spell, mesmerized, like a magician's assistant. If he placed me on a wooden board, balanced between two chairs, and took them away one by one, I would float in the air at his command.

This is ridiculous, Kathy. You've only known Paul for three weeks. You've known Ben most of your life. You're having his baby. He wants you to be his wife. You can't just throw all that away. You gave him your little black bead as a promise.

The moon shone though the curtains, dazzling my eyes.

Are you looking at the moon tonight, Ben? Are you looking at it, Paul? It is just an infatuation, isn't it? I'm being tempted, or tested. Poor Ben. I can't do this to you. I must put an end to it before it's too late.

January 24th 1930

It was nearly two weeks before Aunt Sylvia would let Paul take me up to Haldon Aerodrome. And I had very mixed feelings. I shouldn't have kissed him, I know, but I needed to see him. I really wanted to try flying again more than anything, and without Paul's help, I wouldn't have another chance as Aunt Sylvia and Uncle Jeremy were too busy to drive me up. I'd tried to keep out of his way since that kiss, and I willed myself to put him out of my mind; after all, I'd managed to forget Ben easily enough when I was in Paul's arms. I screwed my eyes tight shut each night, but he just reappeared, like a Hollywood star on a silver screen, or a prince in a newsreel waving at his adoring crowds.

'Kathy, are you ready?'

My heart skipped with joy as he pushed open the front door, and his voice had that instant effect of turning my knees to jelly. I wanted to fall helplessly into his arms, but I managed to say, ‘Good Morning, Paul,’ and gathered my coat in front of me for protection.

‘What’s the matter, Kathy?’ Despite my shield, he hugged me so close that I felt giddy and hot.

How could something so bad feel so good? I could hardly speak as my heart thundered like a Handley Page roaring down the runway.

‘Kathy, I love you,’ he whispered as he led me towards the door. I followed, caught in a trance. Then, as if someone had clicked their fingers, I saw the post had been, and there was an envelope with Ben’s handwriting on the mat. I felt as if I’d been caught in a spotlight, like a prisoner halfway up a twelve-foot wall.

‘No!’ I struggled away. ‘No, Paul. This is who I love,’ I said, waving the letter.

‘But, Kathy, you didn’t seem too worried about Ben the other day.’

I winced as he said Ben’s name, it felt like a razor blade slicing through my heart. ‘No, it was wrong. We shouldn’t have done it. Who knows where it may lead? Let’s not spoil what we’ve got. Our friendship.’ But looking into his cloudy blue eyes, I wasn’t totally sure.

Saying no more, Paul helped me into his car, and I drove through the village and up the hill to Haldon Aerodrome, concentrating on the road, and trying to ignore him sitting in silence beside me, except to tell me to change gear or keep in to the left round a bend. With relief, I parked the car and saw Andrew waiting for me with a helmet in his hand.

‘I didn’t expect to see you again, Kathy,’ he smiled through the window.

‘I really want to learn to fly, Andrew, it can’t be worse than last time.’ I told him, getting out.

‘Are you *sure* that you’re up to it?’

‘Of course!’ I said, crossing my fingers and hoping that I wouldn’t put the baby at risk again.

He grinned. 'My goodness, you are a plucky girl.'

'Thank you.'

Soon, we were racing down the grass runway and up into the air. Any worries about Paul, or apprehension about the baby were swept away by the exhilaration of flying. Flying! Andrew circled the airfield and everything was perfect.

'Let's practise some turns,' he called.

'All right!' I shouted.

We flew backwards and forwards getting tighter each time: whizzing over the hillside, skimming the aerodrome and then zipping towards the sea.

'Well done, Kathy, you flew the last circuit all by yourself.'

'No! Did I?' I yelled, secretly pleased of the practice I'd had in my bedroom.

'Yes, you are a born pilot.'

At last we made our final turn, and gently descending, we landed quietly on the grassy strip and taxied back as calmly as if we'd been for a spin in a car. I waved my scarf in the air, as Paul ran over the damp grass.

'You were marvellous!' he shouted. 'You were really brave.'

'I flew that last circuit all on my own!'

'Good girl,' said Andrew, 'I'm glad you came back. You flew like a real aviatrix today: if you carry on like that, you'll soon have your licence. Did you enjoy it?'

'It was fantastic.' I returned Paul's hug, despite my misgivings. 'I feel like doing it again!'

Chapter Sixteen

February 14th 1930

I heard the post land on the mat, and hurried downstairs. Two cards lay there. *Valentine cards from Ben and Paul?* My heart thumped so much, that I thought it was going to pop through my chest like in those crazy Hollywood cartoons. I bent down to pick up the envelopes, but when I turned them over with clammy fingers, they were for Auntie and Uncle. I wandered up and down the hall, my hands making damp prints as my thoughts twirled round and round.

I'm glad I didn't post that silly card to Paul and make a fool of myself.

I had sent one to Ben though. I'd trawled through all the card shops in Teignmouth, but I couldn't bring myself to buy him one that said 'I love you' or 'Be my Valentine', I wasn't sure that it was true any more. Most of the cards bore hearts and flowers and sentimental verses, but at last I found a jolly toy aeroplane, with a boy at the front and a girl at the back. She held out a Valentine card to him, and he held out a big red heart to her.

'Has the post been, Kathy?' Aunt Sylvia called.

With a heavy heart, I took the envelopes into the kitchen.

'Thank you, I wonder who this could be from?' Auntie raised her eyebrows at Uncle. The corners of her mouth twitched in anticipation. Then she burst out laughing, 'Jeremy!'

The card had a picture of a little boy in a yacht, and she read out the rhyme written on the sail:

'Come for a sail on the sea with me,
And you'll be as happy as can be,
I'm so glad that you are mine,
My lovely, Lady Valentine!'

'It's perfect, Jeremy.' She wiped the tears of laughter from her eyes, and passed it to me. 'You really are the limit. You know that I'm never ever going out in that boat with you.'

How he dared to tease her, I just didn't know. We'd always tiptoed around her at home, and in the shop, wary of her unpredictable eruptions. But he kissed her lovingly, and opened his card.

'Oh look!' He showed us the little blue car with two golden puppies like Rosie's at the wheel. 'The number plate says U 4 ME. Thank you, Sylvia.' And he kissed her again.

'I really wanted to get you a green car like yours, but that's all they had.' She stroked his cheek.

I might as well not be here. My stomach tied itself into a knot. *I'm just an intruder on their first Valentine's Day together.*

We all jumped as the doorbell rang.

'Who can that be?' she said.

I hurried to answer it. A delivery man stood there behind the most enormous bouquet of deep red roses.

'Jeremy, you shouldn't have!' Auntie gasped.

The man held out an envelope: 'Miss Kathy Mason?'

'Kathy? They're for you!' Her face clouded for a moment, but then she took the bouquet, and passed me the card. 'Who are they from? Is it your young man, Ben?'

Feverishly, I ripped it open, and read, 'To My Valentine.'

'I don't know, it doesn't say.' I shook my head. But I did: only Paul had ever sent me flowers. My heart thundered away, what was I getting myself into?

'Let's put these in water.' Aunt Sylvia led the way back into the kitchen, 'I think we'll need two vases.'

'That's rather extravagant of the boy, isn't it,' Uncle Jeremy raised his eyebrows and winked, 'to send you flowers?'

Just then, the doorbell rang again. It was the postman.

'Sorry, ma'am,' he said, as Auntie opened the door. 'This envelope was stuck in the lining of my bag. I thought that it might be a card, seeing as it's Valentine's Day, so I've brought it round special like, ma'am.'

'Thanks very much,' said Auntie, reading the envelope,

‘Kathy, it’s for you, too. I wonder who this one’s from?’

The postman rode off, whistling.

Ben! It was his handwriting. Heart beating, I tore open the envelope, and took out a hand-made card with a pen-and-ink drawing of a Gipsy Moth on the front, with Ben and I sitting in it. Inside the card, the banner fluttered across both pages saying:

Please be my Valentine!

My eyes filled with tears. *Dear Ben, I am sorry. I wish that I’d never met Paul.*

However, despite Ben’s sweet Valentine card, and my guilt, that night I dreamt that Paul and I slept together. I woke up, horrified, in a hot sweat.

But, I kept dipping into the dream all day long, trying to recreate the delicious sensations, like dipping into a box of chocolate truffles which softly melted on my tongue. Sickly, but irresistible: licking my fingers, and filling my mouth, fuelled by the hot desire in the pit of my stomach. All day, my body thrummed. In my dream, I had frolicked in black silk with scarlet bows amongst the softest pink rose petals.

That night, the dream returned full of desire and tenderness. I awoke moaning and aroused: wanting to make it come true, wanting to feel Paul’s touch on my body.

Studying myself in the bathroom mirror, I thought longingly of buying some black silk lingerie so I could romp with him as I had in my dream. I’d always been proud of my boyish shape and I never had to bind my breasts like Abigail to keep them flat. (How she grumbled about the tight lace bandeaus she wore.) I’d been happy in my cotton liberty bodice, but now my breasts had inflated to the size of two reasonable melons, anything would be better than my cotton side-lacer brassiere. Talk about a passion-killer!

Quickly dressing, before I changed my mind, I went downstairs.

'Auntie, I was thinking about going shopping in Exeter today, do you want to come?' I crossed my fingers hoping she'd say . . . what? *No*: then I could go on my own or *yes*: then I'd be absolved from such a wicked plan.

'Good gracious, no!' She threw her hands up in the air.

My temperature rocketed; I would be going on my own after all.

'I've got to deal with these papers for the shop,' she continued. 'The solicitor has kept me waiting for two weeks. I don't know why everything is so slow down here in Devon. In Reading, it's all is done in a jiffy.' She picked up her pen. 'Have a jolly time, dear, and take care.'

So off I went, catching the bus at the bottom of the drive.

I held my head high as I entered Bobby's department store; after all, my aunt ran her own shop didn't she? I found the lingerie was on the first floor, and forgetting to take the lift, ran up the stairs, arriving hot and breathless. The assistant stood guardian over her array of limbless and headless mannequins which were as smooth as Italian marble, and decked in brassieres and knickers in the latest colours of ivory, eau de nil, salmon pink, lemon . . . and black! She stared at me over her spectacles, as if to ask what a woman in my condition was doing there. Losing my nerve, I fled down the street to Colson's.

The lady there was busy serving other customers so I was able to look at what they had. The touch of the silky lingerie sent tingles up my fingers, and I adjusted my turquoise ring to look like a gold wedding band.

'Can I help you, madam?'

I winced. She looked petite and middle-aged, a bit like my mother. I licked my lips nervously, 'I'd like to buy a brassiere and matching French knickers, please.'

'What size?'

'Thirty–four, please, medium cup.'

'You look as if a *large* cup would fit you better, madam.'

I caught my breath.

'Which colour would you like?'

I blushed, and my heart drummed in my chest. *I want the black so much, but I can't.*

'Um . . . cream, please.' Then as she bent down to take them out of the drawer, 'No, black!' I tried to smile confidently.

'Certainly, madam.'

She brought out a set decorated with tiny red bows, just like in my dream. I held out my left hand to feel them, and with a shock noticed that the little turquoise flower had twisted its way back to the top of my ring.

There was a pause as the assistant's eyes settled on my hand.

'I'll take these,' I blushed.

It took an age for the money which Mother had given me for "emergencies" to trundle along in the little brass canister to the cash desk and back, and I could feel my face getting redder and redder. *I bet she never envisaged an "emergency" like this!*

I couldn't wait to get back to Hillfields and try them on. Soft, silky and delicious, they clung to my full body. My face flushed back at me from the mirror. But, I longed to see Paul again.

That evening, Uncle Jeremy looked over the top his newspaper. 'Did you have a good day in Exeter, Kathy? Paul has been round looking for you. I thought you were trying to avoid him.' He raised his eyebrows. 'He wants you to go with him to Haldon tomorrow, and see him fly.'

'I honestly don't know what I want, Uncle. I thought I loved Ben, but when I'm with Paul, I'm under his spell.' I shrugged my shoulders.

'You be careful, my girl.'

'It's funny, Uncle, but Auntie said that to me too.'

February 17th 1930

I spent another night tossing and turning, and by the time I'd dropped off at last, Mabel was knocking on the door with a cup of tea.

I bathed, and bubbling with excitement and apprehension, I slipped into my new silk brassiere and French knickers. They felt wonderful and secret under my clothes. I knew that it was wrong, but I couldn't help it.

I waited by the window in the dining room until Paul's little red car turned up the drive, and I hurried out to meet him.

'Kathy?' It was as if he knew what I wanted.

'Yes?' I wanted him so much.

'Let's find somewhere where we can be alone.' He took my hand and led me back to his car. After that dream, I wanted him far more than Ben, and I couldn't help myself.

'Where can we go?'

'To my house in Teignmouth.'

'Your house? I thought you lived at the hospital.'

'No, father bought me a little cottage: two up, two down so I could be nearby. I'm supposed to let out the other room, but I haven't got around to it yet.'

'But, we can't go there, we'll be seen!'

'Don't worry, Kathy, it'll be fine.' He kissed me.

The cottage huddled on the shady side of the street where the pavement glistened with damp. Whilst Paul unlocked the door, I shrank down in the passenger seat. And, when the coast was clear, stole in behind him.

'Well, at least the fire hasn't gone out!' He threw on some fresh logs which spat and sizzled, their flames lighting up the wintry gloom.

'Come here,' he said, taking me into his arms.

I didn't need any magic; I was already under his spell. He lowered me onto the sofa, and kissed me. On my lips. On my throat. On my neck. Delicious feelings overwhelmed me. I quivered with anticipation. He slipped his finger inside my blouse, and touched my skin. Electric charges shot straight down to my toes. He carefully undid the top buttons, and kissed me. I caressed his head, and his hair tickled my palms.

I wanted to give myself to him completely. Then, I felt a little nudge inside my stomach. The baby. I'd made this mistake once; I wasn't going to do it again. I pushed Paul away and sat up, fastening my buttons.

'What are you doing, Kathy?' He tried to pull me down again. 'What's the matter? I thought you wanted to . . .'

'I did, Paul, but I can't.' I stood up and straightened my skirt. 'It's not fair to Ben and the baby.'

Paul frowned, 'You mean, Ben, the one who got you into this mess, and wouldn't stand up for you and get his parents' permission to marry you? The one who went away and left you to come down to Devon on your *own*? Does he even care about his baby? I bet he doesn't even know that you've been learning to fly in your condition.'

'He does, actually. And you didn't stop me from flying either, and you're a doctor!'

'Kathy, listen . . .' He touched my arm, but I shook him off.

'Ben and I have known each other since we were little. Yes, of course, I wish he'd tried harder to persuade his parents to let us marry. But, the fact is I'm having his baby and we are going to get married in August when he's twenty-one. I can't let him down.'

Paul was stony faced. 'But you've let me down, Kathy. You let me believe that you were in love with me.'

I sat there, and gazed into the fire as he went outside, banging the door, to get some more logs. My new black brassiere strap cut into my shoulder, and I tried to loosen it. *How far would I have gone? Would I have gone all the way? Would he have really wanted me like this: pregnant with another man's child?* My hand went to my mouth. *Was I a loose woman? First Ben and now Paul?*

I conjured up a picture of Ben on that last summer's day. *I certainly loved him then, but I love Paul now. I love them both. I don't know what to do. Can you really be in love with two people at once?*

'Sorry, I can't stay here, Paul, I've got to go,' I said when he reappeared with an armful of wood, and wrapping my coat around me, I left him alone.

Chapter Seventeen

I walked down towards The Endeavour Inn. I knew that Uncle Jeremy often met Bill Canlan there; perhaps I could get him to take me home. I peeked around the door. The pub was full of fishermen, sailors and boatyard workers leaning up against the bar, or crowding around the brass topped tables. The sounds of their voices filled the air, laden with beer, fish and smoke, and poured out into the street. I wrinkled my nose. Uncle Jeremy spotted me in the doorway and came out, followed by Bill.

'Kathy? What on earth are you doing here? I thought you were up at Haldon with Paul.'

'I was with Paul, Uncle, but then,' I flung around for an excuse, 'he had to deal with an emergency in town. Now I've missed the bus, and I wondered if you could give me a lift home.'

'Yes, of course,' he said. 'But we were just going to inspect the new passenger launch, would you like to come?'

I looked round, half hoping Paul had followed me, but he was nowhere to be seen. I sighed, not knowing what I wanted.

'Come on,' said Uncle, taking my arm. 'It's only around the corner in New Quay. What would you have done if I wasn't here?'

'Waited for the next bus, I suppose, but I'm glad you are here, after all.'

'There she is!' Bill, with a ruddy weather beaten face like the South Devon cliffs, pointed at the sparkling white boat, bobbing in the gentle swell.

I shaded my eyes: 'She floats then?'

'Of course.' Uncle nudged me.

He traced his fingers over the name *Lady Jane,* painted in red and gold swirly letters on the bow, and smiled to himself.

'Oh, you've changed it,' I said. 'I thought she was called *Lady Valentine*.'

'She was, but I did it in honour of your lovely aunt.'

I raised my eyebrows.

'Didn't you know?' Uncle chuckled. 'Your aunt's first name is really Jane, but she prefers to be called by her second. She feels it more suitable for literary circles.'

'Really, well I never knew that.'

'Perhaps there are more things you don't know about her.' He raised his eyebrows. 'She's quite a dark lady!'

What did he mean by that?

'Are you ready, Captain?' Bill stood to attention, and gave a mock salute.

'Aye, aye!' said Uncle Jeremy.

Bill pulled his peaked cap down over his eyes to keep out the glare and started the engine, whilst Uncle undid the ropes and leapt up the gangplank, more like a man in his forties than in his sixties.

'Are you coming, Kathy?'

'No, I'm not dressed for it, I can't.' I shivered. 'I'll wait here.' I'd noticed a bench in the sun, and I wanted to sit down, and wrestle with my thoughts.

'Just come for a little maiden voyage?' he called, as the engine shuddered into action, and the propellers churned up the water into a bubbly foam.

The temptation proved too much. 'What sort of engine is it?' I shouted.

'Petrol marine, modified from a motor car engine!'

'I'll come!'

Uncle helped me in. 'Here, let's put this blanket around you to keep you warm.'

I snuggled up underneath it, on a jaunty blue and white striped seat with the matching canopy flapping over my head.

Bill thrust the boat into reverse, and backed away from the harbour wall, the sharp fumes filling our nostrils. Once clear of the other boats, he powered it forwards towards The Point.

'Well?' asked Uncle Jeremy.

'It's wonderful, where did you find it?'

'Abandoned, at some old yard up the river. Bill's renovated the engine and replaced the boarding. I've been nailing down loose planks and giving it a few coats of paint.' He patted me on the knee. 'Kathy, are you listening?'

'Yes.'

'What is it? Have you got something on your mind?'

Bill stood at the wheel, eyes on the other craft on the river.

I watched the dinghies zip by in the wind, and took a deep breath of sea air. 'Uncle, you were right; I am in love with Paul. I'm in such an awkward situation, because I love Ben too.'

'Have you talked to your aunt about this?'

'No, she's too busy; she never seems to have any time for me.' I pulled the blanket up to my chin. 'I didn't think growing up would be so complicated. Where did I go wrong? I love Paul here. I thought I loved Ben at home. How do I know who I really love?'

Uncle lit his pipe, and the smoke blew away in the wind. 'Let me tell you a little story:

One August when Paul was small, I was sent on relief to the Plymouth branch of the bank. The summer sun poured through the windows, and we sweltered behind the counter. A young woman came in. She wanted to exchange some francs which I dealt with. We also exchanged a few pleasantries, and she left. I thought no more of it. But, later as I returned to my rooms in The Barbican, I saw her again, leaning on the railings, watching the sailing boats setting out to sea. I raised my hat to her, and she smiled back.

'The next day was a Saturday, I had been planning to go home to Carah, my wife, but as Paul had developed chicken pox, and I hadn't had it, I decided to stay over the weekend.' He shook his head, and studied the horizon. 'It was a big mistake.'

'Why, what happened?' I interrupted.

'I went for a walk over to The Ho, to sit on a bench and read the newspaper. Someone sat down beside me, and when I looked up, it was her! Of course we talked innocently. Her family lived near Plymouth, and she had married an officer in the French

Navy, but she no longer loved him. No, she wasn't Carah; she was just a beautiful, young woman. And, yes, I was wrong. I don't know what happened. We spent a pleasant half hour in conversation. Then, I really don't know what got into me; I asked her to join me for lunch, and she agreed. Oh, we toyed around with some Brixham crab, and potatoes, but I could feel this magnetism. I could feel this desire. Her presence was bewitching. She knew it too, and we were captured, under a spell.'

I nodded. 'That's just how I feel with Paul.'

'As if in a dream, we stole back to my rooms over a cake shop; the very smell of baking takes me back to that day: coffee, chocolate, almonds, spices, warm fruit. Anyway, I don't have to tell you any more. It happened. I didn't know that there was a child. The woman, Anna, didn't know where I lived either. She sent a letter to the bank where I'd been working, but it didn't catch up with me until years later.'

'What are you trying to say, Uncle?'

'I'm trying to say that I'm ashamed that I deceived Carah, my wife. I have never forgiven myself. She went to her grave never knowing.'

'What about the child?' I felt my baby flutter inside me.

'I never replied; I don't know what happened to her.'

We both stared out over the sea, lost in thought. I tugged at the biting, black brassiere strap again under the blanket. *What a fool I've been to even think that Paul and I could ever have a future. I was so happy with Ben before.*

Paul arrived the next day whilst we were having Sunday lunch, and Aunt Sylvia insisted that he sat down, and ate with us. Without being rude and leaving the table, I had no escape. I pushed my food around my plate and tried not to catch his eye. However, whilst the table was being cleared, he whispered, 'Kathy, I must speak to you . . . alone.'

I sighed, and rested my forehead on my fingertips to stop the pain that gathered there.

'I can't talk to you, Paul.'

'Please, Kathy.'

I grasped the air in my fists as if I was reining in a horse.

'Let's go for a ride in my car,' he suggested.

'No.' I folded my arms. 'Can't we talk here?'

'We could go to Haldon and get some fresh air?' he said, playing his trump card, knowing I couldn't resist the excitement of the aerodrome.

So reluctantly, I nodded: I had to put an end to it all somehow.

Up on the moor, the rain that had been holding off all morning, blew in from the sea, and we sat in the car as the windows steamed up and cocooned us in a foggy cloud of our own.

He tried to put his arm around my shoulder, but I shook it off.

'No, Paul.'

'But, Kathy, what is it? I'm sorry if I've been too forward, but I love you so much.' His eyes looked as grey as the sky.

'It's not you, it's me. I encouraged you and I shouldn't have. I've made myself cheap. If that's at all possible: I've made myself cheap enough already.' I stroked my rounded tummy.

'I love *you*, Kathy; it doesn't matter about the baby.'

'It does. My baby needs its own father. I can't deny it that. It'll be born in a few months. I can't carry on with you, Paul.'

'Do you love me, Kathy?'

The rain lashed against the windows, and seeped in through the gaps the wind had made between them and the hood. Involuntarily, we moved closer together to keep dry, and I brushed some raindrops off my lap.

'Yes, I do.' I looked into his cloudy eyes. 'I do. But, that's the problem. I love Ben too. And my place is with him. He wants me to marry him. I can't have you both.'

Paul took my hands in his, and fondled them with his thumbs. 'I mean it when I say that I have never loved another girl as much as I love you. You're different, Kathy, you sparkle, you're alive.' He pressed my fingers to his eyes, and they came away damp. He kissed them, and gripped my hands. 'Kathy, I can't live without you.'

'Paul, I'm ashamed of what I've done. I should never have come to your house. Goodness knows what might have happened . . .'

'I would have made love to you, Kathy.' His eyes were dull like the sea in a storm.

I closed my eyes. 'I wanted you to, Paul, you don't know how much. You weave enchantments around me whenever I see you or think about you. I'm living under your spell. But I've got to wake up. This baby is real, Ben is real: he's waiting for me. I didn't come here, looking for this to happen. Ben's always been my friend; he's the father of my child, and I *want* to marry him.'

Paul held my hands. 'Kathy, *I* want to marry *you*. Marry me! Marry me straight away, we don't have to wait!'

'Paul,' I stroked his hair, his face, 'Paul, I love you, I think I always will, but I really love Ben too. It's a different kind of love. Our love is magical, but the love between Ben and me is real; we're going to have a baby. I will never forgive myself for betraying him.'

Relentlessly, the rain blew into the car as the wind buffeted it about.

'Come on,' said Paul, 'we're going to get drowned out here; I'm going to try and drive into the hangar.'

'You're crazy!'

'No, I'm going to try.' He forced open the car door and ran to the hangar. It took all his strength to slide the huge door across as the wind whipped his coat and hair. Then he battled his way back to the car, drove it in, and slammed the door shut behind us. Although the steel building creaked and groaned in the wind, the whistling in our ears stopped. The rain beat down on the high roof, but at least we could open the windows and breathe. I moved away from Paul, but the damp from the seat soaked through my coat.

In the gloom, we could make out the shapes of about half a dozen Gipsy Moths resting on their tails.

'What are we going to do, Paul? Won't they wonder where we are in this storm?'

'Yes, but they know that we came up here. They'll think that we're sitting it out.' He edged closer again. 'Let me hold you, Kathy.'

'But, Paul . . .'

'I won't do anything; I just want to hold you. I love you so much. I want this to remember you by.'

I rested my head on his shoulder, and he put his arm round me and caressed my hair. I wanted it to last for ever too, but I knew that it had to end. The rain continued to batter the hangar. I wriggled a bit. 'The seat's digging into my back.'

'Let's get out, there's some tarpaulin there beneath that wing, there'll be more room.' Paul attempted to fashion the tarpaulin into a kind of bed, lay on it, and patted the space beside him for me to join him there.

'I can't do it, Paul. It's got to end.'

His face crumpled. I stood and watched him sink his head into his hands. I yearned to sit beside him and comfort him.

Instead, I wandered over to the cockpit of the nearest plane. Someone had left some stepladders beside it so I climbed up and looked in at the instruments. *Could I get in there? I'm getting bigger every day.* But, I squeezed in and lowered myself down. The compass pointed north. I traced my finger around the dial. *North-east, that's where Ben is in Lincolnshire. That's where I should be. With him.* I couldn't see Paul beneath the wing. I closed my eyes and imagined flying this little plane up over the heart of England and on to the east coast. *How long would it take? How far is it?*

Eventually, Paul's head appeared beside me.

'Kathy give me one last chance, please?' Dark shadows smudged underneath his red eyes.

My whole body cried out to lie with him on the makeshift bed, no matter what might happen. My arms ached to hold him, and my eyes stung with tears. I tried to struggle up, but a little foot dug in under my ribs. *The baby.*

'I can't, Paul, my place is with Ben. We can still be friends; you're my cousin-in-law, aren't you?'

He smiled, but with his lips together forming a tight line. Sighing, he helped me out, and we sat in the car until the rain stopped, surrounded by the grey, grounded Gipsy Moths.

We were as silent as the grave on the way back to Hillfields. The bleak road stretched ahead, and I could see Paul's stony white face out of the corner of my eye.

Uncle Jeremy came to the door, and put his arm round me, as his son reversed his car into a large puddle. The wheels spun, and together, we watched the Austin Seven splash away down the drive. Paul didn't wave.

'You've really told him this time, haven't you?'

'Yes.' I bit my lip. 'I still love him, Uncle Jeremy.'

He squeezed my shoulder, 'Yes, I know, Kathy, I know.'

The small car disappeared into the road, and Uncle shut the front door. I shuddered as if a guillotine had chopped my heart in two.

'I've been thinking Kathy; you should have a friend to come and stay. Is there someone you'd like?'

I sighed, 'There is Ben's sister, Abigail . . .'

'Write and ask her; I'm sure Sylvia won't mind.'

'No, she doesn't seem to notice what I do.'

Chapter Eighteen

I've done it. I've told him. I think that he understands it's final this time. I rammed a brown carrier bag stuffed with silky lingerie into the dustbin, and dropped the lid down with a dull clang. *I'll always have a place in my heart for Paul, but he's not the one for me. Maybe if I hadn't been pregnant? Or if I'd come to stay with Aunt Sylvia for a holiday? Who knows? But, Uncle Jeremy was right; I haven't been fair to Ben. I've got to think of him now.*

The storm had blown itself out, although rain still dripped from the trees as I wandered up the garden through the watery shafts of afternoon sun. I had brought my writing paper and pen with me and sat at the table in the summerhouse; it was a bit damp and musty, but I was tired of my own room and all the hopes and dreams it had contained.

Dear Abigail,

How are you? I haven't heard from you for a long time. I am well, and I'm now about six month's gone. The bump shows quite a bit and Auntie won't let me near her new shop, so I've been learning to drive and I've been up in a Gipsy Moth three times.

I chewed my pen, and decided not to tell her about the crash, hoping that Ben hadn't told her either.

I do miss you, and I wondered if you'd like to come and stay here in Devon for a week or two? It's so lonely on my own without you and Ben. He still writes to me nearly every day, but I'd love you to be here so we could have some fun. Do let me know if you can come.

Lots of Love,
Kathy

I had to wait a week for her reply and I watched out for the post every day. Letters came from Ben, but at that moment, it was Abigail I wanted.

Dear Kathy,

Thank you for your letter, I'm glad you're keeping well. I would love to come and stay, but my diary is a bit busy at the moment. I could perhaps come when the weather's warmer. Mother and Father are going on a Mediterranean cruise later in the spring to build up her strength. I've got no desire to admire all those ancient ruins with them for two whole weeks, so that would suit me perfectly. I'm sure they wouldn't miss me at all.

How can you dare to learn to drive? I'm sure that any car would be like a battered tin can after I'd finished with it! And flying? Kathy, are sure that you ought? What about the baby?

Please take care, my darling, and I'll be in touch nearer the time.

All the very best,
Your friend,
Abigail

It was only the beginning of March and spring seemed such a long way off. I went to see if Mabel had the kettle on, but I found her crying in the chair by the Aga, with Rosie nuzzling her lap.

'What ever's the matter, Mabel?'

'It's the puppies, Miss Kathy.'

I looked round and saw the empty basket. 'Where are they?'

'They've gone, miss. Mrs Trevelyan arranged for Mr Kingston to have them. Going to train them as gun dogs, he is.' Mabel fondled Rosie's silky ears, and the dog looked up at me with soulful eyes, under a wrinkled brow.

Mr Kingston? The man in the paper shop.

'Poor Rosie.' I stroked her head and she licked my hand. 'I loved your little puppies.'

'Well, they did make an awful mess, and get under my feet so, Miss Kathy. I shan't miss that, but I shall miss them.'

Mabel wiped her eyes. 'I hope Mr Kingston looks after them. I don't suppose they'll be in the kitchen by the fire; kept in one of his outhouses, more like.'

'Oh dear, I hope they'll be all right. You know, nobody tells me anything, Mabel. I'm always the last to find out.'

'Let me make you a nice cup of tea, Miss Kathy.' Mabel sniffed and got up to draw the kettle onto the hot plate.

I felt a little sick, and rubbed my tummy. *I couldn't possible give my baby away. How awful to be one of those girls who have to give up their babies, or to be thrown out onto the streets and have to fend for yourself. At least Aunt Sylvia lets me stay here. But, I bet she can't imagine how Rosie must feel to lose her puppies; she's never had a child of her own.*

'Here you are.' Mabel handed me my tea.

'Thank you, where is Aunt Sylvia anyway?'

'She's gone with Mr Trevelyan to look at a motor car in Newton Abbot. A Morris Cowley, I think.'

'What? I didn't know that either. I suppose that she didn't want me to go with them. *The embarrassment of it all!*' I flounced around the kitchen as if I was her. 'I'd have loved to have gone.'

'Yes, well, she does need a car of her own. She says Mr Trevelyan is always down at the boatyard when she needs to go somewhere. She hates catching the bus, you know.' Mabel sniffed. 'She says you never know who's been sitting on the seat before you.'

I laughed, it was so like my aunt to say that.

Two horns sounded; one loud, like a cruise ship, and the other quieter, but more insistent like a ferry.

'The new car!' Mabel and I shouted together and rushed outside.

Drawn up, next to Uncle's green Alvis, was a little Morris Cowley. Uncle had the bonnet up, studying the engine.

Aunt Sylvia got out. 'Isn't it lovely, Kathy? Do you like the crimson paint? I would have preferred Oxford Blue, but it was this or the brown.'

She let me sit in the driver's seat, and showed me the little dickey seat for an extra passenger or luggage. I hadn't seen Aunt Sylvia so excited for a long time.

It wasn't the old style Bullnose car, which I thought was much sportier, but she seemed to be pleased. 'Could I have a go? I have driven Paul's once or twice.' I blushed as I mentioned his name.

'No, certainly not. I'm not letting you drive my brand new car.'

Uncle Jeremy put down the bonnet and helped me out.

Why doesn't Auntie trust me? I'm sure I can drive as well as her, if not better.

March 31st 1930

Abigail arrived at last. Uncle Jeremy drove me down to the station to meet her. I made sure he didn't forget this time.

As the train pulled in, she leant out of the window.

'Coo-o-ee! Kath-ee!'

Two porters rushed to carry her bags, and she advanced up the platform like a film star, snug in her fox fur, whilst I brushed some specks of soot off my borrowed coat.

'Kathy, you do look wonderful.' She kissed me on the cheek, and a cloud of Chanel No. 5 enveloped me and made me wrinkle my nose.

'You look wonderful too.' I'd forgotten how much she resembled Ben, not her colouring, but her bone structure and expressions. The blood rushed to my cheeks, and my heart skipped a beat. I added shakily, 'This is Mr Trevelyan, Auntie's husband.'

'Please call me Uncle Jeremy; Kathy does.' His blue eyes twinkled like Paul's, and I was struck how much the two of them looked like the boys I loved.

'My goodness, Kathy, how big you're getting!' She patted my tummy. 'Just think, it's my little niece or nephew in there; I wonder which it'll be?'

We snuggled together in the back of Uncle's car like old times.

'So, what have you been doing down here in Devon?'

'Oh, I've been learning to fly and drive, and I've been out in Uncle's new boat.' I really couldn't tell her about Paul. What would she think?

'You're just the same, can't keep away from anything with an engine, can you?' she giggled.

'No, I can't.'

She inspected my hands, 'Well, at least you've got rid of all that oil around your fingernails. You're looking quite ladylike. And what a dear little ring.'

'Thank you. What have you been up to?'

Abigail tugged the hem of her hyacinth blue dress, then tapped her fingers on her handbag.

'Well . . . I nearly got engaged.'

My jaw dropped open. 'What? Who to? Why didn't you tell me?' I gasped.

'I wanted to be sure it was going to happen before I told you, and then . . . it didn't.' She shrugged her shoulders, and pouted.

'Oh, Abigail, what happened?' I held her tiny hand.

'His name was Robert. I met him on New Year's Eve.'

'At Maureen's party?'

'Yes, he was a friend of her brother. I danced with him, and after we'd sung *Auld Lang Syne*, he asked if he could take me out.'

My cheeks burned. *That's exactly what happened to me and Paul.*

'Are you hot, Kathy, shall I open the window?'

'No, I'm fine. Go on.'

'Robert was awfully decent, and I was tremendously keen on him. He had a little M G Midget runabout, and he took me to the pictures, and to some dances. We had such a wonderful time. He was such a catch.'

'But what went wrong, Abigail?'

'I was head over heels in love with him, and he talked of marriage.' She pressed her fingers to her lips, and her eyes filled with tears. 'He came to ask my father's approval, and Father said 'yes'.'

'I . . .'

I wish they'd let Ben marry me so eagerly.

'What, Kathy?'

'Oh, nothing.'

'Then,' Abigail continued, 'it was awful. Mother and I were out in town, searching for a dress for the engagement party, when we saw him with his arm around another girl.'

'No!' I tried to breathe deeply to stop my heart thumping right out of my chest. *This is what I have done. I have done this too.* I tugged off my gloves, and yanked at my scarf.

'*And,* he kissed her, right there in the street. Oh, Kathy, my knees gave way, and I fell on the wet pavement and ruined my new coat from McIlroy's. Mother helped me up and then stormed over, and gave him a piece of her mind.'

'But couldn't it have been his sister or a cousin?'

'Not when he kissed her on the lips.'

'Oh, Abigail, I'm so sorry.'

And I'm sorry for kissing Paul too.

'I should never have gone out with him. I've never had a proper boyfriend before; I think I'm too intense, I frighten them off.'

'Don't be silly.' I squeezed her arm. 'Who was this girl any way?'

'A local councillor's daughter.' Abigail screwed up her nose. She fingered the little gold locket around her neck. 'You know why I wear this don't you?'

'Yes, it's waiting for a picture of your true love.'

'My true love,' she echoed. 'I thought I'd found him, but I haven't yet. You are so lucky, Kathy.'

'Well, actually, Abigail . . .'

If I could only tell you what I've been up to . . .

'Here we are.' said Uncle Jeremy, turning into the drive. 'Ah, there's Sylvia at the door.'

'Abigail, how lovely to see you again. It seems ages.' Auntie kissed her on the cheek, and ushered her inside. 'What a lovely little suit. Wherever did you get it from?'

'Heelas's,' Abigail smiled.

'I thought so, it's lovely. The colour matches your eyes.' Auntie tucked an arm in hers, and led her into the sitting room. 'Would you like some afternoon tea? Come and sit here on the sofa next to me, and tell me all about your journey.'

I followed them in and sat alone on the armchair. I felt empty and sick inside. *Why was Auntie making such a fuss of Abigail? Why doesn't she make a fuss of me?* I massaged my tummy, and for the first time, began to realize what a disappointment I must be to her. Under different circumstances, I would be the one basking in her attention.

The excitement of Abigail coming to stay drained away.

Mabel brought in the tea tray with scones and clotted cream. To me, they were hard and tasteless, so I sipped my tea, and it scalded my tongue.

'You must come and see my new premises, Abigail. I've been up to town and ordered some exciting new books for the Easter visitors; I'd like your opinion of it all.'

'Will you be open by then, it's very soon?' Abigail dabbed her mouth with a serviette.

'Yes, I hope so.'

'How jolly! We'd like to come, wouldn't we, Kathy?' She turned to me. 'Have you seen it?'

'No, I . . .'

Auntie interrupted, 'As things are, I don't think Kathy is going to be the greatest asset to my business.'

'But surely, Mrs Trevelyan, Kathy can come and have a look before it opens?'

Auntie sighed. 'I suppose so, but you'd better wear something loose, Kathy, we don't want anyone noticing that you're in the family way.'

My cheeks flushed red, as Auntie flicked through some book catalogues with Abigail, stopping now and then to point out some fashionable new author.

I wasn't expecting this. Auntie's making more fuss of Abigail today than of me in the whole time I've been here. She's obviously the niece, or even daughter, that Auntie has always wanted. She used to bring books home for me to read, but I was always too eager to escape over to Ben's garage. I wish that I'd taken more notice.

'Well, I'm sure you'd like to unpack, Abigail. Kathy, would you like to show her up to your room?'

'Yes, Aunt Sylvia,' I sighed.

'Good, we'll have dinner at seven. I believe that Paul, my stepson is coming.'

Oh no, I don't want to see him. What if Abigail notices there's still something between us? I closed my eyes. I felt like packing my bags and running away.

Chapter Nineteen

Upstairs, Abigail smoothed out the creases on her bed. 'This is simply lovely, Kathy.'

I smiled; it wasn't her fault that Auntie had a soft spot for her. 'Yes, we can have such fun tucked up our beds on cosy nights, whispering in the firelight.' I lifted up the gold bedspread. 'Look, I've tidied all my *Autocar* magazines off the top of your bed and piled them underneath; Auntie doesn't know, but I expect Mabel does. I'll put my things on this side of the dressing table, and Auntie has taken her spare clothes out of the wardrobe to make room for yours.' I opened the door with a flourish.

'I have been looking forward to seeing you again, Kathy, I've really missed you.'

Hot tears stung my eyes.

'What ever is it?' she asked.

I sat down beside her, and she hugged me tight. She seemed so small and fragile compared to Paul or Ben.

'I've missed you too,' I sobbed, 'I can't tell you how much.'

'Ooh! What was that?' She rubbed her side.

'It's the baby kicking,' I sniffed. 'Give me your hand.'

'Oh, Kathy, it's lovely. Does Ben know?'

'Yes, I think so,' I nodded. *Had I actually remembered to tell him in my letters?* 'The doctor listened to its heart through a sort of trumpet.'

'Ooh, let me try!' And she rested her blonde curls on my bump here and there until she found the spot. 'Kathy, it's going swish, swish: swish, swish: swish, swish! I wish you could hear it too. I must tell Ben when I write to him.' Her eyes sparkled. 'He told me that you're going to get married when he's twenty-one, whether our parents like it or not.'

'That's what he says.'

She frowned. 'Don't you want to, Kathy?'

'Yes, of course, but it seems such a long time away.'

'This is an absolutely wonderful house.' Abigail looked out of the window as she came down the stairs. 'What beautiful views.'

I peered out over her shoulder, 'Yes, they are.' I'd never really stopped to admire them; I'd always been too busy thinking about Paul to notice. Then, I gasped, he had arrived already and was taking off his coat in the hall. *Oh no, he's here. What am I going to do?* He turned to me, his eyes grey, but lighting up to an iridescent blue as if the sun had come out from behind a cloud.

'Kathy, there you are, I was hoping that you hadn't got one of your headaches.' The sound of his voice nearly broke my heart.

'No, I'm fine. I'd like you to meet Ben's sister, Abigail.' I raised my eyebrows and nodded my head to make the point.

'How d'you do?' He shook her hand.

'Very well, thank you,' Abigail smiled.

Auntie and Uncle sat at each end of the table with Abigail beside me, and Paul opposite. 'Did you know, Father, The Prince of Wales is flying down to Haldon at the end of May?'

'Really?' Uncle Jeremy picked up his soup spoon.

'Yes, it was in the newspaper.'

'Oh, why?' I asked, forgetting that I was trying to ignore Paul.

'To visit the new Torbay Hospital, and the Bath and West Show.'

'Is he coming in his own Gipsy Moth? I'd love to go and see him.' I couldn't help asking.

'Yes, he'll be flying it himself.'

Aunt Sylvia buttered her bread roll. 'Who'd want to fly in a rickety, noisy aeroplane? Give me a motor car, or a train any day. Far more fitting for royalty.'

'My brother's learning to fly in the RAF,' Abigail offered.

'Really?' Paul glanced at me, pretending he didn't know.

My cheeks were on fire. I was really trying to shake off his spell, but every time our eyes met, I saw a flash of magic there, and I longed to be under his enchantment again.

'He's at Cranwell, isn't he?' Aunt Sylvia asked.

'That's right,' Abigail beamed.

'You're not keen on all things mechanical too, like Kathy, are you?'

'Goodness no, I'd love to be an actress, but I don't think I'll ever be discovered and whisked off to Hollywood. I'll just have to marry a film star, then I could sit by the pool all day and go to the parties at night.'

'It's my ambition to fly to America.' Paul's eyes shone.

'Yes, I'd love fly . . .' I began.

But, Abigail had turned to him. 'Would you?'

'Yes, Charles Lindberg crossed this way in less than a day and a half. I would love to soar on the wind over the Atlantic and land in New York to a ticker tape welcome, though I think I'm a bit late for that.'

'Wouldn't it be dangerous?' Abigail rested her delicate chin on her hands.

'Not if you planned your trip properly. You'd need to take enough fuel, water and provisions.'

'There's nowhere to land if you had a problem, is there?' Her blue eyes opened wide.

'Well, no.'

Why is Paul talking to Abigail? I felt hollow inside.

'Amy Johnson's proposing to fly all the way to Australia.' I tried to get back into the conversation. 'That's even further. I'd like to do something like that.'

'Don't be silly, Kathy, you've hardly learnt to fly, and look what happened when you did,' Auntie said.

I prayed she wouldn't mention the crash.

'And anyway, how on earth can you go off round the world with a baby?' Her bracelets jangled in agitation.

'Why not?'

'Well, it's not the done thing for a young mother, is it?'

'Amy Johnson's perfectly respectable.'

'Kathy, it seems to me that you should put all those foolish thoughts out of your head, and grow up.'

I pushed back my chair and stood, but I had to grab the table for support. I felt as if I'd been battered from all sides: Paul, Abigail and Aunt Sylvia. Only Uncle gave me a sympathetic smile, whilst the others looked at me in surprise.

'Excuse me,' my voice trembled, 'I have a headache, I think I need to go and lie down.'

I threw myself on the bed, forgetting for a moment the baby trapped below. *The baby!* I hastily turned over and felt my tummy. *Have I hurt it?* I wiped away hot tears with my sleeve. I rested my head on the pillows and pressed all over my bump. It felt very still. I held my breath until at last the baby kicked, and I rested my hand on the spot in an effort to hold on to its little life.

What am I going to do, baby? I love your Daddy. He was my first love. We had such fun growing up together, and now he wants to marry me. I want to marry him too, I think . . . but I love Paul. And I can't marry Paul because of you and your Daddy. Are you as confused as me?

Pictures of Ben and I growing up sprang in front of me like an old fashioned lantern show: falling off our bikes; grazing our knees; sailing homemade boats in rock pools; constructing Meccano aeroplanes and cars, and in every scene: Abigail playing alongside us with her dolls. *If I hadn't got pregnant, if I hadn't met Paul, I'd have been perfectly happy.*

Paul is a magician. Everywhere he goes; people are captured under his spell. He has that easy way about him; he can talk to anyone. Excellent attributes for a doctor, but now, Abigail is entranced too. I spied her pots and potions on the dressing table: Chanel No. 5, Ponds Cold Cream, Bourjois rouge, Max Factor lipsticks; even they were crowding out my brush and comb.

Why does Auntie dislike me so much? She agreed for me to come here after all. She could always have said no. I'm hardly her companion, am I? I never see her. Well, she's wrong about flying. I will have more lessons one day; why shouldn't I? I've survived a crash. I'm a modern young woman.

A little foot played on my palm. *Baby, are you listening? You sleep when I'm walking about, and wriggle when I'm trying to go to sleep myself. You make me want to spend a penny, and you give me indigestion. You've taken over my life too, haven't you?*

I pulled the eiderdown over me and closed my eyes.

But, there was a tap on the door.

'It's only me,' said Abigail. 'Are you asleep? I've brought you a cup of cocoa.'

I struggled to sit up. 'Thank you. I could just do with that.'

Abigail perched on the bed, her hair looking like spun gold in the firelight. 'Do you want me to draw the curtains?'

'Yes, please, I didn't realize it had got so dark.'

'Poor, Kathy, your aunt doesn't understand you, does she?'

I shook my head, and sipped my cocoa.

'I don't know what's got into her.' Abigail stood up and went to the window. 'She didn't used to be like that before.'

'No, she's cross because I'm pregnant. And, Mother dumped me here. I suppose that *was* unfair when she was newly married.'

'But she's spending all her time setting up her new shop. Doesn't she have any time for Uncle Jeremy?'

'She sees him at mealtimes. I don't know, perhaps marriage is different when you're older. He's always at the boatyard.'

'Ooh! Do you think that they've made a mistake?' Abigail's eyes opened wide.

'I don't know. How do you know that you're marrying the right person?'

'Well, you certainly are, Kathy; Ben is the perfect one for you.'

'Are you sure?' I could feel the colour in my cheeks. 'Your parents don't seem to think so.'

'I'm sure. You should see yourselves together. They'll come round, I know. You'll prove them wrong, mark my words.'

She drew the curtains, and twirled round with a smile spread wide across her face. 'Oh I say, Kathy, he's adorable!'

'Adorable?' I knew exactly who she meant. My heart sank into my empty stomach, and I felt the colour drain out of my face. I gripped the eiderdown.

'Those eyes. Have you noticed them, Kathy? They're magic. I go all weak when he looks at me.'

What can I say? Yes, he's gorgeous? I'm under his spell too? I can't tell her. I feel so helpless as if my mouth has been gagged, and my hands tied. What would she say if she knew how close we'd come to . . .?

'I've asked him if he'll take me for a spin in his little Austin Seven.' Abigail hugged herself.

My mouth dried up, and I had to make some more saliva before I could talk. 'What did he say?'

'Yes!' Abigail beamed. 'He's awfully decent. But he said I'll not have to mind my hair blowing about in the wind. Can you lend me a scarf, Kathy? I don't think that I brought one.'

She danced around the room. If I hadn't have been so consumed with futile jealousy, I would've thought how enchanting she looked.

'Have you noticed how blue his eyes are? They twinkle like little stars. He's a doctor isn't he? I'm sure my parents would approve.'

'What are you saying, Abigail?' I couldn't believe my ears.

'He's the one. He's the one, Kathy. I'm going to make him mine.'

'And what does *he* think about this?' I couldn't keep the chill out of my voice, but she was oblivious.

'Oh, he doesn't know yet. But I'm not going to let him get away like Robert.'

She might as well have thrown a bucket of cold water over me. Her words soaked through, and washed out any hope I had of keeping my love alive for Paul, if only in secret.

'I have heard he's quite a charmer,' I said, remembering Auntie's words. 'There've been quite a few nurses at the hospital that have had their hearts broken.'

'So? He's unattached now, isn't he, so he's fair game.'

How can I say how much I love him still, and how much I want him to be mine? It's only because of Ben and the baby that I've him turned away. Please don't take him away from me altogether.

Then Abigail frowned, 'Kathy, he told us about your flying lesson. Why ever didn't you tell me that you'd crashed? Did you tell Ben?' She looked straight into my eyes.

'Of course! He wasn't very pleased though.'

'I should think not. Are you sure that the baby's all right, Kathy?'

'Yes, it's fine, we just glided down, and got out before the fire.'

Abigail gasped, 'The fire? What are you talking about?'

'The plane burst into flames after we got out. It was fine. I'm fine.' I gripped her arms, 'Please don't tell Ben, I don't want him to worry.'

'I won't, but Kathy, do be careful. You could have killed yourself.' She hugged me tight. 'You are hopeless. You can't keep away anything with an engine, can you?'

Can't keep away from Paul.

Abigail sat on the floor, and rested her head on the bed. We remained there, watching the flames licking away at the coals, lost in our own thoughts.

April 1st 1930

Aunt Sylvia drove her little red car to her shop in The Triangle, with Abigail and I squashed in the back.

'Now, Kathy straight inside. I can't have you being seen near my new business.'

Abigail squeezed my hand. 'Here, let me hold the door for you.'

'Phew, it's not so easy when you're seven months pregnant.'

'Shh, Kathy! Anyone might hear you.' Aunt Sylvia glanced around as if looking for spies.

'There's no one about, Auntie.'

'I don't know what I'd do if it got out that you were in the family way.'

'But, people were talking about me in the doctor's months ago.'

'No! Why ever didn't you tell me?'

'What was the point? It wouldn't have changed anything, would it?'

Auntie drew her lips into a thin line of disapproval.

Abigail and I sheltered by the shop's arched Victorian window. A new blind, pulled down about a quarter of the way was printed with *Sylvia Trevelyan – Women's Bookshop and Library.*

Fumbling for the keyhole, Aunt Sylvia opened the door, and flicked on the lights. We screwed up our noses at the smell of fresh paint, and Auntie wedged the door open with a spare tin.

'You can help me with these sheets if you like, girls.' She tugged one off a bookcase in the corner and inspected the shelves to make sure they weren't damaged, and we swept one away from the counter revealing wooden trays for the library tickets, and some drawers for the stationery.

'Here's the stock room.' Auntie opened a door at the back of the shop. 'Would you like to get the boxes of books out, Abigail?'

'Ooh, yes!' she said, rushing in. 'Look here, Kathy, I love this Agatha Christie. Did you know, Mrs Trevelyan, I've read it three times already?'

'Really, doesn't it bother you that you know whodunit?' Aunt Sylvia smiled.

'No,' Abigail shook her head, 'I find a new clue every time!' Then she pointed at the blind. 'I think it's wonderful that you're going to have a subscription library for women.'

'Yes, it was very popular in my last shop. Not all women can afford to buy the books they want, like you, dear. Now that we have the vote, we must educate ourselves as much as possible. Not that I'm sure Agatha Christie will do the trick!'

'You used to have all the Huntley and Palmer girls queuing round the corner when one of her new books came out, didn't you?'

'Yes, Abigail, those were the days.'

'I used to love coming into the shop on Saturdays with Kathy, and writing out those little tickets to put on the shelves about your recommended books,' Abigail smiled. 'Kathy hated it, she was always itching to get finished so she could see Ben,' she added, opening a box, and beginning to arrange the books on the shelves. 'I think we should turn out some of the covers. They're much more attractive than the spines of the books.'

'That's a good idea, Abigail, it will look much more interesting,' said Aunt Sylvia, following her example.

Abigail always tries to please everyone. My head started to swim. *I can't compete with her.*

'Kathy, sit down, dear; you look a bit pale.' Aunt Sylvia appeared concerned for once. 'How about doing a little sticking for me? The cover's got ripped on this book. I've got some gummed paper tape somewhere.'

'You know I'll only mess it up, Auntie.'

'Nonsense girl, here you are.'

I tried to hold the edges of the cover together as I ripped the tape with my teeth and licked it. 'It's not very good, I'm sorry.'

'Here, let me have a look.' Auntie bustled over. 'It's not the tidiest repair I've ever seen. Do it like this.' She took the scissors and began to cut some strips.

'Golly, I'd forgotten you were left-handed,' I said.

She looked at me over her glasses, then licked a strip and placed it on the tear, pressing it down with her long red nails. 'There!' She admired her handiwork and placed the book on the shelf. 'I will have to reduce the price though. That's a pity.'

Abigail arranged a display of notebooks with colourful spines. 'Shall I put them with the pots of pencils? The ladies will probably need both if they want to write something.'

'Excellent! If you stay down here in Devon, I'll give you a job.'

Abigail shook her head and smiled.

I don't really want a job either, but I wish I could do something right for a change.

'I'd love a cup of coffee, wouldn't you?' I couldn't bear the sisterly camaraderie any longer.

'Yes, Kathy, thank you.' Aunt Sylvia nodded. 'There's a gas ring and a kettle upstairs. How about having some cream cakes from Ashley's?'

'I'll go!' I offered, slipping out of the door before Auntie could stop me, as Abigail waltzed round with another armful of books.

Chapter Twenty

With a box of cakes tied with ribbon from Ashley's, we climbed up the narrow stairs and perched on bentwood chairs in the small office to drink our coffee.

'Abigail tells me how much she likes my stepson, Paul.' Aunt Sylvia bit into a chocolate éclair.

'Yes, he's gorgeous, isn't he?'

Oh, not this again! I felt indigestion gnaw at my stomach.

'He's taken you up to Haldon once or twice, hasn't he, Kathy?' Auntie added, scooping some chocolate off her nose with a manicured finger, and licking it.

'Yes, he has.' I couldn't help sighing.

'What's wrong, Kathy?' Abigail frowned.

'Oh, nothing, just a bit of wind.' I rubbed the aching spot below my ribs.

'I hope he doesn't drive *me* to the aerodrome. I'd rather go to some pretty cove with a picnic.'

She's stealing Paul away from me. I know I've turned him down. I've shut the door: he's free. He can do as he likes, but I can't bear anyone else to have him!

I like Abigail, I love her, she's like a sister. But why is she after Paul?

'What do you think, Kathy?'

'What?'

'What do you think about going down to the Tea Gardens at Labrador Bay on your birthday?'

'Oh, I don't know.' *I'd forgotten all about my birthday.*

'Have you been paying any attention? Mrs Trevelyan suggested that we make up a party and go there for one of their famous cream teas.'

I smiled blankly, 'That would be nice.'

April 12th 1930

I wasn't looking forward to it, but Paul arrived on my birthday to take Abigail and me to the Tea Gardens at Labrador Bay. Uncle said that he'd bring Auntie later after they'd been to the shop.

The sun shone warmly for April, and our cotton frocks flapped in the breeze as I waited by the passenger door.

But Abigail grabbed the handle. 'Can I sit in the front, Paul?' she asked.

He looked at me over the top of the car, and raised his eyebrows, almost pleading for me to sit beside him. *Jeepers! Does he still feel the same?* But I had to tear myself away for the baby's sake. Here was a new day, a new year; I was nineteen, almost grown up: a good time to start.

'I don't mind.' But the minute I'd said those words, I wished I hadn't.

I climbed into the back, and sat there watching Abigail's blonde curls bobbing about next to Paul's familiar head. My fingers itched to tickle the soft short hair behind his ears, and my lips longed to say I was only joking, that I really wanted to sit beside him after all.

The old smuggler's cottage clung to the sloping cliff face, and pine trees framed picture postcard views of the sparking sea. A perfect birthday, if only . . . if only I was here with Paul. Alone.

What a mess! I sat back and closed my eyes. The waves breaking in the bay and running up the beach seemed to be saying:

Last summer . . . Ben.

I've got to try again . . . Ben.

I've got to learn to love you again . . . Ben.

I fingered the amethyst brooch in the shape of a little Gipsy Moth that he'd sent me for my birthday to try to summon up some determination.

But, my thoughts were interrupted by Abigail trilling, 'Listen Paul, just listen to the gulls!'

'They're not all gulls, you know.' His warm voice replied.

I opened my eyes, shading them with my hand.

Abigail leant close to him, and I could almost feel the static, and see the sparks she gave off. 'Aren't they?'

'No, can you hear those over there, down the cliff calling 'Kittee-wake. Kittee-wake?' He stretched his neck and ruffled imaginary feathers, 'Well, they're calling their own name.'

'Really? You're joking!' She squeezed his arm, and I squeezed my eyes tight to shut out the picture.

'Shall we go for a walk after tea, Kathy?' Paul touched my shoulder, and an electric shock raced up and down my arm. I took a deep breath, and opened my mouth to say 'yes', but Abigail frowned:

'I think the path might be a bit too steep for you.'

'Yes, you're right,' I sighed. 'Well, I think I'll take some pictures then.' I picked up the new Brownie box camera Uncle and Auntie had given me. 'Stay there, just as you are, Paul.'

'Ooh, let me be in it too!' Abigail squashed up even closer, and put her arm round him.

Their lovey-doveyness made me feel if I'd been punched in the stomach. Painfully, like a fighter returning from his corner, I heaved myself out of my chair and turned to face them. I held the camera at waist level, or where it should have been, and suffered another blow as I saw his familiar face in the viewfinder, with Abigail's cheek pressed close to his.

'Have you wound it on?' He pointed at the camera.

'No. Just a minute.' I waited until number two appeared in the little red window. 'Ready?'

'My face aches with smiling!' Abigail laughed.

Click.

Letting her take Paul away from me was like doing several rounds with Jack Dempsey.

'Listen, Kathy; that sounds like Father's car.' Paul disentangled himself from Abigail's embrace, 'What can he be doing here?' And he hurried round to the front of the building.

He was gone for quite a few minutes, but I couldn't bring myself to talk to Abigail. Then I heard another man's voice.

Is it Ben? My heart stopped.

'Dad? Mother? What are you doing here?' I blinked. I didn't recognise them at first; they seemed smaller and greyer, but I sprang up, despite my size, and hugged them.

'Happy Birthday!' they laughed and cried at the same time.

Even though they'd sent me away, it was such a relief to see them, like coming home, kicking off my shoes, and putting on a pair of comfy slippers.

'Good gracious, Kathy.' Mother held me at arms length. 'Look at the size of you.' In comparison, her petite waist, adorned with a bunch of imitation violets, appeared unimaginably fragile, as if she could bend and snap like a slender branch.

'We have missed you, love.' The worry wrinkles on Dad's forehead deepened for a moment, before the laughter lines around his eyes crinkled up again, and he patted me on the back.

Aunt Sylvia and Uncle Jeremy, coming up behind, dragged two other tables and chairs over so we could all sit down.

'I couldn't let your birthday go by without seeing you.' Mother dabbed her eyes. 'It was Daddy's idea to come as a surprise.'

'Yes, we got the first train this morning, telephoned Sylvia when we got to Teignmouth, and here we are.' He winked at his sister-in-law who pursed her lips.

'I thought that you'd forgotten me because if this.' I stroked my bump.

'No, darling, we haven't forgotten you. It's just that it was best for you to come here to stop all the neighbours gossiping.' Mother took my hand.

'Yes, but you didn't think about my customers, did you?' Aunt Sylvia retorted.

'We didn't know that you were going to open a new shop, did we?' Mother shrugged, and I felt as if I was luggage being sent from one railway station to another.

'Look, Kathy, we've brought you some presents.' She gave me two packages.

I opened the smaller one, 'Ooh, it's some Californian Poppy. Thank you, Mother; it'll remind me of you.' I showed everyone the little bottle with its red cap.

I weighed the second lumpy present in my hands. 'What can this be?' I asked, carefully unwrapping it on the table. 'It's a picture frame, how lovely. Did you make it, Dad?'

I held up the sunburst frame made out of beech and rosewood. In the middle of the rays was a photograph of Mother and Dad outside our house. 'You are clever, thank you.'

He stroked his moustache. 'Kathy, it's to let you know that we are thinking about you, and to remind you of home.'

My fingers made hot, wet prints on the frame.

The waitress appeared to take our order. The breeze rippled her long black dress and white apron, and teased her lacy headband.

'That'll be lovely then.' She bit her pencil. 'A pot of tea for six, and six Devonshire teas. Thank you very much.'

I traced the outline of the frame in my hands. The lines led inwards and down to Mother and Dad. They were the centre of my world once, but they'd made me move on. Dad stared out to sea through the shady trees, his mouth in a hard, sad line. Mother held my hand tightly, as if I was a balloon tugging away on a string.

'Ah, here comes the tea,' said Uncle Jeremy. 'Sylvia, will you be mother?'

'I love Devonshire teas, don't you?' His teeth sunk into the cream, and his lips caught the sweet crumbs.

Aunt Sylvia sliced her scone in half. 'Have you seen Ben's parents recently, Emily? Do you think they'll change their minds?'

Mother dabbed neat little blobs of jam and cream on her plate. 'I've seen Mrs Hunter in passing. She didn't stop to talk.'

'Mother and Father won't talk about it. They'd prefer to think that nothing's happened.' Abigail spread jam on her scone. 'I think they should have let Ben marry poor Kathy straight away, and not put her through all this bother.'

Paul batted away an early wasp that had come out of hibernation.

'How's Ben getting on at Cranwell, Abigail?' Mother asked.

'Oh, very well, he's been doing some long distance flights and manoeuvres. He should be qualified by the summer.' Abigail smiled, 'Paul is learning to fly, aren't you, Paul?'

'Yes, I am. Up at Haldon Aerodrome.'

Abigail took his hand, and looked into his eyes, 'You're going to take me up there aren't you?'

You told me you'd rather go for a picnic in a secluded cove!

'Abigail has been such a help in the new shop, Emily. She really has a flair for the book trade.' Aunt Sylvia beamed. 'It's pity she can't stay longer.'

'That's wonderful, but Abigail doesn't really need to work, do you, dear?' Then Mother glanced at me. 'I hope that Kathy has been helping you too.'

'Yes, she has been down to the shop, but I can't possibly have her there when we open. What on earth would my customers think with a girl behind the counter in her condition?'

I flinched as if I'd been stung. 'I'm going for a little walk.'

'Let me come with you.' Abigail began to get up too.

'No, I just want to take some pictures.' I set off along the cliff path, imagining what they were saying behind my back.

'Poor old Kathy.'

'She's probably a bit upset.'

'I wouldn't like to be in her shoes.'

I didn't care. The rocky steps wound down the cliff face, edged with little primroses rooted in sandy cracks. It looked too steep to get down to the sea where the waves crashed against the red sandstone. So I sat down on a tussock, out of sight of the tea party. The roar of the waves filled my head, and the bright sun made me squint. Shading my eyes, I could see right across Lyme Bay, where bright yachts skimmed over the water.

Why does Aunt Sylvia say such things?

Oh, I'm so tired of being pregnant, I wish I could take off this bump and put it down for a while so I could run down to the beach and paddle in the sea.

'Aah!' I grabbed my stomach as a pain gripped me like a tight corset.

'Are you all right?' Abigail bent down beside me, her face shading me from the sun.

'I don't know. Why did you follow me?'

'To make sure you didn't slip down the cliff. I'll go and get Paul. Stay there.' She peeled off her cardigan, and wrapped it round my shoulders. I shivered despite the warm afternoon, and lay back against the scorching rock face. The pain tightened under my bulge. Something wet escaped down below. *Is it blood? Oh no, what's happening? Is the baby coming?*

Soon Paul appeared, and knelt down beside me. 'Kathy?'

I bit my lip and closed my eyes, thankful that he was there.

'I'm just going to feel your tummy.' His calm, gentle hands worked their way over my bump.

'There,' he said, 'don't worry; I don't think you're losing it, but we better get you home.' He scooped me up and carried me back to the others. Under other circumstances, it would've been wonderful to be in his arms.

'Kathy, what have you done?' Mother sprang up. 'I should never have let you go.'

'I'm all right now, I feel better . . . urgh!' I groaned as the pain took hold again. 'What's happening, Paul? Are you sure I'm not losing it?'

'I'll get my bag from the car,' he said.

'It's here, Paul.' Uncle Jeremy handed it to him. 'And I've got this blanket from mine. Lay her down. Here, on the grass.'

Mother stroked my forehead with feather-light fingers, and Dad knelt beside me.

'Let's feel your pulse.' Paul took my wrist. 'And listen to your heart.' The large stethoscope uncoiled as if it was alive.

'Is the baby all right?'

I held my breath as he listened to its little heartbeat with a trumpet. 'Yes, it's good and strong.'

'What about the blood?' I asked.

He felt my stomach again. 'I think you'll be all right. You just need a few days rest and then you must take it easy, Kathy.' His blue eyes melted my heart. 'Let's get you home, it's the best place to be.'

'Do you think it was the crash?' I whispered.

'Well, I don't suppose that it helped,' he smiled.

Thinking about it afterwards, I remembered Aunt Sylvia sitting on her chair, smoking a cigarette in her long black holder, and studying a blackbird pecking at some fallen crumbs.

Chapter Twenty-One

April 13th 1930

'I feel as if I've been sent to my room like a naughty child,' I said, as Mother came and sat on my bed.

'Well, darling, if you must do these reckless things.'

'Maybe I was silly to climb down the cliff, but I want to fly more than anything.'

'Yes, I know, dear, but we can't always do everything we want. Your job now is to bring this little baby safe into the world. I wish I could stay, but Dad has to get back for a new building job. I've brought you these.' She handed me a carrier bag. 'Just a few little matinee coats, vests and bonnets. I had to do something, I've missed you so much.'

'Thank you.' I pulled them out. 'They're lovely.'

Mother leant forward, Californian Poppy filling my head. 'Do you think you'll be keeping it?'

I stopped with a little vest suspended in mid air.

'What? What do you mean?'

'Do you think you'll keep the baby?'

'Of course, Mother, it's mine.' *What is she thinking about? I'm not giving up my baby. Not after I nearly lost him yesterday.*

'But, what if Ben can't marry you.'

'He will, he's promised to when he's twenty-one.' I dropped the vest on my lap. 'What are you saying, Mother?'

'I'm just saying that things change.'

I picked up a bonnet that looked small enough for a baby doll and stretched it open with my fingers. 'Absence makes the heart grow stronger. That's what Grandma always says.'

'But sometimes, it grows stronger for someone else.'

I blushed. *How can she know?* 'I don't understand, what do you mean?' I twisted the ribbon between my fingers.

'What if *Ben* has found someone else whilst he's been away.' Mother buttoned up one of the matinee coats. 'Someone who isn't pregnant and whom he hasn't got to marry, like you.'

My heart pounded. *I never thought of that.* 'But Ben loves me. Look at all these letters.' I opened the drawer beside my bed, and a few drifted to the floor displaying pen-and-ink Gipsy Moths with my name fluttering on the banners.

Jeepers, I've been so wrapped up with Paul. What an idiot. I've been messing about with him all this time, thinking at the back of my mind, that if it all goes wrong, Ben will be there. He will still be there, won't he? I stroked my tummy.

'Now, never mind Ben, Kathy, I'm very concerned that there's something going on between you and Paul.'

My cheeks burnt. 'No, there's not. Where ever did you get that idea?'

'I've noticed the way you look at him.' Her green eyes searched mine. 'You appear to be completely under his spell.'

I thumped my fist down on the bed, making the baby clothes fly into the air.

'Apart from Uncle Jeremy who's dear and kind, Paul is the only one who makes life worth living down here. But, you'll be pleased to know I've told him to leave me alone. Are you happy now?' I looked at her straight. 'On top of that, Abigail's arrived and she's deliriously falling in love with him already.'

'Let her have him, Kathy. Don't get in the way.' Mother gathered together the baby clothes and folded them up. 'For Heaven's sake, don't get yourself into any more trouble.'

I shut my eyes and took some deep breaths.

'Have you ever loved anyone else apart from Dad?'

'No, I haven't.'

'So, you can't know how I feel, can you?'

She frowned. 'In my day, you didn't get yourself into the family way until you were married. You kept yourself to yourself. I never dreamt of letting a man touch me, not even your father, until this wedding ring was firmly on my finger.' She rolled it about from side to side with her thumb. 'I love you, Kathy, you know that, don't you?'

'Why did you send me down here then?'

'We had to. What else could we do?'

'You've seen Auntie; she ignores me most of the time. Look how she was yesterday, she's much rather have Abigail who's 'awfully decent' and an asset to her new shop.'

'Kathy! After all she's done for you.'

'I hardly see her, Mother. We hardly speak.'

'She's taken you in and sheltered you.'

'Only because you asked her to.'

'Oh, my poor Kathy.' She took my hand. 'I'm so sorry that you're unhappy.'

Dad knocked on the door.

'Come on, Emily, we've got to catch the train.' He put his arms out and hugged me. 'Goodbye, love, chin up.'

''Bye, Dad.'

'Well, I have to go.' Mother took out her hankie and wiped her nose. 'Take care, Kathy, remember what I said, won't you?'

A prisoner confined to her cell, I spent the next few days in my room. I missed going out in Uncle's car, I missed going to the aerodrome, and most of all, I missed Paul. Abigail did bring me *The Great Gatsby* to read, but the glittery life in Long Island was a million miles away from a seaside town in Devon.

April 14th 1930
Another letter arrived from Ben:

Dearest Kathy,

I'm so sorry that I can't get any extra leave for Easter, but we have an important exercise coming up, (all on the q.t.) and we have to practise for it. There isn't time for me to get down to Devon and back, so I'll have to stay here. There'll be Easter services and parades to keep us busy.

I love you Kathy, I know that we're so far apart, but I think about you every minute of every day. I cherish your little black bead. I still have it around my neck and it reminds me of you and the promise I made to you. I'm looking forward to having you in my arms again so much.

See you soon, it won't be long, Darling, I promise.

Yours for ever and ever,

Ben

I wasn't too disappointed; I wasn't ready to see him yet. I used the letter as a bookmark, and it was still there on page seven of *The Great Gatsby*, two days later.

I'd been promoted to lying on the sofa. My body pressed a permanent shape on the dark brown velvet cushions, and my long legs stretched over the leather armrest, but I preferred it to being all alone in bed in the quietness of my room. I really began to miss the tennis and cycling I used to do at home, and my legs ached with idleness. I read the paper, quite dull except for a piece about the Duchess of Bedford's flight to Cape Town which she hoped to complete in nineteen days. *All these women flying around the world: Amy Johnson, the Duchess of Bedford and Lady Bailey. And I'm stuck here.*

I asked Mabel to turn on the wireless, but the soprano made my head ache. Despite the fact that my body was in enforced repose, I still couldn't stop the turmoil in my mind.

I've trampled all my rosy hopes and dreams into a dirty puddle. I've made a mess of everything in my life so far by getting pregnant. I've upset my parents and been sent away from home, and now I'm here with my aunt who finds me a great burden. I may have ruined any chance of a happily married life by falling in love with Paul. I've very nearly rejected Ben, probably the only one who could make my 'happy ever after' happen. Why did I encourage Paul? Why did he fall in love with me? Why did I get pregnant in the first place? Why me? Why is Abigail everything I'm not? Does Paul really love her? Does Ben still love me? The questions whirled around my head like muddy water stirred with a twig, but there were no answers.

April 19th 1930

On Easter Saturday, Aunt Sylvia and Abigail starred in the grand opening of the new shop. She had been so unbearable all week with talk of the arrangements, and talk of Paul, that I was actually looking forward to her going home on Monday. However, they came back for a late supper, full of excitement about their day.

'Oh, Kathy, you should have seen all the balloons outside the front door.' Abigail kicked off her shoes and rubbed her feet. 'Mrs Trevelyan even climbed up the stepladder to tie the banner.' She spread her arms wide. '*Grand Opening Today! Books for Women!* I wish I'd taken your camera.'

'How wonderful.' I tried to smile.

'I couldn't have done it without Abigail's help, you know.' Aunt Sylvia flopped into her armchair. 'There was quite a crowd, lots of nurses from the hospital too. Paul must have told them.'

'The shop was packed,' Abigail joined in. 'Your aunt and I worked as a team. I packed the books in the new paper bags. Have you seen them, Kathy?' She held up a brown bag with *Sylvia Trevelyan – Women's Bookshop and Library* printed boldly in black. 'And Mrs Trevelyan rang up all the sales in the till. Ching!' Abigail turned an imaginary handle in the air. 'I had no idea it would be so busy. It was such fun.'

'You were marvellous,' Auntie smiled, 'Thank you, Abigail. Here's a little bonus.' And she handed her an envelope.

'Oh really, Mrs Trevelyan, you shouldn't, thank you.'

'No, it's a pleasure. You did so well selling those Katherine Mansfield short story collections. Just the thing for women down for the holiday weekend.'

'I did sell some of those Virginia Woolf essays too for the more discerning woman!' Abigail laughed. 'Oh, Kathy, you are so lucky to have an aunt like Mrs Trevelyan: it's like having another mother. Our mother never had much time for us. We had so many nannies instead; I don't think that they could cope . . . Oh my goodness, here's Paul.' She patted her hair, and smoothed her skirt.

I searched Abigail's bright face to see if there was any clue as to what was going on between them both, but her innocent blue eyes smiled back, not giving away any secrets, even though each night I watched her go to sleep clutching her pillow.

'Hello, everyone.' He hovered in the doorway as if he didn't want to favour either of us. 'I've just come to get some mending that Mabel was doing for me.'

Abigail raised a fine eyebrow. 'I'm very good at sewing on buttons.'

'Thank you.' His eyes twinkled. 'I'll remember that.'

The baby's elbows and knees dug into my ribs like Tom in *The Water Babies* climbing up a chimney.

'A reporter came from the paper, and took our picture, didn't he Abigail?' Auntie said, oblivious to my discomfort.

'Yes, will you get an extra paper and send me one, Mrs Trevelyan?' she said, picking up a carrier bag and shaking out what appeared to be a flowery blue suit with trousers. 'Do you know what these are, Kathy?'

I shook my head. 'Are they pyjamas?'

'They're *house* pyjamas I got them at the shop next door. They cost fifteen shillings as a two-piece, but I paid a guinea and bought the jacket too. I'll try them on after supper so you can see them.'

Later, Abigail smoothed her trousers down from her trim waist to her hips, and twirled in front of the mirror, making them flare out at the bottom like a skirt. 'They're a delightful fit, aren't they, Kathy?'

'Yes, they're lovely. I can't wait until I can fit into something so slimming.' I sighed.

'If it's a nice day tomorrow, I might wear them to the beach with Paul,' she glowed.

Again, that stab and thrust in my heart. *I must give him up. I must stop thinking about him. I've been trying to. Let's see how many seconds I can count without thinking about him.* I shut my eyes. *One . . . Two . . . Three . . . Fo . . .*

'Paul says he'll pick me up at ten o'clock.'

My eyes sprung open as if I'd been stung by a wasp.

'Did I tell you, we had lunch together yesterday?'

The wasp tormented me again.

'Yesterday? No? Where did you go?'

'To The Royal Hotel.'

'The Royal Hotel? They'd never let me in there in my condition.'

'Sorry, Kathy,' she said, swishing the trouser legs to and fro. 'We had fried fillet of plaice and ice cream. Then we took a little walk along the seafront.'

I swallowed. *That's where Paul and I went on New Year's Day.*

'It was lovely, Kathy. The sea whooshed right up and splashed over the wall. He had to hold on to me to stop me being washed away!'

He had to hold you?

'And I shouldn't tell you this, but we sat on a seat at the end of the promenade, you know, where the trains go under the bridge into the station.'

Our seat.

Abigail flopped beside me on the bed. The flowers on her house pyjamas brought out the blue in her eyes, making her look gorgeous. 'And guess what?'

'What?'

She leant nearer. 'He kissed me.'

'He kissed you?' My heart missed a beat, and my palms began to sweat.

'Yes, well, he needed a little help, so I pretended that some sand had blown in my eye, and asked him to have a look. Of course he couldn't see it, so I told him to come closer. He came so close that I could feel his breath on my lips. I gazed into his eyes, and the kiss just happened.' Abigail kissed the air.

I felt as if I'd been stung by a thousand wasps. My skin prickled all over, and I actually began to scratch my arms.

I never thought it would be so painful to give him up.

'Oh Kathy, I think I really love him. Those sparkling eyes are captivating; I just melt whenever he looks at me. I can't bear to go home on Monday. What ever shall I do without him? You will look after him whilst I'm away, won't you?'

My mouth was too dry to speak, so I nodded.

'I do hope that your aunt will let me come back soon. I can't wait Kathy. I should love to come and live down here in Devon and be Paul's little wife. I could travel home to Reading when I wanted, but I think I should be perfectly happy here. We could buy one of those dear little bungalows they're building up above the village. I can sew some curtains, and make jam, and be a doctor's wife.' She bounced up and spun round again.

I found my voice at last. 'Abigail, does Paul know all about this? Has he talked about marriage?' I scratched my arm really hard. *He did ask me to marry him once.*

'No, he hasn't, but I'll soon talk him round. He's the one for me, Kathy; I just know it. I've been so jealous of you and Ben going to get married.'

'We don't know for sure, do we?'

'My parents won't be able to stop you when he's over twenty-one, will they?'

'I hope not.' I crossed my fingers.

'I want to have a little baby like you. They'll be cousins, think of that. It'll be divine.' She whisked downstairs to show Auntie her pyjamas.

I sighed. *Perhaps Paul didn't really feel anything for me after all. Perhaps I've made a fool of myself as Abigail's about to.*

I thought about Ben's letter, and slid it out of my book.

'I love you Kathy, I know that we're so far apart, but I think about you every minute of every day. I cherish your little black bead. I still have it around my neck and it reminds me of you and the promise I made to you. I'm looking forward to having you in my arms again so much.

See you soon, it won't be long,'

I could hear his voice. *He is the only one who truly loves me.*

But, I felt all alone.

Chapter Twenty-Two

April 20th 1930

On Easter Sunday afternoon, I lay on my bed under the eiderdown and drifted in and out of a deep sleep. I really missed lying on my front, and the baby squashed me if I lay on my back, so I lay on my side, put a pillow under my bump, and hugged another one. I pretended it was, who? Paul lying next to me on his sofa? Or Ben lying on a tartan blanket?

I dreamt I was at the railway station, meeting one of them off the train. I didn't know which. The station clock said fourteen minutes to eleven. I'd missed it! I began to run through the passengers to the platform. Knots of people got in my way; families, elderly couples. *Didn't they have a train to catch?* Others streamed past in the opposite direction. Then someone barged right into my stomach with a large parcel. Ooof! I woke up.

The muscles below my tummy tightened and a pain gripped hard. Surely I'd imagined it, but no, there it was again, a raw, ripping pain, just like before at Labrador Bay. To my relief, it faded away, then it came again, only harder. *I must get some help. I can't get out of bed; it might make it worse. I might even begin to bleed.* Sweat poured down my forehead, and I wiped it away with the sheet.

'Help!' I called out several times, but I couldn't make anyone hear.

Beside my bed was a small bookcase with a lamp on the top. With all my strength, I reached out to push it over. It wouldn't go. I struggled up higher in the bed, the pain clenching harder than ever, and pushed again. It toppled slightly, but wouldn't budge. Just as a new pain took hold, I gave one more final shove and the bookcase, lamp and books went crashing down. It seemed that within a minute, Mabel was up the stairs.

'Miss Kathy! What ever have you done? Are you all right?'

'I'm sorry, Mabel. The pains are coming.'

'I'll get your uncle and aunt; they're in the summer house.' Then, she shouted from the open window, 'Help! Mr Trevelyan, you must get Dr White!'

Within seconds, they rushed in the back door.

'What's happened?' Uncle called.

'Miss Kathy has the pains, sir.'

'I'll get on the phone right away.'

To my surprise, Aunt Sylvia came up and sat on the bed.

I frowned as another pain took hold. 'Do you think the baby's coming?'

'I don't know, dear, just try to relax.'

'I can't. It's too soon for the baby. I've still got over a month to go . . . OH!'

Uncle Jeremy came in.

'I'm sorry, Kathy, but the doctor has been called away to an emergency on the golf course. We'll have to take you to the hospital. Do you think that you could get in the car, my dear?'

I groaned, but what else could I do, so I nodded.

'Let's wrap you in some blankets and we'll take another to put over your knees.' Auntie tugged some down from the wardrobe.

'Ready?' Uncle Jeremy gently swung me up into the air.

I felt safe in his arms as he carried me down the stairs. He managed to get me in the car, then slowly stood up straight and rubbed his back. 'Phew, you're heavier than I thought.'

He drove us along the river to the new hospital, whilst I clung to Aunt Sylvia as the pains took hold.

'I'm really going to lose it this time, aren't I?' I shivered so much that my knees knocked together.

Then motoring right up the drive to the front door of the hospital, Uncle Jeremy tooted his horn.

Aunt Sylvia tapped him on the shoulder. 'What are you doing? There are sick people in there.'

'I know, but I want Kathy to be seen as soon as possible.' As he got out and ran up the steps, a young nurse emerged to investigate the commotion. Her starched apron and white winged cap flapped like the seagulls crying above, and threatened to make her fly away with them.

'What ever is the matter, sir?' She craned her neck, like a small white heron, to look past him into the car.

'It's my niece: we think that she's having labour pains.'

'Well, I'm afraid we don't have a maternity ward here. Have you tried to contact your own doctor?'

'Yes, but he's out at Haldon on another emergency.

'My son is a doctor here, Dr Trevelyan?'

'Oh.'

'Please could you find somebody to look at her?'

'Very well, I'll see what I can do. You had better come in.'

With Uncle's help, I made it up the steps and into the reception hall. The red and blue tiled floor floated before my eyes, and the sharp smell of disinfectant cleansed my nostrils.

'Wait there, please.' The nurse indicated some straight-backed chairs.

I lowered myself gently next to Uncle Jeremy, and Aunt Sylvia sat on the other side. The large mahogany clock ticked loudly as the thin red hand counted out the seconds on its white face. I felt as if I was locked inside the clock itself and cut off from that ordinary Sunday afternoon where pleasure boats sailed up and down the Teign in the late afternoon sun.

Eventually the nurse returned. 'I just need to take some information, and then the doctor will see you. Name?'

'Miss Mason.'

'Miss?' Her keen blue eyes went uncontrollably to my left hand, where my little ring was trying hard to look like a wedding ring, and then my stomach.

'Yes,' I sighed.

'So, you're not married then.'

'No.' The colour rose to my cheeks.

The short blonde waves bent over the form, and the nurse wrote neatly on the top 'Unmarried Mother.'

'Date of birth?'

'April 12th 1911.'

'So you are nineteen?'

'Yes, just.'

'How many months along are you?'

'Nearly eight. Will I be all right? Am I losing my baby?'

'My niece has already had one scare.' Aunt Sylvia sniffed.

'I'll just go and see if the doctor's ready.' The nurse rustled off down the corridor.

'I'm sure that was one of the nurses who came to opening of the shop,' Aunt Sylvia murmured.

'Ohh!' Another pain took hold.

'Yes, they came when I was putting up the banner, and asked when the shop would open.'

At that moment, the nurse came back. 'The doctor will see you now.'

'I'll stay here.' Uncle Jeremy picked up a magazine.

The nurse helped me along to a spotless consulting room, scrubbed white and smelling strongly of methylated spirits. I shuddered at the sight of a trolley full of glistening medical instruments. Outside, the sunlight reflected off the cars on Shaldon Bridge and dazzled my eyes.

'Can you get onto the bed?' The nurse offered a helping hand.

'I think so.' But I struggled, and despite my long legs, my cumbersome bulge got in the way. Once up, I balanced uncomfortably for ages until at last the doctor bustled in.

'This is Sir Rupert Alexander.' The nurse straightened her apron.

'What have we here, then? Unmarried mother, eh?' He leant over to examine me. The breeze from the window blew a cloud of his cologne over my face and made my eyes sting, and his steady breath irritated my stretched stomach as he listened to the baby's heartbeat.

'No problems there; heartbeat as strong as an ox. Let me check you, my dear.' He felt my pulse, timing it by his pendulous gold watch which he flicked back into his waistcoat pocket. Then he took a rubber cuff and wrapped it around the top of my arm.

'I'm just checking your blood pressure.' He pumped it up until I thought my arm would explode. 'Well, my dear, it is a little high; I think that we should keep you in overnight just to make sure that it goes down again.' He nodded to the nurse.

'Do I have to? The pains aren't so bad now.'

'We need to keep an eye on you.' He replaced his stethoscope around his neck. 'You need lots of rest.'

'So I won't lose the baby, then?' I half whispered.

'No, not if you're careful.' He came up level with my face. 'What are you going to do with it anyway, have it adopted?'

'Oh no! I'm getting married. I'm going to keep it. I could never give up my baby.'

'Are you? Well, I should have a good hard think about it, a young girl like you.' And he swept out again.

The nurse helped me off the bed and waited as I put my clothes straight.

'You really must take more care, Kathy. I'm sure that your air crash didn't help.' Aunt Sylvia stood up. 'Well anyway, you're here now; I'll go home and get your nightdress and sponge bag.'

The long narrow ward had a row of large Georgian style windows, and was empty for the Easter weekend, except for one elderly lady in the far corner. The nurse handed me over to Sister: a taller, older woman who showed me to a bed facing the river.

'Put this on.' She swirled the blue striped curtains round the bed, and offered me a white gown that tied up at the back.

'But, my aunt's bringing my nightie.'

'There's no time for that, we must get you in to bed.' She gave a firm nod.

Reluctantly, I undressed and put the gown on. It didn't meet behind, and the cool air chilled my bottom. Sister tied up the tapes and ushered me between the starched scratchy sheets.

'Hmm, no wedding ring I see,' she said, tucking me in tightly.

I checked my little turquoise ring and sighed: the blue flower gleaming up at me hadn't helped a bit. I lay back on the hard pillows, and watched the curtains breezing in at the window opposite. Only a couple of hours ago, I was safe in my own bed.

Later, Abigail brought my overnight bag. 'I offered to come with Uncle Jeremy so I could see you. You do look pale, Kathy.' She noticed my untouched tray. 'Didn't you want any supper?'

'No, I didn't feel like it.'

'Poor you. I'm sorry I've got to go home tomorrow and leave you all alone. Thanks immensely for inviting me; I've had such an adorable time helping your aunt open the shop and, of course, with Paul. I'm never going to forget our romantic picnic today. Smoked salmon and cream cheese sandwiches will always remind me of him. You know? I'm going to write to him every day. I'm going to miss him so much.' She held her hands over her heart. 'It won't be half so nice at home without him, Kathy.'

Oh, Abigail! How can you waltz in here and take him over like this? I can't bear you singing his praises all the time.

After she'd gone, I dozed off to sleep. A few hours later I was woken up by a quiet commotion around the bed of the old lady who had evidently taken a turn for the worse. I drifted off again, only to wake in time to see the doctors and nurses leaving the ward. Then I thought I was dreaming; illuminated from behind by the light in the corridor, I saw the silhouette of a doctor and nurse in an unmistakable and unforgettable embrace. The nurse was the petite blonde that I'd seen before, but the profile of the young doctor made me call out.

'Paul?'

They spun round in horror.

I sat up so fast that my stomach muscles clenched and I groaned in agony.

'Oh my God, Kathy!' He came in as the nurse scurried off.

'Paul? Why were you kissing that nurse? Abigail thinks that you're in love with her. Jeepers, you even took her on a picnic this afternoon.'

He came over, and perched on the bed. The mattress bent under his weight. 'Calm down, Kathy or you'll make yourself ill.'

'I am ill; I've got high blood pressure.' My hand shook as I pointed to the door. 'That's the nurse; the one that helped us this afternoon.'

'Kathy, I'm sorry. Her name's Patricia.'

'Patricia?' The name sounded like icicles thrusting into my heart.

'Sorry, Kathy, I loved you so much.'

'You *loved* me?' My mouth dried up and my throat tightened. The baby kicked me hard under the ribs.

'Yes, I'm sorry.' His blue eyes glimmered in the dull light from the corridor. 'I was so upset that you didn't want to marry me.'

He reached for my face, but I grabbed his wrist to stop him. 'I'm sorry, Kathy. It is so hard to have to tell you, but let me try to explain. Patricia's usually on the night shift. Her father's a surgeon. I've worked with her for quite a long time. She was the one who suggested that Sylvia should open a shop.'

'Full of good ideas, is she?'

'Don't be like that, Kathy.' Paul ran his hand through his hair. 'We just used to chat through the long dim nights here, listening to patients coughing or calling for bedpans. She told me all about her boyfriend who left her to go Oxford and whom she hasn't seen since; he never even wrote. I told her all about you, Kathy. Oh, I don't know, talking about you and our problems just brought Patricia and me closer together. And gradually, I've fallen in love with her. Perhaps I did make a mistake with you. But I truly did love you so much: you filled my every waking moment. I don't know; it hurt so much that I couldn't have you.'

'Is that why you didn't tell me?'

'Yes. I didn't know how.'

'Did you really love me, Paul?'

'Yes, oh yes, I still do in a way. You're so lovely.' He put his hand out again, but I turned away. 'It's not the same with Patricia. It's a different sort of love.' His hand traced the blue woven stripe in the blanket instead. 'I can see us getting married. I can believe in a future together.'

' . . . That you couldn't have with me.'

A tiny bit of magic still shimmered in his eyes like the sky after a firework display and I felt like the charred remains of an empty rocket, trodden in the mud.

I took a deep breath. 'And to think she took all my details as cool as ice. Did she come and tell you?'

'Yes, she realized who you were.'

'And yet it didn't stop you mauling her in the corridor right outside my ward.'

'Please, don't do this; I want to be your friend, even if we can't be together. I'm so sorry, Kathy.'

'What about Abigail? She's set her sights on you.'

'That's just harmless fun.'

'I don't think she sees it that way. Is that what you do; have several girls on the go at once?'

'I'm sorry.'

'No wonder Uncle and Auntie told me to be careful. Why did you ask me to marry you? Did you mean it then?'

'Yes, I did. When I said you were the only girl that made me feel that way, I meant it. It was too much when I couldn't have you.' He smiled, 'Kathy, we can still be friends. I can see you when I come to visit Father and Sylvia.'

'What would be the use?' I twisted the sheet round my fingers. 'Oh, I've been so stupid.'

Overnight, the rain lashed at the windows and permeated my nightmares until the tea trolley rattled round at six o'clock.

'Milk and sugar?' A new chirpy nurse poured out a cup.

'Thank you.'

The nurse went off to rip open the curtains and my heart sank when I saw the wet, watercolour sky. Then the sun rose and tinged the grey blue clouds with silver and pink, and gilded a Gipsy Moth fiery gold as it flew up the river.

I'm sorry, Ben, I thought, let's try again.

Chapter Twenty-Three

April 22nd 1930

I am so bored and I've only been home twenty-four hours.

Feet up on the sofa, I made several overstitches on the back of the linen tray cloth Abigail had left for me to embroider. *She only went home yesterday, but I miss her.* I turned it over to follow the blue transferred pattern.

Auntie's busy back at the shop after the Easter weekend, Uncle Jeremy's sailing with Bill Canlan, and even Mabel's visiting her sister. I stabbed at some blue and yellow petals with my needle. *I can't even dream about seeing Paul any more.*

I attempted the pink centres in a sort of circular blanket stitch, and at last, got into the rhythm of the embroidery. *If only Life was like this: clear blue lines to follow until it was finished, and a choice of harmonious colours to fill in the detail. Ow!* A drop of blood soaked into the linen. *No, Life's more like that instead.*

Thoroughly fed up, I threw the tray cloth aside, and glanced out of the window to see the telegram boy cycling up the drive.

My heart pounded. *A telegram? Who's it for? What could have happened?* I eased myself off the sofa, shuffled along the hall, and warily opened the front door.

'Telegram for Miss Mason?'

Me? I've never had a telegram addressed to me in my life. It's always for Mother or Dad when someone has died. Has something happened to Grandma? My hands shook as I signed for it and clutched the buff coloured envelope. I turned it over and over, as the boy whistled his way back down to the road. I remembered Grandma's white face when a cousin was lost in the Great War. *Jeepers, I hope Ben hasn't had an accident.* With clammy hands, I ripped it open. My eyes tried to focus on the words, and after several seconds, they swam into view.

DEAREST KATHY = ABIGAIL TOLD ME YOU WERE IN HOSPITAL = FLYING DOWN ON SATURDAY = ALL MY LOVE BEN +

What? I had to read it again to make sure I hadn't imagined it. I sat on the hall chair, shivering. *Ben is coming to see me on Saturday.* I spread the telegram flat on my lap, and read it a third time to make sure.

Thank goodness he's all right. I put my hand to my mouth. *Wait a minute, Saturday's only four days away. What am I going to do?*

I hauled myself upstairs and took out my pile of letters. A photograph from the Church Picnic last summer fell out. I couldn't bend to pick it up so I got down on my knees. I touched Ben's happy face in the picture. He'd sat on the sands and I'd knelt behind him. Closing my eyes, I remembered my arms being tickled by the gentle stubble on his chin. We'd smiled at the camera, unaware of what was to come.

What am I going to say to you? I haven't seen you since Boxing Day. My heart thumped wildly. *Oh, what if you meet Paul? You're bound to.* My head throbbed; I remembered Paul's kiss, and the hot desire. *Paul filled my soul with magic. I'm still helpless whenever he comes near, never mind that Patricia.*

Then, the silhouette of them kissing flashed up like an advertisement at the cinema. *He'll never be mine, will he? He has totally forgotten about me. Can I finally escape from his spell? That's where I've been: under his spell. It wasn't real. Ben's real.*

The baby squirmed, and I massaged my tummy. *You're real, aren't you? Well, little baby, your Daddy's coming to see you, and I'll do my best.*

I took out my writing pad, and chewed my pen. I started several times, but screwed up the pages. *What do I say to someone that I've betrayed?*

Dear Ben,

What a surprise your telegram was. I wondered what had happened at first; I thought you'd been injured or something. How are you flying down? Are you coming on your own? Where will you stay?

I'm looking forward to seeing you on Saturday so much. I miss you, and I'm very lonely now that Abigail's gone back home.

Please let me know when you're arriving.

Lots of Love,

Kathy

His reply arrived on the Thursday; the envelope had a Gipsy Moth flying past a signpost to Haldon Aerodrome.

Dearest Kathy,

I hope the telegram wasn't too much of a shock, but I was so excited that I had to tell you straight away. I've been chosen to go with a flight to Haldon Aerodrome to scout out the airfield for the visit of the Prince of Wales in his Gipsy Moth! We will take three Moths and I'll be able to fly some of the way myself, I'm not sure how much. I couldn't believe it when they asked me. It's beyond my wildest dreams. I can't wait to come and see my girl again.

We'll be arriving on Saturday afternoon. We're staying at the clubhouse, and leaving on Sunday morning. I do hope that you can come and see me, or I can come and see you. What an opportunity!

Kathy, I do love you so and I can't wait for Saturday. You don't know how much I miss you.

All my love, for ever and ever,

Ben

Aunt Sylvia and Uncle Jeremy sat at the kitchen table having breakfast as I read the letter. 'Ben's scouting out Haldon

Aerodrome on Saturday for the visit of the Prince of Wales. So that's what the telegram was all about.'

'Well, I never did.' Auntie poured out some coffee. 'When is he arriving?'

'In the afternoon.' I was sure they could hear my heart beating loudly.

Uncle Jeremy's eyes twinkled. 'Would you like me to drive you up there?'

'Yes,' I said, whilst the fish in my tummy swirled round as if caught in a maelstrom. 'It's so long since I've seen him.'

'Where's he going to stay?' Auntie asked.

'At the clubhouse.'

She sipped her coffee. 'How about him coming back here for dinner?'

'Really?' Are you sure?'

'Yes, of course, why not? You're going to marry him, aren't you? And his sister is perfectly respectable.'

I hoped to goodness that he wouldn't find out about Paul.

I didn't have many clothes to choose from for Saturday, and the weather could be quite changeable up on Haldon Moor, so I paraded in front of my mirror, trying to make the best of what I had:

This blue dress is too frumpy; I look about thirty years old. I wore that skirt when I went to Paul's house. I can't possibly wear it again. I threw it to the back of the wardrobe. *My bump sticks out in this dress; it's too clingy, and I cannot wear that floaty blouse with the big bow; I look like a fat pussy cat.*

Auntie knocked on the door. 'Can I come in, Kathy?' She waved a carrier bag in the air. 'I thought you might like this.'

I pulled out a creamy gold dress which fell loosely from the shoulders, with a matching jacket. Both were trimmed with black beads, like the one I gave Ben.

'It's lovely, Auntie, but . . .' I frowned.

'I'm sorry, Kathy, but I didn't approve of your relationship with Paul, even if I encouraged you to go with him in the first place. He seems to be out of the picture now, and your young man's coming. I know how much you love him, and I just want to help you look your best.'

'But, I can't afford this.'

'It's a present.'

'Thank you.' I held it up in front of me.

I'd better do this beautiful outfit justice.

Uncle Jeremy drove me up to Haldon. The sun burnt in a clear blue sky, and I was glad I'd worn my hat.

'Let's get out of the heat and have a glass of lemonade.' He led me to the clubhouse.

'Good afternoon, Mr Trevelyan. Good afternoon, miss. Where's Doctor Trevelyan today?' Peggy came over to take our order, and frowned a little when she saw how big I'd become.

Uncle and I looked at each other and smiled.

'Miss Mason's *fiancé* is flying in today.'

'Oh,' she tapped her pencil on her pad, and sniffed. 'That's nice.'

The ice cubes clicked and cracked in my lemonade as we waited for the planes to arrive, and Uncle chatted to me about the Puss Moths and Avro Avians on the airfield. I could hardly listen. It was like sitting in a dentist's waiting room with a bad toothache, dying for the tooth to be pulled, but dreading the pain.

Why am I so nervous? Will Ben still love me when he sees me? Will he know what I've done? I didn't really do anything wrong with Paul in the end; I only kissed him. There's no harm in that, is there? But, what might have happened? I can't bear to think about it.

I took off my jacket and fiddled with the little black beads.

The time ticked by on the large mantle clock. He was due at three o'clock, and as the hands measured out the seconds and the minutes, my heart thudded faster and faster.

I wish I was anywhere rather than here. I wish I really was at the dentist's; at least I could just lie there and not worry about how to act or what to say.

Then at two minutes to three, we heard the insistent, unmistakable humming of the Gipsy Moths, just out of synchronisation, so you could make out the thrum, thrum, thrum of each engine.

'They're here!' Uncle Jeremy hurried me outside.

The planes swung round and landed one, two, three in an arrow formation, the red, white and blue RAF roundels catching the sunlight like the markings on a real moth's wing.

The ground engineers rushed out to fix the chocks, and the men climbed down, hidden under leather helmets, goggles and greatcoats.

'Which one is Ben, Uncle? I can't tell.'

'Well, if you don't know, my dear, what will we do?' he chuckled.

My fish darted about as if being chased by a shiver of sharks, but the baby lay completely still, as if waiting for something to happen.

The men marched together in twos towards the clubhouse, and the senior officer called them to attention, and saluted Andrew who stood ready to receive them like the King inspecting his troops.

'Flight Lieutenant Archie McCall, sir.' The officer snapped his hand smartly down by his side.

'Good afternoon.' Andrew, who had put on his best suit and medals in honour of the event, smiled broadly and shook hands. 'Welcome to Haldon Aerodrome.'

'Thank you, sir. Thank you for letting us stay.'

'That's no problem at all. We're happy to have you on such an important occasion.'

The officer saluted again. 'Fall out,' he commanded his men.

'Jeepers, there he is.' I pointed a shaky finger. 'On the far side at the back. Is it him? It is!' I thought my heart was going to stop. Frozen, despite the warm spring day, I was rooted to the spot. My mouth went dry, I couldn't speak, and my head swam.

'Kathy!' Ben sprinted over, wrapped his arms around me, and clung on like a drowning man in a stormy sea. Disregarding the wolf whistles of his friends, he kissed me long and hard. And it was right. It felt right as I melted into that sure loving kiss, and melted into his arms, with tears pouring down my cheeks.

'I love you, Ben.'

'What's wrong, Kathy?' he said, wiping the tears away with his fingers.

'Nothing.' I looked into his dear eyes and smiled. 'Nothing. It's so wonderful to see you again; I've missed you so much.'

'I've missed you too,' he whispered into my hair. Then he gently touched my tummy. 'How are you? And our little baby? My goodness, you're so big, and look at the black beads on your dress; just like mine.' Smiling, he fished out the ID chain with my little black bead from inside his shirt. His eyes, warm and loving with little lines crinkling up at the corners like autumn leaves, shone with a clear conscience, innocent of desire for someone else. The familiar smell of cologne masking a whiff of oil comforted me, and I relaxed in his arms.

Uncle patted him on the back and shook hands. 'Wonderful to meet you at last, Ben, good man. How marvellous to get a chance to do this trip.'

'Pleased to meet you, Mr Trevelyan.'

'Oh, call me Uncle Jeremy, Kathy and Abigail do. How is your sister, by the way?'

'Fine, thank you very much. She really enjoyed her stay with you.'

'Well, tell her she's welcome any time, lovely girl.'

'Officer Cadet Hunter. Fall in.' Flight Lieutenant McCall called him to attention.

'Ask him if you'd be able to come to dinner, Ben,' Uncle called after him. 'My wife and I would be very pleased if you could.'

Ben marched smartly over to the Flight Lieutenant who didn't look much older than him, and whose boyish face was barely masked behind a neat brown moustache. After a few words, the officer glanced in our direction and gave Ben a wink. He returned to us, breathless.

'I can come, the boys want to go down into Teignmouth tonight; they hope to borrow a van, so they'll drop me off and pick me up on the way back. Will seven o'clock be all right Mr. Tre . . . I mean Uncle Jeremy?'

'Yes, of course, we'll see you then.'

Ben held my hands. 'I wish we could spend all afternoon together, but we've got to check over our planes for tomorrow.'

'Yes,' I said, 'I wish we could too.' And I really meant it. Seeing Ben again was just what I needed. I hadn't realized how much I'd missed him. How stupid of me.

We were just leaving when the Flight Lieutenant came over to us with Andrew.

'We're going to have a spot of tea in the clubhouse. Mr Trevelyan? Kathy? Would you like to join us?' His accent reminded me of Mother's Aunt Margaret from Edinburgh.

'Thank you very much, Flight Lieutenant er . . .?' Uncle asked.

'Please call me Archie, all my friends do.'

'Well, that's very kind of you, Archie. Come along Kathy, I'm sure you could do with a cup. My grandmother in India always used to say that it warms you up when you're cold and cools you down when you're hot.'

Chapter Twenty-Four

Ben walked beside me, hand in hand, with a big grin on his face.

'Oh, Kathy, I've been waiting for this moment for so long. I can't believe it's really you.' He let Uncle and Archie go on ahead, and turned and enveloped me in his arms. 'Kathy, Kathy, I love you so.' He kissed me, and I wanted him to drink me all up.

In the clubhouse, Archie pulled the chairs into a circle and introduced us to the other airmen, whilst Peggy bobbed about serving cups of tea.

'Of course, what we need is some transport.' Archie sat back and crossed his legs. 'Do you know where we can find a van?'

'Perhaps one of the ground engineers . . .' Uncle Jeremy stirred in his sugar.

'Excuse me, sir,' Peggy stood to attention, 'but my Jim has a little van that I think you could borrow. He's over in the hangar. I'll go and ask him.'

The hangar. I remember the last time I came to Haldon with Paul and we sheltered from the storm. In fact, I've never been here <u>without</u> him, until today. And here's Ben sitting right next to me, in the same chair that Paul sat in when I told him all about the baby. I shut my eyes as the room tilted.

Ben squeezed my hand. 'Is something wrong, Kathy?'

I shook my head, 'I'm just so pleased you're here.'

'Tell them about your flying lessons, Kathy.' Andrew tapped my arm.

The boys turned to me in amazement.

I looked at Ben who raised his eyebrow. 'I'd like to hear all about your little exploits too,' he nodded.

I bet you would! I'd better keep Paul out of this!

I'm sure my cheeks turned the colour of a boiled beetroot. I swallowed, and something tickled my throat and making me cough and my eyes water.

'Yes, I've been up with Andrew three times,' I managed to say. *Pictures of Paul hurrying across the field and watching me fly flickered in front of my eyes.*

'You were very brave when we had that little fire.' Andrew shook his head.

Ben's jaw dropped. 'What little fire? What happened, Kathy? You didn't tell me about that.'

'I didn't want to worry you.' I patted his knee. 'The plane crash-landed and after we'd climbed out, it burst into flames. That's all, we were fine, but the plane wasn't.'

'Kathy, you're joking, aren't you?'

'No, it's true.'

'But, the baby, is it all right?'

'Yes, I think so.'

'That's not why you were in hospital, is it?'

'I'm not sure, the doctor said that my blood pressure was up a bit.'

'She's a plucky young lady,' Andrew smiled, 'but I'm not so sure that I'd have taken her up if I'd known about her condition.'

'I wish I could have some more lessons one day.' I sat up straight. 'I want to fly to Australia like Amy Johnson.' Some of the boys nodded in agreement, but others shook their heads as if it wasn't a suitable ambition for a young lady.

'I know, Kathy,' said Ben, 'but I don't think you should take any more risks for quite a while!'

'He's right, women should stay at home where they belong,' said one of the Cadet Officers. 'There's no knowing what trouble Miss Johnson might get herself into: crocodiles, volcanoes, or even lost at sea.'

I shrugged my shoulders; flying to Australia was the least of my worries.

Uncle Jeremy broke the silence. 'How is your flying coming along, Ben?'

'I flew all the way from Cardiff, so that's a start,' Ben smiled. 'I'm going to do the return trip, aren't I, Archie?'

'Yes, that's right. All this flying clocks up your hours, Ben. I expected to fly more when I became a Flight Lieutenant, not less!'

Uncle put down his cup. 'Thank you very much for our tea, most enjoyable. We'll see you about seven, Ben?'

'Yes, of course, I'm looking forward to it. See you soon, Kathy.' Ben kissed me again as the boys whistled loudly.

At seven, on the dot, I heard a horn outside. I peeped around the curtains to see Ben waving goodbye to the airmen as the van they'd commandeered from the aerodrome rattled down the drive.

'Ben, so lovely to see you. Do come in.' Auntie was at the door already. 'We've heard such a lot about you.'

I hurried down the stairs and Ben's eyes sparkled when he saw me. 'Kathy! There you are. I thought you were hiding from me.' He kissed me on the cheek, and whispered, 'I've missed you all afternoon.'

As we sat round the table, I couldn't believe that he was there beside me, and I had to touch his leg now and again to make sure he was real: his serge uniform, prickly, yet warm under my fingers.

'So you had a good flight, Ben?' Aunt Sylvia passed him some bread.

'Yes, we did it in stages, and I flew the last one.'

'Well, we're very pleased to have you here. Perhaps now you can persuade Kathy to stop doing reckless things!'

I gasped. She was only joking, of course, but I felt dreadful that, being so reckless, I'd deceived him. How nearly everything had crashed right out of the sky like my Gipsy Moth. What on earth had possessed me?

Ben took a sip of wine, and winked at me over the rim of his glass.

My face turned red. I felt as if I really had gone all the way with Paul, and that I had a scarlet letter stitched to my dress. Thank God, I'd thrown that silky lingerie in the dustbin. What would he think about that if he knew? Dear true Ben, he would never have dreamt I would have got up to anything like that.

Suddenly, the room began to spin around me, and I pressed my fingers to my forehead in an attempt to keep it still.

'Do you feel poorly, Kathy?' Aunt Sylvia reached across and patted my arm.

'I'm fine,' I whispered, 'I just need a little air.'

Creeping quietly to the door, I escaped outside and sat on the edge of an ornamental urn full of overblown tulips. The sun dipped low in a sky emblazoned with crimson and orange which made the flowers look as if they were on fire. Already, the mist crept up the valley. The air smelt fresh and earthy after the warm day, and gradually everything stopped revolving. *Ben's here. I can't believe it. I haven't seen him since Christmas.* I fiddled with a black bead on my dress, and thought about how I'd been under Paul's spell, and how near I'd come to throwing my future with Ben away. The sun slipped down behind the hills, and I shivered.

I felt a hand on my shoulder, and almost jumped out of my skin, but it was Ben.

'Kathy? What's wrong? Have I done something to upset you?'

'No, I'm just tired; I felt a bit giddy. I couldn't sleep last night and I'm over excited, that's all.'

He took me in his arms. 'Kathy, I love you. I've missed you so much. Every day has brought me one more step closer to when I could see you again.' He tenderly kissed my lips.

A big tear rolled down my cheek.

'Oh, Kathy, this isn't like you.'

'I know, my emotions are all mixed up, perhaps it's because I'm having a baby.' I pulled out a hankie and blew my nose.

'Come on inside, and get warm.' And, with his arm around my shoulders, Ben guided me back into the house.

The airmen were due to collect him at ten o'clock, and I watched the hands slowly creep up to the hour, and then tick right past. Ten minutes later, Ben looked through the curtain to see if he could spot them.

'My goodness, it's thick fog out there! I don't think there's much chance they'll be coming for me now.'

'It happens quite often after a warm day with clear blue skies.' Uncle Jeremy joined him at the window. 'I dare say that they won't be here until the morning in this weather. You'd better stay, Ben. I wouldn't like to drive out there myself tonight; I don't think you could see your hand in front of your face.'

Aunt Sylvia took charge. 'You can sleep in the spare room. I'll find you some clean pyjamas.'

Oh my goodness! Ben's sleeping here!

I tossed and turned as much as my large tummy would let me, but I couldn't get comfortable. *I should really tell him about Paul and what we did. But how can I?*

After a few hours, I suddenly saw the wedge of light around my door get wider, and Ben's silhouette appeared in the middle.

'What are you doing?' I whispered.

'I couldn't sleep. I went to the bathroom and saw that your door was open a little. I just had to come and see you.'

'You mustn't. What if Auntie finds you here, she'll turn you out into the fog, and make you find your own way back to Haldon.'

'Shh!' Ben crept in and sat on my bed.

'No, Ben.' I pulled up the covers, like a protective wall.

'Kathy, I've got to talk to you. I've been looking forward to seeing my girl so much. I've bored everyone silly at Cranwell with my talk about you. They even joked that I was chosen to fly on this trip, just so they could come with me and see what all the fuss was about.'

Dear, familiar Ben. I could see him better as I got used to the gloom. He appeared older: his face was filling out and I could make out the hint of a frown between his eyebrows.

'Kathy, I've missed you so much, I adore you, and I want to marry you with all my heart.'

I couldn't stop the tears trickling down my cheeks.

'Don't cry, Kathy.' He carefully blotted them with the corner of the sheet. 'It can't be much sport to put up with being sent away from home because you're pregnant. I wish my parents had let me marry you straight away, then we could be together, go to sleep together, and wake up together every day. That day will come, Kathy, I promise. As soon as I'm twenty-one, we will be married, just wait, and be strong.'

The sobs wracked my body so much that the springs below me creaked and groaned.

'Shh! Kathy, what ever is it?' Ben lay down beside me on my narrow bed and held me in his arms. His embrace was sure, safe and sound. He pulled the covers over us and waited. Gradually, the mad gulps stopped. He kissed my hair and stroked my tummy, so gentle and comforting.

'I can feel our little baby, Kathy. What shall we call it?'

'I don't know. I haven't thought about it really.'

'How about Charles, if it's a boy, after Charles Lindbergh?'

I stared at the ceiling imagining myself soaring across the oceans in my own Gipsy Moth. 'Or Amy, if it's a girl, after Amy Johnson?'

'That's better.' His warm hand soothed my skin. 'That's more like the old Kathy.'

His hand moved to my breast. My palms prickled as I massaged his back, and my mouth tingled as I lifted up my face to his. This time, this time it was better than before. Yes, there were electric thrills and my body throbbed with pleasure, but this was deeper, more complete, more real, more meaningful than I'd ever dreamt of or anticipated with Paul, and more than the feverish events of that warm, late summer afternoon.

This is real. We're meant to be together, we're meant for each other. We know each other so well.

'I love you, Ben,' I whispered as I stroked his hair, and we lay, wrapped together as if nothing was ever going to tear us apart.

The bedroom, the house, Aunt Sylvia and Uncle Jeremy, and even Paul, all twirled away and left us at the centre of a whirlwind. There was no one else apart from Ben and I spinning together with the past few months forgotten, and our future yet to come.

We lay there as one, and dozed off, safe in each other's arms. I slipped into a dream; one that I'd had quite often since I'd come to Devon.

I was floating down the aisle of a church. The intoxicating scent of lilies filled my head, and I looked down to see half a dozen large flowers in my arms, tied up with ferns. I was anxious that my ivory silk dress wouldn't be stained with the green sap. A cool breeze chilled my arms under the lacy veil, and I could see a frill of lace above my eyes, which tickled my forehead. I couldn't scratch it because, apart from the flowers, my other arm was held tightly by my father, stiffly dressed in pin-stripe trousers, tailcoat, winged collar and bow tie. The organ music rose and propelled us forward.

I felt my tummy and it was quite flat. Where was the baby? Had I had it? The music soared as we approached the altar. The sun poured in through the eastern window and dazzled my eyes. I squinted to see the groom waiting beside the vicar, but as he stood in the shade, I couldn't see who I was marrying.

The service began, and I tried to glance sideways to guess his identity, but when it came to the place where we turned to each other to make our vows, his face was still hidden in the shadows. It was as if I was looking at his reflection in water; sometimes he looked like Paul, but then the features would dissolve and reassemble themselves as Ben.

Which one was it? In previous dreams, my panic had risen as the wedding continued. *I can't marry this man; I don't know who he is!* The vicar intoned the sacred vows, and motioned me to repeat them.

I heard my voice saying, 'I, Katherine Mary take thee . . . Who are you?' I tried to pierce the darkness, then turned to my father, 'Daddy, help me!' But he stared steadily ahead, and loosened his collar with a finger. And I always glided back up the aisle married to a man with no face and no name.

But this time, the groom took a step forward into the sunshine. The hazy face settled and I could see first of all the brown wavy hair, then the round face, and lastly the smiling brown eyes. Like the hero-pilot of a war film, Ben emerged from the mist, and I threw myself at him. I could hear the vicar saying, 'Please restrain yourself, young lady.' But I didn't care, I was marrying Ben, and I kissed him fully on the lips.

I awoke to find the fog had cleared and the moon beaming in through the window. I kissed Ben on his ear, on his cheek, and again on those delicious lips. He woke up too, and covered me in kisses.

'This is what I wanted, Kathy. Oh, this is what I've been waiting for.' He reached for something on the bookcase beside my bed.

'What's that?'

'Aha! It's a surprise.'

'I didn't see you bring anything in.'

'No, I didn't want you to; I didn't know if the time was right.'

I opened the little box. A gold ring shone in the moonlight; a solitaire diamond, with three small diamonds decorating the shoulders on each side.

I looked into his bright eyes. 'It's beautiful. Thank you.'

He took my hand and examined my turquoise ring. 'What's this, Kathy? I noticed you wearing it earlier.'

I frowned. 'It's been awful, Ben, being unmarried. The things people say, especially women. I had to buy it.' I twisted it round. 'See, if I do this, it looks like a wedding ring. But it hasn't made that much difference. Everyone in Teignmouth seems to know who I am anyway.'

'I'm sorry, Kathy, you've been through so much. I am going to make it all right just as soon as I'm twenty-one.' Taking off the turquoise ring, he gently pushed the diamond one onto my finger and it sparkled in the silvery light. 'I have your little black bead to remind me of you, so I thought you'd like this to remind you of me and our wedding promise.' He kissed my hand. 'You'll always be in my heart, Kathy.'

I hugged him, gaining strength from his body. *This is how it should have been. This is how it will be.*

'I love you, Ben. I love you.' The baby, little Charles or Amy, seemed to turn a somersault inside.

'Oh no! That's the boys!' Ben shot out of bed as we heard their van coming up the drive. He gave me one last kiss, and tiptoed off to put on his uniform. 'Thank your aunt for letting me stay. I'll see you soon; it won't be long. I love you so, Kathy.'

'I love you too.'

And he was gone.

I stroked the warm sheet where he'd been lying and my ring glistened in the fading moonlight.

Chapter Twenty-Five

April 27th 1930

At breakfast time, I made a show of picking up my cup with my left hand, but Aunt Sylvia didn't notice. So I patted my hair into place, and the diamonds caught the sunlight and made it dart around the kitchen like a hundred little rainbows.

At last, she paid attention, 'What ever have you got there? Let me see.'

I held out my hand and wriggled my fingers.

'Keep still. Oh Kathy, that's lovely. An engagement ring?'

I nodded.

'When did he give you that then?'

'Just before he left, Auntie.' I made my eyes wide and innocent.

'Oh.'

I could see what she was thinking. 'He just popped in to say goodbye; it wasn't the right time last night.'

'Well, you're really going to marry him now. I was a bit suspicious that he hadn't given you a ring before.'

'There wasn't time, Auntie. He had to go away.'

She stood up. 'I must go and telephone Emily, and tell her the good news.'

'No, I want to tell her myself.'

The telephone was the one extravagant concession to the twentieth century that we had in our house. Dad had it installed so Mother could deal with any business enquiries. Now, with my heart thumping loudly, I clasped the receiver, waiting for her to answer.

'Hello?'

'It's me, Kathy.'

'Oh, I didn't expect it to be you! Is everything all right, dear?'

'Yes, I . . .'

'You're not having trouble with the baby again?'

'No, Mother, everything's fine. I . . .'

'Why are you telephoning me then?'

'I'm trying to tell you, Mother, Ben's given me a diamond engagement ring.'

'A ring?'

'Yes, we're engaged.'

'No! I don't believe it!'

'Yes, really.'

'That's wonderful, Kathy. He means to marry you, after all.'

'I'm so excited.' I stretched out my fingers again and made it sparkle by pushing it to and fro with my thumb. 'We're going to get married after his birthday in August; his parents won't be able to stop him this time.'

'Kathy, that's wonderful news, I can't wait to organize this wedding at last!'

'I know, Mother!'

'Let me speak to Sylvia, I need to sort out a few things.'

Happily, I handed over the receiver.

My heart raced, I wanted to run. I wanted to fly. I felt like dancing along the promenade, despite being nearly eight months gone, and telling the whole world that I loved Ben, and showing them my dazzling ring. *That would make Aunt Sylvia burst a blood vessel!* I chuckled. *I'd better go for a walk instead.*

I wandered down the drive under the fresh green leaves, taking off my cardigan and carrying it over my arm. I crossed the road, and squeezed through the kissing gate into the meadows which led down towards the river sparkling below. I knew it would be silly to go too far, so I sat down on a log under two trees which had grown up side by side, their branches entwined to make one shady umbrella. *Ben and I are like this. We've known each other since we were small and we're part of each other. If one of these trees was to be chopped down, then I bet the other would just fall over and die; they depend on each other so much.*

It was Sunday, and the church bells rang out over the fields. I imagined emerging triumphant through the old oak door on our wedding day amidst a cloud of confetti, arm in arm with Ben: his wife at last!

A Gipsy Moth droned across the sky and I followed it until it disappeared behind the leaves above my head. I thought of Ben flying back to Cranwell, and wondered how far he'd got.

I admired my ring again, turning my hand from side to side. *It even makes me look elegant. I'm glad Mother was so delighted. I don't know how she's going to plan our wedding without Mrs Hunter knowing, but I'm sure she'll find a way.*

I'll be Mrs Hunter too. Mrs Benjamin Hunter. How do you do? I practised shaking imaginary hands.

Then, I closed my eyes and tried to recapture my dream, the lovely part when I realized it was Ben at the altar; his face, the one I loved so much, emerging from the mist. I relived the delicious hours we'd spent wrapped up together in my bed. I couldn't wait to see him again. It all felt so right, just as it had that late summer day on the tartan rug.

Jeepers, I haven't thought about Paul all morning. I'm free of his spell at last.

After lunch, I decided to write to Abigail.

Dear Abigail,

I have such wonderful news! Please don't tell your parents, but Ben has given me the most beautiful diamond ring!! It's sparkling on my finger as I write. I can't believe it!

I can't wait to be married in the summer either. Will you be my bridesmaid? What colour dress would you like? I think that a powder blue would suit you down to the ground.

Please keep an eye on Mother; I think she'll be in seventh heaven now she's got a wedding to organize.

Do hurry and write to me soon, and tell me what you think.

Love from,
Kathy.

Then, for something to do, I began to sort out my newspaper cuttings on the bed. I'd been collecting them since December, and amongst them I had a picture of Amy Johnson in overalls, astride a Gipsy Moth, another of her in a leather helmet and goggles with an article declaring her intention to fly solo to Australia in a 'secret plane', and one at the Tring gliding club, with the comment that she might attempt to cross the Channel in a glider.

I arranged and rearranged them in my scrapbook, but couldn't decide on the layout. I kept admiring my glittering ring instead. *I want to fly again like Amy Johnson, but right now marrying Ben is much more exciting. I'll be complete at last. This wonderful ring makes all the difference. It says: I may not be married right now, but I have a fiancé who has promised to marry me and he will very soon.*

I flicked through the Sunday paper looking for any more news of Amy's solo flight. Yes, there it was: she'd bought a De Havilland Gipsy Moth which she would call Jason, and hoped to set off on May 5th. I got out my scissors, snipped round it and stuck all the pictures in, trying not to get glue and ink on Aunt Sylvia's golden counterpane. I sat back turning the pages and imagining flying ten thousand miles all on my own. Would I really want to go that far without Ben?

'Ring . . . Ring . . .' The telephone echoed through the house.

Slowly, I slid off my bed to go and answer it when I heard Auntie's voice.

'Abigail, how are you? You want to speak to Kathy?'

By this time, I was down the stairs. Auntie stood in the hall, wearing her wide straw gardening hat, and a floral cotton dress. She had the telephone receiver in one hand and the other gripped the glove she'd taken off. Her face was ashen.

'Kathy, there's been an accident. Here, sit down, my dear.' She pulled out the little red chair and I lowered myself down. She wrapped her gloved hand around my shoulders; it smelt of earth and green weeds, and handed me the phone. Her breath had condensed in the little cup that she'd spoken into and made tiny droplets of moisture.

'Abigail?'

'Kathy?'

'Yes, what on earth's happened?'

'Oh, Kathy, it's awful, there's been an accident.'

'Who's been hurt? Not Mother? Is it Dad? Has he fallen off a ladder again?'

'No . . . I'm afraid it's Ben.'

'Ben's had an accident?' I whispered, as if speaking loudly would make the unthinkable really true. 'Is he all right? Has he been hurt? What's happened to him? Is he all right, Abigail? Tell me he's all right.'

'Their planes collided in the fog over the sea.' I heard her swallow.

'No!' My heart squeezed into a tight knot. 'Are they searching for him?'

'Kathy, I don't know how to say this; he's . . . Ben's missing, presumed drowned.' There was silence, then Abigail gulped back her tears.

'What? You're joking, he can't be! He was here this morning. I've just written to you to tell you about the engagement ring he's given me.' I held my hand out so it caught the light. 'Tell me you're joking.'

'No, I'm so sorry, Kathy. It's true.'

'But if he's missing, *presumed* drowned, he might not be! He might come back. He might! They might find him after all.'

'They couldn't find any sign of wreckage, Kathy. They think that it's more than likely that he's gone down with it. I'm so sorry.'

Auntie knelt beside me and held me tight, listening into the earpiece.

'What happened?' My voice sounded as if it was coming from a long way off.

'Poor flying conditions and pilot error,' Abigail sobbed. 'That's what one of Father's old colleagues at Cranwell said.'

'But how?'

'They came down over the Bristol Channel.'

'That's only about an hour's flying time from here.' *That must have been about seven o'clock in the morning. I was still in bed*. I pictured the crumpled sheet where he'd lain, and my hand, awkward with the new ring, smoothing out the warm creases.

'Are you sure?'

'Yes, two of the Moths collided in a dense patch of sea fog, and it seems that the other one flew straight into them. Although two airmen were picked up by a passing fishing boat and taken to Ilfracombe, no one else survived. They couldn't find Ben at all. I can't believe it, Kathy, I can't.'

I felt completely numb. *It's not true. Not Ben. He was here this morning.*

Auntie squeezed me tight, and took the receiver.

'Abigail, dear, I'm so sorry. Please give my condolences to your parents. Thank you, yes, I'll tell her. Goodbye. 'Bye.'

A dull ching sounded as she replaced the receiver. For the first time, I noticed Uncle Jeremy standing in the kitchen doorway.

'I'll get you a glass of brandy, it'll do you good.'

Auntie held my hand in hers and stroked it with her thumb.

'Poor, Kathy, this is awful.'

'No, they've made a mistake. They must have done. Ben's not drowned. He's not. It's not true. We're going to get married.'

'I'm afraid it sounds as if it is, my dear. Abigail told me that the RAF is going to give them all a memorial service at Cranwell.'

'Cranwell? I can't go there. It's too far.'

'I don't really think that it would be advisable go at all in your condition, especially if his parents don't approve.'

'Oh, Auntie!' The tears spilt down my face. 'What about the baby? What am I going to do?'

'I don't know, Kathy. There's no need to think about it now.'

I rocked to and fro, cradling my tummy, until Uncle came back with the brandy.

'Here you are, Kathy, it won't make things better, but it'll help.'

'It's a punishment,' I sniffed. I couldn't help it; all the guilt of the past few months was too much. 'It's a punishment. I was never meant to marry Ben at all, was I?'

Aunt Sylvia rubbed my back. 'Poor Kathy, please don't say that, it's not a punishment.'

'It is.' The tears made my face feel distorted and ugly. 'I let Ben get me in the family way. I didn't stop him. If I'd have said no, then I'd still be at home waiting for him to come back and everything would've been as it was before. He'd never have flown down to Devon to see me, and he'd never have been drowned. I've got what I deserved.'

'No, dear, it's not all your fault. It takes two to tango. It's sometimes impossible to refuse.' She glanced at Uncle Jeremy.

I struggled upstairs, lay on my bed, and hugged the pillow. *It's not true; they've made a mistake. Ben was only here this morning.*

I tried not to think of the accident, but pictures crept into my head, and projected themselves onto the ceiling. Ben at the controls flying to Cardiff. The other planes disappearing into the fog. Calling out into the white impenetrable light. His engine drowning out the sound of the others. Straining to tell where they are. Shouting to Archie. Not hearing his reply. Feeling sick with fear. Spinning through the damp, cold air and falling into the icy sea.

In my dream about the fighter planes, it must have been Ben that crashed after all.

I couldn't sleep that night, watching the light around my bedroom door, and waiting with heavy eyes to see Ben's silhouette again, but it never came. I stroked the same sheets that we had lain on together for those few short hours, and I buried my nose in the pillow and smelt his cologne, and that faint whiff of oil. It reminded me of those Sundays when I helped him tinker with his beloved Norton.

More pictures rolled round my head: the summer's afternoon on the tartan rug; the time he turned up when I'd taken all those Beecham's Powders; running through the snow on Boxing Day; arriving in a Gipsy Moth, only yesterday.

Ben, I wish you were here now. I've only seen you five times in the past eight months, and for four of those months I've been enchanted by Paul. I didn't deserve you, and now you're gone.

I rubbed my eyes with my wet hankie until they were sore.

The baby squirmed around inside. Its elbows and knees pushed through my skin like someone pulling on a tight sweater.

What am I going to do about the baby? If I'd married Ben, it would've been all right. Eventually, everyone would have forgotten that the baby was born before the wedding. We could've settled down here in Devon, and no one at home would've been any the wiser.

I'm glad that I've finished with Paul, now that I know what a bounder he really is. Poor Abigail! Patricia is welcome to him.

But am I any better than him for deceiving Ben?

The baby's not going to have a father now. Ben was always there, even if I did play around with Paul: I never really worried about the danger he was in before. What did Dr White say? Oh yes, it's best for the baby to have a father and a settled home as soon as possible. But what am I going to do? Sir Rupert Alexander, at the hospital, said I should have a good hard think about having it adopted. Oh, I can't go through with that. I could never give my baby away. My hand cradled one of its little knees protectively.

But, how can I give it a home? Mother will never take me back with a baby. She'd never be able to look the Flower Club in the face again. Aunt Sylvia wouldn't like me to stay here either, although she was kind this afternoon. What am I going to do?

The moon that witnessed Ben and I lying in its silver light last night, sailed out from behind a cloud and shone on my ring. I shut my eyes and imagined magical little moonbeams sparkling around the room like fairies. *I wish they could wave their wands and bring Ben back, and then everything would be as it was this morning when those rainbows flashed around the kitchen.*

Chapter Twenty-Six

April 28th 1930

I woke up with the rain hammering on my window. In my dreams, my fingers slid down a seaweed-covered rock as I tried to hoist Ben on to it, and stop him from drowning. My eyes stung from the salt water, and an aircraft engine throbbed in my head as a plane circled to find us. But the headache, and my wet pillow, proved I'd been crying most of the night.

I felt all alone, like the time I walked home in the dark when I was about thirteen, with only a torch to guide me. I shone it up and down the road, but its faint light didn't penetrate the gloom. The deep pools of blackness between the streetlights scared me, and I couldn't see what lurked in the shadows amongst the bushes. If there had been a murderer, there was no one to call anyway; the houses were set too far back from the pavement. I heard a thud behind me and I whipped round, but my torch showed nothing but a ripe crab apple rolling on the ground. Then I heard a bike squeaking and creaking along. I didn't dare turn again, but walked on, keeping my eyes on the circle of torchlight in front of my feet, whilst the bright beam from the headlamp crept alongside me in the road. My heartbeat filled my ears.

'Kathy, is that you?'

I peeked sideways, and clamped my hand over my mouth. 'Ben, thank goodness it's you. You scared me.'

He got off, and walked along beside me, wheeling his bike with one hand and putting his arm in mine to keep me safe. All my fears flew away. The dark didn't seem so frightening any more because of him.

If only he was here now, I wouldn't feel so afraid of the future.

I didn't want to get up. I couldn't face Uncle and Auntie. I didn't want to talk; I just wanted to come to terms with it all in my own time. I just wanted Ben. I'd hardly thought of him all spring, it had been Paul. Paul. Paul. How blind? How selfish had I been?

Now that I realized how much I really loved Ben, he was gone. I hugged the pillow tightly, trying to squeeze some memory of him out of it, but only a single, white feather fluttered out, hovered in the air and twirled down onto the eiderdown, like his plane had spun out of the sky into the sea. And the baby fidgeted as if anxious to know whether I could bring it up alone without Ben to be its father.

The grey day droned on and merged into evening with heavy dark clouds hiding the sunset. I imagined Ben washed up below some forbidding granite cliffs on the North Devon coast, gasping for air. But, a picture of his lifeless body kept surfacing instead.

Mabel had brought me trays of food, but I couldn't bring myself to eat.

'You must keep up your strength, Miss Kathy, think about the baby.'

I rubbed my tummy which rose like a small hill under the bedclothes. *It's Ben's baby: it's all I have left of him.*

She hovered by the door in the twilight. 'It'll do you no good to starve yourself. How about I boil you a nice egg with some soldiers to dip in it, would you like that?'

'All right, thank you, Mabel,' I sighed.

And it seemed as if she was back in no time with a boiled egg, slices of toast and a cup of Horlicks.

'This will do you a world of good. You'll feel much better.'

'Thank you.' I said, balancing the tray on my lap, as best I could.

Mabel turned at the door. 'You'll get over it, miss. You'll get over it. It doesn't seem so now that you will, but I know. My Jack, he went down just before the Armistice. It was dreadful, everyone cheering in the streets, but him not coming home. But I got over it. It took time. They say time heals, and it does.'

After another sleepless night, I dragged myself into the bathroom, and bathed and washed my hair. I had to make some effort to look reasonable for Aunt Sylvia and Uncle Jeremy. But, as usual, she'd gone to the shop, and he wasn't due back until lunchtime.

I waited in the kitchen with Mabel and Rosie. The golden retriever rested her head on my lap, and looked up at me with her soulful eyes, as if she knew how I felt. I stroked her warm, furry head.

'Dogs are always faithful, aren't they, Mabel?' Rosie's floppy ears felt like velvet. 'They're always pleased to see you, however bad you're feeling.'

Mabel took the roast pork out of the oven to test if it was done. 'Mm, sage and onion always reminds me of Christmas,' she said.

Last Christmas Day was so lonely, but the thought of seeing Ben on Boxing Day was like a star in the dark sky. Now the starless sky is more than I can bear.

Rosie trotted over and scraped at the back door, asking to be let out.

'Why don't you go and play with her in the garden, Miss Kathy? Stretch your legs a bit.' Mabel slid the sizzling pork back into the oven. 'This won't be ready for a while.'

I didn't want to. I didn't have any energy, but I couldn't resist those doggy eyes staring at me like deep pools of dark chocolate.

Sighing, I opened the door. 'Come on then, Rosie.'

She rushed past me and bounded up the garden, searching for her favourite ball of well-chewed leather under the remains of some bedraggled tulips. She pranced back, holding it high in the air, and dropped it at my feet. Picking it up with my finger and thumb, I threw it across the lawn, and like lightning, she brought it back. Feeling weary already, I spotted the deckchairs in the summer house, and pulling one to the open door, I sat down. For a while, the game continued with me throwing and Rosie fetching until she found an interesting smell near the rose bushes. Then she spent several minutes making forays underneath, and leaping backwards when the thorns scratched her nose.

Glad of a moment's respite, I sank back into the chair and closed my eyes. A cool breeze blew in around me, and I hugged myself to stop shivering.

Oh, Ben. I wish you were here to keep me warm and safe. I don't know what I'm going to do without you.

I pictured his smiling face on that last morning when he gave me my ring. I twiddled it to make sure that it was still there, as I had done so many times over the past couple of days. Apart from the baby, it was all I had.

Then, Rosie barked, and I looked up to see her defending her garden against a supercilious marmalade cat prowling along the fence. 'Rosie!' I shouted. 'No!'

The cat disappeared, tail in the air, over the other side and she trotted up and dropped her ball at my feet. Stroking her head, I noticed the corner of an envelope sticking out of the skirting board, just beside me and I tugged it out.

It was addressed to Aunt Sylvia from Mother: I'd recognize her handwriting anywhere. The damp had smudged the postmark, but I could just make out November 1929, and the ragged edge showed it had been opened. I began to take out the letter, wondering if it was about me being pregnant, and curious what Mother had said. But, of course, I knew I shouldn't and decided to put it back where I found it. However, the glue holding the envelope had come unstuck, and the soggy paper came apart in my hands letting the letter drift to the floor, writing side down. I stared at it for a moment or two and then picked it up and turned it over. Rosie nuzzled my hand as I read.

Dear Sylvia,

I'm writing to ask you if Kathy could come to spend a few months with you as she has fallen pregnant. Unfortunately, I don't think the father's parents will let them marry because they are keen for him to finish his officer training in the RAF, and his mother's recovering from TB.

Well, you were right about that, I thought.

As you can imagine this is a very distressing time for us, and we do not want to cause any scandal. It would be very kind of you if you could look after her until the baby is born sometime in the late spring.

My hand travelled to my huge stomach. Spring had arrived, but I still had a good month to go. Then I read the next bit:

Please take Kathy in, because, after all, she's your daughter, not mine.

I felt sick. 'No! No. It can't be true,' I whispered. 'Aunt Sylvia can't be my mother. Why didn't they tell me?'

I had to read the last sentence again. ' . . . *because, after all, she's your daughter, not mine*.' Clapping my hand to my mouth, I sank back into the deckchair, my heart beating like a piston engine.

Rosie gave a short bark, and picked up her ball.

'Not now, Rosie.' But I threw it anyway, and she hared down the garden.

If I'm Aunt Sylvia's daughter, not Mother's, who's my father then?

'Miss Kathy!' Mabel called from the kitchen door. 'Lunch is ready!'

Stuffing the letter in my pocket, I hurried back to the house, not sure what to do about it. Aunt Sylvia and Uncle Jeremy were already sitting at the dining table.

He patted my shoulder as I sat down. 'How are you, my dear? You look a bit peaky. Would you like to go for another sail in my boat some time? That would put some colour in your cheeks.'

'No, I'm all right, thank you, Uncle.'

The secret I'd uncovered in the summer house was as hard to swallow as the sour chunks of grapefruit in my bowl, and although I sprinkled some sugar on the top, it didn't make me feel any better. And the indigestion which had got worse as the baby grew, gnawed under my ribs.

I watched Aunt Sylvia cut up her pork, with her knife in her right hand. *Nobody would guess that she was left-handed like me.* Then the heat rose through my body. *No wonder I'm left-handed; she's my mother!*

I took a deep breath, 'I've got something to show you.'

They looked up, forks poised in the air.

I pulled out the letter from my pocket.

'What have you got there?' she asked.

'A letter.' I straightened it out to show them.

Her jade green eyes stood out against her pale face, and her fork clattered to her plate as she recognized the envelope. 'Where ever did you get that?' she gasped. 'It's mine. Give it to me this instant, Kathy. Where did you find it?'

'In the summer house.'

'That's were I must have left it,' she whispered. 'I wondered where it had gone.'

I licked my lips to moisten them. 'Aunt Sylvia, it says that you are my mother. How can you be? Why didn't you tell me?'

Tears welled up in her eyes. 'I'm sorry, Kathy. I'm sorry.' She took my hand. 'Yes, it's true. You are my daughter.'

I stretched my shoulders back and rubbed the spot just under my ribs where the indigestion cut in like a knife. In less than three days, I'd become engaged, I'd lost my fiancé, and now I'd found out that my mother wasn't my mother after all, but my aunt, the one who hadn't exactly made me welcome, *was*.

I got up. I just had to get away from there. Anywhere. Auntie's crimson Morris sat on the drive, so without thinking further, I grabbed the keys from hall table, squeezed in the car and drove away.

Chapter Twenty-Seven

There was never any doubt where I should go. I was going home. It never crossed my mind to go to the railway station and catch a train, or attempt to drive all the way there by motor car either. No, I was going to *fly*!

I found Aunt Sylvia's car easier to drive than Paul's Austin, and the electric starter meant that it didn't need cranking. I don't think I could've done that anyway with my big bump, but I did crunch the gears a bit at first. Soon, I raced up the road to Haldon between the familiar deep, earthy banks, whilst I focused on flying home and getting some answers to all the questions buzzing around my head.

Mother, how can it be true? How can I be Aunt Sylvia's daughter? I know that I haven't been the perfect girl, but I am yours and Dad's, aren't I? I want to come home to see you. I want to talk to you. Why did you send me away to this nightmare? Mother, I'm coming home. And I put my foot down to make the little car go faster.

Was it only on Saturday that I came up here to meet Ben? I'd felt as if I was going to the dentist, rather than seeing the man I would marry. The diamonds sparkled on my finger. I squeezed my eyes tight to force back the tears, opening them just in time to avoid a low branch which nearly thwacked me on the head as I drove under a tree. The tears, unleashed, poured down my cheeks.

Ben, I should have been thinking about you this year, not Paul. What a waste of time. I wiped away some tears with my sleeve. *I didn't appreciate you being there in Lincolnshire. Waiting for me. But now you're gone for good.*

I ploughed the car through the deep gravel, and parked beside the clubhouse. For a second, I held my breath: *There's a red Austin. Is it Paul's? That's all I need.* But it wasn't; just a similar one lined up with the other cars and vans watching their owners take to the skies. I sighed with relief.

Then I caught sight of a Gipsy Moth weaving in and out of the wispy clouds, dipping and looping; catching the afternoon sun on its silver wings.

I wonder if that's Andrew up there? He said I was a born pilot. I can fly. I know can do it. I'm going to fly out of here. I'm going home. I know you're not there any more, Ben, but Mother is. My mother is.

As I squashed my stomach past the steering wheel, and climbed out, Uncle's Alvis crept slowly up and parked beside me. *Oh, no! Uncle Jeremy, you don't have to come and rescue me. I can do this on my own.* Then, I noticed the driver:

'Aunt Sylvia?' I gasped, grabbing the car door to steady myself. 'What are *you* doing here?'

'I want to talk to you, Kathy. Please, don't do anything rash.'

'I'm not.'

She raised her fine eyebrows. 'You weren't thinking about running away in an aeroplane, were you?'

I opened my mouth.

'You'd never be able to cram yourself into a plane for hours on end in your condition.' She patted the seat beside her. 'Please come and sit in here, Kathy, there are so many things I want to say.'

'No. I'm going to . . .' *Why did she have to turn up?*

'Who were you thinking of borrowing a plane from anyway? You can't just grab the keys and drive away, like you did in my car.' Her green eyes flicked over the Morris, and came back to gaze into mine. A frown pinched across her forehead.

I clenched my fists. My feet were itching to run. I wanted to climb into the nearest plane and just go. But she was right. Who would spin the propeller? I couldn't even crank a car engine. Should I remove the chocks first? Where would I re-fuel? I didn't even have a map.

Reluctantly, I clambered inside the Alvis. The seat cushioned my back and I realized how much it'd been aching. I couldn't bring myself to look at Auntie. We sat there watching a red Moth taxi down to the end of the runway, turn, and breeze back, lifting into the air like a ladybird as it swayed from side to side, heading northwards over the hills. I wished it was me. More tears trickled down my face, and I wiped them off my chin. *Ben flew off that way on Sunday morning.*

'Kathy? Please don't. Here take my handkerchief.'

I caught a whiff of Chanel No. 5 as she pulled it out of her handbag, and it made me feel sick. 'How can you be my mother? I don't understand. You didn't even bring me up. You haven't taken any time to be with me here. You don't seem to care about me at all.'

'Kathy, I care about you more than you'll ever know.' She reached something from the back seat. 'Look at this.' She handed me a photograph of me as a baby, framed with forget-me-nots.

I glanced at the chubby cheeks and pouting mouth and gave it back to her.

'We've got the same picture; it's Mother and me. She calls me her little Russian princess because I'm sitting on a fur coat. It doesn't prove anything.'

'Look more closely.' She thrust it back.

'What? What has this got to do with it?'

'Look again.'

I did, and my heart almost stopped when I recognized the tall young woman in the picture. 'Oh, it's *you!* Why did you have your photo taken with me as well?'

'Look at the back.'

I turned it over and there in my mother's beautiful handwriting were the words:

Dear Jane,

I promise that I will look after your little baby, Katherine Mary, as if she were my own.

Edith Mason.

I frowned, puzzled for a moment. *Dear Jane? Of course, Uncle's boat is called the Lady Jane. He said she was quite a dark lady, now I know just what he meant.*

I glared at her. 'Oh, yes, you're known by your second name because it's more appropriate for the *literary world*. And did it seem more appropriate for someone in the *literary world* not to have an illegitimate daughter too?'

She smiled. 'Don't say that, Kathy, you know as well as I do how people regard unmarried mothers. You've had a happy childhood, haven't you? A mother, and a father? A good school? A warm home? Good friends? I can see that you have from knowing Abigail all these years. I couldn't have given you all that. I don't know how I should have coped.'

'You could've given up your job, and been a real mother to me.'

'But how would I have paid the bills, or kept a roof over our heads?'

'I don't know.' *I don't know how I'm going to do that myself now Ben's gone.*

'Kathy, we had those photographs taken as a symbol of the fact that Emily was going to bring you up instead of me. It was our little ceremony, and the next day, she and your father moved to another part of town taking you with them. So Kathy, I know exactly how you feel, I have been through it all, and it has been hard seeing you suffer in the same way that I did.' She gave a watery smile, and patted my knee. 'I can't believe that you're really my daughter, either, because I've had to pretend that you weren't for so long.'

'Why haven't you ever loved me, warmed to me? What have I done wrong?'

'Nothing! I couldn't begin to love you too much in case I gave myself away, and you found out. I know that you used to hate coming and helping in the shop, and couldn't wait to run off to see Ben, but just having you there was everything to me, even if you were grumpy.

'And when you came to stay in Devon, I wanted to hold you and comfort you, but I couldn't, so I just got busy with my new shop and kept out of your way.' She held my hands and rubbed them with her thumbs. 'I'm sorry, Kathy, please forgive me.'

I noticed that her skin was exactly the same colour as mine: a golden tone instead of pink like Mother's. I felt as if the very foundations of my life had suffered an earthquake and had settled painfully into a new formation deep inside.

'But, what about my real father, who is he?'

'I knew that you'd ask that.'

'Well?'

'He's . . . Oh, how am I going to say this?' She waited as another aeroplane rumbled past us and up into the sky.

'Go on. Tell me he's a famous author or poet.'

She screwed up the handkerchief she'd been twisting around her fingers. 'It's Joseph,' she whispered, her face sagging as she released the terrible secret she'd kept for nineteen years.

'Joseph . . .' My temperature rose. Beads of sweat began to trickle down my forehead. I swallowed; my mouth was almost too dry to speak. 'Joseph Mason? My father?'

She nodded, spreading out her crumpled, damp handkerchief on her lap and tracing an embroidered rosebud with her finger.

I grabbed her arm. '*Dad* is my father?'

'Yes, Kathy, now can you see why I had to give you away? I couldn't look after you and, there was no future for Joe and me.'

'Did . . . does Mother know?'

'Yes, she's a saint, Kathy. I don't know how she coped bringing up her husband's child. She must love us so much to put everyone else first, instead of herself.'

The baby, which seemed to have been holding its breath until now, squirmed under my ribs, and I rubbed the painful spot.

'So, they didn't have any children of their own?'

'No, they'd tried for years, so although she had to put up with the humiliation of her husband having an affair, she did get a little baby to love. I don't know whether that made up for it though.'

'How did it happen? Can you tell me?' I studied her tired green eyes. 'Was it just once like Ben and me?'

'Just once?' She turned her head away and gazed at Dartmoor looming on the far horizon. 'No. It went on for several months.'

'Aunt Sylvia!'

'It's awful, Kathy, you really shouldn't have to hear this. Emily had several miscarriages and had to rest. She used to go down to your father's workshop to do the books for him, but when she couldn't manage any longer, I would call in to help on the way back from my shop. It was all innocent at first; I just did the accounts. But he was really upset about Emily losing her babies, and he confided in me. Over the months, one thing led to another.' She screwed up her handkerchief again. 'And, you came along.'

'Oh my God! What did she say? What did she do?'

'Oh, she was distraught at first. I've never seen anyone in such agony; after all I was having the baby she wanted so badly. But then she came to realize that she could look after you, and keep her husband. Funnily enough, her health returned and she became her old self.' Aunt Sylvia shrugged her shoulders. 'I believe they've been happy.'

I smiled ruefully, thinking about the arguments they'd had over me being sent to Devon. No wonder Dad didn't want me to go.

'So that's why she wanted to send me away to you?' I touched her arm. 'Has he ever had anyone else?'

'No, he loves her, he always has.'

'It's funny how you can love one person and still be enchanted by another though, isn't it?'

'You mean you and Paul, don't you?'

'Yes,' I sighed.

'Kathy, I'm sorry I've been such a failure.'

'Perhaps if you'd taken more interest in me over the past few months, I wouldn't have got involved with Paul. I don't know. It wouldn't have stopped Ben being drowned, would it? All the time I've been here, I've been so mixed up, so confused, and now this.'

I was desperate for a cigarette, and rummaged in my handbag. All I could find at the bottom, wrapped up with a comb in a dirty hankie were the ones Paul had given me. I crushed the packet in frustration and anger.

'Come on, let's go home, I could do with a stiff drink.' Auntie started the Alvis. 'Will you be all right to drive?'

'I suppose so.' All the fire and energy I'd had as I escaped to the aerodrome, had poured away like lava down the side of a volcano, and as I struggled out of the car, I felt empty like an old, cold crater.

'Are you sure, Kathy, you look very pale.' New lines seemed to have appeared on Auntie's face too.

'What shall I call you?' A searing pain cut across my forehead. 'I don't think that I can call you *Mother*, because that's who Mother is.'

'No, call me Auntie,' she sighed, 'I really don't mind. Then, perhaps, we won't upset her. I'll just have to keep telling myself that you are my daughter instead of my niece.'

I followed her home, foot hard on the accelerator to keep up with the Alvis, and bouncing in and out of every pothole in the road.

How could that woman be my mother? My mother is a homemaker: caring and loving. A real mother, even though she did send me away for fear of what the neighbours might say. Though, I suppose, she must have had enough worries in the past: that they would find out I wasn't her real daughter; that I was the result of her husband's affair with another woman, who, even worse, was her sister. I braked sharply around a tight bend, trying to keep Auntie in sight. The wheels slid out behind me, and it was only instinct that helped me to straighten up and keep in the road.

Aunt Sylvia is so headstrong, a woman in a man's world of business. She fell in love with someone that she shouldn't, and got herself pregnant. I'm not a bit like her. The steering wheel bumped my tummy yet again, and I thought for a few moments. *Jeepers, I am though, aren't I?*

Chapter Twenty-Eight

Thankfully, no one came out to meet us when we arrived back, bumped about and breathless.

Aunt Sylvia pushed open the front door. 'You'd better telephone Emily, Kathy; it's far safer than flying home.'

I hadn't spoken to Mother since Saturday morning when I told her I was engaged, and I couldn't believe that so much had happened since then. She did write a touching letter about Ben's accident, saying, *'Whatever happens in this life has a reason. Remember that, Kathy, even though we can't see it at the time.'* I wondered if she felt blessed for at least having her husband's daughter to bring up, instead of no child at all.

I sat on the little red velvet chair where I'd heard the news about Ben, whilst I waited for the operator to connect us. The telephone rang for ages. Mother never seemed to be anywhere near it, and I imagined her rushing in from the garden and standing in front of the hall mirror to tidy her hair, in case it was a customer, before she picked up the receiver.

'Hello?'

A big lump came into my throat at the sound of her voice. I couldn't speak.

'Hello? Is anybody there?' She gave a snort of annoyance and, turning away from the telephone, called out, 'Joe, is that you? The phone's just rung, but there's no one there.'

I heard his feet echoing on the tiles in the hall; he must have come home early.

'Give it to me, Emily.' I heard his warm voice, some fumbling, then, 'Hello?'

'Dad?' I managed to get his name out. 'Oh, Dad!' I sobbed.

'Kathy? Is that you? Are you all right? We're so sorry about Ben. What a shock.'

'Yes,' I managed to sob. 'But, Dad, there's . . . '

'What ever is the matter?'

'Oh, Dad, I've found out. I know.'

'Know what, love?'

'I know that Aunt Sylvia is my mother. I know everything.'

There was a long silence.

'Kathy, I'm so sorry. I knew this would happen if you went down there to stay with your aunt.'

'But she's not, is she? She's my *mother*. Oh Dad, what a mess.' I felt giddy as if I'd been spinning on a roundabout in the park, and gripped the side of my chair.

'I love you. I'm sorry.'

I could hear the heartbreak in his voice, but I couldn't answer. All the words I wanted to say felt log-jammed at the back of my throat.

'Your Mother wants to speak to you, I'll hand you over,' he said.

'Kathy?' Her voice sounded thin and weak as if she'd diluted it with crying.

'Mother?'

I heard her sob, and whisper, 'I can't, Joe.'

'Yes, you can, love, come on.' I imagined him putting his arm around her. How could he ever have had an affair with Aunt Sylvia when he obviously cared so much for Mother?

I pressed the receiver against my ear, straining to hear her soft words.

'Oh dear, I've been dreading this day for nineteen years. I'm so sorry we've deceived you. I love you, Kathy.'

'I love you too, Mother.'

'I'm sorry we didn't tell you. How could we? We didn't know when it would be the right time. We didn't know what to say. And now this. Oh, Kathy, I wanted you to be mine. I believed that you were. And now, I've lost you altogether. I can't bear it.' She blew her nose.

'No, you haven't. I am yours. You are my mother. You brought me up, and nothing's going to change that.'

I turned round to see Aunt Sylvia poised at the dining room door with what looked like a neat whisky.

'Let me speak to her.'

I handed over the receiver, and listened to her explaining how I'd found out.

'Don't worry, Emily,' she continued, 'I don't think anything's going to change, it's not as if she's a child any more, is she? I'll look after her, just as I said I would.'

Will things change? Will she look after me? I don't even know if I want to get close to her. I don't know how I feel.

April 30th 1930

The day passed in a blur. I fiddled with my engagement ring, letting the diamonds catch the light. *On Saturday, I thought that my future was set fast like these stones, but now it's as if they've fallen out and left gaps with ragged gold teeth: I was engaged to Ben, and now he's dead. My baby was going to have a father, and now I'll have to bring it up alone. Mother was my mother, but now Aunt Sylvia is.*

I tried to read the papers. There were some reports that Amy Johnson had little chance of making it to Australia alone in her Gipsy Moth, even though I believed wholeheartedly that she could. Surely, it was easier to fly there solo, than to sort out the problems I had in my life.

I picked up my embroidery, and tried to untangle the coloured silks, but the muddle of pinks, yellows, greens and blues refused to part.

I went out into the garden and came in again: I didn't know what I wanted or where I wanted to go.

If only Ben hadn't crashed in the fog. If only I wasn't pregnant. If only Aunt Sylvia had kept away from Dad. But if she had, I wouldn't have existed at all.

May 1st 1930

I was glad to see a letter on the mat from Abigail.

Dear Kathy,

I hope that you are bearing up; it's such an awful time for us here.

Mother stays in her room; she is so devastated, and Father marches about all the time, barking orders in such a bad temper as if everyone is to blame about Ben instead of him. And after all, it was Father who wanted him to go to Cranwell in the first place.

I can't bear it. I miss him so much. He was the most adorable brother. Well, you know that, don't you?

We've got to go all the way to Lincolnshire for the memorial service tomorrow. Poor, old darling, I wish you could be there with us.

Anyway, I can't stand it at home any more. I wondered if I could come and stay for a few days on the 3rd, if your Aunt doesn't mind.

All my love,

Abigail

I couldn't eat any breakfast, and sat holding the letter limply in my hands. *The service is today?*

'Who's the letter from, Kathy?' Aunt Sylvia tried to make some conversation.

I held it up. 'Abigail: may she come and stay on Saturday for a few days?'

'Certainly, that will be nice, she's a lovely girl.'

I winced at the praise, but hoped that one day, she would begin to think better of me. 'Thank you, Auntie.'

She must have been aware of my frustration, but she continued in a buoyant mood. 'Come into Teignmouth, Kathy and have a walk along the prom. Some sea air would do you good.'

'No, thanks, I just want to be somewhere quiet today.'

'All right, my dear, must dash.' And off she went to the shop.

Uncle put his hand on my shoulder as Mabel bustled about clearing the breakfast things. 'There's something else, isn't there, Kathy?'

I closed my eyes to prevent my tears escaping, and swallowed. 'Ben's memorial service is today, and I won't be there. What am I to do? I can't stay trapped in here all day with my memories.'

'You could go to the church in the village.' Uncle struck a match for his pipe.

'No, if someone saw me, I would have to explain why I was there.' I shook my head. 'That would make it worse. I can't go to the aerodrome; it would hurt too much, and Teignmouth would only remind me of things I'd rather forget.'

The tobacco curls glowed red as he drew some air through them. 'How would you like to come for a little trip up the river with me for a change? I could borrow one of Bill's twelve-foot dinghies, and I'm sure Mabel would make us a picnic.'

'Would it be safe for me?'

'Yes, I should think so,' he smiled. 'You were attempting to fly home in a Gipsy Moth the day before yesterday.'

In my mind I saw a picture of Ben's plane coming down in the fog, and an idea came to me. 'Could I pick some flowers to scatter on the water for Ben?'

'I think that would be a lovely idea. Wrap up warm; it can be quite chilly on the river, you know, even if it is sunny.'

Grateful for something I could do, I went to look for some flowers. I had thought of the scarlet tulips in the ornamental urn, but they were past their best and when I picked one, all the petals dropped like tears. There wasn't much else except for a few shy, white lilies of the valley sheltering under the rhododendrons. They would have to do. I picked a bunch, and their sweet perfume made me feel light-headed as I walked indoors.

'Let me wrap those in some wet cotton wool to stop them drooping, Miss Kathy.' Mabel's eyes glistened. 'Did you know that lilies mean 'a return to happiness'?'

'No,' I whispered.

And she hugged me tight.

'Here she is! I'll just go and check everything is shipshape and Bristol fashion with Bill. You sit yourself down on that capstan for a moment,' Uncle said. 'I won't be long.'

The oily sea lapped to and fro against the harbour wall, and the boat, named *Windspeed,* bobbed about waiting for an adventure. I wondered if a steady trip up the river with an unhappy pregnant girl would be enough for it. The sun reflecting off the water and shiny brass fittings, made me squeeze my eyes tight, and the sweet smell of the lilies in my hands blew into my face on the breeze. *Would there be wreaths of flowers at the service? Did Mother and Dad send one? I haven't have time to ask them.*

'Did you see that, Kathy?'

I blinked open my eyes and then screwed them up again, shading them with my hand, as Uncle shoved an armful of cushions and rugs into the boat.

'No, what happened?'

'That man over there knocked his binoculars into the water and his wife hit him with an oar. They'll have a fine trip.'

Wife. The word echoed in my head. I'd never be Ben's wife now. The flowers trembled softly in my hands.

'Come on, my dear; let me help you climb in. It will rock a little, but the sooner you sit down and make yourself comfortable, the better.'

Sitting in the bottom of a small dinghy with the boom hovering beside my head wasn't the best place to be when I was the size of a baby whale, but I didn't care.

I watched the sea gulls swooping down to snatch scraps of mackerel from the quay as Uncle got ready to cast off. I'd love to live on the wind like them, free from all my troubles, I thought, as I tucked the lilies of the valley under my seat to keep them cool.

A couple strolled along the quay hand-in-hand: he in his RAF uniform and she in some cream trousers and a sailor collar. My heart missed a beat. They looked like Ben and me! And as they turned to kiss each other, oblivious to all the activity around them, I felt sick.

'You do look pale. Let's get out of the harbour, Kathy, you'll feel much better when we're speeding along on open water.' He rowed the dinghy out from the quay before setting sail. Eventually, free of the crowd, we zipped along unimpeded, as the gentle waters of the river made a satisfactory swash, swash sound against the prow, and the couple became mere dots in the distance.

'This is more relaxing than the diesel engine, isn't it?' Uncle sat behind me, guiding the tiller and pulling on the ropes. 'You'll have to mind your head when the boom goes over, though.'

I glanced back at him. With his pipe clenched between his teeth, and his blue eyes surveying the river, he looked every inch the sailor, pointing out things of interest: river boats loaded with clay; cormorants and grey wagtails raking for cockles and mussels; children, pretending to be dolphins diving through a rubber tyre; and a heron sweeping up into the air with a fish floundering in its bill. We sailed past the village spread out around the red stone church, and could make out the windows of Hillfields reflecting the May sunshine, then on up the broad, gentle river, lost in our thoughts.

It was nearly eleven o'clock, and I imagined the scene at Cranwell. I'd never been to a memorial service, but I had seen military funerals on the newsreels. Because they were always in sombre black and white, it was hard to imagine on this spring day, with the sun shining on the sparkling blue river and the soft green hills, that something so sad should be going on in a bleak cemetery in Lincolnshire. *Was the sun shining there too? Would there be a military band with muffled drums? Would a bugler play*

The Last Post? I couldn't believe that this was all for Ben and his colleagues. *There would be no coffins draped with Union Jacks. Would they fire some guns and disturb the complete, absolute silence? Would the birds flap out of the trees in alarm?*

I imagined Abigail standing there between her parents, trying not to cry whilst ranks of grim-faced airmen stood to attention.

Uncle Jeremy reached out and touched my arm. 'I think it's time for your flowers now, my dear.'

I brought the lilies out, and their perfume wafted away on the breeze as I jingled their tiny white bells. Gently, I undid Mabel's thread and removed the cotton wool. I threw them into the river where they landed higgledy-piggledy and bobbed about. *This is how Ben drowned in the swirling waters of the Bristol Channel.*

All the memories of my life with him flooded back: as children filling my new Wellingtons with wet mud; Saturday afternoons fiddling with his motorbike; last summer, when innocent friendship had grown into passionate love.

A red Gipsy Moth droned up the river as if in salute.

Things should have been so different.

Eventually, Uncle Jeremy landed us in a small, sandy cove. He secured the rope around an overhanging tree, and helped me make myself comfortable, leaning against a large log, with the cushions and rugs from the boat.

He offered me a sandwich. 'Come on, Kathy, some food will do you good.'

But, the bread and ham stuck in my mouth, I couldn't swallow them. So, I had to have a cup of tea from the flask instead, to wash them down.

He lay on his jacket and shaded his eyes with his hat. 'I'm sorry that you've had such a hard time, Kathy. It's been one thing after another, hasn't it?' He reached for another sandwich.

I nodded. I felt raw inside, as if I'd been ripped apart, and the baby which had been lulled to sleep by the river, now ground down into my pelvis, and kicked up against my ribs.

'It's a shame about you and Sylvia,' he said. 'I had hoped that being down here would have brought you both together, but it seems to have driven you further apart.'

I shrugged my shoulders, and sighed.

Uncle tipped his hat back to squint at me. 'We have been trying for a baby, you know.'

It was as if a loud gong started to reverberate in my head.

'What?'

'Of course, we've not been married for a year yet; it's still early days.'

How old is she? She's older than Mother. She must be nearly forty! Surely, she's far too old.

'Sylvia managed to recover from the tragedy of giving you away,' Uncle continued, 'and built her life around her career to blot out the past. When we married, she gave up her bookshop in the hope that she might be able to have a family at last, but nothing happened, so that's why she's opened a new one down here. When she heard that you were in the family way, she also thought she was pregnant, and was delighted that you could share your time together, but it wasn't to be. Every month, she's been so disappointed, and . . . I must admit, I'm glad to get away to the boathouse sometimes. I love her though, with all my heart.'

'I wish I'd known about everything. I can't believe that Mother, Dad and Auntie all kept it a secret from me.'

'She's always cared for you, Kathy. Always sent money each month to help pay for your upkeep.'

'That makes me sound as if I'm a public building! Why couldn't I be normal like all the other girls? Just normal. One mother. One father.' I jabbed the sand with a stick to make two eyes. 'Some brothers and sisters of my own.' I drew a smile underneath to make a happy face. 'But, now I know why I didn't have any of those,' I said, scrubbing the picture out.

Uncle Jeremy got up. 'Look the tide's beginning to go out again; we shall have to hurry before the mud is exposed and we run aground.' He gathered the flask and sandwich papers, hauled me up and helped me into the boat. Then, he pushed off and climbed in. 'There's a following wind too,' he said, tugging the sails as the dinghy fairly flew down the river towards Teignmouth.

There was no sign of my scattered flowers.

Chapter Twenty-Nine

May 3rd 1930

Abigail and I sat up in our beds on the Saturday night, cradling mugs of cocoa.

'We'd better drink this before it gets cold.' I stirred the milky froth into the chocolate until it disappeared. 'I don't really feel like it though.'

'I don't fancy any either; I really don't feel hungry. I've hardly eaten all week.' Abigail's face was as pale as her pillowcase.

'Poor Abigail, I noticed you playing with your dinner.' I stroked the mountain in the bedclothes made by my tummy. 'Mabel's been watching over me like a mother hen; she's made me munch my way through three meals every day for the baby's sake.'

Abigail half smiled, and placed her mug on the bedside table. 'It's so nice to be here with you again, Kathy. I really needed to get away; it's been awful at home. But what about you? I'm sorry it was me that had to tell you the sad news. I really wish it wasn't true. It's such rotten luck.' She leant over and picked up her handbag from the floor. 'I've got something for you,' she said, handing me a little brown packet.

'What is it? Oh, drat! I've spilt my cocoa on the sheet!'

Abigail hurried to get a wet flannel to wipe the mess away. 'Open it and see,' she called over her shoulder.

I felt the package. 'It's all angular and hard.'

'Hurry up!' She came back, the light flickering in her eyes for the first time since she arrived that afternoon.

I dug my fingers inside. 'Oh, it's one of Ben's Meccano aeroplanes,' I said, pulling it out, and caressing it.

Abigail mopped up the cocoa. 'I squirrelled it away for you before Mother began to sort out his things.'

Somehow, it felt warm as if Ben had just finished it.

I hugged her, 'Thank you so much!'

She climbed back into her bed. 'You know, I keep remembering all sorts of little things about Ben that I'd thought I'd completely forgotten. My first memory ever is of him pulling me along in a little wooden wheelbarrow. I can feel the bump, bump, bump over the grass, and I can see him jogging along in front of me. He wore a green sweater with a hole where his grazed elbow poked through. Even now, that mix between fear and excitement makes me laugh.' She dabbed her eyes on the sheet. 'It would, if it wasn't so sad.'

I fingered the little plane. 'Do you remember us filling up my new Wellingtons with wet mud? I was so proud of them and begged to be able to come over to your house to show Ben. They were black and shiny just like his. I felt so grown-up. Then we had a big discussion about how waterproof they were, and he suggested that we test it by filling them up with sloppy mud.'

'Yes, I remember. Didn't it occur to you that jumping in a puddle would do the trick? I couldn't understand why on earth a *girl* would want to get herself dirty. Maybe he was jealous that your boots were shinier than his?'

'I don't know. But I remember how jealous you were when he won the prize at Sunday school for the best drawing.'

'Yes, I'd spent ages on mine, and he goes and dashes his off at the last minute before Church, and won. Who ever heard of the animals arriving at Noah's Ark on a circus train?' She shook her blonde curls which even after a day's travelling, still looked perfect. 'He said he did that so he'd only have to draw their heads and necks. I think he just wanted to get something mechanical in the picture.' She smiled with tears in her eyes.

'He is . . . I mean, he was good at drawing.' I pulled his last letter out from under my pillow, and showed her the Gipsy Moth on its way to Haldon. 'He was so excited to be chosen to come to Devon.'

Abigail handed it back. 'I was really jealous of you too, Kathy, you know.'

'Really?'

'Yes, he was my brother, but he always spent more time with you. He never seemed to have any for me. He never wanted to have tea with my dolls, or even to play schools. I used to spend ages setting up a classroom, and all I had to teach were my dolls and good old Teddy.'

'I'm sorry; I just wanted to be outside doing something, or finding out how something worked. You used to come with us, though didn't you?'

'Yes, I couldn't bear being alone. Now, I will be alone without him. He used to be such a shield against Mother and Father. He would always try to make peace and smooth things over.' She pointed to my bump. 'But, what are you going to do without Ben? What about the baby, Kathy? It must have been so hard waiting for him for so long, and now he's gone.'

'Yes, if I hadn't been going to marry Ben, I might even have married Paul.' I examined the ring on my finger; I hadn't taken it off since Ben put it on for me. Then I looked up, Abigail's face had turned whiter than white, she opened her mouth, but no sound came out. I thought she was going to faint. It seemed like several minutes, but was probably only a few seconds until, like someone trying to wake from a nightmare, she managed to speak,

'Paul? What are you talking about?'

My temperature soared like a geyser. 'Oh no, I shouldn't have said that. I didn't want you and Ben to know.' I flapped the bedclothes up and down to cool my body. 'I've felt so terrible about this. I'm sorry, Abigail, but when I first came here, I fell hopelessly in love with him. I didn't mean to, I was completely under his spell.'

She jumped out of bed. 'Kathy, how could you? What about Ben? What about your baby?' Her blue eyes burnt like flames of gas in her angry white face.

'I tried so hard to ignore him. I'm so sorry.' I swallowed, as a sick feeling rose in my throat. 'I managed to break away in the end; but I was totally entranced. Abigail, you should be so wary of him.'

'I don't believe any of this bunkum! How could you? How could you, knowing that Ben was pining away for you, breaking his heart all alone at Cranwell? You've deceived us both. Why didn't you tell me when I was here before?'

'Because it was all over by then, and you appeared so keen on him. At first though, he said he really loved me; he'd never loved anyone as much before. I was flattered. I was enchanted. I didn't know what to do. I didn't mean to fall in love with him. I'm so sorry. I feel dreadful.'

'Do you still love him?'

'No, of course not. It wasn't real; it was infatuation. I can see that now. I'm going to stay true to Ben's memory. There couldn't be anyone else.' I hauled myself up on the pillows. 'Don't set your sights on him any more, Abigail. He can't help himself when it comes to girls; he just leads them on. I didn't realize how bad he was. I'd better let you know he's got another girl now, Patricia. Ugh, her name always makes me shiver. She's a nurse at the hospital. I actually saw them kissing outside my ward.'

Abigail flopped on her bed. 'Oh, Kathy, I'd been hoping to see him again. He only sent me one letter; now I know why.'

'I'm so sorry.'

'I'm never going to find the right boy, I'm going to be an old maid, left on the shelf for ever.'

'And am *I* going to find anyone like *this*, on my own with a child?'

'Oh, gosh, I'm sorry, too.'

The silence hung between us.

Then the baby began to kick, digging into its favourite spot beneath my ribs. 'There's less than a month to go before it's born. I have no idea what happens, or how to do it. It's not the sort of thing you talk about, is it? All I've seen is Rosie having her puppies. That's all I know.'

'Well, Maureen's sister, Beatrice, told her all about it. Perhaps if we'd had older sisters . . .'

'But, did she tell *you*?' I turned to her, anxious to know what really went on.

'Are you sure that you want to know?'

'Yes. I need to.'

'Well, she said there was a lot of mess; if you're going to have it at home, you should put newspaper on the bed, to soak it up.'

I blanched. 'What mess? What's going to happen? I thought the baby just came out when it was ready.'

'Well, apparently, the baby's in a sort of sack of water. When that breaks, it makes quite a puddle, and there's often quite a bit of blood.'

'Why didn't anyone tell me about this? I had no idea. Does it hurt much?'

'Yes, Kathy.' Abigail frowned. 'The labour pains are rather like a bad monthly pain until you're ready to push.'

'But it's not that bad, is it?'

'She said Beatrice's baby felt all knobbly like a Savoy cabbage.'

'Jeepers!' I gasped. 'Oh, I don't think that I can do this. Like a *cabbage* of all things?' I crossed my legs.

'It weighed ten pounds. Remember how the Sally Allies fed her up? She'd had the pains for so long, that she didn't have enough strength to push it out.'

'So what happened?'

'They called the doctor, and he had to use some forceps. She said they looked big enough to bring a baby elephant into the world. I don't know exactly what they did with them, but it was born within seconds, like magic.'

My whole body ached at the thought of it. 'I wish that I could just have an operation, and that it would all be over when I woke up. It can't be that bad, surely? I really can't ask Aunt Sylvia.'

'What about your mother? I couldn't talk to mine, but surely you could?'

I caught my breath, ‘Oh, Jeepers!’

‘What is it, Kathy? It’s not starting now is it?’

‘No, you don’t know, do you?’

Abigail shook her head in bewilderment.

‘Hasn’t Mother told you?’

‘No?’ She frowned.

‘Oh, Abigail, this is even worse, it’s terrible: I’ve found out that Aunt Sylvia really *is* my mother!’ I covered my mouth with both hands as if to keep the terrible secret in.

‘Aunt Sylvia? *Mrs Trevelyan?* No, she can’t be!’

‘She is! I found a letter from my mother asking her if I could come and stay and reminding her that, after all, I was her *daughter!*’

‘It’s not true, is it?’

‘Yes, I’ve spoken to Mother.’

‘What will it mean, Kathy? Are you going to come and live in Devon for good?’

‘Good Heavens, no. No. She’s hardly been like a mother to me, has she? In fact, sometimes I think she’d rather have *you* as her daughter.’

‘Don’t be silly, Kathy.’

‘Look how she took you to help her open the shop. That should have been me.’

‘Yes, but you’re not interested in selling books, are you, you silly thing? But, I suppose that she would have asked you, if you hadn’t been pregnant. Oh, I’m sorry, Kathy. That was cruel.’

I waved her comment away. ‘That’s not all. Guess who my father is?’

‘I’ve no idea. Nothing would surprise me now.’

‘Dad.’

‘Dad? You mean your father?’

‘Yes, that’s right.’

‘What, your father *is* your father?’ Abigail jumped off the bed again. ‘I don’t understand.’

'Dad and Aunt Sylvia had an affair when Mother was ill because she'd had so many miscarriages. She got pregnant with me, and so Mother and Dad brought me up.'

'Oh, Kathy!' She sat on the bed beside me. 'But that seems quite a sensible solution. Everyone was happy?'

'Yes, but I didn't know. All my life has been a lie. Everyone has pretended that I was my mother's child. I even think they came to believe it too.'

'Didn't you have any idea? After all, you are tall like your aunt, and come to think of it you do look rather like her.'

'Yes, but I thought that was because she was my *aunt*. Most people resemble some member of their family, don't they? I also have Mother's nose and chin.' I rubbed them thoughtfully. 'Mother has green eyes, and I thought that combined with Dad's brown ones, I'd got hazel.'

'But, Mrs Trevelyan has green eyes too.'

'Yes, and we are both left-handed.' I turned my hand to and fro and frowned at my diamond ring.

'Oh, I say, Kathy,' Abigail bounced up and down. 'I've had the most wonderful idea! Why doesn't *she* bring up your baby for you?'

'What? Aunt Sylvia?'

'Yes, it would make things even between you.'

'But she's got her shop, she hasn't got any time.'

'Maybe . . . maybe, *I* could run the shop. I'm sure she'd trust me.' Abigail smiled confidently. 'That would leave you free to do whatever you wanted to do. Learn to fly if you liked.'

'No, I couldn't let you do that. She wouldn't want to be shackled with my baby. Uncle Jeremy said she'd been trying for one herself.'

'What? Isn't she a bit old now?'

'She's had several miscarriages, that's why she opened the shop to take her mind off things.'

'Well, that's it then, the perfect answer.'

'I'm not sure if I want to give my baby away.'

‘But, you wouldn’t really, she is its grandmother after all.’

‘Well, I know how I felt, finding out after so long that I’d been deceived. How would you feel if you found out that your mother wasn’t your own after all these years?’

‘I’d be as pleased as Punch! I’d rather have Mrs Trevelyan any day!’

My head began to ache. ‘Let’s go to sleep now, I’m too tired to think.’ But, I couldn’t stop myself, and as Abigail turned off the light and settled down in bed, thoughts flooded into my mind.

I want to learn to fly so much. Every day Gipsy Moths drone and buzz across the sky. I want to be up there with them. I want to see the world as Ben did. I want to explore like Amy Johnson. I want to be free.

I remembered my flying lessons; the thrill and the excitement of actually leaving the ground and soaring through the sky. *Through the sky!* That’s where I belong.

Right on cue, the baby began to grind around again, muscling its shoulders deep inside, and exercising with hobnail boots against my ribs. I rubbed the painful spot.

Oh, Baby, you’ve been with me for eight months. I can’t give you away, can I? You’re part of me, part of Ben. You’re all I’ve got left of him. Yet, Uncle Jeremy said, that I’d had a happy childhood. Could I give you such a happy time? Would it be fairer to let Aunt Sylvia bring you up? Give her a chance too? Can I trust her? Would she make a good mother? And pictures of how she’d been too busy for me since I arrived in Devon came into my mind; she’d even forgotten I was coming.

I don’t know. I just don’t know.

Chapter Thirty

May 4th 1930

Aunt Sylvia put down her knife and fork, and picked up her wine glass.

'Congratulations, Paul, and you too, Patricia.'

Uncle Jeremy raised his glass. 'Congratulations.'

Abigail and I had been struck dumb with the news we'd just heard. *Paul and Patricia were engaged!*

They'd arrived just before lunch, making Mabel rush round, laying more places at the table, and putting extra vegetables and potatoes on to boil.

If Abigail always looked like a freshly wrapped doll, then Patricia, (that shiver again) looked like a freshly wrapped doll, dressed up as a nurse. Even out of her uniform, she looked starched, scrubbed, and pressed. She stood ramrod straight beside Paul, a matron in the making, in her navy crêpe de Chine suit with white collar and cuffs. She gave me a polite nod as we were introduced, and I wondered if she remembered me from the hospital visit. I suppose she had good reason to.

However, she'd kept her left hand tucked away, and it wasn't until we had begun our main course, that Paul cleared his throat, and announced that they were to be married.

I glanced at Abigail. Her face was a picture of anger, and disbelief, the agony clearly showing in her eyes as she watched Patricia's platinum ring sparkle, the round blue sapphire, reflecting the happy couple's eyes, surrounded by twenty-two tiny diamonds. 'One for each year of my life,' she tinkled, as Paul turned his magical gaze upon her.

Then he looked at me, and I could see a little frown between his eyes. 'Kathy, you have something to celebrate as well, don't you?'

'What's that?' I couldn't think of anything at all that needed celebrating.

'You're part of the family now: my stepsister.' He raised his glass.

I felt the colour drain from my face.

'Really?' I took a sip of water. 'How do you know, anyway?'

'Father told me.'

Uncle Jeremy looked a little sheepish.

'Well,' Paul grinned, 'if my father is married to your mother, you must be.'

Aunt Sylvia, who, up until now, had been laughing and was delighted with her stepson's news, turned a deathly pale, and glanced at Patricia and Abigail. 'We haven't been talking about it, Paul,' she whispered.

'Well, perhaps you should,' he said, and sipped his wine.

At last they left, and Aunt Sylvia urged us to have some coffee with her in the sitting room. I didn't want to, but there was no choice.

'I'm sorry you had to hear all about this, Abigail. He really shouldn't have broadcast it like that to all and sundry.' She pressed her fingers to her forehead.

'Please don't worry, Mrs Trevelyan, Kathy told me last night. I think it's charming. How wonderful to be able to be mother-and-daughter after all this time.'

Aunt Sylvia and I looked at each other helplessly.

'And it's especially nice,' Abigail continued, 'because you'll have Kathy's baby to look after, if you can't have your own.'

Aunt Sylvia, lost for words, looked from me to Abigail, and to Uncle Jeremy. 'What *have* you been telling them, Jeremy? No one knows apart from you.'

He laughed nervously, 'People must have wondered why there's no sign of any children yet, and why you've been busy opening another shop. Perhaps Abigail has a point. Perhaps you should bring up Kathy's child, especially as you missed *her* childhood years.'

But she shook her head.

'Wait a minute. What about me?' I raised my hand, the diamonds sparkling. 'I may want to bring up my own baby by myself.'

'But, how can you, Kathy?' Auntie's fine brows knitted together. 'Where will the money come from? Where will you live? Surely you're going to have the baby adopted?'

'Adopted?' My mouth went dry again. 'I can't give my baby away to a stranger.' I took a deep breath. 'It's my baby. It's all I have of Ben.'

Abigail got up and put her arms around me. 'I'm sorry, Kathy.'

Aunt Sylvia took my hand. 'Kathy, I know someone from the Adoption Agency who comes into the shop. I'll get her to come round for tea one day and talk to you.'

'No, thank you, I don't want to talk. I'm going to keep it. It's mine. Uncle Jeremy, they can't make me give it away, can they?'

'Kathy,' Uncle Jeremy picked up his pipe. 'I should at least listen to what Sylvia's lady has to say. You don't have to take her advice, you know.'

I rubbed my huge tummy and wondered what I was going to do.

May 7th 1930

On Wednesday afternoon, steely rain clouds, rolling in from the west, swallowed up the sun which edged them in gold, like grand invitations. Aunt Sylvia switched on the light, and within a few minutes, the rain poured down outside. She peered into the gloom. 'Oh, there's the bus, she'll be here in a minute. Poor woman, in that deluge.'

Abigail and I followed her as she rushed to the front door, and flung it open.

'I'm so sorry, Mrs Dawson. We should have come and met you in the motor car.'

'It's no problem at all, my dear.' Mrs Dawson shook her macintosh outside. 'Quite used to it. When I was in the Land Army during the War, we worked in every kind of weather; rain or shine,' she beamed at us. 'Now, shall I go in here?'

'Yes, of course.' Aunt Sylvia took her raincoat. 'This is my niece, Kathy, and her friend Abigail.'

'Hello, my dear.' Mrs Dawson shook my hand. 'Oh, you are like your aunt.'

Aunt Sylvia pursed her lips. 'Do sit down.'

'Thank you.' Mrs Dawson made her ample form comfortable on the sofa.

'Now, as you know, I've come along from the Adoption Society. Our aim is to provide a good life for unwanted children, by finding a home for them with childless couples. Now, I understand that this is what you would like, Miss Mason?'

I felt my face glow red, and my heart thumped against my ribs.

'You can trust us to adhere to the utmost secrecy because, my dear, most of our adopting families are from the middle classes, and they dread their neighbours finding out that their children were born out of wedlock.'

I glanced at Aunt Sylvia, but she kept her eyes firmly on our visitor.

'And,' Mrs Dawson continued, 'they usually tell them that their real parents are dead, so they don't find out the horrific truth about their origins.'

'They tell them that their parents are *dead*?' The colour drained out of my face, and my cold, clammy hands stuck together. I thought I was going to be sick.

'Yes, dear, these respectable people must keep up appearances.' Mrs Dawson straightened her jacket. 'I must also say that secrecy also protects the family from the interference of the natural mother who, if she could trace them, would be unable to resist making contact.'

'But, what if I don't like the new parents?'

'Well, I'm sorry, my dear, if you entrust us to find your baby a new family, you give away your right to know where it has gone. We have to protect them you know.'

'What about me? You can't take my child and destroy its identity. You can't take my child and hide it from me!' I said, nearly on fire.

'Let me assure you, Miss Mason, the Adoption Society ensures that natural parents do *not* retain any contact or knowledge of their children.' She opened her large leather bag to get out some papers.

I couldn't stop myself. 'I want my baby to know who its mother is.' I raised my eyebrows at Aunt Sylvia pointedly. 'I want it to know what a wonderful father it had. I want to see my baby grow up. I want to see its first smile, its first steps, and its first day at school.' Abigail grabbed my arm to steady me. 'I want to keep it. It's *mine*. *No* one is going to bring it up except me. I don't care what everyone else thinks. It's my baby. It's part of me. And it's all I have left of Ben.'

'Kathy.' Aunt Sylvia stood up, nearly knocking over the tea tray. 'Calm down, this won't do you any good.'

'Well, my dear,' Mrs Dawson shuffled her papers. 'Let me tell you this. Giving up your baby can help someone else's pain: mothers who have lost their babies, or who are unable to have them in the first place. Surely it's better for your baby to be brought up in a family that wants it and will look after it properly?'

Abigail looked from Aunt Sylvia to me, and nodded.

I understood what she meant, and I sighed as my baby squirmed around. 'But, you don't know for sure, do you? I want to know exactly what happens to my baby.'

'I don't think that you're ready to make any decisions yet, Miss Mason. Let me see you again in a week, or two.'

'Won't you stay for a cup of tea, Mrs Dawson?' Aunt Sylvia looked as angry as the clouds outside.

'No, thank you, Mrs Trevelyan, I'll see myself out.' And she went, shutting the door firmly behind her.

'Kathy, what ever were you thinking of? You were very rude.'

'I want to keep my baby, Aunt Sylvia. I'm going to do it on my own, even if you didn't.'

I felt the child inside me limbering up for the battle.

That night, after tossing and turning for hours, I had a nightmare. I was cuddling the heavy, warm weight of the newborn baby's body close to me, as I kissed its feathery hair. Its soft breath caressed my skin, and its sweet, milky smell filled my head. Then, Mrs Dawson wrenched the baby away from me as it nestled so safely in my arms. 'No!' I screamed. 'Please don't take my baby away!' She grinned at me like a manic Cheshire Cat.

Then Abigail cradled me, and rocked me back to sleep.

May 8th 1930

The next morning, she had a letter from her father begging her to go home. Her mother was inconsolable about Ben's death. He didn't know what to do with her.

'I'm sorry, I'm going to have to go, Kathy.' Abigail's tear-stained face looked drawn and haggard. 'Can you manage on your own?'

I nodded, but my head ached with lack of sleep. 'Come back soon.' I tried to smile.

I watched her pack the clothes she had only recently put away. 'Abigail, you're my only shield against the world too. You are my link with Ben, and you stood by me when I fell pregnant. What will I do without you?'

We clung onto each other for dear life and, for the millionth time, I wished I hadn't got myself in such a mess.

With Abigail gone, the thought of adoption scared me so much that as soon as it surfaced, I pushed it to the back of my mind. I didn't want to think, or even talk about it, and kept well out of Aunt Sylvia's way, only appearing for meal times and then scuttling away like a crab to the sanctuary of my room.

I took some old newspapers up with me for something to read, but they were all boring: politics, finance, and diplomacy. Then I spotted an article asking: What *could* Amy Johnson, an inexperienced female, be thinking of to attempt to break Bert Hinkler's record flight to Australia in sixteen days? Surely it was an impossible ambition for a young woman to achieve?

I hadn't given Amy Johnson a thought in the past few days, so I decided to see if there was anything else about her pioneering journey.

Scanning the paper for news, I found a small paragraph: Amy had taken off in her Gipsy Moth on May 5th. Heart beating, I realized she was already on her way.

Ten thousand miles to the other side of the world. I should love to do that; I should love to be anywhere but here. I wish I had her confident smile. I wish I could be making flying history like her.

I stole downstairs to Uncle's study to find an atlas, and hurriedly spread it open on my bed. The names of all those foreign places, like those on the wireless dial, filled me with excitement, and for about half an hour, I was lost in flying around the world. Discovering mountains, rivers, seas and plains I would never explore, and cities I would never visit, unless of course, I did learn how to fly. *But, I'm not going to do that, am I? My baby comes first.* Thoughtfully, I cradled my tummy.

Nevertheless, I cut the articles out and stuck them in my scrapbook. *What an adventure through sun, rain, wind and fog, beating off wild animals and natives? Even crossing the Equator. All alone in a little Gipsy Moth, just like the one I flew at Haldon.*

I felt extremely close to Amy. I could shut my eyes and imagine that I was tucked into a cockpit like hers, gripping the joystick, my feet on the rudder pedals and the wind rushing past and playing a joyful tune in the wires, whilst I fixed a course south-eastwards to Australia.

Chapter Thirty-One

I hurriedly flicked through the rest of the papers: on the first day Amy reached Vienna, whereas Hinkler had managed to get a hundred miles further to Rome, but on the second she had pushed on to Constantinople, whilst he had only got as far as Malta. *Hooray!* I traced a trembling finger over the map. *She's trying to beat him by daring to fly over the mountains, whilst he flew over the Mediterranean.* I forgot all my problems as I feverishly looked up the faraway place names in the atlas. Then, I drew tiny pencil crosses on the cities and towns which I joined together with faint dotted lines. *I hope Uncle doesn't notice. I can't make out anything on the poky maps in the papers. I wish I'd paid more attention to Geography at school; it was never such fun as this. It's like exploring another mysterious world.*

In the morning, I rushed downstairs as soon as I heard the papers flop on the mat. Then I carefully opened them and looked for any news of Amy Johnson, before just as carefully folding them up again, and placing them on the breakfast table for Uncle Jeremy. I found out that she had a real chance of reaching Karachi, and therefore, beating Bert Hinkler's record time to India, and I danced like an elephant around the kitchen.

May 11th 1930

By now she was headline news: after flying at eight thousand feet above the snow-capped Taurus Mountains, she'd arrived in the north-west Indian city at last. I found myself rubbing my eyes, gritty with imaginary sand as I read about how she'd been grounded by a storm in the desert. She'd had to use her luggage as chocks to stop her Gipsy Moth being blown away whilst she sat there, revolver ready to protect her against wild dogs. *Jeepers!*

At night, I had long, colourful dreams of flying endlessly into the sunrise. Clouds of orange, lavender and pink swooshed past the wings of my plane. Exotic birds circled above me in the sky, whilst dangerous crocodiles and sharks brooded below, waiting for a tasty meal. But, I wasn't scared at all, and flew on, and on, over snowy mountains, sandy deserts and wide blue seas until a land appeared on the horizon. There I could see bouncing kangaroos, and koala bears waving from eucalyptus trees: *Australia!*

I never tired of those dreams, and could revisit them again every night. But the strange thing was, I never actually landed on that tropical shore; the dream slipped away at that point, or I woke up, frustrated and longing for my journey to end.

Battling with my own problems, and trying to keep them tucked away at the back of my mind, I spent hours poring over the atlas, searching for foreign cities, or tiny islands. I lugged encyclopaedias upstairs too, though I knew I shouldn't in my condition, so I could discover more about these mysterious places. Often, I'd get caught up in reading about some war, invasion, or rice production figures before hastily returning to Amy's flight. When a Gipsy Moth droned by outside my window, reminding me not only of Amy, but also of Ben and his baby, I would stop and stroke my tummy. I knew that I would have to make a decision about its future, but I wasn't ready yet.

I felt so akin to that ordinary girl, the typist from Hull, that it was almost as if I knew her personally. I imagined climbing into the heavy leather, wool-lined flying suit, with a cumbersome parachute on my back; tucking my hair inside my helmet and pulling down the goggles to protect me from the deafening, blinding wind. I stood beside her under the tropical sun when she was photographed in baggy khaki shorts, and felt the blistering heat burning my face. I cocooned myself in the cockpit with her, living for the moment, with no thought for the future, apart from arriving safely and breaking Bert Hinkler's record.

Anxious for the news each evening, I waited by Uncle Jeremy's wireless, for the latest instalment of her adventure as she flew across India searching for Allahabad. But, the newscasters spoke in such a monotone, that they might have been reading the shipping forecast. *Don't they know how important her mission is?*

In my imagination, I scanned the ground as we hunted for the ancient city, and reassured her as she made a difficult landing at Jhansi, damaging a wing. We then followed the wide Ganges to Calcutta. It was like reading an adventure novel, and in fact, I had to go and find an exercise book so I could write it down in my own words. I drew my own maps too, much clearer than those in the papers, and stuck them in my scrapbook. I knew this was all a conscious attempt to push the problem of the baby into my *un*conscious.

Therefore, as the monsoon caught up with her, I pursued Amy Johnson down the Bay of Bengal to Rangoon through a blanket of thick clouds and a deluge of torrential rain which swamped her as she tried to find a way through the Arakan Mountains. At ninety miles an hour, she must have been terrified that she'd crash into a rocky ridge. However, to my relief, she made it through.

She was reported to be so pleased that a woman could succeed in a man's pursuit, in a world dominated by men. I know just how she felt. Even though women like her who were over twenty-one had the vote, they still weren't considered the equal of men, and had to work even harder to make their mark. So, I'm sure she took great pride in changing the plugs each evening, and draining the oil to make Jason ready for the next day's flight, not to mention, filtering her own petrol too.

At Insein, five miles north of Rangoon, she had the amazing luck of crash-landing (without her plane bursting into flames) onto the playing fields of the Government Technical Institute where her repairs, which would have taken three weeks in England, were made by the skilled people there in next to no time. But, she had lost her two-day lead over Bert Hinkler. Now they were level pegging.

I was so desperate for her to win. I willed her on as she set off again through heavy rain and cloud, climbing nine thousand feet over the mountains to reach Don Muang military aerodrome, twenty miles from Bangkok, only to be besieged by insects. As I went to sleep that night, I imagined them whirring and buzzing around my room, like questions about my baby's future.

May 18th 1930

The news came through that she'd been hampered by bad visibility flying down to Singapore, and had to make a landing in soft sand at Singora on the east coast of the Malay Peninsula. She had lost the chance of beating Hinkler's record now and I felt like shouting: *Come on Amy! Don't give up! You'll still be the first woman to fly solo to Australia!* But, it was rotten luck all the same.

Leaving Singora, Amy had to take off from a street crowded with curious local people, and I imagined the wings of her Gipsy Moth skimming their heads as they craned to see her, oblivious to the danger they were in. She landed at Singapore, four hundred miles away, wearing her khaki shorts amongst the elite of society all dressed in their Sunday best, but I'm sure she didn't care.

The next day, she decided to take a short cut over the Java Sea to Surabaya in the Dutch East Indies, but more heavy rain and thick cloud meant she was flying directly above the waves, lost in the brooding darkness of the storm. The reports said that in desperation, she prayed to be shown the way out. Miraculously, a gap in the clouds appeared and the sun shone through, painting a vibrant rainbow against the slate grey sky, and leading her to safety.

Amy and I have got a lot in common. She's the plucky girl in her tiny aeroplane made out of wood and linen, lost over a foreign sea, and trusting in God to see her through, and I'm also lost in a situation of my own making. She chose to fly to the other side of the world and therefore suffer its consequences, and I chose to lie with Ben, and I, too, am suffering the consequences. I wish I could be free to fly like her, even if it means flying low over the angry Java Sea and its hungry sharks. I trailed my finger over the map I was drawing. *Please God, guide me, like you are guiding Amy, to chose the right path.*

With relief, I read that Amy had landed on a sugar estate, two hundred miles west of Batavia, damaging Jason's wings which had to be mended with sticky tape, of all things. A Dutch airmail pilot guided her to Surabaya, in eastern Java, where amazingly, a local Gipsy Moth owner provided her with a new propeller. The papers pointed out that by that time, Hinkler had arrived at Port Darwin, and Amy's chance of the record was truly over. She must've had been deadbeat after all that she'd been through. *Keep flying, Amy; don't give up!* I wrote in my book. But secretly, I wondered if she'd ever make it.

A faulty magneto meant that she spent another night there, and had time to gather herself together again before setting off for Atamboea on the island of Timor, her final stop before crossing the treacherous Timor Sea to Port Darwin, on the north coast of Australia.

Later, locals on Sumbawa caught sight of her plane flying over.

Then: she disappeared.

Newspaper correspondents and radio bulletins could only guess where she was. I even caught Mabel dusting the wireless set that evening, waiting to hear if there were any fresh sightings.

'Poor girl, fancy coming down there in that jungle. Who knows what wild animals might eat her? Tigers or leopards. They should never have let her go. What if she's come down in the sea? All those hungry sharks.' She rubbed a stubborn spot, then gasped, 'Oh, I'm sorry, Miss Kathy, I'd forgotten about your young man.'

I smiled bravely; nothing that anyone could say would make any difference.

'It's so dangerous,' she carried on. 'When I went up to the village, everyone in the shop was full of it. Someone said that seaplanes had been sent out to search for her and even steamships had been called into action.'

As we waited, another plane purred its way up the river, and we listened in silence. At last, the bulletin came on, but the newscaster couldn't tell us any more than Mabel's rumours.

I prayed as I went to sleep that she would soon be found. It's strange, but I prayed for her more fervently than I'd prayed for Ben or myself.

Maybe if she achieved her goal, then so would I.

It wasn't until the next morning that news came through which sounded like a thrilling instalment of a story by H. Rider Haggard. In the sudden tropical darkness, she had landed in a field of giant ants' nests and had been surrounded by natives. By a miracle, they seemed to recognize her and her Gipsy Moth, and guided her to the log cabin of the man they called 'Pastor'. He could only speak a little French, no English at all, but provided her with a meal. She spent the night at the aerodrome and returned to Jason with donkeys carrying cans of petrol so she could set off on her final leg.

Amy had only five hundred miles to fly over the wide Timor Sea, and its hungry sharks, to Port Darwin: journey's end. Would she ever make it? The world held its breath. The Shell oil company positioned a tanker half way across, in case of an emergency landing. But, it made me laugh because the route over the sea in bright sunshine was so boring and featureless after the monsoon and mountains, that she had fun throwing down a cake to one of the sailors on board.

She passed over Melville Island, and saw Port Darwin straight ahead. She was so relieved to arrive in Australia at last, that she could hardly see through her tears to land the plane.

I cried with relief too that she'd arrived safely: the first woman to fly solo to Australia.

Ten thousand miles! Her prayers have come true; now will mine?

May 25th 1930

I sat up in bed surrounded by all the Sunday papers that Uncle Jeremy could get hold of. Amy Johnson may have achieved her goal and been the first woman to fly solo to Australia, but I was no closer to solving my problems. My stomach was huge now and the baby seemed to be nearly bursting through my tight skin. I traced my strange, flat tummy button through my nightie, and rubbed the top of my ribs where the indigestion stuck in me like a propeller blade. *The baby will soon be here. What am I going to do? What would Ben want me to do?*

I adored following Amy's journey; I wanted to be like her, just like Abigail wanted to be a film star. But, how could she ever go to Hollywood and be discovered? There was little chance that could happen, especially with parents like hers, and especially now Ben had gone. I could learn to fly properly, though; I'd already tried. I could be a pioneer like Amy, if only I could get some backing. The baby kicked right up under my ribs. I winced and stretched, trying to pull away from it. *What am I to do with you? Should I follow my dreams, or should I do the right thing? Which is the right thing, anyway?*

I studied my face in the mirror when I went to the bathroom. My cheeks were full and pink with the pregnancy, but my eyes were tired and the skin below them a dark smudge. *Can I really be a mother? Will I be a good one? Can I do it?*

I pulled out the well-thumbed pile of Ben's letters, and looked through them for a clue in all his clever cartoons of the Gipsy Moth flying a banner saying 'Kathy'. He wanted to marry me; he wanted us to have a happy life with our little bundle of love. *Ben, you won't be here, and I don't know if I can do it on my own. You'd want the best for the baby, wouldn't you?* I hugged my pillow, the one he'd slept on. If I had the baby adopted . . . My tears ran slowly down onto the cool linen. If I had it adopted, it would have a father, and the father's love that I couldn't give it myself. I used to love burying my face in the freshly sawn wood and putty smell of Dad's jacket when he came home. I loved playing cricket on the beach with him. Our baby would need a father, wouldn't it?

After all, I was adopted even if it wasn't official, and the mother that brought me up loved me and wanted me more than my real mother. Mrs Dawson said that any mother who was desperate for a baby because she was unable to have one, would love and care for an adopted one.

That's what I should do, isn't it?

Ben, you knew I always wanted to learn to fly like you; fly free like a Gipsy Moth. I think I am going to be like a moth, I've been locked up in this chrysalis, and now I'm going to stretch my wings and fly.

I rubbed my tummy, and the baby squirmed in response.

I am going to have my baby adopted.

'It's not as if I don't love you, baby; I do, but this will be best for both of us,' I whispered.

Once, I'd made my decision, I felt as if I was floating on air.

Chapter Thirty-Two

May 29th 1930
I'm sure I'm doing the right thing at last. I'm sure it's best for the baby to be brought up with a family that wants it and loves it, and maybe I'll be free to explore the world too.

'Kathy, are you ready?' Aunt Sylvia called up the stairs.

I quickly stuck the latest cuttings of Amy Johnson's arrival in Australia, and her triumphant flight down to Sydney in my scrapbook, and grabbing my hat and bag, hurried downstairs as fast as I could.

What sport! Amy's arrived in Sydney and the Prince of Wales is flying in today in his Gipsy Moth. I really want to see him, but I can't help blaming him in a way. If Ben hadn't come down on that proving flight, he would still be alive.

So, it was with mixed feelings that I set out in Uncle Jeremy's car with Aunt Sylvia and Mabel, along with most of the population of the South Devon coast to catch a glimpse of our Royal visitor in his flying machine.

In front of us and behind, a pageant of every kind of vehicle wound its way up to Haldon Aerodrome: cars of all sizes; buses and charabancs hired out for the day; bicycles with bells ringing; motorbikes weaving through the traffic, or balancing precariously, sidecars bursting with wives, children and picnic hampers; delivery vans with exasperated drivers; and horses patiently pulling carts or traps. And we could only go as fast as the slowest of all.

'Are you comfortable in the back?' Uncle Jeremy glanced over his shoulder.

'Yes, we're fine here, sir.' Mabel sat in charge of the wicker picnic basket on her lap. I knew she hadn't needed much persuasion to leave her chores on this special day.

But, a mix of frustration and excitement made me feel anxious and twitchy. I couldn't seem to keep my feet still, and I fiddled with my engagement ring which made little sunbeams dart about over the back of Uncle's seat.

'Look at all this traffic,' said Aunt Sylvia. 'Oh, watch out, Jeremy!' A motor car, struggling to get down the hill against the flow, was causing more chaos.

He steered towards the red earthy bank to make room. 'We'll be fine: His Royal Highness isn't due to arrive until half past one.'

At last we crackled over the gravel into the aerodrome, and were directed to the viewing area by a series of Boy Scouts. Each had his uniform pressed penknife sharp with badges and shoes sparkling in the bright sunshine, ready enough for a Royal inspection.

'Look!' Mabel gripped the picnic basket. 'Oh, look at all the red, white and blue! All the bunting and Union Jacks! Oh, listen to the brass band.'

'Could you just watch your side, Sylvia?' Uncle Jeremy reversed the car onto the grass near the airstrip, and then got the deckchairs out for our picnic.

'Do be careful, Kathy.' Auntie grabbed me as I tripped over a tussock of long grass. 'I knew we shouldn't have brought you. You could just as easily have stayed at home with Rosie in comfort, and watched the Prince of Wales drive past.'

'Yes, but it's not the Prince of Wales I want to see, it's his Gipsy Moth!' I eased myself into the chair as she steadied it.

I was too worked up to eat anything, so I sipped some cool lemonade from the Thermos. 'I think I'll have a look at the stalls and see how much the flags are. We must have some to wave.' I just couldn't sit still any longer.

'Can't you wait a minute, Kathy? I'll go for you when I've finished this.' Aunt Sylvia waved her knife at her plate. 'Please stay here and have a rest.'

'No, I'll go. Don't worry, it's just over there.'

Uncle Jeremy heaved me out of the chair again. 'Good gracious, Kathy, how much heavier are you going to get?'

I straightened up and rubbed a drop of lemonade off my tabletop of a stomach. 'Well, there's only a week to go now.'

Aunt Sylvia caught my hand as I passed her chair. 'Tell me, Kathy, have you decided what to do with the baby? It would be best for it to be adopted, you know.'

'I know, Auntie, and that's exactly what I'm going to do.'

I enjoyed seeing her face turn from concern, to surprise, to disbelief.

'You're going to have it adopted?' She dabbed her mouth with a paper serviette.

'Yes, and I'm going to learn to fly and become a pilot like Amy Johnson.'

And now, she was speechless too.

The stiff breeze which blew in from the sea, tugged at my straw hat, as I wound my way through the picnickers to the flag stall, decorated with fluttering Union Jacks of all sizes, and I bought four small ones.

Just then, the brass band struck up the National Anthem as the blue and silver flying machine appeared out of the hazy sky from Padstow and circled the aerodrome. I hurried back with the flags to the others. All around me, the crowd rose as one to cheer, and I wondered if Amy Johnson had this sort of welcome in Port Darwin.

'Look, there he is! He's sitting in the rear seat!' Aunt Sylvia staggered on the uneven ground in her high heels.

'He's all wrapped up in his great coat.' Mabel waved her Union Jack. 'It must be all that cold wind.'

Glancing up into the sky, I slipped a bit on the grass as I reached my chair, but regained balance in time to take a snap with my Kodak Brownie. 'Just look at that beautiful aeroplane.' I murmured, then: 'Oh no!' I looked down in dismay. A large wet patch was growing on my skirt, and my stockings and shoes glistened wet in the sunshine. In horror, I pulled out the back of my skirt; it was all wet too.

'It's just your waters breaking, my dear.' Mabel calmly began to pack the picnic away.

'My waters? Jeepers! What am I going to do? I'm all wet. What will people think?' I surveyed the crowd in panic.

'Don't worry; it's quite normal.' Aunt Sylvia wrapped the tablecloth around me to hide my acute embarrassment. 'But we are going to have to get you away from here, I think the baby's coming. It's a silly question, but do you think you can walk, Kathy?'

I nodded; my lips pressed together in determination. But, as the first pain tightened its grip, I groaned and cradled my stomach with both hands.

Far too heavy for Uncle Jeremy to carry me now, he supported me in his strong arms, and we agonizingly followed Aunt Sylvia and Mabel as they forged a way through the sea of people. We had to stop several times as the pains washed over me in unbelievable all-consuming waves, like volcanic lava, burning me red hot and raw to the very core where the baby waited, as if ready to erupt forth into the world.

'Where are we taking her?' Aunt Sylvia struggled past a large lady who would not move her chair to let us through.

'Over to the clubhouse.' Mabel took charge. 'There will be hot water, and it'll be cooler and quieter; a bit more private, I should think.'

Carefully, we picked our way among the chairs, tablecloths and picnic hampers, as his Royal Highness climbed out of his plane.

'Can't you see that my daughter is about to have a baby? Let us through!' Auntie commanded, as I kept my eyes firmly focussed on her back, and for the first time, I was glad that she was my mother.

At last, we reached the sanctuary of the clubhouse. Peggy was outside standing on a chair trying to see the Royal visitor, and didn't notice us until we were almost inside the door.

'Good Heavens, Miss Kathy, what ever's wrong?'

'The baby's coming,' I gasped as another pain took hold.

'We must get Dr Trevelyan.' Peggy jumped down.

'No, I can't see him now. I don't want him interfering!' I looked at Aunt Sylvia and Uncle Jeremy for reassurance.

'It's the best thing.' Auntie took my hand. 'The midwife will never be able to make it up the hill in all this hullabaloo.'

Peggy turned to her son who was still standing on his chair. 'Bobby, take your bike and please go and find Dr Trevelyan, he should be over by the engineering shed on that viewing platform they've built.'

'But Mother, I . . .'

'No buts, young man.' She made as if to cuff his ear. 'His Royal Highness will be coming back later this afternoon to fly off again; you can see him then.' Muttering under his breath, Bobby pedalled off in the direction of the large shed.

'Ow!' I held on to Uncle as another pain gripped my stomach. Peggy hurried inside and produced one of the canvas beds that Ben's friends had camped on when he had slept with me at the house. *Oh, Ben I wish you were here.*

Peggy set it up and Aunt Sylvia and Uncle Jeremy lowered me gently down. 'It's a bit spartan, but it'll do,' she said. 'There are some sheets over there, Mabel. Can you see those fresh towels? I'll get some water boiling.'

I lay there, the pains coming each time in more excruciating waves. I had never experienced anything like it. Auntie knelt beside me, soothing my forehead and holding my hand. She hadn't shown such tenderness since Ben died. Uncle Jeremy stood at the door filling his pipe, and looking out for Paul.

All this time, I'd been passive onlooker, but now, with the contractions coming closer and closer, I found myself taking centre stage in my consciousness. Aunt Sylvia's face fading into the shadows, the doorway framing Uncle Jeremy's silhouette, and the bright sunshine outside where the crowd roared three cheers for the Prince of Wales, all seemed part of another world. I heard Peggy and Mabel, murmuring quietly, as they boiled pans of water. *What was that for?* Then, they edged sheets of newspaper covered with brown paper under my bottom. *To catch the baby, and wrap it up? What was it Abigail said?*

Helplessly, I watched the hands creep round the large clock on the wall, telling me that the pains were coming every five minutes now. The camp bed made me feel as if I was in a field hospital in the Great War. I imagined that each contraction was like the thrust of a blunt, rusty bayonet clamped to the muzzle of a merciless metal gun, and I writhed and twisted away from the agony, whilst Aunt Sylvia bathed my feverish forehead with a cool, wet cloth.

I heard her murmur something, and then to my horror and delight, Paul's face appeared in my line of vision, obscuring the clock.

'Go away! I never want to see you again!' I groaned.

But, his hand was gentle on my hot brow. 'It's all right Kathy. I'm here now. I'm just going to feel your tummy and listen to the baby's heartbeat.' And although my whole body fought to resist him, his warm and soothing touch helped me to relax a little when the next contraction came. 'Well, that's all fine, you are doing well. I think you're nearly there.'

'What? I can't be, I've got another week.' I tried to sit up, and swing my legs to the floor. 'I've got to go home.'

Chapter Thirty-Three

Paul put his hand on my shoulder and his warmth soothed me again, despite my determination to escape.

'I can't do it, Paul. I can't. Please make the pain stop, please. I can't do it any more.'

'Just relax when the pains come. Try and breathe steadily: in through your nose and out through your mouth.' His concerned blue eyes looked into mine, as he lowered me back down.

'No, I can't, I can't. What am I going to do?'

Aunt Sylvia squeezed my hand. 'Just a little while longer, you can do it. Just a little while longer.'

'That's it,' Paul encouraged. 'Breathe in . . . and out. Good, you're doing well.'

As I tried to concentrate on the breathing, instead of the grinding pain, I stared into the depths of his eyes, and they gave me strength, until he said, 'Right that's fine; you can begin to push with the next contraction.'

'*Push?*'

Auntie held my hands tightly, as I tried to push with all my might.

'I'm never going to do this again. Never!'

'Come on, Kathy, a big push.' Paul's hand rested on my tummy.

'I am push . . .ing. It's no good; it's my punishment for being unmarried. It's no good; I can't do it! How did I get myself into this mess? Paul, get the baby out. Get rid of it. Oh . . . My . . . God!'

'Good girl,' he said, 'I can see the baby's hair. Come on Kathy, you can do it.'

'I just want to go now. I want to go home. I want to go home, and get back to normal. Aah!'

'That's it. It's coming. It's coming. Keep pushing.'

'I AM!'

Mabel hovered nearby with the clean towels.

There was a feeling of release, but I couldn't see what was happening.

'Push again, Kathy.'

I heard a clear tiny cry.

'It's a girl! It's a girl!' Aunt Sylvia cried, as Mabel wrapped it up. 'Oh, look, Kathy. Do you want to see her?'

All the fight in me flowed away like water through the moat of a seaside castle. 'No.' I turned away towards the wall. 'No, I'm not going to keep her: she's not ever going to be mine. Take her away.'

'Oh, Kathy.' She rubbed my back. 'Oh, my poor girl.'

I heard Mabel take the wailing bundle over to the sink.

'Let me help you give her a little wash.' Peggy turned on the taps. 'Oh, she is a real beauty,' she added in a whisper.

I didn't want to know.

'Yes, isn't she,' agreed Mabel. 'Look at her cute little nose. These dark blue eyes look so serious though, Peggy.' I heard the baby cry. 'There, there, sweetheart, the warm water won't hurt you.'

I put my hands over my ears to try to shut out their voices.

'Let's rip up this towel to make a nappy; I've got a large safety pin here on my apron. You never know when you might need one.' Peggy fussed about. 'There we go. It's a mercy the laundry came yesterday.'

Then, the room was hushed as Mabel rocked the baby.

Aunt Sylvia soothed my forehead. 'Paul's gone to see if the ambulance over on the far side of the airfield can take you home.'

I stared at the wall. A photograph of the clubhouse with a row of jolly airmen sitting cross-legged in front seemed to be from a different world.

I just want to die. I never expected it so be so awful.

Then as each minute passed, although the memory of the pain magically receded like the tide going out, the waves of emotion washed over me instead.

I feel like an empty seashell, all life ripped out of me, washed up on a beach by waves of guilt and shame. I hugged myself tight. *I want to run away, but I can't even sit up. How am I ever going to learn to fly?*

Paul came back. 'The ambulance is coming over, old thing; let's get you in it and down the hill before the Prince of Wales's entourage. You and your baby are certainly going to get a Royal welcome.'

'Don't make me hold the baby, Paul.' My dry, cracked lips stung. 'I don't want to see it.'

When I'd finally got home and into bed, Aunt Sylvia and Mabel had bustled in with a length of linen roller towel and a little brass bell which Auntie placed on the bookcase. 'We don't want you knocking this over again, do we?'

'What's that towel for?'

'We need to bind it around your tummy. Lift her up, Mabel.'

'What on earth for? It's sore enough as it is. I don't want that around me.'

'Everyone does it, my dear, to prevent a sagging figure.'

'Please leave me alone.'

'Now, Miss Kathy, my niece swears it kept her nice and flat.' Mabel's competent hands held me as Aunt Sylvia bound me firmly and fastened the towel with a big safety pin.

Paul knocked on the door.

'May I come in? Ah, the linen roller-towel trick; you'll be glad you did that.'

I grunted a reply, then, 'When can I get up and about?'

'You must stay in bed for at least a week to prevent excess bleeding.'

'You're joking.'

'No, it's very dangerous.'

'I wouldn't bleed to death, would I?'

'Well, yes, you might, so I should be a good girl, and stay put: Doctor's orders. Eight pounds, two ounces is quite a size, Kathy; we've just weighed her on the kitchen scales. Another week; and it wouldn't have been such an easy birth.'

'That was easy?'

'Yes, comparatively so, another seven days and the baby would have been that much bigger.'

Oh, God, I never want to do that again.

'Now, shall we bring her in here?'

'No. I don't want to see her. I told you, I'm going to give her away. Don't bring her in here, please.'

May 30th 1930

The linen towel had annoyed me all night. I pushed my finger under the edge, and scratched where it itched; my soft skin felt crumpled and crêpey, and my stomach concave and hollow. I didn't think about the baby; I hadn't even given it a name. It was no longer part of me, and I had no responsibility for it. It had gone, ripped out like a bad tooth. However, I didn't feel the relief a visit to the dentist brings, or the lightening of my burden. Apart from the afterpains, grinding away inside, and my angry breasts aching unbearably, I felt nothing, an emptiness, a void.

The weather became more like November than the end of May. Heavy black clouds, advancing from the west, brought driving rain which attacked the windows like sharp shrapnel, and ran down them in endless sheets; rivers forming and reforming down the oblong panes. Now and then, globules of icy hail mixed in with the rain and momentarily filled up the window frames like miniature snow drifts. Daylight had been replaced by a grey luminescence which hadn't the strength to fill the corners of the room, leaving them dim and gloomy. Mabel lit a fire to add a little cheerfulness, but the flames struggled to burn the damp, spitting coals.

I lay in bed, pale and ashen, my hard breasts throbbing from the milk which had 'come in' ready for the baby that I didn't even want to see. Drops, escaping under the great pressure, made damp patches on my nightdress despite the muslin squares stuffed down my brassiere.

The incessant sound of rain filled my head, I didn't think about Ben or Paul, I didn't even think about flying. My scrapbook with Amy Johnson smiling smugly from the cover, lay untouched on Abigail's bed where Aunt Sylvia had tidied it away. I felt as if I was in a waiting room; a place where time stood still, and nothing ever happened. I was suspended in a painful present with no hope of release.

Above the raindrops, I could hear the melody of Mabel's soft voice as she tended to the baby in the makeshift nursery next door. 'She's all asleep now, Mrs Trevelyan.'

'Thank you, Mabel. How's Kathy?'

'Still lying there, ma'am.' Mabel rattled the crockery on the tray. 'She hasn't touched a bit of her breakfast.'

Aunt Sylvia's heels tapped across the lino. 'Poor girl, I didn't expect her to take it like this. I've telephoned Mrs Dawson and she should be here directly. I think that the sooner the baby goes to its new home the better, under the circumstances. I was so lucky that Emily looked after Kathy for me. It wasn't like giving her away, which was really important to me because I loved her from the minute I saw her. Do you know, Mabel, she looked just like Emily when *she* was born?'

I did?

Aunt Sylvia continued, 'I can just remember waking up and going into my mother's room and there she was holding this dear little bundle. My sisters and I all took turns in cuddling her. New babies always mean a fresh start, a new story to be told. This time we don't know how or where Kathy's little baby will begin hers.'

'No, ma'am. Oh, there's the doorbell.' Mabel's footsteps scuttered downstairs.

She returned with Mrs Dawson and they all stood outside my door on the landing.

'Good morning, Mrs Trevelyan.'

'Good morning.' I could hear Aunt Sylvia's bracelets jangle as she shook hands. 'I'm afraid that it's raining again.'

'Yes, I must bring it with me. Now, I understand that the baby has come early?'

'That's right, yesterday at Haldon, when the Prince of Wales flew in.'

'Oh, I was there. I've never seen such crowds.'

'Yes, I think that all the excitement brought it on.'

'How is the poor girl?'

'Well, she's taking things very badly, she has completely rejected it.'

'That's not so terrible as you might think: she has agreed to give it away.'

'Yes, but she hasn't even held it. I can't understand why. I would want to cradle it and look into its dear little face and keep that memory for ever.'

I felt sick. *I can't even begin to imagine what it looks like. I don't want to know.*

'Now, Mrs Trevelyan, we do have a small problem with the couple who are going to adopt the child. Er; has she been given a name yet?'

'No.'

'I think that that's probably for the best as the new parents often want to choose their own.' The floorboards creaked as Mrs Dawson shifted from one foot to the other. 'Well, the problem is that they have had to go up to Scotland as they've had a bereavement in their family. One of their parents.'

'Oh, dear. How dreadful.'

'It is. It also means that they will not be back until next week.'

'So, you can't take her away today?'

'I'm very sorry, but no. I was wondering if it was at all possible, that she might stay with you until they get back.'

'Well, I suppose so, but how do you think Kathy will react?'

'I'm afraid that we will just have to wait and see. I'm sure the baby will be safe here in such a well run home.'

'Would you like to see the baby?'

'Yes, if you don't mind.'

'She's just in here. We're using a drawer as a cot.'

'Oh, what a little rosebud!' Mrs Dawson exclaimed.

I pulled up the covers so I couldn't hear any more, but I still caught Auntie asking: 'Would you like to see Kathy now?'

'No, I don't think so today.' They came out onto the landing again. 'She was quite fiery the last time I saw her. She didn't want to give the baby away. What made her change her mind?'

'Oh, she has this madcap idea that she'll learn to fly like Amy Johnson.'

'The young people of today! I don't know what the world is coming to. But, the child will have a better future if it goes to some parents who truly want it.'

Well, at least I'm doing something right.

'Can I leave this book with you by Dr Truby King?' Mrs Dawson continued. 'We give it to all our new mothers so that they follow a strict regime. A structured day is best for a contented baby, you know.'

'Well, if you're sure? Mabel has lots of experience with her nieces and nephews.'

'Yes, if you wouldn't mind, Mrs Trevelyan. It will help the baby settle down in the long run.'

When Mrs Dawson had gone, Aunt Sylvia peeped around my door.

'I thought you might've been asleep, would you like anything, a drink perhaps?'

I felt so sad and empty that I could hardly shake my head.

'Darling.' She came over and stroked my forehead. 'How are you?'

I flinched and sighed.

She picked up my scrapbook, and sat down on Abigail's bed.

'Poor Kathy.'

'I didn't think that it would be like this,' I whispered. 'I feel awful, everything hurts. I thought everything would be better when the baby was born, but it's not, it's worse.'

'Would you like to see her when she wakes up?'

'No. It's strange; I just don't feel anything for her at all. I don't want to see her; she really doesn't feel as if she is mine; that I'm a mother.' I turned to Auntie. 'Did you feel like that? Is it normal?'

'Well, I loved you at first sight; I wanted to keep you, but I couldn't. Joe, your father, thought it was best for him and Emily to bring you up. So they did.'

I stared into the distance. *Aunt Sylvia gave me away, and now I'm giving away my daughter.* I shivered; it was strange how warm the baby had kept me.

June 6th 1930

Even with my eyes shut, I could still see the garlands of pink roses on my wallpaper. *There are five blooms to a garland and three and a half garlands to a strip. I guess there must be about nine or ten thousand garlands, and therefore about fifty thousand roses.* I hadn't left the room for a week.

Although, I had come out of the darkness and gloom of the first few days, and my body didn't ache so much, my mind was still numb.

Mabel brought the papers up for me. 'Look, Miss Kathy, Amy Johnson has been made a Commander of the British Empire.'

'Oh, really?' As I frowned, I could see the worry lines forming between her eyes too. But, I could neither think of the future nor the past. I seemed to have lived in the present in that room for always, and could not imagine a world beyond its four flower-festooned walls.

An hour or so later, I felt that I needed the bedpan, and I rang Aunt Sylvia's little brass bell. But no one came.

Where are they? Mabel said that she was popping out for some eggs. How long ago was that? Perhaps she's bumped into someone in the village. Has Aunt Sylvia gone to the shop? Perhaps it's payday?

Drat, I really want to go; I'll just have to take myself off to the bathroom.

All week, I'd had to rely on Mabel for the bedpan and bed baths, and even though she tried to be kind and cheery, I think we both felt uncomfortable and embarrassed. So, not having got out of bed for days, the roses spun round the room as I tried to push back the covers and swing my feet over the side. Cross with myself, I had to lie down until the flowers stopped pirouetting. After a minute or two, I tried again, and this time managed to sit upright for a few seconds as I gained my balance. I held onto the bookcase and hauled myself up, my knees wobbling like jelly. I lunged for the windowsill like an inexperienced skater, and took deep gulps of the cool air blowing in. Grasping the dressing table, I caught sight of my face in the mirror. *Jeepers, is that me? My face is so thin. My eyes have sunk into deep dark circles.* I blinked, but the strange, gaunt face still stared back. From there, I grabbed the door handle and propelled myself onto the landing, breathless, and holding onto the banisters for support. As I rested, I realized with a shock that I was opposite the baby's room.

Chapter Thirty-Four

Jeepers, the baby! I hurried as fast as I could to the bathroom. With relief, I sat on the lavatory. *It's amazing that I can bend with all this linen wrapped around me.* Then, a picture of the baby's room popped into my head. *I mustn't look into it when I go back. I mustn't. I don't want to anyway.* I splashed my face with cold water straight from the tap, and rested on the bathroom chair for a few minutes to recover. Then, aching with the unaccustomed exercise, I set off back to my bed.

The baby's door was a little ajar and from that angle I could just glimpse a perfect pink leg raised confidently in the air: a signal; a need; a request, like flagging down a taxi. I gasped. I hadn't really thought of the baby as a real, live human being, capable of its own actions; I hadn't thought of it at all. I peeped in.

She lay in her makeshift cot with her blankets kicked off. Eyes wide open, and gnawing at her fist, she stared at the lampshade swaying gently in the breeze from the window. I shuffled over to the bed. *What an unbelievable child!* My hand hovered, not sure how, or even whether, to touch her. Deep, blue eyes turned to me in surprise and expectation, perfect little pink lips pursed and a wet tongue emerged amid a cloud of bubbles. Her raised leg came down to join its partner, and they kicked to and fro as if she was on a bicycle; toes catching on heels as she flung her arms flung wide apart in excitement. Despite all my determination, I couldn't resist smiling at her, and offering my finger to hold. She gripped it as if it was a branch above a raging river. Suddenly, shockingly, my nipples contracted with a sharp pain, and milk squirted out, wetting my nightdress. I jumped a step backwards in confusion, but she kept her strong hold. I'm lucky I didn't pull her off the bed, cot and all. Recovering a little, I smiled and whispered, 'Hello there.' She listened, and considered my voice, her eyes scanning my face for recognition.

Enchanted, I summoned up enough courage to touch her head, it felt surprisingly warm, and as I bent nearer, I could smell the sweet, heady perfume of baby powder and milk. With my finger, I stroked a plump little cheek, and her head turned, rooting for food.

'I haven't got anything for you.' I shook my head at her, and sat for a while in wonder, watching her chest rising and falling under the three tiny embroidered yellow ducklings on her nightie. Her peacefulness and serenity calmed me down as well. I didn't want to leave her, but my eyes began to shut, so I managed to get up and, tired with all the exertion, made my way back to bed.

I must have gone to sleep, for the sun had moved away from the window. Voices chattered downstairs in the hall. *Aunt Sylvia and Mabel must be back.* I heard footsteps coming up, and straightened the bedclothes.

'Hello, Kathy, how do you feel? Sorry I've been so long, Phyllis wanted me to go over some invoices with her, and the girls wanted to know how you were getting on. Look, they've sent you these roses. They go beautifully with your room don't they? I'll put them in water for you.' The smell of the full June roses in all shades of pink filled the air as Aunt Sylvia held them out for me to see.

'Thank you. They're lovely.'

'Perhaps you could write the girls a note when you are up and about. Now, do you need the bedpan?'

'No, I'm all right.'

'Are you sure?'

'Yes, I'm fine.' For some reason, I didn't want to tell her just yet about my trip to the bathroom.

As the day went on, I listened to Mabel gently singing as she went about her business in the baby's room. I became aware of the baby crying for her bottle, and the silent satisfaction as she drank her milk. Her gurgles, as she had her bath or her nappy changed, made me smile. I found myself straining my ears to hear her when all was quiet.

That evening, Aunt Sylvia came up again, 'How about seeing if we can get you up out of bed tomorrow? What do you think? You could sit in the chair and look out at the garden for a change.'

'Perhaps.' I still wanted to keep my secret to myself. 'I'll see how I feel.'

Later on, I felt tired after my adventure, but couldn't settle to sleep. Despite the curtains being tightly drawn against the long June evening, I could still hear a thrush singing loud into the twilight and the warning chack, chack of a blackbird. Next door, Aunt Sylvia talked to the baby softly, then sang a gentle lullaby. Gradually, it became darker, and I slipped into a deep slumber.

I dreamt about happy babies floating in the air like balloons. They had long strings which I held as they bobbed about. Then, one by one, they sailed away, off into the blue sky. I knew there was one special baby that I should keep hold of, no matter what, as the others all tugged away in the breeze. It was the only one left. I wrapped the string around my hand to keep it from going, but the playful wind prised the gurgling baby from my grasp. To my horror it blew away. I ran after it, trying to catch the trailing string, but even though I grabbed it one or twice, it always slipped through my fingers. Frustrated, I made one last attempt to catch it, but the wind blew harder, and whipped it away into the distance over the cliff edge, and across the sea.

I woke up in a panic, my nightdress drenched with milk and sweat. I didn't know where I was for a moment. Then I remembered the baby in the room next door. The relief was immense. The hands on my luminous alarm clock glowed; it was twenty past one. Everything was quiet, I tried to shut my eyes and go back to sleep, but I couldn't; the dream kept replaying itself like a Hollywood movie inside my head. The desperation when I saw the baby flying away was unbearable. *I've got to see the baby.*

With my heart thumping so loudly that I thought it'd wake everyone; I sat up, threw back the covers and placed my feet on the floor. My head swam a bit, but I managed to stand up, and holding onto the furniture, made my way to the door as quietly as I could. The handle squeaked loudly as I turned it. *Jeepers, Aunt Sylvia will be out in a minute to see what's up.* The way to the baby's room seemed interminable; the floor seemed to go up and down like being on board a ship.

At last, I peeped round the door. The moonlight shone through a gap in the curtain onto the bed. As quietly as I could, I made my way over to the drawer. I gasped, and my legs nearly gave way. *It's empty!*

I looked wildly around the room, my eyes straining to see in the dim shadows. Then as they got used to the darkness, I could just make out Aunt Sylvia fast asleep in the armchair by the fireplace, with the baby dozing in her arms. A pang of jealousy shot through my heart like an arrow. I wanted to touch the baby; I wanted to hold the baby. It was, after all, mine. *Mine! Oh my goodness, it's my baby!* The emotions that had been locked up for a week now escaped, and silent tears poured down my face.

With a heavy, painful heart, I watched my mother cradle my little daughter. The mother that had only had me to cuddle for such a short while: and the daughter whom I'd never ever cuddled at all. Quietly, I made my way back to bed, and hugging my pillow, cried myself to sleep.

When I woke again, it was nearly six o'clock. The sun was shining through the gold brocade curtains, bathing the roses that the bookshop girls had sent with a warm rich light. Their colours glowed like strawberries and cream, as their sweet perfume wafted towards me.

It's such a shame that after a day or two of frenzy indoors, their petals will soon drop off and die. Perhaps, I should press some in a book, they're so pretty. I'll be up and about by then.

But, by then, the baby will be given away.

The heady perfume of the flowers became heavy with sadness. *I've wasted all these days feeling sorry for myself.* I lay in bed, wishing that the roses would never die.

The clock downstairs had struck nine before Aunt Sylvia put her head around my door.

'Good morning. Sorry I'm so late, but I had such a bad night with the baby. She wouldn't go to sleep, so I ended up rocking her until she did. I'm afraid that I went off as well, I was so tired.'

The memory of her cradling my baby as she slept, made me feel raw inside.

'Are you all right, Kathy, you look a little pale?'

'Yes, I'm fine. I'm just tired with lying here all the time.

'Well, what are we going to do with you?' Aunt Sylvia opened the curtains. 'Would you like to see if you can get out of bed today?'

'Yes please, I'd like to try.' I just had to see my baby again, to hold her and love her.

'Okay then, here we go, let me help you.' Aunt Sylvia eased back the covers and put her arms round me. 'That's right, up you come.'

Her kindness made me wonder about the love that I'd missed for nineteen years. How different would it have been if she'd brought me up herself?

'Kathy, are you sure you're all right?'

'Yes.' Giddiness made my head swim again, but I gripped her tightly. 'I'm ready now.' With her support, I stood with wobbly legs, and grabbed the bookcase again.

'Let me get you the chair, and you can sit by the window for a while so you can get used to being up.' She placed the bedroom chair by the window and helped me down onto it. 'I'll just put this blanket around you to keep you warm. If you can make it, perhaps you'd like a bath? It is a week now, so you should be safe.'

'I don't know. I don't know if I'm ready yet.'

'Come on, let's try, you'll feel so much better for a nice bath. You sit there whilst I go and run it.'

She went off and I stared at the garden. Uncle Jeremy was tidying the borders and Rosie lay in the shade, snoozing, her tail flicking away any fly that came too close. *Poor Rosie, I wonder if she's dreaming about all the puppies she had to give away? I wonder if she would even recognize them again?*

Aunt Sylvia returned, and helped me to the bathroom. But, the baby's door was pulled shut so that I couldn't see in.

'I'll just get you a clean nightdress from the airing cupboard; that milk is still leaking, I thought it had finished, didn't you?'

'Mmm.' *I'm not going to tell you why though.*

She crumbled a bath cube under the tap, and I turned away to get undressed, as I felt awkward for her to see me naked, but it was heaven to sink into the perfumed water. Then, chatting about Uncle Jeremy going sailing later, she put my dirty nightdress in the laundry bin, and shook out a clean one. And when I dried myself, I was amazed to see my flat stomach; the uncomfortable roller towel was really working.

As I hobbled back to my room, the baby began to cry.

'Wait there.' Aunt Sylvia pushed open the door. 'I'll just see what's wrong.'

'No, I'd like to see her.'

'Are you sure, Kathy?'

'Yes, I feel a bit better now.'

We went in and the little baby, red faced and crying as if her life depended on it, drew her legs up to her chest.

'Ooh, she must have some wind.' Aunt Sylvia picked her up and rubbed her back whilst she grizzled like an angry wasp. There was a big burp. 'That's better isn't it?'

I felt a little faint, and sat down on the bed next to the drawer. 'May I hold her?'

'I don't know whether it's wise, Kathy. I thought you didn't want to.'

'Please, just for a minute?'

Sighing, Aunt Sylvia put the little bundle of warm knitting into my arms.

'Oh, she's so heavy.' I wriggled a bit to get her comfortable; her soft head leaning exquisitely on my breast.

'She's a good size, isn't she?' Aunt Sylvia hovered for a moment as if I was going to drop her, but when she realized that the baby was safe, she added, 'Well, whilst you're holding her, I'll just pop downstairs and get her ten o'clock bottle.'

'May I give it to her?'

'Are you sure?' Aunt Sylvia raised her eyebrows.

'Yes, I'd like to.'

'Kathy, I know that you've been very upset about all this, but you won't go getting yourself attached to her now, will you? It won't do you any good.'

'I won't.' I smiled down at the little baby.

Without a doubt, the next few minutes were the most precious that I had ever had in my life. I gazed into those deep blue eyes, and again marvelled at her little face. *Her chin sticks out. Just like mine.* I opened out her hand and uncurled her long slim fingers. *Just like mine.* My heart jumped. *Jeepers. This really is my baby.* I held her even closer, trying to absorb everything about her. I wanted to keep her with my whole heart.

She lay happily in my arms and looked up at me; she seemed to know who I was and studied my face thoroughly as if to commit it to memory. I cuddled her just a little tighter, and she gave the smallest glimmer of a smile followed by another tiny burp. *She smiled at me. She knows who I am. The little beauty. She needs a name. What can I call her? Mollie? Amelia? Of course, Amy! After Amy Johnson.* And something made me sing a little lullaby which I made up as I went along.

Little Amy, Little Amy; flying around the world,

Little Amy, Little Amy; a fearless little girl,
Little Amy, Little Amy; bouncing with kangaroos,
Little Amy, Little Amy; you know who just loves you!

'You sound happy! What's that you're singing?' Aunt Sylvia returned with the baby's bottle.

'Just a lullaby to Amy.' I couldn't take my eyes off her for a second.

'Amy?' Aunt Sylvia raised her eyebrows again. 'Kathy, you can't give her a name. Her new parents will do that. I knew that I shouldn't have left you alone with her. What did I say? Oh, Kathy you'll only make things difficult for yourself.'

I smiled and held out my hand for the bottle.

Chapter Thirty-Five

'It's the right temperature,' Aunt Sylvia instructed. 'Now, just brush the teat on her cheek, and she'll turn her head and take it in her mouth.'

At the first attempt, Amy began to cry, and Auntie put out her hand to take the milk from me.

'No, I can do it.' *Nothing is going to stop me giving my baby her bottle.*

She sighed, 'Just tip it up a little more, and pull it a bit as she sucks.'

Amy's crying soon gave way to satisfied guzzling.

The milk let down again in my breasts, and I felt my nipples pinch tight. I wanted to feed her; I wanted to feel what it would be like to be as one. I wanted to give myself to my little baby.

'Aunt Sylvia? Can I . . . Can I feed her myself?'

'No, for heaven's sake, Kathy! You'll get too attached.' She dug around in her pocket for her cigarettes. 'I think you have become too fond of her already. I shouldn't have let you go this far.'

'Please.' I felt as if I would burst. 'Please.'

'No, dear, just let her finish her bottle. Enjoy this time with her; don't spoil it by wanting more.' She stood by the window, lit a cigarette, and blew out a perfect circle of smoke.

That night when everyone was asleep, I crept out of bed; I felt stronger now and managed to tiptoe to Amy's room. Just as I peeped round the door to see if Aunt Sylvia was there, a floorboard creaked, and I froze to see if I could hear anyone moving, but all was quiet. I pushed open the door as quietly as possible, and I was in luck, Amy was alone, lying fast asleep in her cot. The moon rode high in the sky and made dark shadows through the curtains, but a shaft of light shone on her face. I was captured under her spell. Watching her sleep, I stroked her chest with trembling fingers and felt her heart fluttering like a little bird. I smelt that intoxicating baby smell. My nipples contracted again. *Should I try? Just once?*

Carefully, I lifted her out of the makeshift cot, and wrapped her in a shawl that lay on the bed. I sat down, and with difficulty, unbuttoned my nightdress and slipped the strap of my brassiere off my shoulder. I murmured to Amy all the time, and stroking her head, woke her gently. I brushed her cheek with my nipple. She responded by opening her mouth wide, taking it in and sucking hard. It took my breath away it hurt so much, but then, there was the total relief, the exquisite feeling of my little baby taking my milk. A feeling of total at-one-ness. Tears of joy overflowed down my cheeks, and onto my breast. *This is what being a mother is all about.*

Because I hadn't been feeding Amy regularly, there wasn't all that much milk there, so I put her to the other breast. As I did so, she kicked the drawer, and the brass handles rattled. My heart jumped in my mouth as the sound echoed round the room, but no one came to see what was wrong. I settled down again with her. *This feels so comfortable, so natural; I could do it for ever. I adore you, Amy, my little baby.*

Just then, Aunt Sylvia peeped round the door, her waves held in crimpers under a hairnet.

'Kathy, is that you? What ever are you doing? Is the baby all right?' She came in. 'Oh Kathy, I told you not to, it'll only make it worse, believe me.'

'I . . . I was only . . . What do you mean? Believe you? Did you feed *me*?'

'Yes, I couldn't resist you either.' She sat down beside me and hugged me tight. 'I stole in just like you. It was heavenly.'

'Auntie, I want to keep her. I love her with all my heart. We can make things work; we'll find some way, we really can.' I battled with my tears.

'No, Kathy, this little baby has been promised to some new parents, they are coming back next week to collect her. I know that you love her, but it really is for the best.'

I shook my head. Amy had finished now, and Aunt Sylvia took her whilst I did up my buttons.

'Do you remember when you were little?' She rubbed Amy's back. 'You had a happy childhood with Emily and Joe, your mother and father, didn't you? Nobody whispered and pointed at you? Other mothers didn't stop you playing with their children?'

'Yes, but, it doesn't have to be like that, things are different now.' I took Amy back and cradled her tightly.

'Are they really?'

'Yes, women have more freedom now after the War: attitudes are changing.'

'Not always, and certainly not down here in Devon. Word gets around Kathy.'

'Well, I'll go home then, and take Amy with me.'

'No, that won't work either. How is Emily going to explain away your baby without moving again? They've built that house themselves, and made it a wonderful home for you. They've given you nearly twenty years of their lives, you can't do that to them.'

'What am I going to do? I can't keep her, can I? I wish that I hadn't scared Paul off. Perhaps I should have married him.'

'That wasn't to be, was it? All you can do, dear, is to make the most of the next week. Make some memories to keep for ever. Remember if the new parents hadn't been called away, we would have never had *this* time, would we?'

'No, I suppose you're right.'

'Come on then, let's change Amy's nappy and we can all get back to sleep.'

'You called her Amy.'

'Did I?' Aunt Sylvia smiled.

June 10th 1930

The morning was fresh and full of birdsong. I sat on the bench in the garden gently rocking the pram we'd borrowed from Mabel's niece, with Rosie dozing by my side. A small green leaf fell from the apple tree and blew onto Amy's cheek; I brushed it off and stroked the heavenly soft skin near her sleepy eyes, hidden under long dark eyelashes. I straightened her knitted bonnet and snuggled the collar of Mother's matinee coat around her warm little neck. *None of these things, including the baby, actually belong to me. They are all borrowed; they are all on borrowed time.*

I struggled to raise the navy pram hood against the cool breeze, and tucked in the blankets dappled with sunbeams, as the bright June sunshine twinkled through the rustling leaves. A blackbird searching for worms, cocked her head on one side, and a robin perched on a nearby branch, even bees buzzed in and out of the lupins: it was an idyllic scene. And among all this peace and beauty, lay the little baby with an uncertain future.

Aunt Sylvia only had a few precious moments like these alone with her baby; me, that is, and I've already missed those first special days. I wish I could keep Amy for ever.

Uncle Jeremy was already out mowing the grass. The relaxing rhythm of the lawnmower going to and fro and the fresh smell of the new cuttings made me close my eyes. It had been a long and wakeful night. *How could I let Amy slip through my fingers? What would Ben think? Would he really want me to have her adopted?* I shook my head. *No, I don't think he would.*

I adjusted the hood of the pram again, and it's rusty screech put my teeth on edge. At that moment, I heard footsteps along the gravel, and I looked up to see Aunt Sylvia walking up the garden path.

'I'm just off to the shop.' She peeped into the pram. 'My goodness, she's such a beauty. Be careful you don't fall in love with her, Kathy.'

'Well, she is my daughter.' I tucked the blankets around her to keep the wind off. 'Auntie?'

'Yes?'

'I've been thinking; couldn't I keep her? I can't bear to give her away like you did.'

'No, of course not, darling.' She put her arm round me. 'Giving her up for adoption is for the best. What about all those flying lessons you were going to have?'

'I can't let her go, Auntie.'

Our voices roused the baby, and she began to grizzle.

'There, there.' I lifted her up and rubbed her back. 'There, there.'

'I can see you'd be a wonderful mother, Kathy, but it's not to be.'

The baby turned her head, and gave me a gummy chew on the cheek.

Auntie patted her gently. 'She must be hungry, but it isn't time yet for her feed, poor little thing.'

'Can't she have her bottle now?'

'No, we've got to wait until two o'clock. Mrs Dawson said that we have to follow Dr Truby King's book to the letter.'

'It's not really working is it?'

'No, she doesn't seem to know that she should sleep all through the night from ten to six, or wait four hours between feeds. I wish that we could just give her a bottle when she wants it, poor darling. Perhaps a few drops of boiled water will settle her down.' The baby grimaced. 'Phew, I think she's filled her nappy; I'll just take her in and change it before I go. Oh no, there's the telephone, I'll go and see who it is.'

'I'll change her.'

'Yes, all right.' Aunt Sylvia hurried off to the phone. 'But please don't get any ideas about keeping her, Kathy.'

'Come on, young lady.' I carried the bundle of baby and blankets into the house.

Am I imagining this? She's calming down. She must know that it's me.

I took her upstairs to change her nappy. I hadn't done it before, and the pins looked so big that I thought I might prick her. Holding my breath, I dropped the dirty nappy into the bucket, and cleaned her up with cotton wool and water. Then I dusted her bottom with talcum powder. She loved being free and able to kick about, so I played with her toes and sang the special Amy song again.

Aunt Sylvia came up. 'That was Mrs Dawson; it seems that the couple will be staying in Scotland for at least another week, as the other surviving parent has been taken ill. She wants us to look after the baby until they come back.' She brushed a stray hair off Amy's forehead.

'What shall we do?' I fastened up her clean nappy.

'Well, we haven't got much choice, have we? At least we know that she's in good hands here. We'll have to rely on Mabel. Don't let yourself get too fond of her, Kathy; you know it's for the best.'

But, I couldn't keep away from Amy that evening, and although, I didn't feed her again, I sat on the bed and watched her sleep.

June 11th 1930

I was changing Amy whilst Mabel tidied away the extra baby clothes her niece had sent. 'Oh dear, she's a lovely baby, but she does take up all my time.'

'Let me help more.'

'No, Miss Kathy, you know what your aunt said. I'm to look after her, so you don't get too attached.' She closed the drawer, and picked up the bucket to take downstairs. 'All this work and I've got to go to the shop now for some sugar. I've run clean out, and I've got to do some baking this afternoon.'

I jumped up. 'Let me go, I could take Amy in the pram.'

'Oh, I don't know, Miss. Are you strong enough? What would Mrs Trevelyan say?'

'I've read that women in the jungle have their babies, stand up, and carry on walking. I don't know why we have to take such care. Don't worry about me; I'll be all right. It's a sunny day. Fresh air is good for babies, isn't it?'

'Well, I do have to get on. Now, you go straight there and come straight back, mind. We don't want you tiring yourself out, when you're feeling so well.'

I bundled Amy into the pram, and pushed it up the garden to the gate. I hadn't been through there since the rainy day in January when I tried to avoid Paul.

What a difference. The bare branches had disappeared under a mantle of fresh green leaves which bobbed about in the breeze as I emerged into the lane leading up to the shops.

I'm a mother. I held my head high as I walked up the road, peeping now and again under the hood of the pram to make sure that Amy was safe and sound. The diamonds shone on my finger. *I have a ring; everything will be all right.*

A woman from one of the cottages was pegging out her washing, and she waved and smiled at me. *I belong. I am a mother like you. This is wonderful.*

I slowed down as I approached the newsagent's, Mrs Brown stood in the doorway, gossiping with some women who were leaving the shop. I kept my head up and walked straight past. They stopped talking, but didn't say anything to me. They didn't need to, their faces showed exactly what they thought.

Then they started:

'Here,' one woman said, 'isn't that the niece of the lady who runs that new bookshop in The Triangle?'

'Yes, as a matter of fact it is,' Mrs Brown replied.

'She's not married, is she? And a baby and all. You'd think that people would have more control, wouldn't you? It's just not respectable bringing their little bastards into the world.'

It was all I could do not to turn round and tell her a thing or two. I had to keep going, my cheeks flaming red. 'It's none of their business.' I muttered. 'Amy would have had a father if Ben . . . or, even if Paul . . . Oh dear, I should have never brought you out, Amy. I'm so sorry. You can't have people pointing at you in the street and calling you names for the rest of your life.'

I couldn't bring myself to go into the grocer's for the sugar, but took the long way home around the village, walking up the drive as Uncle Jeremy arrived home for lunch.

'Well, what are you doing out, Kathy?' He poked his head into the pram, and tickled Amy who gurgled. 'Hello, young lady.'

'I went to get Mabel some sugar. But, oh, Uncle,' I hugged him for dear life. 'Why do people have to say such awful things about me and my baby?'

'Kathy, my dear, that's how things are. People should keep their opinions to themselves, I admit, but I think the idea is to stop girls having babies out of wedlock. She's a lovely little thing, but she needs a real family of her own. That's the best gift you can give her.' He gripped me by the shoulders. 'Be strong, Kathy. I'm afraid that if you don't, the child will be taunted about her family circumstances. She will be shamed and humiliated. It wouldn't be fair on her, would it? I should just make the best of her whilst you have her, poor little mite.'

Chapter Thirty-Six

June 12th 1930

Each morning, Amy felt heavier. She was two weeks old now, and her crumpled newborn face had bloomed into that of a proper baby, like a tiny balloon being gently inflated. Her soft skin thrilled me as I held her in my bare arms after her bath. She fitted perfectly against my body and her soft warm head nuzzled in against my neck. I sang her nursery rhymes, and the special Amy lullaby to help her sleep.

Time rushed past, rather like a piece of music played at top speed. Feeding, bathing, sleeping. Changing, feeding, sleeping. Feeding, changing, singing and sleeping.

But, despite the magic of breastfeeding Amy that one time, my milk finally dried up. So I cuddled her close to my heart, whilst she guzzled down her bottle. I couldn't believe I'd given birth to this perfect baby that I cradled in my arms. I'd never thought of myself as the motherly kind. Good old Kathy, the tomboy: clever with mechanical things, expert on motorbikes, motor cars and aeroplanes, in fact anything with an engine. *What would the girls at Auntie's old shop think of me now? What would Miss Snead think?*

Amy's breathing became deep, and her eyelashes pressed heavily on her cheeks as she fell asleep. I laid her in the drawer, and whispered, 'You are so gorgeous. I love you. I promise not to get too attached, even though Aunt Sylvia warns me all the time that I will.'

I tiptoed off to rest on my bed. Lying on my side, I watched as a few petals fell from the roses. I picked up a handful of the velvety pink curls to smell them. *Mm, beautiful!* Then, I dropped them back on the bookcase as if they were red-hot coals. *When these roses are all dead, I will have to give Amy away. I can't do it. I can't.*

June 13th 1930

Vibrant honeysuckle, climbing up the apple tree, gave off a heady perfume in the morning sunshine. I watched Amy sleeping in her pram, and eventually, my eyes began to close too. An inquisitive bee buzzed around us, and as I shooed it away, I heard footsteps on the gravel again. I glanced round expecting to see Aunt Sylvia.

'Surprise. Surprise!'

'Jeepers, is that you, Mother? What are you doing here?' I jumped up. 'Auntie's at the shop. Does she know you're coming?'

'Yes, of course; but I got an earlier train so we could have some time together. I wanted it to be a surprise.'

'Well, it certainly is.'

With tears in her eyes, she hugged me tight. Her Californian Poppy perfume; her small frame; her brown curls mixed with silver threads: I could hardly believe that she was here in my arms. *This is my mother, whatever anyone else says.*

'Oh, Kathy, I have missed you.'

'I've missed you too.'

'Let me see, is this the little darling?' She peeped into the pram. 'She's an angel. Is she as good as one?'

Disturbed by our voices, Amy stirred, and I rocked the pram gently.

'Yes, but she doesn't like Mrs Dawson's routines.'

'Mrs Dawson?'

'Yes, the lady from the Adoption Society.'

'Oh, Kathy, my dear girl. Sylvia told me that you had to keep her here for an extra week. It must be torture for you.' She hugged me again. 'I know what it's like to lose your babies.' Her face crumpled. 'And now you know that Sylvia is your mother, I'm going to lose you too.'

'No, you're not. I told you so before. You're still my mother, the one who brought me up. You're never going to lose me. I'm afraid that you've got me for ever. Come on, sit down here on the bench.'

She dabbed her eyes. ‘Oh, I’m such a silly goose. What about Sylvia, though? Doesn’t she want to carry on from where she left off, now that the secret’s all out?’

‘Yes, but it’s different. We’re only just beginning to get to know each other better. She’ll never replace you.’ I glanced around the garden to make sure that we were alone. ‘It wasn’t easy when I first came. She didn’t want me to be here.’ I looked at her slyly. ‘Just as you didn’t want me at home either.’

‘That’s not true, Kathy. You couldn’t stay: the neighbours; what would they have said?’

‘Well, I think that Aunt Sylvia was a bit worried about her customers too.’

‘I’m sorry, but you did get yourself into this mess, didn’t you?’

‘Yes,’ I sighed. ‘Let’s not talk about it now.’

Mother rearranged the mauve scarf around her neck. ‘You haven’t written, Kathy. I wouldn’t have known you’d had the baby, if Sylvia hadn’t rung and told me.’

‘I’m sorry. It’s been so hard. At first, I couldn’t even bear to see her, and now I can’t bear to let her go. I really want to keep her, Mother. I wish I could.’ I stroked Amy’s cool cheek.

‘You want to keep her? But I thought . . .’

‘She’s so lovely, Mother. She’s mine. She’s all I have left of Ben.’

‘But, Kathy, what about your flying? Remember how you always used to look up into the sky for aeroplanes when you were small, and tell me that you wanted to fly? I didn’t know what I was going to do with you. Most little girls were content with a dolls’ tea party.’

‘Like Abigail?’

‘Yes.’ There was a flicker of a smile. ‘But, you can’t go flying with a baby in tow. In fact, there’s not much a single mother can do. People will always talk, you know. They’ll wonder where the father is, and put two and two together and make trouble.’

'But, it's not like that. Ben and I were engaged. We were going to be married.'

'Yes, but the baby was born out of wedlock, Kathy, and the truth will out. It always does.'

'You all kept the secret about me though, didn't you?'

'Yes, and now, you've found out. You see what I mean? You won't be able to keep it a secret for ever. This little baby's so innocent, what about when she . . .'

'It's Amy, Mother; you can call her that.'

'Yes, I know, Sylvia told me. After Amy Johnson, I suppose.' Mother raised her eyebrows. 'What about when *Amy* wants to know where her father is? What are you going to say then?'

'I'll tell her the truth; I'm not going to keep it from her. I'll tell her that he was drowned in an aeroplane accident, on a proving flight for the Prince of Wales. She'll be proud.'

'What about not having a father to help bring her up? You've always loved your Dad, haven't you? Sometimes, I think that you care more for him than me. But then, he *is* your father.' She shook her head as if trying to make sense of it all. 'What I mean, Kathy, is that children need both parents, and that's why people expect to see a child with two of them who are married to each other.' She clasped her hands together in demonstration.

'That's what Uncle Jeremy said too.'

'Yes, he strikes me as a sensible man.'

We shaded our eyes to watch a plane drone across the sky, and disappear behind the trees. Amy wriggled in her sleep.

'She's quite used to them, isn't she?' Mother peeped into the pram again.

'Yes, we get quite a few flying over each day.'

'Do you remember Dad taking you to Croydon Aerodrome when it opened? You were about ten or eleven.'

'It was the week before my ninth birthday.'

'Really?'

'Yes, I was desperate to go up in one of those Handley Page bi-planes lumbering along the runway, and taking off like huge geese. Dad said that we couldn't afford it though, and we'd only come to watch. I think that that was the very moment that I decided that I really would learn to fly myself.'

Mother patted my knee. 'There you are, you see. You've always wanted to fly. Are you sure that keeping the baby would be the right thing to do?'

I looked towards the house. 'Where is Dad, anyway, is he here?'

'No, he's making use of these long evenings. He's grateful for all the work he can get now that people are tightening their purse strings. He sends his love though, Kathy. He said he'd like a snap of the baby if you have one.' She frowned. 'She is his grandchild, after all.'

'Mother, she's called Amy.' I smiled. Then, I noticed that she looked drawn, and sad. 'You're not worried that there's still something between him and Aunt Sylvia, are you?'

'Good Heavens, no. Don't worry about that, Kathy. Your father and I are happily married, and so are Sylvia and Jeremy. She's taken long enough to find him, mind you. We thought she would never settle down. It's just that I've tried to put it to the back of my mind for all these years, and pretend that it didn't happen. But now you know, I won't be able to pretend any more.'

'Mother, I'm sorry.'

'It's not your fault, my dear.' She squeezed my hand. 'Now, have you got a picture for your father? You had a camera for your birthday, didn't you?'

'Yes, I did, but I've honestly never thought of taking one.'

'Well, have you got any film in it?'

'Yes, I don't think that I used it all up.'

'Go and get it then, what are you waiting for?'

'What about Amy?'

'She'll be fine here with me, don't worry.'

The house was cool and quiet after the sunshine and rustling breeze. I hurried upstairs to find my camera. *The last picture I took was of the Prince of Wales's Gipsy Moth.*

Just then, I heard Amy cry, and rushed to the window. But Mother was lifting her up, and rubbing her back as she began to rock her to and fro.

Poor Mother, she'd have loved a little baby of her own.

I ran down the stairs and into the garden. 'Thank you. She must be hungry, but we have to wait until her two o'clock feed.'

'No, I think it was just a little wind. It's gone now, look.' Amy lay peacefully in her arms. 'Let me take your picture whilst she's quiet. I see she's wearing one of the matinee coats I knitted.'

'Yes, thank you, they've been useful.' Awkwardly, we swapped baby and camera.

A breeze ruffled my hair as Mother squinted into the viewfinder.

'Do try to smile, Kathy!'

Amy wriggled in my arms at the vital moment, making me glance down at her tiny, scrumpled face.

'Oh, that's a shame, I didn't get your smile.' Mother wound the film on. 'Oh, it's the last one, we'll have to get it developed.' As she ducked further under the shady tree to take the spool of film out of the camera, she added, 'I thought we could go for a walk together along the seafront.'

'Yes, but, what will Aunt Sylvia say?'

'I don't really care, Kathy. I just want to walk along the prom with my daughter and her baby like any other grandmother. Come on, let's telephone for a taxi.' Her eyes glittered.

'But, Mother? I thought that you didn't approve. You sent me away. You want me to give *Amy* away.'

'I know, you're right, but that's why I want us to have some memories. I never thought that my tomboy daughter would ever be the motherly type.'

'No, it surprised me too.'

'But, here you are, and here is Amy. Let's live for the moment and enjoy the time we have with her. Does she need changing?'

'No, I don't think so. I did her just before you arrived.'

'Come on then, off we go.'

I forgot all about having to give Amy away as we sped down to Teignmouth in the taxi. How the driver wedged in the pram, I'll never know. Mother and I grinned at each other; it was almost as exciting as going up in the Gipsy Moth for the first time.

He dropped us in The Den, where we'd parked on New Year's Day, and I blushed to think how entranced I'd been with Paul. So hiding my red face, I busied myself tucking Amy safely back into her pram, and at last, we strolled along the promenade.

'Shall we have an ice cream?' Mother was almost skipping along with delight.

'Yes, if you want to. I don't mind,' I laughed. I'd never seen her like this. It must have been the sea air.

Amy dozed peacefully as we passed shellfish huts, and boats for hire for a shilling. Happily, we licked the melting ice cream off the sides of our cornets and wiped our chins on Mother's snow-white handkerchief.

'You know, Kathy, I've never felt so close to you.' She turned and gave me a shy little smile. 'This is a wonderful day, I'm so glad that I came.'

Eventually, we turned away from the seafront to the photographer's in Somerset Place to take in the film. But as we were crossing The Triangle, a voice called out that made us freeze in our tracks, despite the warm day:

'Emily? Kathy? What on earth are you doing out here?'

Mother nudged me. 'Just keep walking; ignore her. Pretend we haven't heard.'

Footsteps clattered along the pavement after us. 'Emily, stop! For goodness sake, I can't catch you up in these heels.'

Reluctantly, we turned round to receive our fate, and saw Aunt Sylvia hurrying along, her cheeks bright pink with the effort.

'What do you think you're doing? Kathy, you should *not* be out with Amy. What will people think? Emily, I'd have expected you, of all people, to have known better.'

Mother pulled herself up to her full height. 'Why? I want to be out with Kathy and my grandchild. I'm surprised you haven't done it yourself.'

'Excuse me, Emily, but she's *my* grandchild. I'd prefer you not to interfere.'

Mother's eyes glittered. '*I'm* married to Kathy's father so I think that makes her mine.'

'Please,' I whispered, as two well-dressed women passing by shot us a glance, 'you're both making it worse.'

Chapter Thirty-Seven

I can't believe this. They're quarrelling about who is Amy's real grandmother. It's the least of my worries. By Monday, there won't even be a baby to fight over. My tummy felt hollow, yet full of apprehension. Those fishes, that had arrived in Devon with me all those months ago, swirled around faster and faster making me feel giddy.

'Mother, Auntie! Stop, for heaven's sake. Everyone's looking at us.' I marched away with the pram. I didn't know where I was going; I just wanted to get away from that busy shopping street. I reached the seafront and took deep gulps of the cool breeze, as the wind eddied around inside the pram and teased Amy's downy hair. Mother and Auntie were hot on my heels; voices raised with the anger they had suppressed for nineteen, nearly twenty, years.

'She's mine, Emily. I'm Kathy's mother for God's sake. You're just a romantic fool, falling in love with Joe when you could've had someone better.'

'With more money, you mean?' Mother's footsteps hurried along to keep up with Auntie's long legs. 'Someone more *faithful* perhaps?' I turned round to see them squaring up to each other. Mother prodded Auntie's shoulder.

'Don't touch me; this is my best suit.' Aunt Sylvia grabbed her wrist.

'It didn't stop *you* falling in love with him though, did it?' Mother gave one last prod.

Auntie shrugged. 'That was different. Exciting. Passionate. More than you ever had. And you got a child out of it, didn't you? I did you a favour.'

'Let me have you know that Joe and I have been blissfully happy for over twenty years, apart from *your* little intervention.'

In front of us, an elderly couple got up from a shelter and shuffled off down the promenade.

‘Let’s hide in there,’ I pointed, ‘then you can wash your dirty linen in private. I have never seen anything like it.’ I began to feel that I was the mother with two warring daughters.

Behaving like naughty schoolgirls, they sulked on the seat: Mother in one corner and Auntie in the other, leaving me to sit in the middle as the referee. Above the brooding silence, seagulls wheeled round and settled on the roof, their claws scratching above us as they stalked about.

‘You can disagree as much as you like.’ I rocked Amy’s pram so she wouldn’t wake up. ‘I’m not clear about many things, but I am about this: Mother, even though she sent me away, is, and always will be, the one that I consider as my mother, and the one that I’ll call Mother.’ She smiled gratefully at me. ‘Aunt Sylvia, you may be my true mother, and you’ve been very kind to have me here, but you’ll never take her place.’

Auntie frowned and studied her long red nails. ‘I’m sorry, Kathy. I’m sorry. I tried, I really did, but it was all too much. I wanted to have a baby with Jeremy that I could keep before it was too late; I’m not getting any younger. And then you came along; the baby I’d given away. My daughter, yes, but *pregnant*. On one hand, at last I’d got you back all to myself, but on the other, I was jealous. I’ve made such a mess of things.’ She held each hand out then rubbed them together as if she was washing them. ‘I wanted to open another shop to take my mind off falling for a baby. They say it’s easier if you’re not trying. Well, we’re both proof of that.’ She gave a watery smile. ‘But, there you were on the doorstep, like Little Orphan Annie, and I had to take you in.’

Mother stood up. ‘I *arranged* for Kathy to come down to you. It wasn’t as if she turned up unexpectedly. You know, Sylvia, it’s not easy being the youngest. You’ve always bossed me around. You even took my husband, and then left me your daughter to look after. How do you think I felt about that?’

Auntie began to stand up too.

‘For goodness sake, sit down, both of you,’ I hissed. ‘It doesn’t matter. We’re all wasting these precious moments with

Amy.' And as if she'd recognized her name, she started, like a few drops of rain before a storm, to cry. I picked her up and cuddled her. 'I've got to give her away on Monday.' Feeling sick and empty, I kissed her warm little head.

She grizzled, as we sat in silence for a few moments, watching some red sailing boats racing along in the wind. Then, Mother reached out and stroked her. 'You don't have to give her away, dear. Keep her. I know how you feel. I lost all my babies, even you, although you weren't mine in the first place. Come home with me.'

'What? You couldn't wait for me to go away to Devon. You didn't want the shame of an unmarried mother in your house. How can I really keep her? You know I want to, but I can't.'

Mother perched on the edge of the seat. 'How about pretending you're a widow? No one will ever know that you haven't been married.'

'I can't, Mother. Where would I live? People know me at home, and people even know me here. I can't pretend like that. I have thought about it so much, but giving her away is the best thing, then she'll have a family life like I did.' I sighed, and held Amy close.

Auntie patted me on the arm. 'Yes, you're right Kathy. You have all your life ahead of you. Amy will be happy, look how happy you've been with Emily and Joe. You've just said that I'll never take Emily's place.'

A small sharp pain thrust through my heart, and I hugged Amy even tighter. *Will she learn to love another woman more than me?*

'You can have some flying lessons, Kathy, and live your dreams,' she continued, 'though heaven knows why you want to: you wouldn't get me up in one of those contraptions. Amy is a beautiful baby, but you can't raise her on your own. I know that from experience, and I have to admit that Emily has done a pretty good job.'

Mother smiled through her tears. 'Thank you, Sylvia. I do wish though that things were different. We'll all miss little Amy.'

Like a cloud bursting, Amy began to cry in earnest. Aunt Sylvia stood up. 'I think we'd better get her home. I'll go and get my motor car and give you a lift. How did you get here anyway? Not on the bus?'

'No, in a taxi.' I put Amy up to my shoulder and rubbed her back. 'I don't know how we'll get the pram in your car though.'

'I'll come with you, Sylvia, and take this film in to be developed.' Mother smoothed down her jacket and skirt, and off they went as if nothing had happened.

I tried to calm Amy by rocking her, but she screwed up her eyes, and her tongue trembled in her wide-open mouth, as her cries turned into wailing. She sounded like a giant angry bumblebee.

'Oh Amy, little baby, please stop crying,' I whispered, gently jiggling her up and down, but she cried all the more. With relief, I saw Auntie's red car coming along and waved so she'd see me, but as it came closer, I realized I'd made an awful mistake: it wasn't Auntie's red car, it was Paul's.

'Kathy?' He leant over the passenger seat and peered at me. I could hardly hear him over Amy's distress. But my heart beat faster, I couldn't help it. I switched Amy to my other shoulder. My mouth was so dry, I didn't think I could speak.

'Paul!' I managed at last. 'How are you?'

'Fine, thank you. How's Amy? That's certainly a lusty cry. Father's been telling me all about her.' He got out and came round to us, the sea reflecting in his blue eyes. 'Hello, young lady.'

Amy stopped at the sound of his voice for a brief moment, but then started off again as loud as ever.

'I'm waiting for Aunt Sylvia.' I raised my voice above the wailing. 'I'm sorry I flagged you down; I thought it was her car. Both red, you know?'

Stop gabbling, Kathy.

'Well, it's nice to see you up and about.' He fondled Amy's hand. 'She's doing well; she's certainly growing, isn't she?' Then, he looked deep into my eyes, 'If things had been different, then who knows what might have happened?' He put out his hand.

Don't touch me! Remember how fast he was to lead Abigail on. How fast he got engaged to that icy woman.

'What about Patricia?' I shivered, despite the warm day.

'Well, yes.' His hand fell to his side. 'Yes, I am going to marry her, but you know, Kathy, you'll always have a special place in my heart.'

'Will I?' But, Amy wailed too loudly for him to hear.

Another red car twinkled in the sun along the promenade. *Auntie, at last!* She pulled up behind Paul, and got out, followed by Mother.

'Ah, Paul, nice to see you. You haven't been round for a while.'

'I've been busy, Sylvia.'

'Yes, I know, dear. You've met Kathy's mother?'

Mother and I exchanged glances.

'Yes, on Kathy's birthday. How do you do, Mrs Mason?' He shook hands. 'You'll never fit in Sylvia's car with the pram as well, let me bring it round later for you. I can't do it now as I've got to get back to the hospital.' Paul struggled to be heard above Amy's cries.

'Thank you, that will certainly help, 'Auntie said, as Paul conjured the pram into his car, and drove off waving.

'Cheerio!' he called.

Cheerio, Paul, I'm far better off on my own.

Amy cried all the way home; she must have been desperately hungry. I hurried to prepare her bottle, and soon she was drinking contentedly.

'We don't mind if it's not two o'clock yet, do we Amy?' I whispered.

After lunch, I went to lie down whilst she had her nap, and Mother went to see Auntie's new shop for herself.

Despite being so tired, I couldn't drop off to sleep. Thoughts about Amy, Ben and Paul whirled around my head. I looked for something to read. For once, I wasn't in the mood for *The Autocar,* and the newspapers had little more to say about Amy Johnson who was still touring Australia. Remembering how I loved researching her heroic flight, I went to get an encyclopaedia, which felt nearly as heavy as Amy, and tucking the atlas under my arm as well, I carried them upstairs.

Where shall I go when I can fly off alone? America? Canada? Brazil? I can go wherever I like. I will need a job to pay for my flying lessons first though, then I'll have to get a sponsor. My heart beating, I looked in awe at the wide Atlantic Ocean and drew my finger westwards. Amy's plane had flown to Australia in short hops, never far from an aerodrome of the British Empire or, a Shell agent, for that matter. I shook my head; I could never make it to America in a little plane.

I sighed, and wondered if there was anything about Gipsy Moths in the encyclopaedia, but no, it was too old. However, it did have an entry about the moth itself. *Let me see, females are larger than the males, but can't fly. Fancy that? I'm a large female, but that's certainly not going to stop me.* I lay back on my bed and twiddled Ben's black bead. *I was a chrysalis when I was pregnant, changing inside and producing a baby. Now, I've shed that old skin and those awful clothes and, like a gipsy moth, I'm going to pump up my wings and take off into the air all by myself.*

I'll visit romantic places you can only see from the cockpit of a plane. Flying close to rainbows; mountain lakes sparkling under a starry sky; whisking through mountain passes, wing tips skimming the snow; crossing wide deserts and oceans, and landing in secret valleys. Life will be an adventure and I'll be free.

Amy is my world, I'll never forget her, ever, but we would be a burden to each other. I would be her unmarried mother which would make her a bas . . . I can't even think it, let alone say it. She will be far better off with a respectable family that loves her. That's the best gift that I could give her. Otherwise our lives will be an empty chasm. I would have no money and no qualifications. I couldn't even work in a shop, or do a secretarial course. Who would look after her? I can't believe it now, but perhaps we would resent each other in the end. We'd have to scrimp and save for everything. I don't know where the money would come from. I wouldn't even be able to afford the ticket to explore the country by train, let alone fly round the world.

Mother meant well when she said I should keep her, but it won't work. She didn't want me at home when I got in the family way and I can't stay here with Amy.

The diamonds on Ben's engagement ring made fairy sprites dart about the ceiling.

Ben, I wish you were here. It's so hard to make this choice without you. If you were here, then we could get married and keep our little daughter; there wouldn't be a problem. We could be together, live together and you could teach me to fly. Mother or Auntie could look after Amy openly and we could have our adventures together.

I pulled his letters out of the drawer and kissed the picture he'd drawn of me in the Gipsy Moth with our little baby.

Chapter Thirty-Eight

June 16th 1930

I woke to find just a few petals clinging onto each rose: the others lay in crumpled clumps around the vase. I hadn't been able to bring myself to throw them away.

Through my window, small white clouds scudded across the sapphire sky. It should have been a day of promise: a day to go up to Dartmoor and have a picnic, or a day to spend on the beach, skimming stones into the sea. But, after so little sleep and so much crying, my eyes were tired and sore and my shoulders ached from hugging myself tightly.

I looked at the photo of Amy and me that Mother had hurried off to fetch before she left. I fingered it gently: it was only two and a half inches by one and a half. I traced Amy's small round head, and her tiny hand that had escaped from the crocheted shawl. This was all I would have apart from my memories. Not very much for a little life.

I'm glad Mother's gone back home to help Dad in the office. I don't think she could bear to watch me give Amy away without snatching her for herself. I don't even know how I'm going to go through with it.

Amy began to cry for her six o'clock feed and I jumped out of bed. This, according to Dr Truby King, was the last scheduled one that she was due, because within four hours she would be gone. Wiping my eyes on my arm, I measured the formula and the water into the bottle for the last time, shaking it and testing a few drops, mixed with tears, on my wrist to make sure it wasn't too hot. I picked Amy up out of her drawer-cot, and her cries turned to urgent cooing as she realized her milk was coming. I sat down in my familiar place on the bed, it was softer and warmer than the chair, even though it did make my back ache, and brushed Amy's cheek with the teat. *This is so easy and natural now. Why did I find it so hard at first? Why on earth did I miss all those opportunities to do this before?* But Amy couldn't answer these questions and, totally unconcerned and oblivious of the importance of the day, guzzled down the milk.

I tried to commit each second of the morning to memory: Amy's squeaky little swallowing noises, the warmth of her dear body through the crocheted shawl, her heavy head nestled on my arm. The pain was just too great, and I sniffed back my tears and wiped my eyes again on the shoulder of my nightie. When Amy had finished, I held her up in the familiar place against my neck, and rubbed her back, taking deep draughts of the sweet baby smell of her hair, whilst her knobbly knees nudged my tender breasts.

I changed her, it certainly wouldn't be the last dirty nappy, and in the quiet of the morning, it was an extra special time to be alone. I softly sang *Little Amy, Little Amy!* and marched her legs up and down in the air, before wrapping her up again in a nappy that came down to her tiny knees.

I dressed her in a soft vest, the cotton nightie with the little ducks waddling across her chest, and Mother's white knitted bootees and matinee coat. She looked so beautiful, with her dark blue eyes and light brown wispy hair, that I just sat and cradled her until she fell asleep, and then cradled her some more until Aunt Sylvia put her head around the door and told me it was time to get up as breakfast was ready.

Reluctantly, I laid her back in the drawer and went to get dressed in a plain navy blue two-piece which Mother had brought me; it wasn't a day to dress up at all. For breakfast, I prodded a cold and congealed egg with my toast.

The time to leave came all too soon. Aunt Sylvia helped me to pack Amy's things together in a bag, whilst I changed her nappy that one last time. Mabel gave us a royal send off, waving one of the Union Jacks saved from the Prince of Wales's visit. (I never did see him properly.) Rosie pushed her way into the car, sensing my distress. She tried to lick my hands and sniff at Amy as if to say goodbye. But, Uncle Jeremy took her by the collar and handed her, whimpering, to Mabel.

I cradled Amy tightly all the way along the river where the hills rolled off like green waves towards Dartmoor. I was so wrapped up in my thoughts that I didn't bother to glance up when Uncle Jeremy said, 'Look there's an RAF Gipsy Moth flying along the seafront.'

'What's that doing here?' Auntie strained to catch sight of it. 'They only come to Haldon when there's something important on; I wonder what it is? Not another Royal visit surely, or it would have been in the papers?'

I remembered the day that Ben had come to Haldon with such high hopes, and how nervous I'd been. *Ben?* I asked the blue sky. *What would you think if you knew I was giving away your daughter today?* There was no reply apart from the gulls calling to each other. *Well, at least I'll be able to learn to fly now like them, but is it all worth it?* At that moment, I still didn't know.

The journey seemed shorter than usual, and Uncle dropped us off before driving on to see Bill at the boatyard. I don't think he could bear to see little Amy go either.

At Mrs Dawson's office, we were ushered into an oak panelled waiting room: dim, except where the sun's rays shone through the mullioned window. The white-faced pendulum clock ticked loudly, measuring the minutes I had left with Amy. The sounds of the street outside seemed muffled and far away. Aunt Sylvia sat beside me, nervously fingering the lacy frill of the Moses basket, loaned by Mrs Dawson, and clutching the small bag of Amy's belongings. I held my daughter tightly against me and stroked her plump downy cheek.

We jumped when the inner door opened and Mrs. Dawson called, 'Come in, Miss Mason.' I stumbled as I got up, and Aunt Sylvia just managed to grab my arm. Obediently, we entered the room.

'Do sit down. It's a lovely day, isn't it?'

We nodded; our mouths too dry to argue. Defiant, I looked round, but the door was firmly shut. There was no escape.

'Now, you know that we have found a lovely home for little Amy. I can tell you that they are a nice young professional couple who have been unable to have any children of their own. Nurse Shaw will look after the baby until we can hand her over.'

The nurse stepped forward; tall and thin with a mouth like a sharp pencil line. Hot rebellion rose in my heart, I clung to my little bundle as tears welled up in my eyes.

'Kathy, dear.' Aunt Sylvia put her arm around me. 'You know it's for the best. Say goodbye to her.'

As I began to give her to the nurse, her tiny hand escaped again, brushing my arm as a final farewell. I tried to make a picture of her in my mind so I wouldn't forget this last moment.

What am I doing? Somewhere, someone will be rocking Amy. They won't know her special song. Will they really look after her and love her as much as I do? I won't know if she'll live happily ever after. I'm going to miss her first real smile, her first tooth, her first word, her first steps, her first day at school, her first boyfriend: I hope she'll be more sensible than me.

I was jerked back to the present as the outer office door banged, and loud voices echoed from the waiting room.

'I have to see her!'

The door flew open.

'Kathy!'

'Ben?' I nearly dropped Amy with the shock. 'What are you doing . . .? I thought you were . . . Ben, is it really you?'

He wrapped his arms around me. 'I'm so glad I got here in time.'

His warm, strong, living arms, held me and I was comforted by that familiar smell of oil-tinged cologne.

'How? Why?'

Mrs Dawson was on her feet. 'I'm afraid that this is all very irregular and upsetting for the baby. Miss Mason, would you please hand her over?'

Ben stood between us. 'No one's handing over my baby. She is *my* daughter, and this woman is going to be *my* wife!'

It was then that I fainted clean away.

When I came round, I was lying on the sofa in the outer office. Amy was still cradled in my arms, and Ben's dear face was so close that I could feel his hot breath.

'Ben?'

'Yes, it's me.'

'What happened? Are you a ghost? Am I imagining this? Is it a dream?'

He held my hand and stroked Amy's head. 'It's me. I'm here. Everything's going to be all right.' His smile was like the most glorious summer's day.

'This is most irregular . . .' Mrs Dawson stood in the doorway looking confused.

'May I borrow your telephone?' Aunt Sylvia grabbed the earpiece. 'Could you put me through to Canlan's Boatyard, please?' She tapped her painted nails on the desk. 'Is Jeremy Trevelyan there? Good. Tell him to come and pick up his wife and his granddaughter immediately.'

'His granddaughter?' Ben raised his eyebrows.

'Yes, we've got a few things to tell you, too.'

I cannot describe how heavenly it was to snuggle up in Ben's arms on the back seat of Uncle Jeremy's motor car with Amy nestled between us. It was no time for words, only to revel in the unbelievable fact that he'd come back. I cried, he cried, Auntie cried, and Uncle Jeremy wiped his eyes; he must have had something in them.

At Hillfields, Mabel came to the door and threw her hands up into the air, shouting for joy, 'Oh, the Lord be praised! You still have little Amy. You got there in time, Master Ben. The Lord be praised!' And she hugged all three of us.

When we were all settled in the sitting room, with a bottle for Amy, and a large pot of coffee and plate of biscuits for us, (I ate at least four; I hadn't felt so hungry for ages), Ben told his tale.

'Well,' he said, 'I got washed up on Lundy Island.'

'Lundy? Where's that?' I said, lifting Amy up to my shoulder to rub her little back.

'In the Bristol Channel, near Ilfracombe.'

'I hoped that's what had happened, but they said you were lost.'

'Good Heavens, however did you get there?' Uncle Jeremy asked. 'Weren't you heading for Cardiff?'

'Yes, but we got lost in some awful sea fog. It came down as we left the coast. We tried to fly lower to get under it, but as we were almost skimming the water, we had to climb up into the cloud. You've no idea how frightening it is to be travelling through that clinging whiteness. I think you can actually see more in the dark: lights ashore, ships that sort of thing. We could hear the other planes, but that was all. We had to make sure that we didn't get too close.'

'Were you flying it yourself, Ben?' I said, marvelling that he was back and sitting right next to me on Auntie's sofa.

'Yes, I was, but at the time I really wished I wasn't.' He squeezed my hand. 'I tried to hold my compass course north-east, but I lost my bearings and must have drifted westwards instead. Then I saw that the fuel was getting low. Of course we couldn't land on the sea, so I decided to circle and turn back. The other machines were following, and that's when it happened. They collided with each other and went straight into us. And that's all I remember until I woke up on a rocky shore.' Ben rubbed his forehead. 'I didn't know where I was.'

'What happened next?' Auntie sat on the edge of her chair. 'Did someone find you?'

'At first, the sound of the sea gulls filled my head. It ached terribly; I must have banged it on a rock or something. My wet uniform clung to me, and my body shivered and shook so much I thought for a moment that I was still in the aeroplane. Eventually, I managed to open my eyes. The jagged rocksI lay on disappeared after about two yards into thick fog, and the sea crashed relentlessly not far from my feet. I wondered if it was going out, or coming in to sweep me back into its depths.'

We sat silently, eyes fixed on Ben.

'There seemed to be a small man in a dark raincoat with whiskers lying near me, I tried to call out to him but he didn't reply. Then, to my amazement, he slid into the sea, and I realized it was a seal. I lost consciousness again, and the next thing I knew, I was being dragged over rocks and stones up a steep path and then over some short grass to a stone cottage.

'I didn't know where I was at first. I couldn't remember anything after the crash. I still can't.' He shook his head. 'But from the dim light of the smoking turf fire, I could see that I was lying on a bed of goatskins in the corner of a small low room.

'A woman, I don't know how old she was, could have been anything from forty to sixty, raised my head and gave me some water. Heaven knows I'd drunk enough of the sea, but I was thirsty. She was dressed in colours of the earth, a brown tweedy skirt and a thick green jumper, I don't think I saw her in any other clothes all the time I was there, and she had a long plait of brown hair which hung over her shoulder like a fisherman's rope.

'Megan, she told me her name, nursed me all through the fever which started the next day, no doubt because of the chilling I got in the water. She said it lasted a week and she bathed my head with apple cider vinegar which she made from the wiry apple trees dotted around the cottages. They had been built for the workers in the quarry, now long gone. When I began to feel better, she strengthened me with soups, using the vegetables she grew on a small sheltered patch beside her cottage. I don't think that I've eaten so well for a long time,' Ben smiled.

'One sunny day, I felt well enough to sit outside with her and watch dolphins dipping far out to sea, and wild black rabbits eating yellow dandelions from her hand. She didn't tell me why she lived there, but she said that she had been there for a long time. Perhaps she had run away from a cruel husband, or father, she wouldn't say. But, she told me about Lundy and tales of pirates and shipwrecks, and I supposed that with my aeroplane accident, she could add me to her list.'

'But, why were you away so long, Ben?' I couldn't resist asking.

'Well, after a few warm days when I began to get my strength back, the weather changed again, and fog clung to us for another week. The fire was so smoky, it was foggy indoors as well as out.

'Megan had no contact with anyone else living on the island, and kept close to the old quarry. Perhaps she had a deep dark secret, but I never found out what it was. To be honest, I never saw another living soul, until the day that a small sailing boat landed on the shore, and a man got out with a large camera, tripod and binoculars, and set to work photographing the puffins nesting on the cliff face.

'Of course, I knew that I had to leave and get back to land, so thanking Megan and leaving her in the little stone cottage, I climbed down the steep path, and introduced myself. I must have looked a bit wild as my hair had grown and a beard had sprouted on my chin, but he recognised my uniform and agreed to take me back to Ilfracombe that afternoon.

'I've never felt so sick in my life. Major Grimes, as he introduced himself, told me that the Bristol Channel met the Atlantic Ocean there, making the sea so rough and I spent most of the voyage hanging over the side.'

'Poor Ben!' I kissed his cheek.

He took me to the coastguard station and they got on the telephone to Cranwell and told them I'd been found. My parents and Abigail came down the next day.'

'Abigail? I didn't know she'd seen you. Why didn't she tell me?'

'I didn't want her to. I wanted to come and tell you myself. So, the RAF boys have made a special trip to bring me down to Haldon.'

'How did you find me at the adoption office?'

'Andrew drove me down to Hillfields, and Mabel told me where you where. It seems as if I was just in time.' He took Amy in his arms, and she studied his face calmly. 'Why were you having our baby adopted, Kathy?'

I hung my head; all the bravado about learning to fly seemed insignificant now. 'I wanted what was best for Amy.'

'Amy?'

'Yes, after Amy Johnson. Did you know that she is the first woman to fly all the way to Australia?'

'Yes, I have caught up with *some* news since I've been back on the mainland.'

I shrugged my shoulders and smiled. 'I thought it was the perfect name for her.'

'But, why were you giving her away, Kathy?' He kissed her head.

'I don't know, I didn't want to, but without a father to help bring her up, it would have been for the best. I wouldn't have been able to give her the family life she deserved.' I looked to Auntie for support, as Ben walked stiffly over to the window, looking so thin, despite all Megan's vegetables.

Then Amy began to grizzle, so I rubbed her back to comfort her and calm myself.

I've done it. I've ruined everything. Ben's alive and he's caught me giving his baby away! What ever must he think?

Chapter Thirty-Nine

Those old fish churned around in my stomach. I bit the inside of my lip to stop myself crying. 'I'm sorry, Ben. I . . .'

Slowly, he turned round, tears streaming down his face. 'My brave Kathy.' He put his arms around Amy and me. 'I love you both. I'm so glad to have you. I'm so glad that I got back in time.'

'I love you, Ben.' The relief flooded through me like a glass of warm red wine.

'Kathy, *I'm* sorry you had to make that terrible decision on your own. How awful for you to face being an unmarried mother bringing up Amy all alone. Look how you had to hide down here in the first place. You didn't want to come, did you?'

Auntie blew her nose on Uncle's handkerchief. 'She didn't want to give Amy away either, Ben. I'm afraid that I encouraged her.'

'The poor girl's been through so much,' Uncle added.

'I am sorry, Ben. I didn't want to have to give her away, but I thought it would be better for her to grow up in a family like I did with a mother and a father and no one calling me awful names.'

Ben frowned. 'Why on earth would they call *you* names, Kathy?'

'Because,' I raised my eyebrows at Aunt Sylvia, and she nodded, 'because my mother wasn't married, and I was brought up by my aunt instead.'

'Your mother's your aunt?'

'Yes,' I smiled, looking at Auntie, 'and my aunt's my mother.' I held up my hands in amazement.

Auntie straightened her skirt. 'You might as well know, Ben, that twenty years ago, I had an affair with Kathy's father. My sister, Emily, was childless, yet she made the ultimate sacrifice and agreed to bring up her husband's baby, knowing full well the circumstances of her birth.'

I looked into his deep brown eyes, trying to read his thoughts. 'Don't you see, Ben? I was happy. You know that I had a wonderful childhood, especially with you and Abigail. Not only would your parents never have let me play with you if they'd have known, but I wouldn't have even lived in your neighbourhood in the first place. Aunt Sylvia wouldn't have been able to afford it.'

Auntie lit a cigarette, and inhaled deeply. 'It meant, Ben, that I could follow my dreams and open my first shop. I'd always wanted to be in charge: buy my own stock of books and sell them to women who wanted to buy them and read them, and to lend them to women who couldn't afford to buy. I wanted Kathy to follow her dreams too.'

'That's it, isn't it, Kathy? You've always wanted to learn to fly, haven't you?'

'Yes,' I whispered, 'I've always wanted to, ever since Croydon Aerodrome. I remember ducking as a silver De Havilland that had survived the War, flew overhead, and watching open-mouthed as the pilot put it through its paces. I wanted to be him as he drew a pattern in the sky, like I did at home with my crayons, of endless loops, twists and curls. I wanted to know what it was like to be up there, looking down below, and I wondered if the pilot could see me standing with Dad, sheltering my eyes with my arm.'

'Kathy, your dreams will come true. I promise you.'

'Really?'

'Yes, they will, but I've got something that I want you to do first.'

'Oh, what's that?'

He got down on his knee. 'Kathy Mason, I want to make an honest woman of you: will you do me the pleasure of taking my hand in marriage?'

'But . . . How . . . I thought . . .'

He put his finger on my lips.

'My parents are so relieved and glad to have me back alive that they've agreed to us being married as soon as possible!'

'As soon as possible? Really?'

Ben nodded.

'Jeepers!'

'Well? Will you?' He shook his head, smiling.

I couldn't have been more surprised if the Prince of Wales, himself, had got down on one knee. Nothing had been further from my mind that morning when I was saying goodbye to Amy for the last time. 'Yes, of course. Of course I'll marry you.' And he gave me the most wonderful kiss.

'Oh, my dears.' Aunt Sylvia gave us a hug. 'Now, Kathy, what are we going to get you to wear?'

I laughed and thought about how pleased Mother would be. Then it struck me: 'What about Mother and Dad? I'll have to tell them! Can I use the telephone, Auntie?'

Ben settled back down again with Amy who began to slumber in his arms, and I went into the hall and sat on the little red chair, my heart beating wildly.

Mother's only been gone a couple of days. What on earth is she going to say?

'Mother?'

She answered the telephone straight away, as if she'd been sitting in the hall, waiting all morning. 'Kathy, dear, how are you? Oh, my poor girl. I wish I could have been there with you. Oh, Kathy, I'm so sorry.'

'But, Mother . . .'

'I do hope that Sylvia's looking after you. I'll try and come down soon for a few days. Have you decided when you're coming home? No, that's too soon to ask.'

Just then, Amy began to cry again and Ben brought her to me.

'What's that? It sounds just like a baby. Where are you?'

'At Auntie's. It is a baby, Mother; I was trying to tell you. It's Amy.'

'What, haven't they taken her? Fancy, letting you down again. Oh, Kathy, that really is the limit.'

'No, Mother, they're not taking her at all.'

'What?'

'I'm keeping Amy.'

'No? Why? How?'

'I'm trying to tell you.' The receiver felt hot and slippery in my hand, and the warm Bakelite smell tickled my nostrils like pepper and made me sneeze.

'Bless you,' she said, 'but what's happened?'

'Ben's alive! He's been marooned on Lundy Island. He's here now with Amy. Mother, we're going to get married!'

I heard some fumbling at her end as if she was getting out her handkerchief.

'I can't believe it, Amy, I mean, Kathy. Oh, I'm all confused.'

'Ben's here, Mother, speak to him.'

Ben handed me Amy, and took the receiver. 'Mrs Mason? Yes, it's really me. I got back from Lundy a couple of days ago. Yes, my parents have had a change of heart, so we can get married if you and your husband will give us your permission. Yes, I understand, that's very kind of you. Yes, it's wonderful to be back, thank you.' Grinning, he gave me the telephone.

'What did you say to him, Mother?'

'I said that I'd have to check with your father, but as far as I was concerned, I'd give you my blessing. Oh, Kathy, I'm over the moon!'

'So am I, Mother, so am I.'

'Dad's only working on a house up the road, so I'm going to run up there and tell him straight away.'

'Really?'

'Yes, I'll get him to telephone you and speak to Ben. Oh, this is such wonderful news. Goodbye!'

'Well?' Ben's eyes glistened.

'She's going up the road to fetch Dad so you can ask him properly.'

'Do you think he'll say 'yes' this time?'

'Of course!'

Within no time the telephone rang making us all jump out of our skins, even though we'd been sitting on the edges of our seats. I rushed to answer it.

'Dad?'

'Ah, Kathy, this is such good news. Let me speak to the young gentleman, then.'

Ben took the receiver. 'Mr Mason?' He stood to attention, as if being inspected by a Wing Commander. 'May I ask for your daughter's hand in marriage?' He winked at me, then Dad said something, and he replied. 'Yes, that's what I thought. Straight away. As soon as possible? Saturday, 12th? Yes. Thank you, Mr Mason. Yes, I will. Yes, goodbye.'

'What did he say? Saturday 12th?'

Ben picked me up and spun me round, 'He gives us his blessing on the condition that we get married as soon as possible, and if we have the Banns read for three Sundays, we can get married on July 12th!'

'But what about your parents?'

'I'm sure it'll be fine. They *want* us to be married, Kathy. They want to see their little granddaughter grow up! Oh, I do love you.'

Epilogue

July 12th 1930 Amy Johnson is sailing home from Australia today.

Here I am floating down the aisle. Four weeks ago, I was preparing to give my baby up for adoption, now she's swaddled in a lacy gown and bonnet, safe and sound in Mother's arms. I'm holding my lilies away from the ivory silk dress that Aunt Sylvia helped me to choose. It's cut on the bias and clings to my body, emphasizing my flat stomach and full breasts that having Amy has given me. The cool breeze of this summer morning ruffles my veil, and Dad, washed and brushed, marches beside me in pinstriped trousers, tailcoat, winged collar and bow tie. I glance at him and smile as the organ music swells and fills the church.

The sun shines brightly through the eastern window, throwing Ben into silhouette. But as I draw level with him, it lights up his face; warm and loving, pleased to see me. 'You look gorgeous!' he mouths, and squeezes my hand.

I feel faint with love and desire. There is a delicious sickness inside, and my head is spinning. I can hardly follow the service at all, just making the responses as the Vicar turns his solemn gaze on me.

' . . . Till death us do part.' The words stick in my throat, and the Vicar repeats them.

Death has almost parted us, Ben; I don't think that I could go through that again.

'Kathy?' the Vicar is insistent.

'Till death us do part.' I whisper, trying hard to swallow my tears.

Like the hero-pilot in a war film, Ben emerges from the mist, and I throw myself at him. I can hear the Vicar telling me to restrain myself, but I don't care. I am married to Ben and I kiss him fully on the lips.

He pushes the gold wedding ring firmly onto my finger, and I'm never going to take it off.

We sail back up the aisle: past Mother, still holding our angelic Amy, and Dad; past Aunt Sylvia and Uncle Jeremy, and past Ben's parents. Although appearing aloof at first, they smile warmly. Perhaps they are a little wary of how things will work out, but I'll do my best to make them like me and be a good wife to Ben.

And the flying? Well, tomorrow, we're going to leave Amy with Mother and Auntie, and fly to the French coast together for a short honeymoon. I hope that they'll all behave themselves. Then, Ben is going to leave the RAF. His father's said he will help him set up an air courier business down here with Andrew, and I'm going to get my licence and be a pilot too. Who knows? I may be able to fly to France, all on my own before long, as Mabel's niece has said she'll look after Amy with her children when we need her to.

I throw my bouquet to the bridesmaids; well there is only one: Abigail, resplendent in figure-hugging pale blue silk. Everyone cheers as she catches it, and I hope that she will be as happy as we are.

Then we all look up as an RAF Gipsy Moth hums its way across the sky towing a banner saying:

'Kathy Hunter - Girl of the Skies!'

That's me!

Cover design by magicat45degrees@googlemail.com

Follow my blog at jeanbullswritingblog.blogspot.com